Twitter

www.

~

26 MILES TO THE MOON

ANDREW MALES

Britain's Next
BESTSELLER

First published in 2015 by:

Britain's Next Bestseller
An imprint of Live It Publishing
27 Old Gloucester Road
London, United Kingdom.
WC1N 3AX

www.britainsnextbestseller.co.uk

ISBN 978-1-910565-24-7 (pbk)

Cover designed by Claire Yeo

Dedication

For Nan

Acknowledgements

Top billing goes to my wife, Michelle, who supported me from my initial ideas all the way through to publication, with her guidance, support and patience...a *lot* of patience. Just behind her is my daughter, Amber, who came late to the party in 2014, but gave me just about enough sleep to make this book happen.

Thanks must also go to Mum and Dad for being great throughout this process. I also hold Dad entirely responsible for any puns I added into the dialogue, having been subjected to so many of his over the years.

If this book ever flies off the shelves, it will be in no small way due to the talent and dedication of my designer and cousin, Claire Yeo, who produced the wonderful cover and chapter headings.

Steve Pocock always believed in the story and encouraged me throughout my journey, and the two New York City Marathons we ran together provided some of the inspiration for the story. I ran both races for the charity Dreams Come True, who also helped promote this book. Special thanks goes to Sarah for all her efforts and support.

I wouldn't have had this fantastic experience without my publisher, Britain's Next Bestseller, so I'm grateful to

Murielle and the team who gave me the opportunity.

A big thanks to the early readers for inflicting upon them what I know now were very rough drafts. Your feedback - good and bad - helped so much in its development and gave me the confidence to keep going.

My novel would also be an embarrassing mess if it weren't for my official editors, Alex Norris and Emma Peyton, my unofficial one, Steve "Chief" Cooper, and someone who fixed many errors before my first submissions, Marion Lang.

Finally, thanks goes to the rest of my family, friends, colleagues and randoms who made this book possible. Whether you ordered a copy, spread the word or just smiled and nodded when I mentioned my book for the gazillionth time, it all helped me get to the finish line.

The Heroes Who Made This Book Possible

Michelle Males, Amber Lucy Helen Males, Ann Males, Simon Males, Michelle Smith, Chris Smith, Rachel Smith, Mary Males, Terry Hammond, Tom Yeo, Piper Yeo, Sarah Strange, Richard Strange, Ted Must, Stephen & Pat Powell, Amanda McIntyre-Brown, Roger Brown, Aunty Rosie, Adam Carpenter, Lynne Fountain, Raymond Fountain, Charlotte Dixon, Chief, Krista McManus, Stephen Pocock, Ella Pocock, Harry Pocock, Michael Pocock, Stephanie Pocock, 'T' , Sally Liddle, Marie Williams, Simon Williams, Kim Williams, Izabella Williams, Amelie Williams, Donnie Oliver, Freddy James, Bernadette Bullock, Gary Bullock, Olivia Lewis, Grace Lewis, Andy Bullock, Louis Bullock, Rob Fuller, Emma Fuller, Bryan Fuller, Colin Kinnear, C.M. Hobbs, Lee Dowden, Lee London, Sue London, Ben "It's only Cornhill" Smith, Mark Wheaver, Rebecca Phillips, Pamela Johnston, Nicola Kerr, Kate Szymanski, Simon Blythe, Vicky Wykes, Lucy Chaplin, Robert McManus, Nancy McManus, Clive Wrench, Stephanie Stevens, Emma Lucy Stevens, Fiona Parmar, Emma Nuttall, Darcy Everby, James Harley, Jasmine Harley, The Kenyons, Amy Mae Williams, Pete Johns, Sarah Long, Terry Emery, Rob Ingram, Amanda Wright, Andrew Twigg, Dawn McQueen, Geoff Tidey, Lisa Bridges, Michael Kavanagh, Nicola Gore, Peter Bannister, Sandy Reyat, Sherry Hindle, Shirley Green, Joe Hakeney, Glenis Moore, Sylvia Nott, Christine Austin,

Isla Eve Watson, Lucy DeVito, Layla Amy Harris-Cherguit, Jacob Kane, PJ Jovanovic, David McCaffrey, Ryan Mark – Tremor, Julie Timlin, Dennis Snape, Sally Dillon-Snape, Bekki Pate, Marlene Tapscott, Michelle Diana Lowe, Polly Walker, Jill Haine, Issi Doyle, Alice Priday, Justine Machin, Jonny Phang, Rachel Phang, Joshua Phang, Nick Whiteley, Mary Smart, Eric Smart, Nicola Smart, Lucy Smart, Richard Smart, Philip Smart, Robert Ayers, David Sanders, Daniel Rosenberg, Andreas Kavallaris, Simon Garstin, Claire Harlow, John Roberts, Vince Hann, Graham Pett, Jonathon Morgan Alexis Tubawawashidha, Jason Absalom, Adarsh Soman, Hanata Tjaniadi, Rajasree Ganguli, Wieslaw Olborski, Mick Worthy, Sandrine Herbert, Janet Gracey, Ieva, Steve Elliott, Marion Leung, Dave Bagley, Melissa Stone, Michael Frederickson, Nella Buisson, Steven Rouse, Kieran Walsh, Ben Clasper, Ben Walter, Phil Bird, Tom Royds, Satu Jones, Victor Arnott, Andy Jones, Dave Parks, Rupal Bhatt, Daniel A Billing, Mike Connaghton, Nan Cole, Victoria Gilbey, Steve Besley, Christopher Harrop, Claire Peters, Stacey Till, Emma Bottomley, Christian Tye, Paul Hyde, Richard Day, Ganesh Ramani, Emma O'Hare, Helen Battison, Jacqi Chalmers, Jacqi Lee, Jayne Riddell, Jenna Trelease, Judith Jackson, Louise Drewett, Marcus Vere, Chris Deaton, Nige Impey, Owen Smith, Ralph Dring, Renee Kimoto, Urszula, Steve Haywood, Michelle Rowell, Steven Mitchell, Sarah Newman, Anna Wiggett, Barry Blust, Sophie Dean, Stuart MacDonald, Lisa Stevens, Anna Moody, Barbara Kirby, Sarah Kirby, Martin Neal, Sue Fowler, Joanne Sorg, Dreams Come True … and to all those who wished to remain anonymous.

Chapter 1

JON had always liked his bum. One of his better features, he thought. But now, standing naked with his back to half of London, he wondered just how many other people might share his opinion. Four hours ago, it had been just another pointless weekday morning.

'A penis?'

Jon's boss, Henry, closed the blinds, plunging his dingy office into further greyness. Jon stared down at his laptop as Henry rattled in a drawer, snatched a pen and drew a big red penis on a whiteboard, complete with testicles. As their regular one-to-one Monday morning reviews went, this was definitely a first.

'My overpaid, talentless design team get asked to come up with an intuitive interface for our next global software release and my tester spectacularly fails to notice that they have created an icon that looks like a penis?'

Jon studied the grotesque caricature Henry had drawn and compared it to the small, inoffensive blue image on his laptop. 'I'm sorry, but I just don't see a penis,' he said.

'That's just great – our last barrier between us and thousands of users who'll be getting our new version, and he can't even recognise a phallic-shaped icon when he sees one. Brilliant.'

'To be fair, no-one else thought it looked like one. Not even the women. In fact, only you've mentioned it.'

'Really? Maybe that's because I actually *have* a penis,' Henry said as he started to undo his belt. 'Perhaps you come from the Action Man school of genitalia. If you're not sure what one looks like, I'm happy to provide your first glance at a real one.'

'No – it's okay. I get it, I get it.' Jon shifted in his seat as Henry proceeded to lower his zip. 'I'll ask Dan to change the icon to something more...suitable.'

'Damn right you will. And don't worry about retesting it all – I'll do it myself. I obviously can't expect you to recognise such advanced shapes.'

Jon curled his hands into fists behind his laptop screen. 'So what am I going to test?'

Henry turned away, appearing to admire his artwork. 'Oh, I don't know. Go check all the help information that users can access. There must be *some* people who bother to read it?'

Jon took a deep breath. 'Okay, if that's what you want. I'll get right on it.' Jon shut his laptop, walked out of the office and into a debrief from his colleagues on what had already been dubbed 'Penisgate'.

Back at his desk, Jon sighed and dropped into his leather chair, causing it to release a similar sound, as if in sympathy with its owner. He ran his hands through his short, brown hair and grabbed the task list for today, crossing out most of what he had planned. He reached for his phone – Stu always liked to be kept informed of the latest episodes involving his best friend's boss.

'He actually unzipped his trousers?'

'Yep. You'd think he'd be a bit more relaxed with over four weeks to go until the deadline. The guy's more tightly wound than a Rolex,' Jon said.

'Jesus. So, checking the help screens. That sounds like riotous fun.'

'Sod all I can do about it. Sure, we haven't changed any of that in ages, but I suppose I can check it all again.'

'Why waste your time? Why not offer something else more constructive?'

'Like what? Checking the marketing material in case the first characters of each line spell out a rude word when read vertically? The software's fine, it's a small update and I'm happy to count down the minutes until Friday.'

'And next week?'

'And next week.' Jon looked at the demotivational calendar on his desk that Stu had decided was the perfect Christmas present for him. At least the August bank holiday was coming up.

'Team leader position not come up again?' Stu asked.

'Why bother? It would only make it necessary to meet more regularly with Mr Penis Obsessive. I'm better off here, believe me.' Jon began to click randomly through his email folders.

'Well I'm off to lunch with the new recruit,' Stu said. 'Twenty-two, blonde and with a pair so perfect you could write a PhD on them.'

'Jammy git.'

'Luck has nothing to do with it, mate. Some of us are born to spend the day flirting with the cream of the marketing talent pool.'

3

Jon tried to imagine his friend's office. 'Any jobs going there?'

'Yeah, a few, I think.'

'Really? Could you –'

'Nothing for you though, idiot. For a start, you're not going anywhere. Rumour has it you have a nice burial spot assigned to you near the car park.'

'They'd probably charge me rent for it.'

'And secondly, you couldn't handle it.'

'The job? I'm sure I could do some –'

'I meant the women – you'd faint just entering the building. Anyway, I mustn't keep Britney waiting. Or is it Brittany? Who cares? I'll give you my detailed report of her tonight. Later, loser.'

From the direction of Henry's office, Jon could hear snippets of a shouted telephone conversation about a lack of printer paper and threats of Henry cutting down a tree and making some himself. Jon continued going through his emails before noticing one at the top of his spam list.

Write yourself into history!

History. Ten years in this wonderful place was his history. He clicked on the title and brought up a short message:

Write yourself into history!

Act now...and I mean NOW! Reply by 12:15pm or miss out forever on the chance to make Jon Dunn a name that goes down in history.

Jon stared at it. It was from DPI Adventures. Strange. It looked like an official email from a new offshoot of Douglas Peabody International, the global company that recently seemed to be involved in everything. There was nothing that looked dodgy, and when he compared it to one of their emails about his bank account, it all appeared consistent. He knew that DPI were known for their quirky competitions and offers, but this seemed different...*Jon Dunn a name that goes down in history.* The only history-making in Jon's life was years ago, when the local paper published a photo of him coming second in a dog look-a-like competition. *Reply by 12:15pm...*Jon looked at the 'sent' time – 12:00pm. Why would you give people just fifteen minutes to read an email after sending? He imagined some naive, eager trainee being hauled into a meeting to explain why they'd had such a poor response for their new venture.

Act now...and I mean NOW! Jon studied the email address again. Yep, looked fine. At 12:09, Jon was still staring at it. *...or miss out forever...*He looked around the office, at the temp scurrying down the corridor towards Henry's office carrying two boxes of printer paper, the list of 183 help screens lying on his desk and the calendar preaching 'Don't give up tomorrow what you can give up today'. Unsure of what he was hoping for, Jon replied to the email and sent his life on a new course.

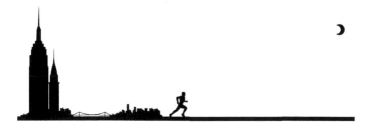

Chapter 2

'JOE? Joe Dunn?' A stomach appeared at Jon's desk, followed a second or two later by the rest of its owner.

'It's *Jon*, actually, Mick.' Mick was the office guy who seemed to do all the little jobs, including twice a day delivering any post that had come in.

'Oh right, yeah, Jon,' Mick said, examining a letter he was carrying. 'Here's something for you. How long you been up here?'

'Me? I'm a newbie, fresh through the door.'

'Really? I've only been here eight months but I'm sure we've met before.'

Jon thought about reminding him that he'd gone to his birthday do just three weeks ago in a pub that barely held a dozen people, but by then, Mick had trudged off, announcing to the department that he'd no doubt see them all again later that afternoon. Jon ripped open the letter before realising that it was another offer to go on a training course that he would never get authorisation to attend. He turned back to his laptop screen just in time to see an email notification. After fifteen minutes, he'd received a follow-up from DPI:

Congratulations! You have successfully replied in time to qualify for the next round. Jon Dunn is still on course to make history!

Simply click on this link, fill in and return this questionnaire by 12:45pm today and, with the right answers, you will be chosen for the exhilarating next round.

Another inexplicably short deadline. He examined the text again – *right answers?* If it was data or opinions, he didn't see how there could be any right or wrong answers. Intrigued, he clicked on the website link. In terms of entertainment, he thought, this was probably as good as it was going to get that day. The link brought up nothing special, just the image of a huge pink elephant from the website Jumbo Surveys, set up by DPI Adventures to collect his answers.

Once started, do NOT leave this webpage until you have submitted your answers.

The first few questions were his name, date of birth, job title, contact numbers and the usual details that were either vitally important for their data capture or just to get you warmed up.

Interests. He ticked 'Sports', hovered over 'Extreme Sports' (did an aborted bungee jump count?), then chose 'Films' and 'Photography'. Was that all he was interested in? He thought back over the last few years – yep, that's probably about it. Jon Dunn: party animal, living life to the max. He ticked a few others just to make himself look a bit more interesting, then unticked them again as he experienced a weird feeling of guilt, as if the elephant were judging him. 12:40 – he'd better hurry.

Favourite charity. He once sponsored his brother in a triathlon for a children's charity, so that would do.

How far is it to the Moon? This was one he knew – *238,000 miles.* Well, on a good day.

When were you last in love? Jon puzzled at the personal nature of this one. Love. Did Sally Collins count, aged nine? Probably not. Certainly his last few relationships didn't quite go the distance. He was about to embark on a complete analysis of his past love life when he realised that he still had another twenty questions to complete. *Never.*

The remaining questions were a mix of the factual and personal. He had no idea of what answers he should be filling in, but when he stared at the summary page at 12:44, he had more than a little feeling of shame at the blandness of his life, laid out in a list. Pressing 'Submit' replaced them with the message, *Thanks for filling in the questionnaire – we'll be in touch very soon to let you know if you've made it!*

Jon tinkered with his own website for the next fifteen minutes, annoyed that part of his lunch break had been taken up by the questionnaire. He had put some good photos on his site, but as always had been disappointed to find no-one had commented on how great they were. He did have one nugget of genius from Stu though, written beneath a close-up of a tulip he was particularly proud of due to the way he'd captured the light. He had written just one word: 'Gay!' Jon was about to delete this masterful critique and think up some suitable revenge when the phone rang. Henry's number appeared on the display, causing Jon's shoulders to slump. He knew he had to take the call – Henry had a sense of knowing when someone was at their desk and avoiding him. Either that, or the rumours of a ceiling spy network were true. Jon picked up the phone but wasn't even given time to open his mouth.

'Jon, Jon, Jon. I've been thinking. Those icons. Aren't they a bit…I dunno, blue?'

Jon had nothing.

'See the thing is, I like green. Green means "go". Go, go, go! Press me. I think they should all be green. What do you think?'

Jon slapped his left hand against his temple. 'But the program's whole colour scheme is based on blue. Our *company* colour scheme is blue. We paid someone thirty grand to come up with a design based on the very fact that the colour that was going to beat all our competitors was blue.'

There was a pause. Jon wasn't sure if he should have been privy to that cost and held his breath.

'But green's so much better, isn't it?' Henry said.

'Well, it's just –'

'Look, get Dan to change them all to green, chuck 'em over to me and I'll make the call. Ciao.'

Fantastic. Despite it clearly not being Jon's role to ask for these changes, he was now going to listen to his own valid arguments against the colour change being thrown back at him from the rest of the team. He made a note to talk to Dan after lunch, before the phone rang again. What does he want now? Jon thought. Let's see how funky the screens might look in Helvetica font? Without looking, he picked up the phone. 'Yes?'

'Hello? Am I speaking to Jon Dunn?' A female voice made Jon sit up. He flicked a glance at the phone display – unrecognised number. 'Speaking. Yes, you are. Speaking to Jon Dunn, that is. Hello. Hi.'

'Great! I'm so glad to get through to you. Brilliant. Do you have any idea why I'm phoning?'

Jon considered this with serious thought. Was she the

twin sister of Stu's new recruit who was asking if he'd join them in their Grosvenor suite's hot tub?

'I'm sure you've guessed – you're in! The DPI Adventures competition – you've made it to the next round. The best round, I might say. It's cool. You're gonna love it! So, so lucky. Well, not lucky, I mean, you got here on your own merit. Great responses to the questionnaire – just what we needed. You're in!'

Jon felt his cheeks flush at the unfamiliar feeling of hearing a girl be excited about him. Or at least something he'd done. Which wasn't much, admittedly, but it had obviously worked. He realised he still hadn't spoken after his clumsy opening, so he thought he'd better reply with something else before she started querying his IQ.

'I, er…okay.' Superb. Thirty-four years on this planet and his speech capabilities barely rivalled a baby chimp with learning difficulties.

'That's all right, Jon, I know this must all be a bit… strange, sudden for you, and that right now you don't have a clue what's coming, but just relax and I'll take care of you. My name's Daisy.'

'Hi Daisy, I'm Jon. But…of course, you know that already.'

What sounded like a genuine giggle calmed him.

'Right. Are you fit?'

'Pardon?'

'Are you fit, ready to move, ready for action, able to jump to it, right now?'

Jon checked he still had legs. 'Yes, I suppose so. But I only –'

'Great. Well, I'm leading the London region of the competition, so meet me at 2pm on Westminster Bridge.'

Jon looked at the clock on his PC. 'Sorry, but I can't possibly make two o'clock. My lunch break is over at half one. How about six?'

'Six? No, no, no Jon. We all have to meet at two. On a strict time limit, you see. Be there or be...stuck testing whatever it is you test.'

Stuck. Perfect word. Game over, Jon realised. 'Just out of interest, what do you mean by we *all* have to meet?'

'All? All the others, of course. It's a game, well, a competition, and obviously we can't have a competition without competitors and, even though people had to be quick and pass the questionnaire, we've got a number of people qualified in London. I reckon you can beat them, Jon. Go for it! C'mon!'

The last competition he'd won was at work last October, as the team who'd been able to drop an egg the furthest without breaking, using a bunch of straws, paper and Blu-Tack. He looked at the trophy still sitting on his desk. 'But I've got work...I can't take an afternoon off just like –'

'Jon? Do you speak or do you squeak?'

'Sorry?'

'You see, all I hear is squeaking. Be there at two or let history happen without you. Bye, Jon. Be there!'

With five minutes left of his lunch break, Jon had finished the list in his head of why he shouldn't go and meet Daisy on the bridge. It was a long list, far longer than the list for why he should go, which, if he was honest, didn't have anything on it just yet. But he knew he could still make it to the bridge in time if he hurried. The list of help screens fluttered as his desk fan swivelled past. This was madness. Henry hated last-minute absences and would go spare at the thought of someone sloping off without planning cover. So why was Jon now writing an email to him saying he had to dash off for 'reasons to be explained later'? What reasons? When later? Too late – the email was sent. Jon leapt up from his chair and marched towards the door. Passing Dan, he said, 'Henry says to make all the icons green and send them to him as soon as they're done. You know, green – go, go, go!'

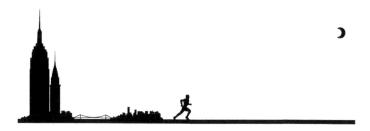

Chapter 3

JON'S body was not altogether communicating with itself very well. Whatever chemical was now swimming inside his head since Daisy's phone call, it was exciting a part of his brain that had been dormant for a while. His legs didn't care what was going on upstairs and, quite frankly, ignored all messages, carrying Jon on a journey towards Westminster Bridge. They ascended the tube escalator, two steps at a time, brushing Jon past people on his right with less interesting destinations ahead. With five minutes to spare, he emerged from a short tunnel and arrived at the bridge, his heartbeat raised and a trickle of sweat running down his back under his white shirt. Now what?

The wide span over the Thames was thriving as always. Big Ben was behind him as heavy traffic queued to cross to the other side. Open-topped red busses were filled with gawping tourists, craning their necks to take in all of the view. He could hear the drones of a bagpipe player serenading passers-by. The London Eye stood on the other side like some cog in a machine yet to be finished. The sun was now making an appearance, warming Jon's hair. Both sides of the bridge swarmed with a random collection of people: the pinstripe-suited typical Englishman; the black-haired Japanese family posing for a photo; the bare-chested, bald man; the immaculately dressed twenty-something woman with a hairstyle that would frighten Genghis Khan; and a short blonde waving a big, square sign as high as she could that said, 'History Makers Here'. Jon crossed the bridge to meet her, and due to the fact that a certain clock behind him hadn't yet loudly announced that it was 2pm, he figured all he had to do now was report for duty.

'I've made it!' he said.

The blonde looked up from a clipboard and smiled. 'And you are?'

Jon recognised the voice and couldn't help being a little disappointed. In his mind, Daisy had been, well, different. Taller and a little slimmer. But she was still cute in her DPI uniform and was smiling at him. 'Jon. Jon Dunn.'

'Ah, Jon Dunn.' She eyed him up and down before scanning her list of names. 'Can I have ID, please?'

'Yes, of course, I –' Jon patted his right trouser pocket and felt only his leg. His mind raced away at the speed of light and swooped down on his desk, his shiny black wallet sitting there in his drawer, next to his phone. 'Crap!' Jon slapped his hand to his mouth, failing to swallow the word. 'Sorry, I mean...I've left my ID at work.'

'Right.'

'No, I mean it. You didn't tell me I had to bring ID.' Jon cursed again, this time silently. He remembered writing the email he'd sent Henry and then dashing off without bothering to check he had all of his usual essentials with him. He fumbled in the rest of his pockets in the hope that pixies had magically beamed his wallet into one of them. The search brought only his train ticket holder, but this also contained some emergency cash and a spare credit card that Jon hadn't even realised he still had. Presenting the card to her, Jon said, 'Will this do?'

Daisy took it and examined the numbered side. 'Mr J. E. Dunn. How do I know it's *Jon* Dunn?'

'I…er…it's me, I swear. Mr Jon Edward Dunn.' A bizarre thought entered his head – had his mum sewn a name label on his shirt? Daisy let out a giggle, making Jon momentarily panic that he might have said that out loud.

'Jon – relax. I guessed it was you. Five–ten, short hair, slim build with a tongue so smooth you could plane doors with it.'

He looked down at the pavement as Daisy reached up to touch him on the shoulder.

'Welcome to the party! You're the last one to arrive, but I'm so glad you could tear yourself away from testing widgets and actually get out into this beautiful day and join us. Go ahead – make some new friends.'

For the first time since arriving, Jon realised he wasn't alone with Daisy. He turned to scan the dozen or so people around him that had gathered in the middle of the bridge. If these had been a bunch of people he'd been introduced to at a party, or perhaps just seen standing at a bus stop, they wouldn't have concerned Jon, but here as competitors, they all looked far superior to him. Which, considering he had absolutely no idea what sort of mental or physical challenge lay ahead, was a little alarming. They just all looked so…ready. Most of them were in business attire, but were so coolly dressed that just looking at them made Jon shiver. All but two of them wore shades, something he wished he had right now as he squinted into the sun. A man to his right towered over Jon, with the chest and shoulders of an Olympic rower. If Jon were about to race a single sculls from here to Waterloo Bridge, then he might as well head off back to work now. A thin woman with a short grey skirt appeared to be barely twenty, but had the look of someone who would quite happily step on your head on her way up the career ladder. He moved into the group for a closer inspection, hoping to find someone who might look a little more helpless than him. Jon felt a finger prod him in the back and turned round to see a vision he thought could only exist on the best air-brushed magazine cover.

'Hello, I'm Summer.'

Long, auburn hair swept around a tanned, flawless face with eyes radiating so much warmth, Jon felt he was about to melt and trickle off into the Thames. Whether he would rediscover the power of speech or if flying cars would be invented first, he wasn't sure. Luckily, she was happy enough to continue alone.

'I know, I know. It's mad isn't it? That we're here, you know.' Summer's eyes flicked this way and that. 'One minute I'm filling in this dumb questionnaire and the next I've signed up for goodness knows what. Don't you just love the unexpected?'

Jon hoped that he would be able to recall his own name soon. For now, he let a sound escape his lips to indicate his agreement, and to reassure her that he had not fallen into a standing coma. She wore a white floaty dress that danced lazily around her slim legs with a neckline cut just low enough to meet the start of her cleavage. She appeared to be about to ask Jon his name, when he was saved, first by the chimes of Big Ben, and then by Daisy's voice.

'Hello people!' Daisy said as she stood on a set of plastic steps and waved both the sign and a clipboard high in the air. 'Gather round, gather round.' Jon followed Summer as she drifted into the small crowd that now surrounded Daisy.

'This is great! Thank you all so, so much for coming. I mean, it wouldn't be much of an event without you all, would it? And we don't want to let down the wonderful city of London, not when there's such a great, fabulous prize at stake.'

Had he missed the announcement of what the prize was? He was still staring at Summer's back, imagining how cool it probably was, not stuck to her clothes. And perfumed, no doubt. Stop it, thought Jon. Concentrate.

'But I'm afraid I can't reveal all just yet.' One or two people let out a groan. 'In fact, even if I wanted to, I couldn't – they haven't even told me.' A look of doubt came across the crowd. 'Don't worry, I'm assured it's big. Very big. Historic. And you'll all love it. But first you must accept a challenge.'

They were each given a DPI-branded phone that contained no data, aside from a single contact number. Daisy took them through the basic operations of the phone, paying particular attention to its camera facilities.

When Jon looked up from his phone, he saw the tall man talking to Summer. How had the bastard managed to trick his lips into forming a coherent sentence with her standing so close to him? Once Daisy had been reassured that everyone was happy with their phone, she jumped back onto her step and addressed everyone once more.

'Hello, hi again. Listen up now, this is very, very important. The time now is 2:10. You have your camera phones and you have yourselves, and that's all you'll need for this task, okay?'

Ten past two, thought Jon. He looked back across to

where he had joined the bridge, wondering how many missed calls from Henry had already accumulated on his phone. Daisy turned over a page on her clipboard and slowly read out its contents.

'By 3:15, in order to be considered for the next challenge, you must have taken and sent to the number in your phone, a photograph of you doing what you consider to be the most outrageous – but legal – pose you can think of. Be creative. A full copy of the rules will be given to you to read and you must sign the declaration form presented to you by the DPI Adventures associate – that's me – in order to participate.' A slight pause. 'That's it. Good luck people and don't forget to sign.'

Outrageous. Jon did landscapes, flowers, architecture, but rarely photographs of other people, let alone himself. Not even hope-that-spot-doesn't-appear-too-large selfies. The only outrageous photo ever taken of him was the infamous eighteenth birthday masterpiece that Stu had so wonderfully taken, forever capturing in time the exact moment his vomit had hit the bonnet of a Mini. Even if he could somehow recreate that now, Jon doubted it would be judged favourably enough for progression in this strange game. Snapping back from this image, Jon realised he was the only person not holding a white piece of paper, so he weaved his way towards Daisy, past the young woman who was scrutinising every syllable of the rules and an older man whose hair was so long, blond and straight it would make most women envious.

'Are you the last in everything you do, Jon?' Daisy was still on her steps and thrust the rules down at him. He took the piece of paper and looked around. A couple of people had already left, jogging off in seemingly random directions in pursuit of inspiration. First, Jon needed a plan. That's what he did every day – made a plan and carried it out. This should be simple – think of something outrageous, work out a plan to achieve it, execute this perfectly crafted plan, and the job's done. But this task required creativity, something Jon tended to only exercise during the family Pictionary session at Christmas. He let one part of his brain read the rules, while the creative cells woke up from their hibernation and attempted to play around with the unfamiliar concept of 'outrageousness'. By the time he'd finished reading the rules and had signed Daisy's form, the best idea that had been presented to him in all its hilarity and originality was to obtain a traffic cone and put it on his head. Wonderful. The competition was quite obviously in the bag.

More of his fellow 'history makers' had dispersed into the London crowd, some heading back over the bridge towards the Houses of Parliament, two gazing over the river looking for opportunities and one approaching a tour bus, gesticulating wildly. Of the remainder still gathered near a bored-looking Daisy, four were talking together, including Summer, who appeared to be leading the conversation. With no other plan of attack and with no better place to be than near her, Jon moved in towards the small group.

'The stupid act itself is not the hard bit, you know, James.' Summer was addressing the half-man, half-engine who had clearly been able to remember his name. 'It's the actual taking of the photo, when you think about it, isn't it?'

'Ah…no self-timer.' The man with obscenely long hair jumped into the conversation.

'Exactly, Pete – which is why you'll need help.' Everyone nodded. 'And trusting strangers with this mobile phone, let alone the shot itself, is not exactly the best idea, is it?' Heads shook with enthusiasm. 'Therefore, we need to work together. So…who's with me?'

Up in the gods, James frowned and looked away. A silence ran amongst the others. Even knowing each other's names, they all knew that everyone else was little different from the oddities that walked past on the bridge, and here they were being asked to trust someone who was actually competing against them. The sound of shuffling feet was only broken by Jon's mouth, making its first solo performance of the day. 'Me! Jon! I'm with you Summer!'

Everyone turned to look at Jon. If Jon could have, even he would have turned round to stare. But he could see envy in their eyes. He'd got in first. Trumped them all, got in while they were sleeping. What were they thinking? Are they mad? Have they actually looked at this beautiful creature and realised that she's asking someone to spend a portion – no matter how small – of their lifetime in her company?

'Cool!' Summer blinded Jon and half of Westminster behind him with her smile. She grabbed Jon's hand and led him away from the crowd at speed, only stopping to toss her copper waves back and shout at those left behind, 'Good luck – you'll need it to beat us!'

Jon felt as if he were being pulled along like a kite. They were almost off the bridge, moving towards the London Eye, when she stretched her neck round and said, 'Don't worry – I've got a plan.'

'Plan?' Jon would have been quite happy to run like this forever.

'Yeah – just as long as you don't mind me getting totally naked in front of you.'

Chapter 4

'**D**MITRI, it's over.' Doug Peabody rested his mobile phone on the highest running track in the country while he slipped on his custom-made orange and green trainers, adjusting the laces. He waited until the tightness felt just right on his feet and the phone's speaker was no longer blasting out the Russian's voice. 'Look, you sat on the fence and wouldn't commit the money. Well guess what? I can pull the offer whenever I like.' More abuse rained into Doug's freshly epilated right ear. Dmitri was an old friend with whom he'd shared many whiskies, but Doug had seen the real side of him since he'd told him of his decision.

'I'm sorry you feel that way, but I have plans. Douglas Peabody International has a strategy.' Doug looked down onto the rooftops of central London. 'I can't keep waiting until you decide whether or not you have the *cojones* to go ahead with this.'

Doug began stretching as Dmitri revealed his own strategy of taking Doug's *cojones* and making them into customised ice cubes for his next cocktail party. He shook his head. What kind of Russian hates vodka, anyway? Even at the edge of the skyscraper, Doug couldn't see any individuals down there, but one thing was for sure – there were people out there more worthy, more willing to help him follow his dream than this fool.

'Cuss me all you want, pal-ski, but it's too late – you're out of it. I've cancelled the contract and started a new process, something totally different.' Doug had been looking forward to this bit since the inception of his idea. 'Nothing on Earth is going to stop me from doing this, and you know what? I don't want yours or anyone else's money. I'm gonna give it away for free.'

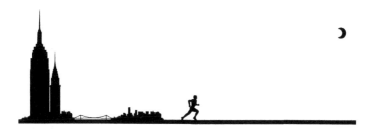

Chapter 5

THE tourists and locals had flocked to the attractions around the London Eye as though they were waterholes in the desert. As it was the summer holidays, the kids were there in their hundreds. Those that weren't already queuing with their parents were dragging them along in the search for ice cream, or to investigate what was so special about the street acts that large crowds were gathered around. In terms of finding a secluded spot for some nakedness, Summer could have picked better. Jon wondered if perhaps he'd fallen asleep at his desk and was dreaming all this. With a jerk, his hand was released from Summer's grasp as she skipped to the edge of the promenade and faced him.

'So, what do you think? Know anything about photos? Composition? Light? Nude models?'

Jon couldn't remember the last time he saw a nude woman, and had certainly never been allowed to capture one on film. 'Um, photography, yeah. I can compose a good shot or two. It's not like we're exactly short of quality subject matter to choose from.' He had meant to say that whilst scanning the picturesque sights around him, but he had been captured by Summer's gaze. She softened her expression and approached him, crossing one slender leg over the other until she was less than half a metre away. 'Wait till you see the subject matter uncovered, honey.'

He wanted to pause time. Release a press statement to the world reporting on the exact wording of everything that had happened so far. Stu needed to be called up and made to listen to this. He was now on a parallel plane, leaving poor old Original Jon stuck in his office going through help screens no-one had updated since the Queen Mother was alive.

'It's gotta have Big Ben in it,' Summer said, pointing at the famous landmark.

'Of course, Big Ben's not the actual name of the tower, just the nickname of the bell inside it.' Jon replayed those words back to himself. Perhaps his mouth was better off alone, without the brain feeding it material like that.

'You know what I mean, Geek Boy.'

'So, where are we gonna find a place where no-one can see?'

'Oh, I don't care about getting seen. Well, I'd rather we didn't get arrested, but I don't mind giving a treat to a few men out there lucky enough to look over at the right moment.'

'What do you mean "we" get arrested? What am *I* doing wrong?'

'I'll tell them you forced me to pose for you.'

'Hey!'

Before Jon had a chance to complain further, he was being dragged off again. He felt like he was back at school, being summoned by the hottest girl in the class who, as part of a dare, had to reveal all to the most innocent of classmates behind the bike sheds. Except with about a thousand witnesses. They stopped at the entrance to a long, empty ramp that made its way down to the river.

'We're not allowed down there, surely?' Jon said. He looked up. 'Plus the bloody London Eye pods go directly overhead.'

'Look, you can see Big Ben, you can get a good angle and it's away from the crowd. The people on the Eye will be looking across at the Houses of Parliament, not down. Relax and set up the shot with my phone. I'll do a special jump into the air. We'll practise it, get the right angle, shape, position etcetera and then I'll strip off, have one take, and get clothed again before anyone really notices.'

Jon watched as Summer did little jumps, arms raised in a variety of different positions, while her dress drifted up to reveal a little more of her perfect legs.

'Are you really sure about doing this?' That was it – his mouth was going on strike. It could not work with this stupidity.

'Yeah, of course, silly. The photo will definitely get noticed. You should see the one I did at the Taj Mahal. You *do* want me to qualify for the next round, don't you?'

Jon nodded.

'And anyway,' she continued, pulling her dress outwards at the bottom on each side, 'just look at all the other crazies around. Who's going to notice little ol' me?'

Just from where he was standing, he could see someone dressed in a ten-foot tall penguin costume, a walking Statue of Liberty and, further up, a fat Spider-Man frozen in action. Maybe they could pull this off without too much attention. With a quick glance round, they scampered down the ramp towards the river, Jon looking for suitable positions to get a good mix of foreground and background. He had missed the Nudes and Timepieces edition of *Digital Photographer Monthly*, but felt sure he could manage without it.

'I think a nice silhouette would be good, given that I'm taking it into the sun. If we can fit in your leap-thingy and the clock face itself, that would be perfect.' Jon zoomed in on some of the test pictures he'd taken. 'Er…Summer?'

'Yes, Jon?' She was doing warming-up exercises as if preparing for the final of the Olympic gymnastics vault.

'Well, I just wondered…exactly in what way will you… er…be facing the camera?'

Stopping with hands on hips, she replied, 'You mean do you get to see my arse or do you get to see the fun side?'

Jon's cheeks instantly became the hottest known objects in the Solar System.

Summer pushed up her breasts and jiggled them. 'I'm afraid I'll just have to risk any lucky sailors going by getting a glimpse of the good stuff. You can settle for the rear.' Summer paused, before nudging her eyebrows up and saying, 'Don't want you passing out at the crucial moment.'

They spent the next few minutes taking photos, practising the move fully-clothed and perfecting the angle. She moved with the grace of a dancer, and her promise of doing the splits naked in mid-air was almost too much for Jon. He felt like the director of a sleazy film, asking his actress to take her kit off and act out a wild fantasy. What was wrong with him? Did he think he'd be whisked off by the lord of the underworld and have his eyes poked out for eternity just for agreeing to help out a beautiful, sexy, amazing woman?

'Are we ready for it yet? Or are your hands too shaky?'

Jon lined everything up. 'Yeah, just there would be perfect.'

'Okay.' She climbed down from the railing she was balancing on and approached him. 'Before I do this, we also have to think of your shot. I have a great idea for you, but you have to trust me. And I mean totally trust me, otherwise it won't work.'

'I...sure. I trust you.' Jon was ready to hand over the keys to his flat, give her his Wi-Fi password and the three security digits of his credit card, but it was the hint of devilment in her eyes that made him hesitate. Before he had time to reconsider, she was unbuttoning his shirt.

'I'm putting a lot of trust in you,' she said, as her fingers worked her way down, 'so if you really want an outrageous photo and for us to go through together, you need to trust me.' By now, she had pulled out his shirt tails and had undone the final button. Placing her hands on his bare chest, feeling a whisper of hair, she looked up into his brown eyes, pupils expanded to the full. 'Do you trust me?'

Jon was going to have a heart attack. Not a painful one though – his entire body had enough natural sedation right now to cope with a crash of rhinos performing Riverdance on his chest. Summer took his silence as an affirmative and whipped off his shirt. 'I'm gonna need this,' she said as she threw it near the edge and then reached underneath her dress, 'but you can have these for a moment.'

True, Jon was not accustomed to being bare-chested out in public, but then he wasn't usually the recipient of a warm pair of white, skimpy knickers in his trouser pocket. A fair trade, he thought, as his heart rate dropped down into two digits again. With the sun still strong in the sky, he was not alone on the male topless front here. He had, however, probably the worst physique on offer of any male here over the age of thirteen, and cursed not having ever stepped into a gym since school. Fortunately, neither semi-naked Jon nor soon-to-be-naked Summer was getting any attention from the throng of people ambling past, as loud music started up nearby and a street dance ensemble drew a large crowd.

Summer was primed and now gave Jon a look of readiness. He was at the highest point of a roller coaster – wanting to admire the view but knowing something was about to take his breath away in a fleeting moment. Crouched low, camera wobbling slightly despite being braced by both hands, arms locked at his side, Jon took a deep breath and waited. He would be taking still photos, but the scene unfolding before his eyes through the camera's screen was destined to shoot to number one in his box office charts and remain there until eternity. Summer faced away from him, undid a zip and stepped out of her dress. A loud drum from the dance troop thudded behind Jon. With a deft flick behind her back, her bra was undone and her back was free. Long, golden legs met a bottom that must have been sculpted by an artisan with a lifetime's knowledge of the mathematics for perfect curves. She climbed up, bent her knees and reached her arms down between her legs. *Boom.* She exploded upwards, flinging the bra high up into the air. *Boom.* Her legs stretched gracefully sideways towards a horizontal split position. *Boom.* She reached the peak of her trajectory, skin surrounded only by the elements, legs in an almost perfect line, arms outstretched until hands met toes. *Boom.* Both Summer and time seemed to freeze, enabling Jon to press the camera's button. He was left staring at the captured image on the screen until it disappeared, ready for another shot.

'Did you get it? Did you? Please tell me you did!'

Summer was hopping beside him in his shirt and nothing else. Grabbing the phone, she moved out of the sunlight to get a clearer view. 'Yes!' Summer threw a hand up in the air, lifting her shirt higher and revealing a thigh. 'That's spot on – we nailed it!' Jon watched her zoom in and out of the photo. He'd given women flowers in the past, surprised them with modest gifts, even paid for a holiday for one girlfriend, but the expression on this girl's face right now was in a different league of honest joy.

'That is one *awesome* photo. Outrageous. A winner!'

'You were amazing. Your legs were...' Jon found a dead end.

'I teach yoga. Being supple has its uses.'

Jon said nothing.

She stood on her tiptoes and kissed him on his forehead. 'Anyway you, it's time we got you covered up again. Here – put this on.'

He was now holding something. 'You're playing, right?'

'Jon...?' she looked at him for an answer.

What was she asking? 'Dunn?'

'Jon Dunn – you said not three minutes ago that you trusted me, did you not?'

'Yes, but –'

'So put it on. It's for the shot.'

'It's a dress.'

'Well it's a shame that clothing recognition is not one of the tasks today, otherwise I'd put you right up there. Yes, it's a dress. My favourite dress, actually, and one which you will be gracefully adorning for your photo.'

'But –'

'And if you even think of disagreeing – especially after what I have just done – then you are in big trouble, Mr Dunn.' She pushed it further against his chest and added, 'Particularly as I'm guessing you got a glimpse or two of the fun bits during my stunt.'

The blood in his body was parting as if he'd swallowed Moses himself – half was ascending back up to his face while the rest headed south. His eyes fought against the invisible magnetic force that can only emanate from a semi-covered pair of boobs two feet away. 'Now, lift your arms up and bend over. It's fairly loose fitting, so you should be able to get into it.' He obliged and Summer did the necessary arrangements.

A dress wasn't too bad, he considered after looking down at himself. Summer would get him in some pose, maybe people would comment, have a little fun at his expense, and then they'd swap back, walk off and hopefully into the next round.

'Right – now the trousers.' She held out a hand towards him.

'Oh, c'mon.'

'Don't be such a wuss. You can't possibly wear a dress with those trousers. Take them off. This shirt doesn't provide one hundred percent coverage to a girl's secrets, either, so I'll need the trousers.'

Indecent exposure or covering up those wonderful legs? Surely both had to be illegal. Jon took out his train ticket holder and phone, slowly removed his shoes and finally his trousers. Summer grabbed them, slipped them on and tightened the belt.

'No time for knickers,' she said.

'So where do you want me?' Jon asked, looking back at the edge and putting his shoes back on.

'Oh no, not here, silly. We have to do something different.'

'I'm a man, wearing a dress and black shoes with your pick of London landmarks as the background. How different do you want?'

'Very.' She pointed upwards. 'There's no better view than from the top of the London Eye.'

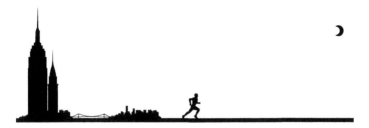

Chapter 6

'**O**i mister – are you one of those…trannies?'

The clothes swap seemed to have favoured Summer more than Jon. Favoured in the sense that she still oozed sexiness in his half done-up shirt, striding around in his black trousers, while Jon looked like he was lost on his own stag do. The little shit of a kid who'd just made the comment, pointing and laughing with his mates, was purely making an observation that everyone else was too afraid to voice.

'Yes, yes he is,' Summer replied. 'He started off as a normal boy just like you but he changed. Watch out – it could happen to you, too.' She gestured effeminately towards the kid.

'Weirdos,' the kid said as he backed away.

They were standing in the queue for fast-track tickets for the London Eye, realising that time was against them if they were to get Jon's shot done before the 3:15 deadline. The queue was long, although it was funny how some people had taken one look at Jon and allowed the pair to go in front of them.

'You're gonna have to pay, by the way,' Summer said, looking away.

'Why? It was your fantastic idea to go on this.'

'My bra is halfway to the North Sea, my knickers are in these pockets, I'm wearing flip-flops, you're wearing my dress and you just saw me naked. Where exactly do you think I would be storing any money?'

The movie clip of her stunning jump began to replay in his mind, before being interrupted.

'Excusez-moi?'

Jon turned to see a French couple smiling at him, camera poised. Before he could recall one of the many swear words his third-year French pen pal had taught him, the photo had been taken and the two were giggling with their achievement. 'Merci!'

Jon folded his arms tightly and gazed at the ticket desk that still had a few people ahead of them. 'Summer – is this all really necessary?'

'Oh take it like a man.' A little titter, only not as cute to Jon now. 'Jeez, it's just a dress. You don't know these people anyway.'

'I look stupid. I'm being ridiculed and everyone is staring. I may as well build my own ticket booth, seeing as I'm now London's newest attraction. At least I'd get paid for this humiliation.'

'Have you stopped to think what delight you're giving to these people?'

'Delight?'

'Look, everyone is here to enjoy themselves, to have fun. They'll go on the wheel, walk along the promenade, go to the aquarium, have their picnics and take home great memories. And seeing a grumpy man in a dress will just add to their day. One of those little things that you tell your partner, friends, colleagues. A tiny observation that creates a smile. You're making a difference to hundreds of people. When was the last time you could honestly say you did that?'

Jon stared at her with all the stubbornness of a kid who'd just been outwitted by his own mum. They carried on queuing in silence until they reached the attendant at the ticket counter.

Summer took the lead. 'Do you give discounts to transsexuals?'

Jon glanced upwards, suppressed a smirk, and dug her in her ribs with his elbow. The ticket lady paused and glanced at her colleague, as if she'd been given a request in an unknown language. For a strange second, Jon thought that he might actually get some kind of reduced rate. He sighed and pulled out his credit card. 'Just two adults, please.'

Tickets and mini guide in hand, the pair worked their way towards the entrance to the Eye. Summer bent her arm and looked at Jon. 'Would ma'am like to be escorted to her carriage?'

Jon focussed on the wheel, but hooked his arm inside hers. She was infuriatingly cute. Despite Jon looking like the world's worst drag queen, paying out for two extra-expensive tickets for something he'd already been on twice, and not having a clue what the point of all this was, he had begun to relax. That was until he heard a voice he recognised.

'Jon?'

There, holding an ice cream in each hand and with two daughters by his side, was Mick. Jon froze as his colleague tried to comprehend the scene.

'What the...?' Mick was looking up and down at Jon in his dress with a face that couldn't have been more shocked if he'd turned up and seen his own gran performing a pole dance routine. 'Why are you dressed as a woman?'

Fantastic. At work, Mick didn't have a clue who he was, yet meeting him randomly by a tourist attraction wearing a dress led to instant recognition. Jon was in panic mode. He had to say something – anything – that would give him half a chance of stopping it getting back to his department, even the whole company. 'You're skiving too. So you can't say anything. Nope. Not a thing, otherwise...'

'Me? I asked for the afternoon off, what with it being so nice and all. Whisked the girls from the ex and decided to come down 'ere.' Mick chomped on a Flake and with a chocolate splutter said, 'Some of us have bosses who are actually sane. Henry? From what I hear, he's going ape looking for you.'

Shit and double shit. A triple scoop of shit with runny sauce to match. Summer was watching with interest but her sharp, witty tongue was apparently taking a rest right now.

'If you'd told me you were bunking off to pursue your sordid, secret other life, I could have covered for you.'

Jon watched Mick's stomach heave up and down as he laughed, while his two kids looked up at Jon with disdain. Jon stared at Summer, his eyes pleading for a rope to help him escape from this ever-deepening hole, but she shot back a look that suggested the only action she might take was to get some popcorn.

'You know what, *Mike*?' Jon said, 'I'm just here having fun. All this is for a laugh, you know? A joke. With this beautiful woman here, who – as a matter of fact – I've just seen naked. Fully.' Jon put his arm round Summer, who duly put her head on his shoulder and beamed at Mick. 'Yes, I've skipped out without telling Henry, but as far as I'm concerned he can paint his penis green, stick it up his arse and write his own help screen on how to do that!' With that, the cross-dressed pair went towards the fast-track queue to get on to the Eye, leaving Mick to watch, yellow dribble hanging from his open mouth.

'Time to execute the next bit of my plan,' Summer said, just before they'd got to the back of the small queue. 'Underpants, please.'

'What?'

'It's simple – you, wearing a dress, in a capsule with over twenty strangers, underpants on head, London stretching out in the background. How much more outrageous do you want?'

Jon thought about it. 'Why can't I wear your knickers instead?'

'The power of suggestion – *your* underpants, meaning you'll presumably be naked underneath. So squat like this and give.' Summer crouched before him. 'Or else.'

'This is beyond a –'

He barely felt her hands race up the dress and grab on to his boxers, so was shocked to see them now crumpled round the tops of his shoes. 'Now all you need to do is step out of them.'

Jon obeyed, and Summer swooped to pick them up and deposit them into Jon's trousers, which were rapidly becoming a mobile underwear drawer.

'This plan of yours had better work,' Jon said, holding his hands in front of his crotch.

'It will, trust me.' They edged forward. 'You were great back there, you know.'

'When?'

'With tubby workmate. Stood your ground.'

'Thanks. He's an arse, anyway.'

'Are you going to be in trouble?'

'Perhaps.' Jon looked ahead. 'Depends where this security guard is gonna stick his wand.'

A man and woman in fluorescent yellow jackets studied them with stern faces.

'Soho's that way,' the man said, pointing a thumb behind him.

'It's okay,' Summer said, 'we're not into anything kinky. It's just a bet, you know.'

'A bet? So who lost?' The male guard's comments momentarily causing a ripple of a smile to appear on his colleague's face.

'Look, we're not doing anything wrong and we have nothing suspicious on us. Well, unless you count these.' Summer whipped out Jon's Scooby-Doo boxers from his pocket and waved them. The guards leaned back, away from the offending object.

'Just keep them to yourself, please, madam.'

With a bit of uncertainty, but with no reason to stop them, they were allowed to filter through to the metal barriers. They now stood on the edge of the platform, waiting for the next pod to rotate round as a host of other people jostled for position in front of them. Jon got the now usual stares but, realising that they'd be spending the next thirty or so minutes in a small space with him, they each looked away whenever he made return eye contact. Summer had taken his train ticket holder and phone in preparation for the competition photo.

'Are you ready for the crowning glory?' Summer was holding his boxer shorts.

'Now?'

'Close your eyes, arms down.'

Jon, arms by his sides stood with his back to the pod that had now come around, as people began to shuffle in. Summer put her arms around his back and slowly kissed him on the lips. It was a kiss that lit him up like a bonus mode on a pinball machine. The score kept ticking up as she moved her soft lips against his. He didn't even notice her unzipping the dress, sending it down around his feet. Eyes still closed, arousal coming up to fifty percent, he only became aware of his undressed state as he felt Summer's hands once again on his chest. When he finally looked again, he saw the devilment back in her hazel eyes, only this time much more than a spark – they burned with mischief.

'See you later, lover boy!'

With that, she pushed him into the pod, so hard he staggered backwards, until he stumbled against the large oval bench in the middle and fell onto it. With a flick of her wrist, she threw him the mini guide which landed fortuitously between his splayed legs, then took out his phone and fired off a photo.

'Got you – here!'

She flung the mobile towards the stricken Jon just as the pod started to move upwards. As it clattered to the floor near his feet, Summer's face swung out of his view and he looked down at the photo on its screen. There he was, on his back, legs spread, butt naked aside from his shoes, mini guide hiding his now rapidly diminishing modesty, with twenty people looking down in shock above him. As he watched Summer grab her dress and escape back down the exit past confused onlookers, wearing and carrying all his clothes, there was only one word he could think of: Outrageous.

Chapter 7

IT'S amazing that something so natural as the human naked form can be both so revered and yet considered so repellent by many. Right now, for his fellow capsule companions, Jon was edging more on the side of the latter. Technically, he wasn't naked – he still had his shoes on – although right now he felt he'd be more at ease with even these off, to at least make it proper naked. Everyone had backed off to the edge of the pod, leaving Jon in the middle like a table centrepiece at a fetish party. Two old ladies were shaking their heads, faces screwed up, although neither appeared to want to look away any time soon. The French couple were also here, the monsieur barking commands at his girlfriend until she produced the camera. Summer was right – Jon was certainly adding to their day.

He didn't think it was appropriate to sit his bare cheeks on the seat provided, nor did he think he could really stand up and stare outside, subjecting everyone to his rear. Still in a sitting position, he gradually slid to the floor, wincing as the cold metal met his bottom. The mini guide – which perhaps now wasn't going to be kept as a souvenir of the day – was his only saviour. He made sure it was firmly in position, before grabbing his phone and slowly shuffling his way back.

'Need a hand, mate?' A lad in his early twenties with his arm casually round the shoulders of another man looked at Jon, eyebrows raised.

'It's amazing what you get in these guides now!' his partner added, bursting into laughter.

If Jon was lucky, by the end of the day he might make the cover of *Time Out* magazine. Three girls, who looked sixteen but almost definitely weren't, tittered and were texting away on their phones. Several other people were chatting in different languages with a variety of disapproving and bemused expressions. 'Ow!' Jon bumped his head on a rail as he reached a point on the edge where people had parted. He carefully got up into a vertical position, facing inwards with his back now pointing out towards the Thames, whilst disappointing the Giggle Sisters who obviously had hopes of capturing a glimpse of the only thing that wasn't currently on show. Jon turned his head around and saw the top of the Houses of Parliament coming up.

'Bad day?' Rhetorical question of the year came from a guy standing next to Jon in his late forties with a crop of grey hair. Jon felt everyone turn their ears towards him, hoping for some narration to the story they were no doubt writing in their heads for future telling.

'Well, let me see…' Jon looked up at the ceiling. 'I have pissed off my boss, everyone at work has probably now been told I'm a transvestite, I have no money, the woman of my dreams has just shafted me and run off with my clothes and I'm standing in a glass pod with a bunch of strangers showing my hairy arse off to the whole of the biggest city in England.'

After what seemed like an hour, his silver friend broke the silence, 'At least it's a good view.'

It was lucky both of Jon's hands were being used to preserve what was left of his modesty, otherwise any news story that was written about him would have contained the words '...suddenly throttled...' He looked back again at the increasingly impressive scene over London. On the plus side, at least his bum was getting smaller to those on the ground. His phone let out a small 'bing!' and vibrated. It was a text from some random number:

'Hi Jon, it's Summer. Soz – it had to be done! I'm in it to win it. Least u got ur photo. Enjoy ur ride! x'

So Summer had planned it all along. Getting a gullible fool like him to take her photo and then led him up the garden path and thrown him in the pond while she trotted off to the next task. Jon read the message again. He had worn a dress. He was now stark bollock naked and being gawped at like a zoo animal because he had trusted her. Jon's heart raced. She must have even sneakily got his number in the queue when she had both phones, just so she could taunt him later. *Enjoy ur ride!* Yep, he'd been ridden – all the way to Humiliation City. The display on the phone went back to the clock, 3:12. Three minutes to the deadline. He brought up the photo again and shook his head. A little voice inside told him that one day he would look back on this and laugh, but it was soon beaten to a pulp by every other voice reminding it of the predicament they were still currently in. His shocked expression in the picture was good, though, and the variety of faces looking at his prone white body could be perceived as comical. He guessed there was no harm in submitting it, so he sent the photo to the number stored in the phone.

Ten minutes later, Jon was convinced the wheel had stopped. Maybe it was just the fact that he was looking at his feet for most of the journey, trying to avoid any eye contact and a potential invite for someone to make a comment, not that they needed any encouragement.

'Oh look – The Gherkin. Remind you of anything in here?' came a man's voice near the door.

'Nah. It wasn't *that* big,' shouted one of the teenagers, resulting in another round of laughter.

Jon thought that perhaps they should hold the next comedy roadshow in this pod. They had all been so very helpful, so keen to come to the aid of a man who was obviously in a sticky situation. Not even a single offer of an item of clothing to help him in his predicament. He could see that even on this hot day there was the odd thin sweater between them. Would it have killed them to spare one? He would have even been quite glad to have the old lady's slip that he could see showing.

'Oi mate – do you want your official photo done? I hear they do a good fridge magnet.'

Jon shot the budding comedian his best f-off stare. His phone buzzed again, this time ringing, so he prodded at a button to answer it.

'If that's you Summer I –'

'Jon? It's Daisy.'

'Oh, er…hi.' Summer had been in his head so much he'd almost forgotten the bubbly blonde who started all of this.

'Are you okay, Jon? Let me tell you – that photo was something else! I was in stitches. I was laughing so hard I think a little bit of pee came out.'

Jon tried to ignore the image that was forming.

'Sorry. Too much information there. I had a spare pair of knick-knocks handy, anyway. So, we've reviewed all the entries and I'm delighted to say…you made it into the top two. You're into the penultimate round!'

Jon didn't feel too much like doing a celebratory dance. 'Great. That's assuming I don't get arrested in the meantime.'

'Huh? You're not still, you know, naked are you?'

'I have about twenty witnesses here that might confirm that.'

'Really? Well, clothes or no clothes, by 4pm you need to get yourself to an address I'm about to send to you otherwise you'll fail, and the other contestant will be declared the winner.'

'You mean Summer.'

A slight pause. 'I can't possibly tell you who you're up against. But I can tell you that they're almost there now.'

'Can I catch her?'

'You won't catch whoever you're up against, but you can still make it in time.'

'And can I still beat her?'

'There's still a chance you could be my winner, yes.'

Jon looked out across the city. 'Is it far from the London Eye?'

'No, you could probably walk it in about twenty minutes.'

'Walk? I'm not going to hang around in this state. I'll do it in ten.'

'Won't running naked be…uncomfortable?'

'Daisy – getting bruised balls will be worth it just to beat that scheming tart. Don't worry – I'll be there.'

Game on. Daisy hung up and then sent him the details of his destination. He had another ten minutes before the capsule 'landed', so he studied the maps on his phone, memorising the route. It would be tight, and would indeed involve him escaping the attentions of the crowd, security and perhaps even the police when he got out, but he was determined not to let Summer win like this. This puppet was going to cut his strings and turn on his master.

As the pod descended towards the platform for disembarking, the girls went to the front. One of them turned to face Jon. 'Let him get off first – I'm not sure if I want that *thing* behind me,' she said, pointing towards his crotch.

'Thanks,' was all Jon offered as a response. He could see through the glass that security was waiting for him, and also a single policeman, presumably having been informed of his dramatic entrance into the capsule. There were going to be questions – questions that Jon had neither the time nor the patience for right now. He stood there, one hand holding his phone, the other keeping the green guide strategically placed, head back and chest out, as if he were waiting for a lift at work on a way-too-casual Friday.

The doors opened. Jon acted as if he were about to step forward to greet the frowning officer, and then did the only thing he could think of – he ran. Throwing the guide at the policeman who, by reflex, caught it, he legged it to his left and down the first part of the zig-zagged sloped exit ramps. As he turned to descend the second ramp, the copper began to chase, but the real problem that Jon faced next was leisure attraction rule number one: always force customers through the gift shop when exiting. It was packed full of people choosing their photos and tacky souvenirs and Jon was about to become a bull within it.

As he approached the end of the penultimate ramp, he realised there was only one course of action to take. He put his hands on the metal rail and sprung upwards. It was only the adrenaline that enabled him to complete his vault over the end gate and into a surprised incoming queue without incurring a major future lifestyle change. Slipping past some horrified, bemused and even delighted faces, he made it out into the open. Free…at least for the moment.

With one hand between his legs – for modesty and athletic ergonomic purposes – he sprinted past the queue, leaving the Eye and Westminster Bridge behind him. He glanced back and saw the policeman giving chase, leaving a trail of shocked onlookers. A man covered from head to toe in grey paint moved only his eyes as he tracked Jon while keeping up his soldier statue impression. Two women dressed in pink t-shirts and matching leg warmers collecting for charity rattled their buckets of change as he ran past, shouting, 'Nice bum!' He ran through a collection of large soap bubbles drifting through the air, bursting on his chest, leaving an oily residue. Another peek behind – his pursuer was even closer than before. Great. Trust Jon to get a policeman who had probably gone under the qualifying time for the Olympic 400 metres. He rushed past kids holding on to their parents' hands.

'Daddy! Daddy! Look at the funny man!'

Weaving in and out of fancy pushchairs, he skipped past tourists trailing suitcases behind them, avoided sellers' goods laid out on the pavements and went past caricature artists too slow to capture this real-life cartoon. Up ahead was a huge crowd that had gathered for another session from the loud dance act. He looked again and saw PC Not-So-Plod just a few metres behind, breathing in short, controlled bursts. Another tourist came into view, orange suitcase dragging behind like a sulky kid. Jon couldn't get caught, not now, not for this. Seconds away from being apprehended, Jon slapped down his shoes harder, caught up with the suitcase, grabbed it and flicked it out and behind him, hauling the poor man backwards and into his chaser's path. The policeman had no chance to react, and was sent flying over both man and case, landing heavily and rolling sideways until he hit a wooden bench. For a few brief seconds, Jon was relieved to see that an officer of the law splayed out on the pavement trumped the naked running man in terms of entertainment. Even the human statues broke character and turned to see what had happened. He put the crowd surrounding the dance group between him and the stricken officer, as various people went to his aid. Jon slowed when he realised his immediate danger had passed, which allowed him to assess the scene once more. He needed a superhero to get out of this one, and suddenly he spotted one: Spider-Man.

'Give me your Spidey outfit…now!' Jon said with his best crazed look, waving his arms at the human statue. Startled by the outburst, in the middle of packing up for the afternoon, the man backed away.

'Just do it!' Jon said. 'Look at me – I've done nothing wrong, and I need your help. That's what superheroes do, don't they? Help people in need?'

He was sure that the half-policeman, half-Terminator would be getting to his feet soon, ready to resume the chase. Whether it was the shock of being mugged by a desperate man waving much more than his arms in front of him, or out of some affinity with his cartoon counterpart, Spider-Man relinquished the pair of trousers. Jon tried to slip them on over his shoes with an almighty tug, but failed to get them over his heels, so he resorted to removing his footwear. Finally, with another sharp pull, he got the blue and red leggings on. For the first time in what seemed like weeks, he was no longer swinging freely in the air.

'Oi!'

Jon spun on the spot to see the policeman standing thirty metres away, looking as if he were ready to not only chase him down again, but this time to kill and bury him on the spot. With no time to put on the rest of the outfit or even his shoes, and thinking that carrying them might slow him down, he decided to donate them to his helper. 'Keep the change,' Jon shouted back after picking up his phone and sprinting off again towards a staircase that led up to the Golden Jubilee Bridge. Bounding up the steps three at a time, he got to the top quickly, but took a lot out of his energy reserves. He paused to catch his breath and to see where the Metropolitan's finest had got to. To his surprise and relief, the policeman was some way behind, due to the severe limp he was now sporting. Jon turned and jogged across the bridge barefoot, bringing up on the phone the details of the next task. Although he felt a bit like a Mexican wrestler who had forgotten to bring his boots to training, it was certainly an upgrade from his previous attire. He still had fifteen minutes. Halfway across the bridge, breathing hard, sun hitting his bare chest, he let a little smile slip from his lips. From desk jockey to indecent, shoeless thief running from the law, in less than four hours.

He soon found his way to his destination in Soho: Isobel's Inks. If Jon had paid a little more attention to the name of the shop as opposed to just getting there, he may have realised why at 3:52 he was standing directly in front of a window with the slogan 'Come In, Sit Down, Pierce Off' underneath a huge neon skull.

Chapter 8

THE naive part of Jon had expected Isobel's Inks to be a nice art shop, or perhaps the finest pen seller in London. When faced with having to enter the type of place he only associated with extreme pain and permanent defacing of one's body, however, he froze with one hand on the tattooist's door handle. As he crept in, a small bell rang above his head, as if a semi-naked, spandex-wearing, barefooted, nervous, pasty man needed any more attention drawn to him. He could smell incense in the air, and hear a distant buzzing somewhere in a back room, neither of which filled him with much comfort. Every inch of the wall was covered by frames containing tattoo designs, mainly black, but some with a splash of red and green. Flaming dragons and angry skulls fought leaping dolphins and delicate flowers. Topless nymphs with disproportional bodies wrapped themselves around heavy weapons. Red hearts, torn hearts, daggers, blood. Apparently anything and everything was available to be scrawled on your body.

A man who looked like he could probably rip off Jon's arm and use it to scratch his arse for fun, put down his magazine and looked up from behind a counter. Every visible surface of his body was covered in tattoos, and judging from the designs, he had something of a dragon fetish. Piercings were also apparently his thing, having more metal on his face than in Jon's entire cutlery drawer. It was impossible to tell his age, unless there was a hallmark somewhere on him. Despite his own most attractive feature being a fish hook through his lip, he regarded Jon as if he were an experiment that they had performed on a wet Wednesday afternoon that had gone horribly wrong.

'This is a tattooist, fuckwit.'

It was Jon's opinion that this greeting was rather needless and hurtful, although it wasn't an opinion that he was about to share.

'Yes, er, I can see that. And…a very nice one it is, too.'

'Comic shop is three doors down, twat.' He went back to reading *Dragon's Digest*.

Ignoring the fact that this subhuman species was obviously an expert in colourful insults, and with his legs feeling as if they might like another little jog right out of here, Jon persisted. 'Look, I'm not entirely sure why I'm here, but –'

'Let me guess – you want a spider's web tattooed on your scrawny little chest? Or perhaps I can do a full-on Spidey mask to cover up your ugly, narrow mug?' The talking tackle box ran his hands down his face, revealing a big-eyed expression. 'Either way, I don't do pussy comic character stuff, so fuck off.'

Jon looked away from the tattooist's stare before it sliced his head clean off. He saw a design of Marilyn Monroe next to Satan, who was having fun impaling his fork in some poor goblin. Jon fumbled with his phone, trying to figure out a way how he could find out what this task was about without it involving him having to conquer this troll. He read the phone message again, and without looking up said, 'Daisy sent me?'

'Daisy? Daisy sent you?'

Jon ducked a little and glanced up. The piercings had rearranged themselves on his face in a smile. 'Well why didn't you say, you idiot? Come on round.'

Jon had clearly said the magic word, as a door was being opened and he was beckoned through by the now beaming giant. 'Daisy's my little girl. Sweet as anything. Takes after me, of course.'

Jon didn't quite know where he was being led, but before he knew it, he was sitting down in an old, black leather chair in a small room.

'I'm Zu, by the way.'

Jon looked at the tree trunk of an arm in front of him and shook its hand. 'Jon.'

'Jon? So you're Jon? I was told about you. Anyway, real name's Elliott. You know, after the dragon in the film.'

Jon gave him a vacant stare.

'You know – *Pete's Dragon*? Mum and Dad loved that film. Thought it was shit myself, that's why I changed to Zu, but I'm kinda hooked on the whole dragon thing, as you might have noticed.'

Now he was sitting down, Jon could see two scaly figures on Zu's legs breathing fire upwards.

'Yeah, I had an inkling.'

'Inkling? *Ink*ling? You trying to be funny?'

Superb. A dragon-man with an eye for an unintended bad pun. Jon didn't reply.

'So, where do you want the sucker, then?'

'Want what?'

'The tattoo, of course.'

'Tattoo?' Jon's face went a previously unknown shade of white.

'Oh, that's right, you don't know, do you? You poor sod. All I know is that my little Daisy Chain – that's what I call her – is part of some oh-so-important competition and told me whoever gets sent here by her before 4pm today has to have a tattoo.'

'On my body?'

A quizzical look. 'Well of course on your body, you total moron!'

Jon didn't know what he found more frightening – the prospect of certain pain and permanent marking of his untouched body, or the fact that it would be performed by a man who seemed to have severe anger management issues.

'I'm sorry, I can't have a tattoo on my body.'

'Where else do you suppose I put it? In an envelope and mail it to wherever your pathetic excuse for a home is?'

'Can't you just do a temporary one for me?'

Zu winced. 'Don't insult my craft. It's needle or nothing.'

'This is crazy! I don't even know why I'm doing this. I'm not going to let you scratch some weird fantasy scene all over my body just so I can attempt to win a competition when I don't even know what the prize is.' Jon went to get up and leave.

'It's not a weird fantasy scene, you Lycra-clad twat. I have to do a logo.'

'Of what?' Jon paused, half out of his chair.

'Of the DPI company. Seems bonkers to me, but I suppose it's free advertising.'

Zu showed him a drawing of the logo. It wasn't too offensive on paper, but Jon didn't have plans to become a walking advertising board.

'I'm sorry, but I can't let you put that on me.'

'Chicken shit?'

'No, it's just – I can't do it, that's all.'

'Aw, maybe Mummy can pay for laser removal after you lose?'

'I'm not letting you graffiti my body.'

Zu leant back against the wall facing Jon, folded his arms and sighed. 'Well, I might as well give you your bag and you can sod off back to the gay superhero meeting you came from.'

'Yeah. Sorry to have wasted your…hang on, did you say bag?'

Zu opened a small cupboard and retrieved a brown plastic bag. 'Well, looks like a bag of clothes to me. A woman who was just here told me to give it to a "Jon" if he ever turned up. I assume that would be you?'

Jon snatched the bag, peered inside and saw some familiar items. 'My clothes!' A plain white shirt had never looked better. He checked his trouser pockets and found to further relief his train ticket and credit card. The elation faded. 'Wait a minute – this woman…was she stunningly beautiful, with a kinda treacherous look in her eye?'

Zu shrugged. 'Yeah, not bad. White dress, bronze hair. Prefer them more rough and ready myself, but she was pretty, I guess.'

'Did you give her a tattoo?' Jon's heart began to speed up.

Zu shuffled his feet. 'Yeah, I may have done a small logo, but…'

'But?'

'Well, it was only on her arm.'

'What's wrong with an arm?'

Zu stepped forward and pushed Jon back in the chair again. 'Dude, the arm is a bit wussy, don't you see? It's fine for women, but this is a competition. I can do one in a much better place, one that would guarantee you'd win.'

Win. Jon realised that he could still beat Summer. He'd got his clothes back, was still in the game and now had a chance to get one over on her. 'Where do you suggest?'

'Back of the neck. Perfect.'

'Why?' Jon involuntarily felt behind his head.

'Hurts like hell. Especially for a skinny prick like you.'

Back of the neck. Well, at least he wouldn't ever see it. Except at the end of a haircut. 'Did Summer – the woman – definitely get one done?'

'Take a look at this if you don't believe me.' Zu showed Jon a photo on his phone. It was quite low resolution, but it was unmistakably Summer wearing the green logo on her arm. He knew he was down to the last two – him versus Summer – and she'd struck first.

'Can you knock me out and do it?'

Zu smiled. 'Admittedly, that would give me some pleasure, but,' he picked up an electronic needle, making a loud buzz, 'I'd get more enjoyment out of you being fully conscious.'

Jon thought of the shop name. 'And Isobel? Isn't she available to maybe take this one?'

'Nan? No, she doesn't help out, it's just named after her. Got more tatts than me, though.'

Pain, glory and a souvenir of this increasingly surreal day, or barefoot back home, untouched?

'Zu?'

'That's my name.'

'Do your worst.'

Chapter 9

ALTHOUGH it had been uneventful, Jon's journey home had been like returning from a masochist party. His neck felt like someone had taken a blowtorch to it, his throat was raw from screaming in pain and the skin between his big and second toes was worn down to the bone thanks to the flip-flops he was wearing. Such was the entertainment provided by Jon – there were even tears just after the hour mark – that Zu had taken pity on him and donated the footwear to prevent a trip home barefoot. He didn't want to ever take off his pants and trousers again, having taken them for granted for so long prior to being stolen. Disappointingly, Summer had taken her knickers from his pockets. Jon was sure she had skipped home merrily from Zu's with a slightly itchy arm, pleased at her day's work in nearly destroying some random bloke's life.

At just after nine o'clock, he flopped down on his bed as if it were his final resting place. There was a shrill *meow* and a cat landed on his chest. 'Easy, Conan. Been quite a day.' Jon began to make a fuss of Conan as he started up his purr engine and rubbed his chin against him. 'Not sure what happens now, though.' After Zu had reluctantly agreed that any further refinement of the logo would not really justify the resulting pain, he'd had a photo taken and had submitted it. Since then, almost three hours ago, there'd been nothing. What had he been thinking? Risking his job and all for the pleasure of public humiliation and a ridiculous tattoo. Still, he admitted, it was something to tell the grandkids, presuming he could ever find a woman who liked strange tattoos. He wondered if he could arrange for its removal before he had to face his own parents. There was one person who it would impress, though, or at least surprise to the point of near fainting. Ensuring the cat didn't slide off the duvet, he grabbed the house phone and dialled.

'All right Stu. How's the new recruit?' Jon let Stu get all his crap out of the way as Conan pussyfooted his way into a trance on top of him. Fifteen minutes later, almost as an afterthought, Stu enquired about his friend's day. 'Another fun afternoon for you?'

'Actually, it was quite eventful.'

'What – did Henry spontaneously combust?'

'No. Well, maybe, I don't know. I wasn't in after lunch.'

'You never said you'd booked the afternoon off.'

'I didn't. I…just took it off.'

'You pulled a sickie? Never. Jon Boy doesn't have the guts to do something as mutinous as bunking off.'

'Well today I did something different, something you'd never do.' Suddenly the pain on his neck thrilled him.

'Hmmm, went to Madame Tussauds?'

'I got a tattoo, if you must know. And got a girl to strip off totally naked for a photo. Add to that a bit of nudity myself in a major London attraction, followed by some light mugging and being on the run from the police.'

An hour and a half later, Jon put down the phone

satisfied that he stunned Stu in such a way he was never going to look at his best friend the same again for the rest of his life.

'Wish I could've seen his face,' he said as the cat woke up and instantly began to paw Jon to remind him of the only living creature in the entire universe he should be thinking of. A quick trip to the bathroom followed, while Conan passed the time before the next period of attention by washing himself. Jon could still taste the toothpaste as he settled down under the duvet when he heard a faint ring. It took him a few seconds to locate the DPI mobile that was on the floor.

'Hello?'

'Jon? It's me, Daisy. You did it! You did it! I'm so proud of you!'

Jon sprung up like a cobra, sending Conan flying onto the floor. 'I won?'

'Of course you won. Back of the neck? You're insane! I've got a small daisy on my hip and it nearly killed me. I spoke to Daddy and he called you a big pussy for all the crying and screaming, but I think you're very brave, Jon, very brave indeed.'

'I beat Summer?'

'You beat all the other competitors. In the final two, your tattoo was judged to be the more adventurous and most painful. Exactly what we're looking for.'

Jon waved a clenched fist until his arm ached. He'd won. He may have got humiliated and suckered by a woman, but for once he had bounced back and triumphed. 'Daisy, I love you. After everything that's happened today, this is just…awesome.'

'Ah, that's really sweet, Jon, but today was nothing.

Today was the easy day. The real stuff starts from tomorrow, and you had really better be up for it.'

'Tomorrow? But I've got to get back to work.'

'Don't worry about that.'

'What do you mean, don't worry? I've no holiday left. I can't take another day sick just for some competition.'

'It will be for slightly more than one day, Jon.'

'More? You haven't met my boss. I can't possibly –'

'Are we back to squeaking again? Now that you've got to this stage, DPI will take care of all that. Trust me.'

Jon thought back to the last time he was told to trust a woman. 'Haven't I won anything yet?'

Daisy gave her trademark giggle. 'You've won an entry to the final round, and therefore a chance to win the dream prize.'

'Which is?'

'Absolutely amazing. Wonderful. A dream come true. Once in a lifetime opportunity'

'Which is...?'

'You'll be the envy of your friends, family, the entire world. The biggest prize in the history of mankind.'

'You still haven't been told, have you?'

A more nervous laugh. 'Not exactly. I'm just a small cog in the London wheel of DPI. It's need to know only, until tomorrow.'

'Do you think it's money? My own private island?' The brain cells were working overtime. 'Does it involve Kylie Minogue?'

Daisy lowered her voice. 'I honestly don't know, but the

rumours here are that Mr Peabody is determined to shock the world.' Before Jon could reply, Daisy returned to full volume. 'But anyway, Jon, you need to get some sleep. It's an early start – you're being picked up at 6am sharp.'

'Do I have a choice in doing this?'

'Of course. Hear what we have to say tomorrow morning, and if you want to be a baby, then you can go back to your little testing job. But I know what you'll do. I believe in you. You can do it – you're my winner!'

She relayed a few other logistical details and then left Jon to rest, not that he thought there was a chance of any sleep after all that. Conan had resorted to scratching the carpet in his indignation at being interrupted yet again. He stopped when Jon shouted at him, but then sat and stared at Jon with the look of an animal that was planning to kill him and his entire family unless he was richly compensated within the next ten seconds.

'Sorry, mate. What do you think, eh? Could I really risk losing my job over this?' He gave Conan some cat biscuits as peace reigned again. 'I can just hear that conversation with Dad. *You know the stable job you always said I was lucky to get? Well, I've just lost it in the vague hope of winning the first thing in my life on my own.*' Then again, he thought, losing his job was perhaps not such a bad idea given his encounter with Mick that afternoon. The day's events replayed through his mind, interlaced with a hundred questions and visions of increasingly inventive prizes, until the early hours when he finally drifted off.

King Kong had been climbing one of the skyscrapers in Canary Wharf with Summer in his giant grasp, pleading for a naked Jon to help her while the *Puff the Magic Dragon* theme tune looped round, as the doorbell rang for the tenth time. Jon woke to confusion and peeked at the clock with fuzzy eyes – 6:03. Who could be ringing at this time? He thought back to the previous night and Daisy's call. 'Shit!' Not bothering to dress, he jumped onto the carpet and dashed to open the door. A young man stood outside in a blue suit with matching tie and cap.

'Jon Dunn? I'm from DPI Adventures. I have strict instructions to collect you and leave for DPI HQ right now.'

Jon yawned. 'By "right now", could you possibly extend that to, say, in fifteen minutes' time?'

'Mr Peabody was very explicit in his requirements, sir. We have to leave now.' He shot a look at *The Simpsons* underwear Jon was wearing and added, 'I have all the clothes you'll need for the day in the car, including footwear, sir. All you need is yourself.'

'I should probably shave, though and –'

'Sir, I have been instructed to leave at the latest by 6:05 – with or without the contestant. If the contestant does not or is not able to travel in the vehicle with me then that contestant must be informed they are no longer in the competition and therefore not eligible for the prize.'

The ever-impatient Doug Peabody and his mysterious prize.

'Can't I just brush my teeth?'

The chauffeur-cum-soldier looked at his watch. 'The limo has full grooming facilities. Thirty seconds.'

'Limo? Wow. Oh well, I'll just come as I am, I suppose,' Jon said as he threw some dried cat food into a bowl and closed the door behind him. 'I've been out in worse.'

True to the driver's word, the limo indeed had everything Jon needed to freshen up. The only missing accessory was a shower, although he hadn't pressed all the buttons inside yet, so he couldn't be totally sure. The drive from Stevenage was going to take about an hour and a half, so he had plenty of time to spruce himself up. The interior had so much space it could probably have transported an entire royal wedding party, and he flicked a couple of switches until it was bathed in purple neon light. The clothing he found was unexpected – an orange tracksuit complete with green DPI logos. There were also black DPI underpants, green and orange DPI shorts and top, and a pair of similarly-coloured trainers that looked like they had been designed by a NASA engineer who'd watched too many *Austin Power* movies. At least they all matched the back of his neck. A quick electric shave, a brushing of teeth and even his first nasal trim of the year via one of the array of gadgets laid out, made him ready for whatever was coming next. And whatever that was, would occur after a little nap.

'Welcome to DPI Headquarters, Mr Dunn.' The limo door was now open, and from his horizontal position, Jon opened his eyes to a pair of black boots, one foot tapping slowly. He yawned, stretched and clambered out into the cool morning air, looking back as the driver closed the door. 'I've left my underpants in there. Sorry.'

'Don't worry sir, I'll have them dry cleaned and sent back to you.'

'Wow. I should have brought the rest of my washing.'

Jon was handed a card. 'You are to have this – it will tell you all you need to know about the meeting. It is 7:40 now, so you have fifty minutes to reach the meeting room. I trust you enjoyed your journey and had everything you needed.'

'Yeah, great, thanks. Wait – fifty minutes to get to the room? Why are we so early then? I could've had a nice lie-in.'

The chauffeur said nothing and just stood there, standing perfectly upright. Jon looked at the card and made his way to the building's entrance after offering back, 'Thanks again. And...at ease.'

Having been asleep for the last part of the journey, Jon hadn't taken in his destination. As he reached the entrance and looked up, he could see an enormous glass building disappearing into the clouds. Home of Douglas Peabody International – where else would he set up offices, other than the highest and most futuristic building around? The card said that the meeting was on the 65th floor. He walked into the lobby and located the reception, whose size and grandeur must have meant it could probably double as an interplanetary space port in a film. He showed his card to a receptionist whose smile was so fixed he was not convinced she was real. She scanned the code on it and read the details on her small screen. 'Jon Dunn – one of the DPI Adventures ten, I see.'

Well at least he now knew for sure how many he was up against. 'Is everyone else here yet?'

'Nope, there's still one more to come after you. The others are on their way up. May I offer you my congratulations on making it to the final, Mr Dunn.'

'Thanks. Not that I know what the prize is.'

'Oh, it's going to be wonderful, I'm sure.'

Jon guessed that she came from the Daisy school of DPI information.

'Here's your security pass. The stairs are to your left.'

'Thanks. I'll take the lift, though.' Jon saw a perfectly

good set of lifts being used a few metres away.

'Mr Peabody has specifically requested that all DPI Adventures competitors use the stairs to reach the meeting. Usage of lifts is strictly forbidden and may result in expulsion from the competition.'

'Are you kidding me? I'm on the 65th floor.'

'You must use the stairs, sir.'

Jon stared at her lips, wondering if they'd ever been together in their entire existence. 'Can't I just go up a couple of flights and catch a lift a few floors later?'

'Sorry sir, the lifts have surveillance and you would be picked up. Especially given your attire.'

He looked at his orange outfit and briefly considered another mugging.

'How quickly can an ambulance get here in the event I have a heart attack?'

'We have a special medic team today on standby for such emergencies.'

'Well, that's just fine and dandy then.' Bastards had thought of everything.

'You have forty-five minutes, so take your time, sir.'

Jon wanted to haul her over the desk and drag her along with him up the stairs just to see if that smile would crack, but instead he trudged off to where she had indicated. He regarded flights of stairs as he did American tourists – on their own, they could be tolerated, but having to deal with lots of them all at once was hell. He stepped onto the first set of wide, white steps and started his ascent, not wanting to look up in the centre of the staircase at what lay ahead, fearing that he might actually see infinity.

5th floor. Already his legs were starting to complain. He peeled off his tracksuit top, wondering if Peabody got off on playing with their lives.

15th floor. Any grooming done in the limo was now wasted in a river of sweat that was cascading down the sides of his face, round his neck and down his back.

27th floor. Jon paused and seriously contemplated continuing in just his underpants.

33rd floor. Twenty minutes into his climb and he was only just over halfway up. He swore that any minute now he'd see his lungs burst out of his chest.

40th floor. Jon sat down on the bottom step of the next flight, regretting that he'd not got a pen to write his last will and testament on the walls. The sound of his heart booming in his ears meant he missed the noise of footsteps coming up the stairs.

'Don't think much of the competition, if they're all as weak as you.'

Had he any muscle tissue still working, Jon would've jumped at the sound of a voice that was now right beside him.

'Name's Nicki.' She paused to catch her breath, which didn't take too long. 'The old git certainly knows how to make us work for this prize.'

She appeared to be in her mid-twenties, slim and sporty. As sweaty brunettes in orange tracksuits went, Jon thought Nicki was quite attractive. On the plus side, Jon could quite clearly remember his name this time; on the negative side, saying it out loud might have killed him there and then on the spot. Instead, he flicked a hand up just enough to give some semblance of an acknowledgement while he sucked in more air.

'You look completely shagged. Sure you don't just wanna quit?' She reached into her tracksuit pocket and retrieved a small bottle of water.

Just as he was about to summon the energy to thank her for the offer of the life-giving liquid, Nicki squirted the entire contents down her throat. 'I'd offer you some, but I've only got another two bottles left and there's still a long way to go.'

'Oh. Okay.'

'What were you expecting, a piggy back?'

'No, I...dunno. Maybe a hand up?' Jon reached towards her.

Nicki looked at his hand as if she were being offered a used tissue. 'Sorry, but you know what this game is like – everything has deadlines and I'm not risking missing out just to help some stranded, unfit arse.' She placed the empty bottle in his outstretched hand.

'Oh. Well I wouldn't want to hold you up.'

'Don't worry, you won't. Gonna push on up. If I don't see you again...have a nice life.'

Jon sat there and watched her small behind bounce up the stairs. He may be dying, Jon thought, but at least he was making friends.

At 8:26, Jon triumphantly emerged through the doors on the 65th floor, sounding and looking like he'd had several organ failures mid-route. Through sweat-filled eyes, he could see bright red lipstick coming towards him.

'Hello again, Mr Dunn. I'm glad you made it in time.'

Jon wiped his eyes and saw that it was the same woman who had greeted him in reception. 'Hi.' He rubbed sweat from his face as he struggled to both stand and talk. There

71

was enough salt on him to keep the entire country's roads free from snow during a long winter. 'Came by lift, by any chance?'

'Of course. Now, you have a couple of minutes to mingle with your fellow challengers and enjoy the view before Mr Peabody requests the pleasure of your company.'

She led him round the corner and Jon found himself looking out across the whole of the city through vast glass panels. He thought he'd seen London up high, but the vista now in front of him made yesterday's view from the London Eye seem like he'd seen the city from the heights of a park swing. Tower Bridge looked as if it were a plastic toy from a Christmas cracker, and the boats mere matchsticks floating on a trickle of grey-blue. Jon was soaring. The city seemed so much bigger. At its low angle, the morning sun streamed through the huge glass windows, and Jon could feel the warmth being absorbed by his jacket. With the other people in identical outfits, Jon was in a corner of heaven's greenhouse with nine other carrots.

'Damn – you made it.' His enjoyment of the view was interrupted by Nicki. 'I assumed I was only going to end up having to beat eight people. Still, by the looks of you I'm not sure you're gonna survive the day anyway.'

Jon ignored her at first and introduced himself to the man by her side, who returned his handshake with a strong grip.

'Hi, I'm Arjun. Have you seen these views? Mental, I tell you. What the heck are we doing here? Don't you just want to smash through these windows and jump out? Crazy, man.' Arjun barely looked at Jon for more than a millisecond as he flicked his eyes this way and that.

Nicki offered her hand to Jon, 'Here, this time you can have it.'

'I'm honoured,' he said, taking it and having his arm pumped for longer than he thought was necessary.

'So, what kept you? I passed you on the stairs ages ago. Still, I must have a few years on you. Middle age does that to a man. Slows you down.'

'Actually, I'm thirty-four.'

'See? Middle-aged.'

Jon was about to protest at this clearly wrong labelling of his age when they were joined by another contestant.

'Good morning, gentlemen, I'm Jermaine,' said a young, shaven-headed man, shaking hands with the men. 'And good morning, lady,' he continued, taking Nicki's hand and kissing it.

'Jermaine, you little charmer,' Arjun said. 'So is that a Lancashire accent you've got there?'

Jermaine winced. 'Yorkshire, please. I take it from yours that you're from the Midlands?'

'That's right. Where our curries are thicker than our accents!'

A fifth orange-clad member broke into their group, wearing a turban and munching an apple. 'Prefer a bit of fruit, me. Name's Barry. All the way from Aberdeen.'

'Wow. Seems like Peabody ensured the whole of Britain got a chance,' Arjun said.

They exchanged a few more pleasantries before they heard the receptionist's voice again. 'Ladies and gentlemen, DPI Adventures finalists. Please all follow me for a short meeting with the owner of DPI himself, Mr Doug Peabody.'

The meeting wasn't being held in a room as such, just

another part of the floor partitioned off from the rest. A large wooden oval table dominated the section with a shine so severe, Torvill and Dean could have re-enacted Bolero on it. The ten filed into the room, each wearing their orange tracksuits, like the Dutch football team minus a goalie. Jon was last in, so walked round to a seat next to what – judging by the sheer presence of it – must have been Doug Peabody's chair. He hadn't had much chance to size up anyone else yet, but looking around, he could see that of the ten, he was one of seven men. Nicki was the first to sit down, followed by a girl with a big blonde ponytail who smiled at Jon. At exactly 8:30, Doug Peabody entered the room, dressed in the same tracksuit, only in black. Ignoring his throne, he leapt up onto the table and crouched, scanning each and every one of the faces in front of him. Throughout the silence, no-one dared breathe out. Doug's stare reached Jon and looked straight into his own eyes, as if testing his character.

'So, this is it.' He rose to his full height, causing everyone to crane their necks. 'You are my chosen ones. One of you...,' Doug swept a finger around the table, 'one of you will make history.' He rubbed his chin, and then, panther-like, jumped down onto the floor. 'But first, I'm sure you're all dying to know what you have to do in order to achieve this.'

Having almost died just to get to this meeting, Jon wasn't sure if he was excited or nervous about what was to come.

'You're all here because you took a risk. Many risks, probably. You saw an opportunity and took it. Having had challenges given to you, you accepted them and then you succeeded. You beat everyone else in your region – just by being here, you're a winner.'

A winner. These words couldn't possibly apply to him, and yet somehow here he was.

'Why did I set such demanding timescales? Because I had to, just to get you here. This time yesterday, you were all losers, you see. All of you.'

Jon glanced round the table. He'd been called a loser before, but was surprised that the term could be levelled at some of the people sitting around him.

'Harsh?' Doug continued. 'Maybe. But that's what I wanted to find – losers, but losers with potential to be winners. Losers who could do so much with their lives if only they put themselves out there, went for their goals. Most people missed our first email deadline as they didn't even see the email in time. They weren't sitting with their computer's email program open, waiting, or grabbing their phone as soon as a little message icon appeared.' Doug got out his phone and pressed a button before holding it out to everyone. 'They weren't slaves to their inboxes, servants to the almighty "bing"'. On cue, the phone let out the shrill notification sound of an incoming email. 'And of the ones who did reply to the initial email, the vast majority had more important things to do than to fill in a long questionnaire on the vague promise of something special.'

Was that Jon? He wasn't a slave, was he? But he knew – and recognised in others' faces here – that the 'bing' had triggered an impulse – one that screamed for instant attention.

'I only wanted people with *potential* get-up-and-go. I wanted people who might be interested in the prize, who I could push, who I could dare, who I could challenge to risk everything when risk was not their game. And through my tasks, with some manipulation, I found you.'

Doug slapped his hands on the table. 'So far, you've probably risked your jobs, embarrassed yourselves and have shown enough desire to win that you've even scarred your bodies for life.'

Everyone appeared to be a bit itchy all of a sudden, rubbing arms and legs.

'Now *that* had to hurt,' said a quiet voice in a Northern Irish accent behind Jon. He turned to see a man with thick black hair and deep eyes point to Zu's creation on Jon's neck.

The head of DPI carried on. 'But there's one more thing you'll need to do to win. One final event, the toughest of the lot. Something to test your stamina, dedication, commitment and will to win.' He gave a discrete nod and the theme from the film *Rocky* filled the room, causing the blonde woman's ponytail to be flicked up in surprise. 'A marathon!' he boomed. 'You're going to run a marathon!'

Doug let this sink in with everyone as he jogged on the spot, then celebrated, mimicking Stallone's famous run up the Philadelphia steps. For a few seconds, Jon had thought he was about to be told that they were all going to challenge for the heavyweight championship of the world, so was partially relieved that it was just a marathon. Everyone else exchanged dubious looks around the table.

'And not just any old marathon...' the music changed to Frank Sinatra, 'it's the New York Marathon! The Big Apple. Central Park, Brooklyn, Manhattan, Queens, Statue of Liberty, Empire State Building – you're gonna see them all in November.'

Doug swayed in time to the music. Arjun was the first to react. 'A marathon? Isn't that like, 26 miles or something?'

'26 miles, 385 yards of sheer endurance, dedication and pain. Nothing that you haven't had to show on your way to the final, just a little more...intense.'

Three seats away from Jon, a man put up his hand to address Doug. 'Er…I'm Tom. I'm sorry, but there's absolutely no way I can run 26 miles.'

'How do you know if you haven't tried yet? You'll get full training. In fact – we're taking you to New York for it. Starting tomorrow.'

'Tomorrow? No way!' said the owner of a Scouse accent that could cut through glass.

'Yes, tomorrow we'll fly you to New York, where you will stay in a luxurious house and then commence training with the best instructor money can buy. Of course, for insurance purposes, you will all have to quit your jobs.'

'Quit? I can't quit my job,' said a girl opposite Jon. 'Do you know how many garages in Gateshead are willing to take on female car mechanics?'

'It's Natasha, isn't it?' Doug said.

'I prefer Tasha. Look, I appreciate the opportunity but it's a bit much to –'

'I can reassure you, Tasha, that we'll provide you with all the money, accommodation, travel, in fact everything you could possibly want out there for the entire duration of the competition. You shall be there for just over three months, and when you return…well, let's just say that we're confident that after what you achieve out there, you simply won't want to go back to your old humdrum existence. We're offering you not only the chance of a lifetime, but the chance for a whole new life.'

'Just by running a stupid marathon?'

'Even if you don't win, the journey will change you. You will see just what you can do when you put your mind to it and really push yourself. You've come this far – haven't you had a wild twenty-four hours? I can assure you it will only get better.'

'Wild' was just one of the words Jon would choose to describe the last day. A marathon seemed suspiciously like hard work, though. He realised he probably hadn't run more than half a mile since he trailed in a distant last in the school's 3000 metre trials at the age of fifteen.

'All you have to do is sign this form, and we'll make the necessary arrangements with your employer,' Doug said, passing a piece of paper to the guy opposite Jon who began reading it. All Jon would have to do is sign his name and he'd be free from Henry's madness, Mick's impending eternal ribbing and hundreds of ancient help screens. One signature and he would also be in the clutches of DPI. Jon broke one of his golden rules of behaviour in a meeting and spoke unaddressed, 'What about the prize?'

Doug looked at him, biting his lip. 'The prize? You'll just have to trust me for the moment. I'll give you more details once you all sign. It's another risk, another test, just for us to make sure you're fully committed and are what we want.'

Jon listened to a few fragments of conversation from the others who were reviewing the form and tried to get a picture of his would-be companions on this adventure. He could now hear that the blonde woman with the ponytail was Welsh, and overheard the Scouser introduce himself as Danny. Natasha was talking animatedly at Jermaine as Nicki – unsurprisingly to Jon – grabbed the form and became the first to sign. Tom followed, shaking his head whilst adding his name. By the time the form had passed through everyone and had reached Jon, it had nine signatures on it. Looking at the form, Jon identified that the Northern Irish accent behind him could be attributed to Kieran. He realised that he was no different from everyone else, and had as much right to be here as they had. Maybe this was what he needed, to be dragged from his job and thrust into something new. The marathon training might even make him properly fit. He could even join a gym back home afterwards and be able to impress the ladies with his new-found stamina. After consideration, the prize was largely irrelevant now. As intriguing as it was, Jon was sure that following his performance on the stairs, beating nine other fit, young wannabes was beyond him. He thought about not signing it, walking out, going home to his cat, facing the interrogation at work and brushing it off and continuing his safe life. But knowing Peabody, he'd probably make him exit via the stairs, after returning his tracksuit and every other item of clothing he had on.

Do you authorise Douglas Peabody International Adventures to make the necessary arrangements for the termination of your employment?

Jon picked up the pen and said to no-one in particular, 'Well, I've always wanted to see Central Park in fall.'

Doug took the form and rose to address everyone. 'Thank you all. I know the decision must not have been easy, but I also know that you won't regret it for a second.'

'So the prize?' Nicki said.

'The prize, yes. The prize...shall be announced in a press conference to the world at 9am today.'

The orange collective let out a prolonged groan, but Doug hadn't finished. 'In which, please be aware, you will all be participants.'

'We're going on TV?' Arjun said.

'Yes.' Doug beamed. 'Get ready to face the millions, because we're spreading the news!'

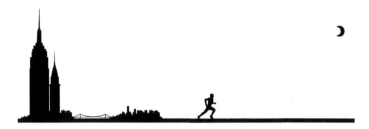

Chapter 10

'THE world needs a kick up the arse.' Despite the warnings of his advisers, Doug thought that as opening lines went, it was a killer. The highest observation floor of the DPI HQ had been transformed into a press conference, ensuring that while all eyes would surely be on Doug, he had the background of the capital. He was positioned behind a glass stand, addressing rows of photographers and reporters jostling for the best position with their voice recorders and microphones held out in front of them as far as they could reach. The media team had done a good job getting everyone here from the TV and newspapers at short notice, and the strict instructions to hype it up beyond belief were carried out without the need for letting staff know the main details. Behind him, five on each side, were his orange-clad hopefuls, sitting beneath two giant screens. He had everyone where he wanted them.

'We are all capable of many wonderful, amazing things. Mankind has achieved so much. Just look at the magnificent building we are standing in today. Technology now is beyond the comprehension of just a few decades ago. But where is the future?' The screens came to life, showing various images of business and entertainment technology.

'Is it being able to access the Internet wherever we are, every second of the day? Is it being able to play games we grew out of in the '80s and '90s in the palms of our hands whilst being squashed, standing up on an hour-long train commute to a boring job?' A few camera flashes went off.

'What happened to our dreams? Our big dreams, the ones I grew up with, the ones we were promised. Where is the adventure, the danger, the spirit to explore?' The screens were now showing images of fast-moving clouds at altitude, exciting a few more of the photographers. 'What about...space?' The screens turned dark and the imaginary camera soared into a starry sky. Doug knew no-one had been expecting DPI to be talking about space, and he got the puzzled and excited looks he'd hoped for. Pictures of Armstrong stepping down from the Eagle formed behind him. 'We were going there when I was a small boy, and reached out beyond our grasp. But we stopped. Forgot about it. Bottled it. We sent robots to Mars, satellites in orbit for navigation systems, built a space station, but what about exploration for us?' He discarded his notes and stepped out in front of the lectern. 'Some other companies are planning to offer visions of space, glimpses if you will. Mere minutes into the dark stuff. For a small personal fortune, you might even get a hotel room a few miles above the clouds. But that's near-sighted, boring stuff. Douglas Peabody International is going way beyond that...it's is going to send a man back to the Moon!'

He thrust his arms out sideways, tilted his head up until it faced the ceiling and closed his eyes while Jamiroquai's *Space Cowboy* blared out all around them, accompanied by clips of various Apollo rockets and spacecraft going to the Moon. He held the pose, picturing the front pages tomorrow as journalists chattered and cameramen bathed him in a frenzy of light. God, this was such a brilliant idea, Doug thought, and he was the only one in the entire world to have the courage to do it. He relaxed his pose and returned behind the stand. Time for the details.

'DPI is funding a rocket that should launch next year. It will carry a small crew not only out of Earth's atmosphere, not only into space, but shooting towards our satellite, the Moon.' Computer simulations of the journey appeared, a large, round Moon getting gradually bigger.

'Let the robots have Mars for now. Let NASA scrape the funds together for getting Americans there sometime in the '20s, if we're lucky. DPI wants men and women to play in the fields we've already found.' The screens' displays were now showing a sweep over the Moon's surface.

'We'll take them round the Moon, over the dark side – the side we never get to see from Earth – and stay up there a while before commencing the return leg back to this wonderful blue planet.'

'Mr Peabody? Will you be actually landing on the Moon?' A journalist at the front held his recorder in anticipation.

Doug had expected this question, 'Tell me – have you ever been *inside* Sydney Opera House?' Bemused looks all round. 'One can still enjoy the pleasures of a stunning location simply by viewing the outside.' Reporters tapped away to capture this quote. Doug pushed on to avoid further examination.

'More details of the technology will be announced soon, but this isn't about rockets, trajectories, logistics – this is about people. Adventurers. Men and women who have spirit, hunger, a desire to be first. I wanted to set a challenge, and these ten fine specimens behind me,' Doug turned and swept his right hand indicating the row of competitors, 'are the people I have specially selected to take up this challenge.'

For the first time, the cameras were not on Doug as they zoomed in on the orange ten on their chairs. The displays now showed a slideshow of each person, their statistics and a brief bio. Doug looked at their faces. Had they twigged yet?

'As you know, I am fond of running, having completed over twenty marathons myself. 26 miles and 385 yards – a supreme test of endurance. They will compete against each other in the New York City Marathon, in November. They will be running for their chosen charities and you can sponsor them right now. Don't worry if you miss the details – they will be published in adverts in every major newspaper over the coming weeks. Please give generously to these fantastic causes that are dear to their hearts.' Doug knew the whole scheme would undoubtedly be seen by many as a publicity stunt, but at least he could also show a caring edge.

'But, ladies and gentlemen, I have not exactly been fair with them. I've been playing a game. You see some of this is news to them as well. What they haven't been told – perhaps haven't even realised yet – is that whilst the crew will be experts, I have one seat available.' Doug looked round. Yes, he could see the dawning. 'You see, the one who comes out on top of the marathon will win this seat, be trained for the trip and therefore make history as the first space tourist to orbit the Moon.' The reporters gathered tight, looking up at Doug, waiting for a gesture of agreement to pounce on these unknowns, to get their stories. That would come later – the poor sods would be ravaged without protection. He looked at his selections. Were they impressed? Were they full of wonder and excitement at this amazing opportunity? One of them was going to the Moon!

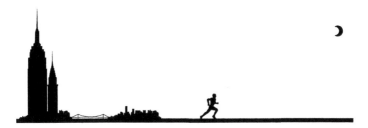

Chapter 11

'**W**E'RE gonna be astronauts!' said the owner of the My Little Pony hair who'd introduced herself a few moments ago. The Press conference had broken up, the TV cameras gone, but the reporters were being kept in a separate room while the would-be astronauts waited for further instruction.

'Only one of us is, actually,' Nicki said. 'So I wouldn't get your hopes up too much, Kerry.'

'It's *Ceris*,' she replied, before addressing Jon. 'Isn't it exciting?'

'Yeah, amazing,' Jon said. 'Always dreamt of going up there. I was looking at the Moon's craters in my telescope only last week. Imagine seeing them up close.'

Nicki exhaled loudly. 'Always had you down as a geek, Jon.'

'Anyway,' Ceris said, turning her back on Nicki, 'I'd love to go, too. As long as I could take Dewi with me. I'm sure he'd love to fly round the Moon.' She produced a small, stuffed red dragon from her pocket and whirled it as if in orbit round Jon's head. 'It would be awesome.'

'Really?' said Tom, who Jon now noticed was a few inches taller than him and wearing a tracksuit that seemed several sizes too big in the chest. 'The way I see it, I've been given the chance to annihilate my body in the quest to complete a distance that public transport was designed for, only to be placed in a small capsule with millions of tonnes of rocket fuel up my arse by a company who knows nothing about space. Personally, I would've preferred money.'

'It's whacky, I'll give you that,' Jon said. 'But to have the chance to go into space...'

'And we're gonna be famous,' Ceris said.

'Hmm. I'm not exactly sure I can handle fame,' Jon said. 'I can just about handle a cat and a flat, and I accidentally set one of them on fire last month.' Singed fur had not been a pleasant smell.

Ceris smiled. 'Oh, you'll be fine. They said that people would be helping us with that part, mentor us, you know.' She stroked Dewi's fur.

'I know a tattooist who'd love that,' Jon said, pointing to the dragon.

'Huh?'

Jon was about to explain when the receptionist came over to address everyone.

'Could you please put yourselves into two equal groups? The PR reps will be with you soon to brief you for the press interviews.'

Ceris wasted no time, gesturing at the others with Dewi. 'Arjun, Tasha, Tom – come over here.' She winked at Jon. 'I used to pick the netball teams at training.' They gathered round Ceris, leaving Nicki, Jermaine, Barry, Kieran and Danny in the other group next to them.

'Do you think they sell spacesuits on Fifth Avenue?' Ceris said.

'Of course – Tiffany's has one with diamond-studded cufflinks with my name on it,' Arjun replied.

'Like DPI can pull this off,' Natasha said. 'It's all a stunt, you'll see. They might get us to run a marathon and promote their company, but none of us are going into space. They'll fake it at best. Bet my life on it.'

'Aren't you a ray of sunshine?' Arjun said.

'All I'm saying is that you can't just build a rocket, point it at the Moon and expect it to work,' Natasha said.

'Do you get many space rockets come in to your garage then, Tasha?' Ceris said.

'Time for your two million mile service, sir. Would you like me to valet the escape capsule?' Arjun said as Natasha glared back.

'Maybe the PR woman can tell us more,' Tom said, as he looked across the room.

Jon watched as a woman in a long, white, sleeveless dress with orange piping down the sides came towards them. She had perfect dark skin and a smile that instantly put them all at ease. She introduced herself as Leona, and took the other group away to be briefed, promising that the other rep was coming over any minute now to deal with Jon's group.

'I'll hand it to Mr Peabody – he knows how to pick his staff,' Arjun said.

Jon was still watching the other group get led away when the second rep in an identical dress appeared behind him. He turned around just in time to hear her address the group.

'Good morning, everyone. My name's Summer and I'm here to help.'

Chapter 12

JON didn't know which way was up. The woman he had thought he had been competing against and had beaten, the focus of his hatred for several hours yesterday, and one of the few women in the world that he'd exchanged nakedness with, was standing in front of him in DPI uniform.

'So, let me see…I have…' she shuffled through a pile of postcards she had on each person, 'Ceris, Tom, Natasha, Arjun –'

'Yes miss!' Arjun put his hand in the air.

'Thank you, Arjun. And…' She looked up into Jon's brown eyes.

'And Jon, I presume.'

'Good guess.'

She broke eye contact. 'Right, just listen to me for a few minutes and I'll go through what the question and answer sessions will be like, and the sort of answers to respond with. I'll also be with you throughout each interview, so don't worry, you'll all be fine. Trust me.'

She proceeded to go over the details, not that Jon was

listening. He was too busy trying to work out what was going on with Summer, and noticing how smooth and tattoo-free her arms were. It took a few seconds for him to realise he was being asked something.

'Jon? Are you okay with that for your charity?'

They had all turned to see his response to Summer's question.

'Er...sorry? I didn't catch that last bit.'

'I know we took some liberties about the charity, taking the name from the questionnaire and springing it on you like that, but we just need to check that you're okay about using your charity for the marathon.'

'Right, yes, sorry. That'll be...fine.'

'Great. I'm sure that –' she pretended to check Jon's postcard, 'Superhero Cross-dressers Anonymous need all the help they can get. Right, let's move, people.'

Summer took them through to the journalists, who she gave strict instructions on the sort of questions they could ask and to go easy as it was the competitors' first time in this sort of environment. She chose Ceris to go first, so Jon, Arjun and Tom stood a few metres away, out of camera shot but still near enough to see and hear everything. Natasha sat on a chair in a corner looking at the ceiling. Jon started to chew on a fingernail as Ceris explained to the press how she had been stuck temping since leaving school, but how much she was looking forward to the competition.

'Wow, look at her go.' Arjun was next in line, just ahead of Jon.

'Who?' Jon said. The lights were picking out a sheen in Summer's hair that he thought was only possible in shampoo adverts.

'Ceris. She's a natural. They love her.'

'Ceris, yeah, suppose.'

'I wish I'd bought a mascot. She's getting loads of cute photos with her lizard.'

'It's a dragon,' Jon said. 'Called Dewi'.

'Eh? Anyways, looks like it's about to be my turn. Time for the world to meet its new star.'

Ceris finished waving to the cameras and made way for Arjun. Jon now stood at the front of the queue, just minutes away from fame.

'Nervous?' Tom said behind him.

'A bit.'

'It's like a combination of waiting for a job interview and to take your driving test, with a blind date thrown in.'

'You're not helping, Tom.'

'Sorry. Summer seems cool, though. At least we haven't got Leona.'

'Summer's trouble,' Jon immediately said. 'I'd rather have Leona.'

'Leona? No way. I met her on one of the tasks, thought she was one of us. Totally embarrassed me in the end.'

Jon spun round. 'In what way?'

Tom dug his hands into his pockets and let out a breath of air. 'Let's just say I ended up on one of Bristol's top tourist attractions with a severe lack of clothes.'

'Don't tell me – she still managed to take your photo?'

'Yeah. Didn't understand why at the time.'

'All part of the plan, wasn't it? Get us to do something stupid, appear to double cross us, and –'

'Before you know it, we're being branded like cows just

to get one over on them,' Tom said, nodding. 'So, you too?'

'Yep, with Summer.' He went back to watching her with Arjun. None of that spontaneity in London had been real. Perfectly choreographed by DPI, designed to give maximum humiliation.

'Bet they had a great laugh thinking up the ideas,' Jon said.

'Reckon so. Clever, though. Suckered us into getting a ridiculous tattoo. They probably had model reconstructions of the events, Plasticine figures of us and all sorts.'

Jon thought about Peabody's words, '...*with some manipulation, I found you*'. Found me and turned me into a blob of brown putty, ready to mould into anything they like. Now, in a few minutes, Jon would be diving off into the public eye. Summer was supposed to be his safety cord, but seemed just as likely to leave him plummeting to the ground. Jon thought back to Natasha's doubts over DPI, Nicki's performance on the stairs, and watched Arjun's enthusiasm electrify the room. He was Jon Dunn. Expert at nothing, mid-table potential at the very most. He glanced behind to the door they'd come through. If he ran now, would anyone really care? Perhaps he could still smooth things over with Henry at work, apologise to Mr Peabody in writing for pulling out and then get his stupid tattoo removed. The stairs were calling. He began to back away.

'Sorry, Tom, but I...I've got to get some water. You take my place.'

'No way. I'm not prepared to go next. Ask Tasha to get you a drink.'

He was about to brush past Tom, ignore Natasha and break for the door when he saw Ceris throw something at him. 'Catch.' Dewi landed in his hands. Nicki was with her, and they both laughed.

'That's for good luck,' Ceris said. 'He doesn't usually take to strangers, but he says you're all right.'

'Thanks,' Jon said, now motionless.

'You'll be fine. Show them that awesome tattoo. The back of your head will be more famous than the front.'

'Which is definitely for the best,' Nicki said, pulling a face.

Jon was about to offer Dewi back to Ceris when he felt a hand on his shoulder from behind.

'Need a comforter?' Summer said.

Jon turned round. 'I, er...it's not mine,' Jon said, handing it back to Ceris.

'A bit scared, are we?'

'No. It's just...I've never been interviewed before.'

'Relax. It's just a few, easy questions, not an interrogation.'

Before he knew it, Summer had whisked him away, seating him behind a small desk that faced four journalists.

'So Jon – how do you feel about running a marathon?' the first reporter said.

'Er...I...I dunno.' Jon played with his hands.

'We hear you've haven't really done any running before. Why do you think you can win this competition?'

'Well, I don't.'

'What Jon means is,' Summer said, 'that he doesn't know what he is capable of until he tries.' A few unsure nods. 'But he has naked ambition.'

Not even the Mona Lisa had a smile that subtle.

'What about the chance to go to the Moon?'

'I'd love to go.' Jon paused and looked towards Summer. 'If it ever goes ahead.'

'You see?' Summer gestured towards Jon. 'Even *they* can't believe how wonderful the prize is and how DPI has pulled it off.'

Jon wondered if she had a script for every possible response.

'How about your tattoo? We know it was part of the competition, but why did you get it done on the back of your neck?' the third reporter said, poised to write down Jon's reply.

'I was tricked into it. You can't trust anyone around here.'

'It was a test, that's all,' Summer said. 'Part of the competition, and one that Jon passed magnificently.' She turned towards Jon. 'Besides, once the race is over, you can always grow a mullet to cover it up.'

Jon opened his mouth to reply but Summer grabbed his shoulders and spun him around so that the cameras could take the shot of the tattoo.

The rest of the interview was fairly straightforward, with nothing Jon could do to even cause the slightest of ruffles in Summer's perfect hair. He answered all the questions, posed for some more photos – forward facing this time – and by the time he was finished, he was sure that the newspapers would have this particular challenger down as a quiet oddball, with long odds of winning. Nothing new there, then.

Jon wanted to catch Summer on her own, but the rest of

the morning was spent in the two groups, finding out more information about the New York training, arrangements for tomorrow's travel and reading a full printout of the rules. The marathon was to be their full focus for the next three months, and it was DPI's deepest desire to get everyone in shape to make it a competition like no other. They were expected to do weekly blogs of their experiences and training, and take part in warm-up races in New York. There were timetables for every single day from tomorrow until race day. Nothing, they were told, could be deviated from, due to a strict training regime. Sightseeing? They'd see plenty of New York while running round it. DPI were not only effectively employing them now, they were dictating their lives every day for the next quarter.

At 11:30, Jon was laden with bags of paperwork, instructions, maps, programmes, schedules and souvenir DPI gear. Most of the group had now gone, but Jon was admiring the city below bathed in gold from the high sun. It was a long way down, back to the normality of the streets he would soon be swapping for the noisy avenues of New York. He watched cranes at work, changing the skyline even further. London was growing up fast.

'Hey, daydreamer,' Summer said behind him. Jon spun round. 'I'm off now, but will see you across the pond in a short while.' She turned and went to walk away.

'Is that it?' Jon said. 'No apology? Not even an explanation?'

Summer returned to face Jon. 'What do you want me to say? I'm sure you've figured out by now that I was just part of the game.'

'Game? This whole thing is stupid. I don't even know what I'm doing here. I can't run a marathon, and no-one will give a damn about how I get on in training.'

'Wow.' Summer put her hands on her hips. 'Aren't you Mr Glass-Cracked-And-Completely-Empty?'

Jon looked back towards the window as Summer put a hand on his shoulder.

'Look, whinge and stomp your feet as much as you like. Yes, you got played, embarrassed and manipulated. But can you really tell me this isn't the most exciting thing to have ever happened to you?'

'Well, er, I don't know…' Jon was saved by Nicki who had approached them.

'Sorry – I do hope I am not interrupting anything,' Nicki said.

Summer took her hand away from Jon and faced Nicki. 'No, I was just giving this one a pep talk. He was crying because he was going to miss his cat. I'll leave you both to it. Good luck with the training.'

Nicki and Jon watched Summer walk back towards the lift.

'You two seemed cosy,' Nicki said.

'Me and Summer? You've gotta be joking.' Jon returned to the view of the city below.

'Not what it looked like from here.'

'Nah. She's probably got half a dozen men down there wrapped round her finger.'

'Guess you could get a bit of an advantage, getting in with the DPI staff.'

'If you're worried about me beating you, I can assure you that won't happen.'

Nicki laughed. 'You? Beat me? I've seen two-year-olds climb stairs better than you. No, I just want to make sure that it's an even competition.'

'Look, there's no way I'll be going to her for help.'

'You better not. I know you'll probably need all the help you can get, but just do it fairly, right?'

'What exactly are you doing here, Nicki?' Jon said, looking intently at her. 'I mean, you seem competitive, enthusiastic and fit – if you're so fantastic why are you in a competition with a bunch of so-called losers?'

'Got my boyfriend to do my entry for me. He saw the email come in and did it on my behalf. I was far too busy to bother. Didn't know anything about it until he took the call and quickly explained. As soon as I learned it was a competition I was right on it.'

'So...you cheated, you mean?'

'I think of it as manipulating the system. Who gives a toss, anyway? We're all here now.'

'It's not exactly in the spirit of what Mr. Peabody wanted.'

'Rubbish. The only thing he cares about is money and how to make it. The whole competition is for exposure – surely even an idiot like you can see that.'

Jon shook his head and walked off. Nicki followed him just behind until they reached the lift doors where Leona was waiting alone.

'Looks like we're the last ones. You got all the info you need from us?' Leona said to the pair.

'Yep – pick up 6am for the 10:20 flight. Bring your suitcase and dreams,' Nicki said.

'Correct,' Leona said, smiling. The three got in and descended to the reception. As the lift came to a halt and the doors slid open, Leona got out first and turned back. 'Oh, one more thing Jon – Summer said for me to tell you that if you wanted that naked photo of her, let her know and she'll email it to you.'

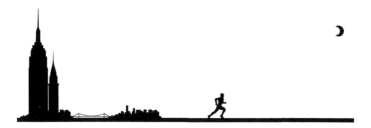

Chapter 13

'IF it doesn't hurt, you're damn well not doing it right.' Jackson, the fitness instructor, was taking them through their first training session in Central Park. Jon had envisaged their first morning in New York being a gentle jog round part of the park, a seminar on healthy eating and perhaps even a massage for those who hadn't run outside since their school cross-country days. Twenty minutes into the session, and all they had been asked to do is to stay in one spot and contort their bodies into positions that Jon thought should only apply to master yoga teachers. DPI wanted to ensure everyone was fully trained to the same standards to ensure a fairer race, and to create more competition. The group's sole trainer was Jackson Jones, chosen mainly for his reputation of training the reluctant – from bad kids thrown into an exercise programme to avoid jail, to obese people who were trying to avoid the grim reaper. He was something of an American TV star, which also helped to generate interest in the competition this side of the Atlantic. His six-foot-four frame allowed him to project his voice well, and he continued to shout at his ten new recruits. 'I can hear your mumblings, you British pussies! You think stretching is painful? Perhaps unnecessary? This is *saving* you pain, people. This will make you stronger.'

The ten would-be runners were all lying flat on their backs in their orange DPI running vests, facing a clear blue sky as the morning sun shone through the tall, leafy trees, pricking at their faces. Unfortunately, Jon was unable to take in this wonderful view as his eyes were screwed up tight in response to his left leg being lifted up towards the sky by Jackson in an attempt to make it go at right angles to his body.

'The classic hamstring stretch. Let me know when it hurts more than you can bear,' Jackson said.

'Hmhhhhmmggrrhhhhh!' At an angle of forty-five degrees, Jon felt like his leg was being stabbed repeatedly, so he hoped that this guttural outburst was a clear indicator that any further bending back of his leg was likely to make him black out.

'Jon – you're about as supple as Pinocchio. We're gonna need to do some severe work on that.' He slowly put Jon's leg down and walked off to his next victim.

The session was being held in a corner of the Great Lawn, a vast patch of green within Manhattan's most famous and most-visited park. A few pockets of people were dotted around, mainly locals taking the chance to relax before a busy New York day ahead.

'You okay?' Ceris said, a couple of feet away from Jon.

'Aside from the backs of my legs feeling like someone is carving them up for a Sunday roast? Yeah, smashing.'

'I prefer a nice bit of Welsh lamb, myself.'

Jon looked at the sports watch that they'd all been given. 'What time is it back home? It's 8:20 here now.'

'Oh, let me see, add five hours...so that would be... lunchtime.'

Jackson cast a shadow over them. 'Did somebody mention lunch? Blondie – by the time I've finished with you this morning, food will be way down your list of priorities. You'll be dreaming of a shower and a big ol' comfy American bed first. Not that you'll get either yet – your ass is mine for the afternoon, too.'

'So when do we get to do some proper running?' Kieran said. 'Don't know about anyone else but I'm ready to go.'

'You're ready when I say you are,' Jackson said. 'You ain't even close yet.'

They were taken through the rest of the stretches, all the time Jackson bellowing out the different muscle groups each exercise was working on. Jon hoped that there wouldn't be a test at the end of it, although he could at least calculate the number of muscle groups there were simply by counting the number of areas in his body that were complaining of being woken from their long-term hibernation. He looked around at the other nine finishing their stretches and was confident by their lack of sweat and casual rubbing of limbs that he was definitely hurting the most.

'Do we get to do press-ups?' Arjun said as he waited for the next instruction. 'I'm dead good at them. Bet I could even give you a run for your money, sarge.'

Jackson walked over to him and looked him up and down as if he was sizing up a branch to snap in two for a fire. 'Where does your good-for-nothing self come from?'

'Birmingham, sarge.'

'Birming-ham, I see. Well, Arjun from Birming-ham, two things: One – never call me "sarge" again. Two – if you want, I can set up a fair contest to have a one-on-one push-up challenge with me.' He leaned in closer. 'But, I would need to have one arm tied behind me with Ceris and Nicki standing on my back.'

Arjun's face froze. 'Tell you what sarge – I mean, sir – I'll come back to you on that one.'

'You do that.' Jackson backed away, ready to commence the next stage of the training. 'It's shake 'n' bake time people. C'mon!' He shook his arms down by his sides, wobbling his head and twitching his legs at the same time. 'Need to relax those muscles, so give 'em a good shake.'

Ten orange jellies wobbled in obedience. Jon had the advantage of being at the back of the group so no-one else could see him. He hoped he didn't look as bad as Tom, who was jiggling around in a cartoon zapped-by-lightning way.

Jackson held up his hands, 'Okay, that's enough now. All that orange is making me want some juice, so unless you want me to squeeze you all out, I suggest you all follow me for a gentle run around the park.'

'At last, some action,' Kieran said, but not loud enough for Jackson to hear.

'Right – take a bottle of water each. Arjun – you follow me, the rest of you arrange yourself in single file. Try to keep up but no overtaking just yet.'

The two of them headed off the grass and onto the nearby path. It was a slow jog, and Jon seized the opportunity to ensure he would definitely not be last for their first ever run together. Before his muscles could realise what was going on, he had sprung forward and caught Arjun just ahead of Nicki. A few minutes in, and Jon was quite enjoying the jog. A warm morning, running slowly through a huge park in one of the world's greatest cities, in new clothes and running shoes provided to him for free, with the benefit of also getting fit. Grey squirrels darted between the trees, cyclists created a breeze as they sped away. A woman in a tight top and small shorts ran past in the opposite direction, her music player drowning out the distant sounds of the Manhattan rush-hour traffic. Jon hadn't seen much of the city due to a long sleep soon after landing yesterday afternoon, but so far this was his favourite place. He hadn't given much more than a glance at the timetable yet, although he knew there was something every day, so a gradual build-up of distance seemed reasonable. He could cope with gentle morning jogs, and the inevitable, gradual lengthening of them as they worked their way towards a marathon distance. Perhaps he'd even get better at the stretching.

'Everyone all okay back there?' Jackson's enquiry was loud enough to be heard by the Statue of Liberty. 'That's the warm-up section done, now for the main event of the morning. Let's pick it up, people!'

Jon watched as Jackson's dark arms pumped hard and propelled him twenty metres further forward, followed by an eager Arjun two seconds later. The gap between Jon and those in front increased.

'Hey, Cockney boy! Move those Dulux-white legs of yours or let a real runner through,' Nicki said, now alongside him. Jon upped his pace to what seemed to him a near sprint to catch Arjun again, before matching the new pace. He gulped in large breaths of air, his cheeks expanding as he heavily blew each one out again. A tightness gripped his calves and his shins began to complain with each impact on the concrete. At least he wasn't running barefoot this time, he thought. Nicki had gone with him at the same time and was now tucked in even closer behind. His chest started aching as if he were just recovering from bronchitis and sweat was forming on his forehead. Jon hoped that this pace wouldn't have to be maintained for long, otherwise he might join John Lennon on the list of Brits to die in this city.

Wide avenues gave way to smaller paths as the orange train continued its way through the park, past baseball pitches, mums with prams and roller-skating teenagers. Tom was at the back, slightly lagging behind, and just above Jon's breathing he could hear Natasha and Ceris pointing out some of the sights along the way. Arjun was now a little further ahead of Jon, with Nicki now literally breathing down Jon's neck. Jackson decided that running forwards was not a challenge whatsoever for him at this relatively sedentary pace, so he turned round to face the group and started running backwards.

'Who's at the back? Tom? Tom can you hear me? Everyone listen up. This is where it gets interesting. Tom – I want you to run up here to the front, and once you reach here, I'll shout and the person who is then last runs up to the front. We'll keep doing this until I'm back leading you all. Everyone ready? Tom – are you ready? Go!'

Tom started to jog faster, gradually overtaking Barry and Natasha.

'Kick those legs and get up here! We'll be out of Central Park before we finish, at this rate.'

Tom increased his speed, and with a fixed grimace, he finally made it to the head of the queue.

Jackson continued to run backwards, now in second place. 'Barry – now show us what you Scots have got.'

The exercise continued, Jon eventually ending up in the last position after Nicki sped off from behind him. She looked in control, with plenty to spare. Jon, on the other hand, was eating well into his reserves already.

When Nicki got past Kieran to lead the runners, Jackson shouted to Jon, 'Go!'

From Jon's position, the front now seemed like it was in another borough of New York. He moved out to overtake Arjun, but took at least ten seconds just to draw level.

'Are you trying to hold his hand, Jon? Get up there! I've seen glaciers move quicker than you.'

Jon put his head down, increased his stride length and made some progress. He wasn't sure what would happen if he didn't make it to the front, but if it was anything like the forfeits at school, he'd be running in his pants that afternoon. The thought of this drove him on, and by the time he'd got a sympathetic smile out of Ceris as he went past, he realised there were only four people to go. The back of Nicki's head was his goal now and he pushed on through the pain to reach it, focussing on her brown hair bobbing with every step. As he moved parallel to her, huge mouthfuls of air were being sucked in and expelled by his cheeks as he strove for as much oxygen as his muscles demanded for the manoeuvre.

'Stop to tie up your shoelaces?' Nicki said, with little effort in between her controlled breaths. Jon knew he didn't have a spare ounce of energy for a verbal response, so he decided to reply with his legs. With a final effort, he edged past and moved out in front. He'd done it. From what seemed a mile back, he'd made it past everyone. He felt as if he was leading the 1500 metre Olympic final, runners trailing in his wake. Mission accomplished.

Jon felt a head rush and then everything went white.

Chapter 14

'LET me know when he wakes up so I can kill him.' Nicki sat on the grass nursing her arm as Jon lay on his side, Jackson kneeling down beside him. Jon came round with what initially looked like the world's scariest nurse staring at him.

'Jon? You okay? How many fingers am I holding up?' Jackson said.

'Four. Yeah, I'm fine, I think.' Jon sat up. 'What happened? Did I make it to the front?'

Nicki shoved her elbow near his face. 'Look! Look what you've done! You bloody fainted right in front of me and caused this.'

Jon looked at the small patch of blood on her elbow. 'Oh. Sorry.'

'Sorry? I fell right over you, you moron. If I get a scar from this…'

'Sorry. I really am. Don't know why I fainted.'

'Maybe the fact that you're a Cockney wimp who has more chance of becoming king than finishing this marathon?'

'Hey!' Jon began to get on his feet. 'I'm not from London. I'm from Stevenage.'

'Well, wherever that is they don't breed athletes, obviously.'

Jackson stepped in between them, 'Cool it, you two. By the looks of it, there's no real damage done. Jon, you seemed to land on the grass, so aside from the stains giving you the full DPI colours on your shirt now, you look fine. Here, take some of your water.'

Jon gulped down half of his bottle. Jackson took Nicki away from Jon and began cleaning her wound with water and items from a carrier he wore round his waist. Most of the group were doing various stretches against trees or on the grass. Jermaine came up to Jon and patted him on the back. 'Don't worry about it, my friend. It's the heat – we're not used to it being so hot this early. Jet lag, too. I'm sure you'll be fine.'

Arjun joined the pair. 'That Jackson seems a right fitness freak. Not sure that I wouldn't have fainted as soon as I'd got to the front. Reckon you did us all a favour.'

'Thanks. Don't think Nicki quite appreciated it.'

'Her? She'll get over it. Never seen someone get so angry over a graze. Thought they made them a bit tougher in Nottingham,' Arjun said.

Jackson had finished with Nicki and was now on his mobile, his voice no less loud on the phone than it was in a training session. 'Everythin' ready? Equipment laid out? Everyone there? Cool, we'll be over in five.' Jackson hung up and addressed the runners. 'I have a surprise for everyone. Seeing as our little jog was curtailed by Mr Headrush, I've brought something forward. You'll be able to sit down and rest your legs plus have a little fun. We'll have a brisk walk back to the lawn.'

Jon walked with Tom and Arjun towards the back of the group following Jackson.

'Great start to the training, Jon,' Tom said.

'Not exactly what I'd hoped for,' Jon said. 'Barely nine o'clock and I've already been unconscious, hurt more muscles than I thought I actually had in my body and Nicki wants to kill me.'

'So did you say you were from Stevenage? I live in Bristol, but I'm originally from Hitchin.'

'Ah, Hitchin, our wonderful neighbours,' he replied. 'Of course this does now mean I have to beat you.'

Tom smiled. 'It doesn't count if they have to carry you across the line. Anyway, I think we'll have our work cut out to beat Arjun and a few of the others.'

Arjun put his arms around the pair. 'C'mon, we've got three months yet, anything could happen. Even Nicki might mellow out.'

They carried on a bit further, the Central Park human traffic increasing as if it were the fitness capital of the world. Fifty metres from their destination, Jackson yelled out, 'Play time!'

The sight that greeted them was surreal – a side-on perfect line of big orange space hoppers to their right, with a row of photographers pointing long lenses a hundred metres to the left. It looked like a pretend firing squad from the 1970s.

'We're not using Swiss balls – we like to be a bit more creative. This side of the pond we call them "Hoppity Hops", but as a British company, DPI has specially commissioned these logoed versions, so I guess I'll have to go with your "space hoppers". Either way, they're a great way to exercise.'

Natasha, Ceris and Arjun rushed to be the first to try out their new toys.

'Hello, my trusty steed. I am Prince Arjun, your noble rider,' Arjun said, sitting down on a hopper, grabbing the rubber handles with one hand and slapping its side with the other. The girls bounced around him on their own hoppers with whoops of delight.

Kieran ran up and kicked a space hopper a short way across the grass. Nicki sat on one and waited, while Jon made sure he chose a position well away from her. It had been a while since he'd ridden one, and had grown considerably larger since then, but he guessed it was like riding a bike. A big, rubber, bouncy bike without any wheels. After his efforts earlier, he decided to take just a few cautious bounces, trying to forget about the press photographers down the field. He was sure none of this was going to make the headlines of the tabloids, let alone the broadsheets, but it was still strange to think of him being in the public eye.

Once everyone – aside from the stationary Nicki – had had their fun, Jackson took them through some exercises with the hoppers designed to tone them up. Jon was made to lie on it on his front and use it to support his legs in a press-up position. It seemed easy at first, but gradually each push up from the ground got slower as Jon's years sitting at a keyboard took their toll. They then switched to lying on the floor on their backs, passing the ball from outstretched arms above their heads, to between their raised feet, lowering their legs before bringing them up again and repeating. A line of ten DPI logos at various heights all captured by the cream of the media. After twenty minutes of exercises, Jon was feeling like he'd just received a chop in the stomach from Bruce Lee. Jackson proceeded to line them up on their hoppers and told them all to sit and wait.

'Ladies, gentlemen and others. I hoped you all enjoyed that workout, but now we come to serious stuff. No marathon competitor should stand on the start line without a few races under their belts, so welcome to your first race of the training programme.'

'No way!' Natasha said.

'Brilliant. Let's get it on!' Kieran said as the chatter levels increased.

'Quiet, please. This is a landmark point in your progress. It's quite simple – a race to the finish line, a hundred metres down there. The winner gets to do twenty press-ups.'

'Huh?' Danny said. 'How's that an incentive?'

'All losers get to do forty. Now take your marks...'

Jon gripped the handles tightly. Barry and a focussed Tom were to his right, everyone else to his left.

'Get set...'

He set his feet into the turf and stared at the finish line and the cameras behind it waiting their arrival.

'Go!'

'Yeehaw! Giddy up, horsey!' In the centre, Arjun took a massive bounce to take an early lead. Jon was quick to start but had decided to go for a steady approach in terms of raw pace, whereas Danny and Arjun were going at it as if they were trying to escape from a bank robbery in the world's worst getaway vehicles. Ceris and Natasha had already bounced into each other and were struggling to get upright again. About a third of the way down, Jon was in seventh place, pushing hard, looking at the ground in front intently with each bounce. He didn't see himself pass Barry who had wobbled and had to stop to steady himself. Danny had moved across to be next to Arjun in the lead, and Nicki was closely tracking them to her right.

'And it's Orange Rum by a nose,' Danny said as they approached halfway. Still looking down, Jon was unaware that he was veering diagonally to his left, moving nearer to the centre. The initial adrenaline had worn off and his arms and stomach muscles began to ache with each bounce, but he kept up his steady pace and had moved up level to fifth place with Kieran on the far side.

'C'mon, Tango!' Arjun said to his rubber mount as it lifted off the ground in wild bounces. One launch into the air was too energetic however, and it sent his body flying towards Danny who could do nothing to get out of the way. They both fell sideways, still stubbornly holding on to their handles as Arjun twisted round and landed in a heap almost directly under Danny's hopper. The Scouser finally let go and fell to the ground, shoulder first, followed by a face plant in the grass, muffling his vociferous complaints. With thirty metres to go, Jon was now third, having edged ahead of a slowing Tom. Due to his unintentional diagonal path, Jon had been surprised to pass so close to the stricken pair and had looked up to see Nicki was only a couple of metres to his left now, in the lead with Kieran to her left, just slightly ahead of Jon. The photographers were much closer now and he could even hear their shutters closing rapidly as they captured the action. He inhaled sharply and pushed himself down harder on his hopper. One glance sideways saw that Kieran was losing rhythm. Jon was up into second place with just fifteen metres to go. Nicki bent round to see Jon slapping his trainers into the ground to bring him level with the next bounce. The surprise on her face was quickly replaced by the narrowing of her eyes as she took up the challenge and pushed for home. Jon matched her efforts. The hoppers squashed down in unison, stretching the DPI logos between their legs as they bounced together, almost touching. Techniques were abandoned as they wobbled erratically in their determination, their feet shooting up in the air. With just a few metres to go, Nicki stared straight ahead but shot out a leg to her right and struck Jon's hopper, nudging him sideways away from her. She braced herself with her left foot when it landed on the floor to counteract the action, and pretended not to notice Jon lurching off-balance to his right. As she crossed the finish line, Jon was left outstretched on the grass behind her, his hopper bouncing away from him. With the cameras clicking, she immediately got off her winning mount and rushed over to Jon.

'Are you okay? I lost my balance and I think I might have clipped you.'

Jon was on his back, his head on its side as he watched everyone else bounce their way over the line. He turned to look up at a face whose eyes betrayed her worried expression. She was holding out a hand. A little dazed, Jon took it, and was yanked up by Nottingham's finest. She put an arm round Jon, and photographers captured the hug as she whispered in Jon's ear, 'That's for the scar.'

Nicki had the honour of counting the group through the extra twenty press-ups she had immunity from, posing once in the middle of their circle with the winning hopper held above her head at the media's request. Jackson had even presented her with a small medal, promising everyone a much better one when they finished the marathon. After completing his set, Jon lay face down on the ground, wondering if his arms would ever work again.

Now that the staged shoot had been completed, Jackson asked the photographers to leave them alone to resume the rest of the day's training.

'Nice grass stains.' Ceris sat down next to Jon. 'Looks like you've been rolling around with a girl all morning.'

Jon let out a little smile. 'Well, me and Maid Marian had a couple of tumbles today, I guess.'

'She's a tad competitive.'

'That's a bit like saying Danny's a tad Scouse.'

She laughed. 'So what do you think so far? Do you think they'll knock us Brits into shape?'

'I'm not sure about this Englishman. I hear there's a Welsh girl who's got a chance, though.'

'Me? I don't know about that. It's early days. If Arjun runs as fast as his mouth then he'll be a challenger. So could you, if you train hard.'

'Nah. I'll be pleased if I just don't come last.' Jon adjusted the laces on his trainer.

'Look, we all got here the same way and none of us are exactly prime athletic specimens. You don't know your potential until you push yourself.'

Jon wondered whether he had ever pushed himself, or indeed been pushed, in his entire life. 'Are you saying that I might be the male equivalent of Paula Radcliffe…it's just that I don't know it yet?'

'Maybe. She was always amazing in the New York marathons. None of us will become elite athletes in just three months, but you could practise her head bobbing movements – that would be a start.' Ceris exaggerated Paula's trademark head wobble. 'Whoa! That made me dizzy. I don't know how she did it.' She ended up spinning her eyes around and flopping her head on Jon's shoulder. A welcome sweet scent met his nostrils, and although the touch between them was brief, it invigorated Jon somewhat.

Jackson surveyed the scene in front of him. 'So what did we all learn from that race?'

A few seconds of silence.

'How to look a prat on a kid's toy in the middle of Central Park?' Natasha said.

'That Nicki rides it hard and fast?' Kieran said, just before Nicki motioned her foot towards his midriff.

'How about that speed and power doesn't always win?' Jackson answered his own question and pointed to Arjun and Danny. 'You two went off like men possessed and then paid the price. Nicki and Jon had good, steady techniques, paced themselves and only went a little crazy near the end.'

'Didn't Pass-Out Boy over there finish last in the end, though?' Danny cocked a thumb in Jon's direction.

Jackson stepped towards Danny. 'I saw that you had more grass in your mouth than a cow in a new field when you went down, so you can keep quiet. The point is, that every race will have different tactics, different strategies. Don't go off too gung-ho and don't mess around at the start otherwise you'll never recover. Any questions?'

'Yeah,' Tom said. 'Is every morning going to be like this?'

'Of course not,' replied Jackson. 'Today's just a warm up, a light day. Have five minutes' rest and then I'll introduce you to some of my favourite exercises – the ones that'll make you scream for mercy.'

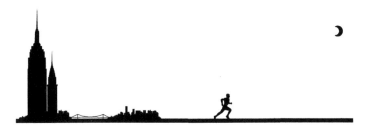

Chapter 15

'**M**UM, I'll be fine,' Jon said down the phone for the fifth time in as many minutes. It was his fourth night at the DPI Adventures House and he knew that despite plenty of texts and emails, the call to his parents had been overdue.

'But I hear Central Park can be very dangerous,' Jon's mum said.

'We only run in daylight and there's ten of us together. Plus no potential attacker would dream of taking on the fitness instructor for fear of being killed by enforced sit-ups.'

'Are you staying somewhere nice? Not in the Bronx, are you? And please tell me you're not staying in the Devil's Kitchen.'

His mum's experience of New York consisted of films she'd stumbled on when watching TV on Sundays, and – a little worryingly in Jon's opinion – her entire collection of *Sex and the City*.

'It's called Hell's Kitchen, and no, I'm nowhere near there or in the Bronx. It's a huge house on Long Island, actually. Very cool.'

'Long Island? Do you mean the Hamptons? It's very swanky there. Have you been invited to any parties?'

'It's not the Hamptons, just Long Beach. It's on the other end, not too far from JFK.'

'Well you being near an airport is not much use to us now, is it?'

'DPI are very strict on visits, I told you. No family, friends or partners are allowed. You know I would pop home at least once if I could, but there's nothing I can do about it. DPI doesn't want anyone else here to distract us from our training.'

'Hmm. So you say.'

'Mum –'

'So are they feeding you?'

'No Mum, they're starving us. I expect by tomorrow I'll be dead.'

'Don't say that, Jon. I meant are they providing you with food or are you eating out all the time? New York has some lovely restaurants.'

'Don't think we'll get to dine out much. DPI provides all the food and has even given us our own chef to cook everything for us.'

'Oh, well that's fantastic.'

'Not really. They get to say what we eat and when we eat, for three whole months.'

'But it will all be good stuff, right?'

'Yeah. Nothing that's not nutritional and beneficial to a marathon runner. Not sure why DPI didn't just secure the rights to a wonder pill and saved all the hassle.'

'Well, at least it'll be better than your usual cheesy beans on toast.'

Jon sighed. 'That was just a one-off when you surprised me that time. I can cook, you know. I do a mean lasagne.'

'I'm sure you do, love. So what about the other runners? Any nice girls there?'

'Well, there's one girl here from Nottingham who probably wouldn't spit on me if I was on fire, and a Geordie who's definitely not my type, but Ceris is all right I suppose.'

'Well don't you make a fool of yourself though, love. Don't go chasing after anyone who you can't get.'

Jon rolled his eyes. 'I'll probably be chasing after all of them in the marathon, the boys as well.'

'What? No, you can win this. Three months, good food, lots of exercise – you'll be running faster than everyone, I'm sure. But…'

'But what?'

'Well, if you do win…I'm just not sure about this space nonsense.'

'Look Mum, even if I had bionic legs, I doubt I would win, but in the unlikely event that I do, you can worry about that later. It's not for ages, anyway.'

'And what was all that talk about the police? Did you get arrested?'

The London Eye chase seemed a long time ago to Jon. One or two newspapers had discovered the story upon researching the contestants after the press conference. 'DPI sorted it all and explained the circumstances. No charges were made, so you can stop looking for me on *Crimewatch.*'

'It said you were running around naked. I don't think that's advisable, love, even in August.'

'No, Mum. So is Dad there?'

Even talking to his dad was better than discussing the events of London with his mum. Goodness knows what the press might have found out about the events leading up to it. The last thing he needed was his own mother worrying about his apparent fetish for wearing women's clothing.

'So how's fame and unemployment?' His dad's voice suddenly bellowed in Jon's ear.

'I'm not jobless, Dad, just…taking a career break.'

'You know you could have applied to NASA if you wanted to go into space. They always need testers.'

'I think Human Resource software is a little different from multi-billion pound rocket navigation programs.'

'But at least you're doing something interesting with your life, for once. Was the selection process just random?'

Jon slumped back on his bed. 'No, it was quite involved, really. They obviously thought I had what it took.'

'Good. Never thought you had it in you. You really think you'll be able to run twenty-six miles?'

'Why not? I've got until November to train for it. Stranger things have happened.'

'That's a long way to run, though.'

'How would you know? When was the last time you did any exercise?' Jon could accept his Dad's disappointment in his career due to his own success in business, but advice on physical achievements was pushing it.

'Your mum and I go for walks every Sunday.'

'Yes, to the pub. Down the road.'

'It's still exercise.'

'If you think that's exercise, you should have taken part in Sergeant Pain's sessions today.'

'You were never that good at physical education at school, if I remember.'

'This is more punishment than education. Anyways, how's Conan?'

'Cat's fine. Think he misses you, though. Mum does, too.'

'It's only been four nights.'

'Yes, well, it'll end up being three months, which is a long time. Especially as we can't even visit until the day of the marathon.'

'Don't you start as well.'

They chatted for another ten minutes about the competition and things back home before Jon made his excuses, hung up and went downstairs to join the others.

'What do you reckon, Jon? Hit the city tonight?' Kieran said, sitting opposite the girls in the living room.

'Are we allowed out?' Jon asked.

'Allowed? This isn't a prison camp, we can do whatever we want,' Kieran said, throwing a cushion across the room towards the girls.

'Watch it – that cushion might be bugged, you know,' Natasha said, filing her nails.

'If it was,' Danny said, 'then it might pick up some pillow talk, eh?'

Jon sat down as everyone groaned. 'It's just that DPI

have been pretty clear that while our free time after dinner is ours, they – and I quote – "seriously advise against any activities that involve the consumption of alcohol of any kind".'

'Who said anything about alcohol? I'm just suggesting a night on the town,' Kieran said.

'C'mon, Jon,' Natasha said, 'do I look like a girl who'd go out and consume alcohol of any kind?'

'Don't answer that one,' Barry said as he put down a peach he was halfway through. 'But I'm up for it, and I don't even drink.'

'I'll be good,' Arjun said. 'Strictly lemonades all night.'

'I don't know guys...I'm shattered after today. Legs are killing me,' Jon said.

'Ceris will rub them better in the limo,' Kieran said, before ducking the return cushion. 'Go on – once the cameras are here it'll be impossible to sneak out.'

Jon couldn't disagree. DPI had arranged for a documentary to be made of the experience, and the TV crew were due sometime next week. Whilst not exactly *Big Brother*, there wouldn't be much that escaped the cameras. 'Where would we go?'

'Where else would you go in New York on a Saturday night?' Kieran said. 'Manhattan, baby! I know this great cocktail bar off Times Square. Went there last year on my twenty-fifth birthday. They do killer mojitos.'

'That sounds a little like alcohol to me,' Jon said.

'Look, we'll have a couple of drinks, nothing too bad, see the lights, relax and come back before midnight.'

Jon looked at everyone's expectant faces. 'Oh, go on then. A small trip out won't hurt.'

And that conversation was Jon's last memory of the night.

Chapter 16

IT had been a long while since Doug's bed had been covered with so many newspapers on a Sunday morning. Amber burst into the room and carefully placed the front covers of a tabloid in one of the remaining gaps on the duvet.

'That's the last of them now, Daddy.'

'Well thank you, my little peach. Good work.' Doug surveyed his reading for the rest of the morning. His view had always been that anyone who said they didn't care what the press thought of them was lying.

'You're really popular this week. I've never had to pull out so many pages for you.' She lifted up the cover of one of the tabloids which had gone with a less-than-enthusiastic headline of "Space Crazy". 'Is it true you're sending someone to the Moon?'

Doug took the newspaper, deciding to read some of the more negative ones first to get them out of the way. 'Yes, we're going to build a big rocket and fly all the way there and get them home again.'

Her eyes grew wide as the engine of her imagination hurtled her through the journey. 'Can we go, too?'

'Maybe one day, when you're older.'

'But I'm six! And I'll be seven in October. That's older than almost all of the kids in my class, you know.'

'Seven? Well in that case, maybe I'll have to put you on our special top secret training programme. Come here and I'll tell you all about it.' Doug lifted up the duvet and she climbed into the bed. 'But first you must promise not to say anything to anyone.'

'I promise!'

'Sworn to secrecy?'

'I swear!'

'May your dolls be locked away in the prison of the trolls for a hundred years if you tell?'

'They may!'

She was the picture of innocence, from her long blonde hair to her cherub face.

'You see, the Moon is just the start. We can build bases, laboratories, launch pads for future missions beyond the Moon.'

'You mean to Mars?'

'Yes, Mars, and some of the other planets. We'll need pilots, of course.'

'I can learn how to fly.'

'And scientists.'

'We learn science at school!'

'Really clever people.'

'I can play chess!'

Doug took her through the details of his dreams, sharing

the images he'd had at her age. He watched the wonder grow on her face as he explained the huge distances, the perils of space journeys, the extreme conditions of the planets. The room became the Solar System as they stretched out their hands to position the imaginary route of the exploration.

'We need to go faster, Daddy! Faster and further!'

'We will have to, if I am to see my grandchildren on Titan.'

Amber looked at him. Doug could almost see her count his forty-nine years. With watery eyes, she said, 'Daddy, won't you be really old when I'm living on Titan?'

For a split second, the sadness of reality pricked at their bubble. Doug refused to let the outside in again, and put on a face of mock incredulity. 'Me? I plan to live forever and visit all my children and grandchildren and great-grandchildren all over the Solar System.' He tickled her until she wriggled out of the bed, running off promising to look up Titan on the Internet and to give him a full report by the afternoon of what would be needed to set up home there.

It was nearly ten o'clock by the time he'd finished reading the tabloids. They covered the entire spectrum of responses, either completely ridiculing his Moon plans as unachievable, or going so overboard to suggest that DPI was well on its way to make NASA extinct. *The Sun* had leapt on board with it, having a centre-page pull-out of a cartoon diagram on how DPI was going to launch, achieve orbit and then return. The *Daily Mirror* had praised Doug's idea, but doubted its feasibility, saying that if the Moon was indeed made of cheese it would have fewer holes in it than DPI's plans. The marathon concept had been a hit with most people, though. 'The Great Space Race' in particular caught Doug's eye, and he was sure that he would recommend that title to his PR team. Both papers had stories of the ten competitors – 'The Moon Runners' – along with a table of their latest odds for triumph. Doug felt a genuine excitement for them, and a little twinge of envy at what they were going to achieve. Your first marathon was always the best, Doug thought. Not knowing if you could really do it, blissfully unaware of the total pain that was ahead. The thrill of rounding the last bend and seeing the finish line, that first medal round your neck. Now he was adding the experience of a lifetime to the winner – something that properly deserved that label. He didn't really care which of them won, just as long as they represented the company well, and he was sure that the interest they would generate would keep him and DPI in the news for many months.

The broadsheets, as expected, took a more balanced view. NASA apparently wasn't happy with DPI's plans, especially the negative press that was being generated focussing on the lack of progress since the Apollo program. A stout defence based on the success of the Shuttle missions and the unmanned exploration of Mars did little to placate the critics in comparison to what relative newbies DPI were doing. NASA had opened their attack with a we'll-believe-it-when-we-see-it argument. There were also the protesters, campaigning on what a huge waste of money the whole thing was. Hadn't we already gone to the Moon? What was the point in going and not even landing on it? Doug grabbed a pen and put a ring round one article that argued that DPI should be putting the money into Africa. 'Short-sighted fools,' Doug said out loud to no-one, and activated his voice recorder on his phone to dictate a response he would send to PR. 'If we sunk money into Africa, in the future when mankind is on the brink of disaster with nowhere to go, I'm sure the tens of billions left to perish will be heart-warmed to know that we saved a few million lives, and that now they are all happily able to be alive to witness the gradual collapse of humanity.'

The most interesting articles, however, regarded the Internet conspiracies. These ranged from the bizarre – the construction of a Michael Jackson statue to be dropped onto the Moon's surface – to the more sinister – the questions over DPI's real intentions and the use of the experimental human space monkey that the despicable competition was going to choose.

So far though, Doug thought, things were going nicely. DPI stock had risen well and all the newspaper financial sections were in admiration of their plans in terms of the coverage and excitement they had generated. The marathon was all in hand and PR were lapping up the various publicity opportunities with the contestants. Had it been over two years since he'd read that damning article in *The Daily Telegraph*? He'd known that the paper had been right – that DPI had survived the rapids of uncertainty but were now moored up in stale waters, going nowhere fast – but it had been another thing reading it knowing that the rest of the world would now know it too. By chance, the papers back then were also reporting on NASA cuts and abandoned future missions, and it was the combination of these two that had sparked his original idea. Recently though, he felt like he'd given his local pub football team a fortune and announced to the world that they would be bringing home the Champions League in a few years' time. He thought of Amber, and her delight at hearing all his plans. Picking up *The Sun*'s diagram of the DPI-branded rocket, he wondered how they'd got their information on how it was all going to be put together. Especially given the fact that after his recent calls from the project team, Doug didn't have a clue himself.

Chapter 17

JON was dying. In fact, he felt that there was a good chance he was already dead. He could sense he was horizontal, but that was as far as his knowledge stretched. Somewhere in another world, he could hear voices.

'Is he still not up yet? I can't wait to show him the photos.'

'Wait till he sees the one of him and Tasha singing.'

'Should've shaved an eyebrow.'

'Kieran! That would've been cruel.'

'Do you think they'll get the sick smell out of the limo?'

'Best get us a new car, I reckon.'

'C'mon – we'd better leave him.'

Jon fell deeper towards the clutches of death.

A lifetime or so later, he heard an explosion of noise as someone charged through the door.

'Good morning, Jonny Boy!'

Jon opened his eyes just in time to see Nicki slap him hard on each cheek.

'Wake up, loser,' Nicki said as she began hauling him

131

out of bed. 'The TV crew are here and they need every one of us up in fifteen minutes. I thought you'd appreciate a little help.'

'Huh?' was all Jon could muster.

'TV, you know – the documentary? They've come early. DPI thinks there's enough interest in us to start now, apparently. But,' she said as she pulled him into a sitting position, 'I'm not quite sure why they'd bother with you.'

Before he knew it, Jon had been dragged out of his bedroom and was now standing on something cold, vaguely aware that he was just in his boxer shorts. He looked up to see jets of water spray out onto his face. It was like being stabbed by icicles.

'I'm sure I'm not the only girl who's forced you to take a cold shower,' Nicki said, holding the shower hose and watching him jump around.

Jon felt a bit more awake now. He also felt he might slip into a cryogenic coma any second, and that his head might suddenly pop due to the high-pitched screams that were coming from somewhere in the room. It was only when Nicki had turned off the spray and the screams turned into a low moaning that Jon realised the source of the noise was in fact himself.

'Sounds like your karaoke singing. God only knows how anyone voted you above me last night,' she said, before grabbing his arm, pulling him out of the shower cubicle and putting a large white towel around him. Jon's core temperature was now raised to something slightly above absolute zero.

'Bedroom. Now.' Jon was pushed back along the corridor towards his room.

'Underpants off. Don't worry, I won't look. It's probably

microscopic anyway after that shower. Dry yourself off and wear these.' Nicki had rummaged in Jon's drawers and dug out some boxers and running kit. She stood with her back to him, facing the door, as he fumbled around trying to work out how his two legs fitted into the holes in his boxers. He finally put them on, not knowing if they were inside out or even upside down. They appeared to cover everything, so he went on to the next round: his shorts. These were more difficult – they had a lining and a drawstring, and the orange colour was far too bright. The shuffling and grunting made Nicki turn around. 'Bloody useless baby. I've seen my boyfriend struggle the day after the night before, but you really are something else.'

Jon resigned himself to being pulled around, legs out, arms up, until he was fully dressed.

'Right – downstairs.'

'N–' Jon's throat closed up. He swallowed as if he'd just eaten a small piece of molten lava. He could taste aniseed. Feeling his chin, he managed to force out, 'Need. To. Shave.'

'Fine. The state your face is in, you need all the improvement you can get. You've got five minutes,' Nicki said, this time dragging him across the landing back towards the bathroom, electric shaver in hand.

Looking at his reflection in the mirror, it was with a little regret that he turned on the shaver. He had hoped to have enough time before the cameras were there to get a full beard going and surprise everyone back home. He thought that it might get him more coverage as the bearded runner, or at the very least give him a topic for his blog. In its current state however, it had to go, so he attacked one side of his face, wincing at the loud hum. Half way through, the buzzing slowed and stopped. Jon looked at the shaver and saw the light flashing to indicate a dead battery. He searched for the power lead, then realised it must be in his bedroom, so he started to shuffle his way back, until he heard a familiar voice.

'Hey, big boy.'

'Summer?' Jon stood in his Darth Vader boxer shorts, a wet towel over his shoulder and facial hair that looked like he'd had an accident with some Fuzzy Felt and a tube of glue. 'I…wasn't expecting you.'

'No kidding,' Summer said, smiling as she approached him. She put both hands on his unevenly-shaved cheeks and rubbed. 'Is this a New York fashion I haven't heard of?'

'What? Oh, crap. Yes, I, er…shaver. Ran out of battery. Didn't quite finish the job.'

'Maybe you should leave it. Create a statement, perhaps even start a trend. Who knows? They love British fashion over here. With a bit of PR creativity, that half beard and you could go far.'

'I'm not sure the world's ready for that. I'll shave it off.'

'I reckon you'd look good with a beard, a full one.'

'Really?'

'Yeah, a real man grows a beard.'

'Wish you'd told me that before I started shaving today.'

'Why? Would you have grown one for me?'

'No, not for you. Why would I grow one for you?' Jon looked away and continued to his room, Summer following. 'Besides, I'm not really talking to you.'

'Funny, feels like a conversation to me.'

'Yeah, well, you surprised me.'

Summer leant against the door frame. 'So now you're

going to ignore me? Your PR rep? Your only barrier between you and the world?'

'I can always use Leona.'

'Leona, right. She's an angel, of course.'

Jon thought back to what Tom had told him at the press conference about the rep getting him into his own embarrassing situation. 'Looks like I can't trust either of you. Maybe I'll be fine on my own.' He started to look for his shaver lead.

'It's okay, you can trust me, Jon'

He sighed. 'Summer, what are you after?'

'Relax Jon, I'm not after anything. I'm just playing, having a little fun.'

'Like in London?'

'London was…a mission. One that we both passed.'

'One of us had slightly more fun at the expense of the other.'

'You'll get over it, I'm sure,' Summer said, finding the shaver lead and throwing it at him. 'Anyway, I was just rounding up the troops. See you downstairs to discuss the documentary.'

Fully clothed and clean shaven, Jon flinched at the round of applause that greeted him on his arrival at the foot of the stairs.

'Hey – it's the Sambuca Kid!' Danny said, giving Jon a one-arm hug.

'Wow, if they ever do a zombie remake of *Chariots of Fire*, you've got the lead part,' Arjun said.

'What was I drinking?' Jon asked, almost afraid to hear the answer.

Natasha was the first to reply, 'Two beers, one mojito and three flaming sambucas. Hardcore southerner, eh?'

'Told you that you shouldn't have bought those last two shots for him, Tasha. How's your hand, Jon?' Ceris said.

Jon looked at his left hand. 'It's fine. Why?'

'Try the other hand.'

Jon gazed at the palm of his right hand. A large red circle looked back at him. 'How?'

'You really don't remember?'

'No. I –' and then he saw a flashback of a struggle, a panic, flinging his hand against the bar and the sound of breaking glass. He looked at his hand again. The perfect circle of a shot glass rim. He winced.

'There we go,' Kieran said. 'The look of total recall of a drunken night.'

Jon remembered Danny showing him how to put the sambuca flame out with his hand over the shot glass. He remembered the warning against too much suction and the high temperatures. His hand gave a little throb as he recalled the heat and the pain.

'Great,' was all Jon could muster, wondering how many other disfigurations to his body he could manage within the next week.

He sat in the living room, staring at his hand, as the documentary production team took everyone through how the program was going to be made. It was going to be broadcast in England every Wednesday evening, covering the previous week's activities.

'Shame we didn't have the camera earlier – could've done a spin-off of *The Walking Dead*, the state he was in,' Nicki said, pointing a finger at Jon.

'Don't tell me you were actually having fun?' Summer said, looking at him.

Jon only offered a sarcastic smile in response.

'Anyway,' Summer continued, 'from now on, I'm going to have to request nicely that you all keep any raucous festivities to a minimum. You are all representing DPI now and the cameras will be with you. DPI will look very seriously on any inappropriate behaviour.'

'So we're not allowed fun any more?' Natasha said.

'That's not what I said. Of course you're allowed to have fun, but DPI is paying a lot of money for all this and they do not want their good name to be tarnished by the odd silly misdemeanour.'

'But the cameras won't be there all the time, will they?' Danny said.

'That's not the point. Mr Peabody takes marathon training very seriously, and for you to be ready in just thirteen weeks' time will take a lot of commitment. We want you to all line up at the start on Staten Island fully fit, fully trained and ready to compete equally with each other. Do not do anything to endanger this goal.'

'He sounds like a control freak to me,' Natasha whispered.

'Why do we all have to be equal? Surely some of us are going to end up being more naturally gifted at this and therefore be favourites to win?' Tom said.

Natasha jumped in with a reply, 'It's because they want the excitement, the thrill of the unexpected. Who's gonna win? Every part of the UK will be interested in their regional hero, so everywhere will be exposed to DPI. Follow your man or woman and buy DPI products while you're there. If it's a two-horse race then the interest dwindles. Basically, we're advertising puppets.'

'It's not like that,' Summer said. 'Look, I'll be frank – DPI has bought into all of you and wants to maximise the exposure by ensuring that you're all in the limelight. It's obvious we didn't ask you to do the tattoo just for a dare – it's also fantastic advertising for us.'

'So I'm right?' Natasha said.

'But it's so much more than that. Mr Peabody genuinely wants you to compete to the best of your ability. He's providing the best nutrition and the best exercise regime. What's the point of doing all that and allowing you to mess it up by getting drunk and injuring yourself?'

'And of course heaven forbid we show up the whiter-than-white DPI.'

Summer let Natasha's remark bounce off the walls a few times. 'Look, the show might get picked up by one of the American networks, and if it does, you will all be under scrutiny here. Would you let a bunch of people with your name tattooed on them loose in the city to do whatever they want for three months? Or would you produce guidelines to exercise some control to avoid any issues?'

Jon surprised himself by joining in. 'I'm sure we'll all behave ourselves. It seems fair from their point of view, when you think about it. Guys, we can still have a laugh but just make sure I don't touch any sambuca from now on.' The rest of the group smiled.

'Thanks Jon, exactly. You're going to need to relax and I will make sure you have fun. Have faith in DPI, please, and we guarantee you'll enjoy the whole experience.'

Summer closed her folder to end the session. The gathering disbanded, despite Natasha and Tom looking as if they wanted to continue their battle with Summer. Jon went into the kitchen for a drink, opening the fridge that was large enough to step inside and train for an attack on the North Pole. He poured himself some orange juice and was distracted by the sight of Summer and Leona through the window. He couldn't tell what they were talking about, but Summer had shaken her head a few times. When Leona came back into the house and left Summer outside alone, Jon took his chance to go out and join her.

'Tough crowd, eh?' Jon said as he stepped onto the patio.

'You lot? Well, I suppose I should have expected it. It's all a bit different for you and we haven't exactly been given much of a chance to train you up yet,' Summer said.

'You mean brainwash us.' Jon put his arms out forward and swayed like a zombie.

'DPI isn't all bad, you know.'

'So you admit they're a little bit bad?'

'Your Jedi mind tricks won't work with me – you forget who you're talking to.' She stuck out her tongue.

'However, it doesn't help me trust DPI when I don't even trust the employee who's supposed to be looking after us.'

'Look Jon, I was just doing my job in London. I had to be undercover otherwise it wouldn't have worked.'

'But why me? Why put me all through that? And don't give me any of that "But didn't you enjoy wearing a dress and almost getting arrested for indecent exposure?" crap.'

Summer gave him a look that said she was about

to say exactly that. 'You volunteered, remember? You were the only person who wanted to come with me when I suggested we team up. It was a test of trust and cooperation. Everyone else shot off to do their own thing or didn't dare contemplate teaming up with someone who they thought they were up against.'

'Nah, I only volunteered to save you from that big guy with the muscles.'

'Oooh, James, wasn't it? He was quite hunky. Yes, I could've had a lot of fun with him, I reckon.' She gave him a little nudge with her elbow as she pretended to dream away in the distance.

'Alas, you ended up with me.'

'Yes, you. See, you may have only volunteered to save me from the man of my dreams, but you also showed a lot of trust later and helped me with my photo.'

'But did you have to make me wear a dress?'

'Yes.'

'And strip me naked?'

'Yes.'

'And run off with my clothes?'

'You got them back.'

'I think you're missing the point…'

'No, you are.' Summer held his arm and took him a few metres away from the house. 'Peabody wanted daredevils, people who were not afraid to take risks, people who were willing to do whatever it took to get through to the next round. But he didn't want the usual nutters who would apply to something like this, he wanted to coax out the ones who had it in them, but they just didn't know it.'

'So I became your project? What about everyone else in the group in London?'

'We had to pick someone somehow.' Summer chewed on her bottom lip. 'Peabody has a lot of great ideas, but is not a man to hang around – he wants things done now, and doesn't always help us with how we are to achieve them. He says that it's our job to sort that out.'

'Unlike my ex-boss who probably would have gone down there himself.' Jon desperately tried not to think of Henry instead of Summer in her photo, otherwise he feared breakfast would make an unwelcome reappearance.

'Anyway, the photo and tattoo tasks were mandatory, but we were under pressure to ensure we got a suitable candidate, that who we picked was right for the programme. I couldn't just leave that to luck – I wanted my candidate to earn it, so I decided to grab the first person up for it and just work with that.'

'But what if I hadn't have gone through with it? Missed out on the photo? Who else would you have picked in the time allowed?'

Summer smiled. 'Me and Leona had a theory – show a guy your naked body and he'll do anything.'

Jon opened his mouth to argue, but closed it again.

'We also had a bet on how far we would go ourselves, and how far our chosen one would go.'

'Ah,' Jon said, 'that's why you were so excited after I took your photo.'

'Leona and Tom were good, but we gave it large. Well, so to speak.'

Jon blushed a little.

'So yes, my delight was genuine.'

'Well something of you has to be.'

Summer cupped her breasts with both hands and jiggled them. 'Aren't you forgetting these? I'm sure you had enough of a look to see they're the real thing.'

Jon was mesmerised for a second before responding, 'I'm not sure. I've had forensics study the photo all week and I'm waiting for the results.'

'Watch it…or I'll get a full size poster of you in all your glory and hang it up inside the house.'

'So it was my destiny – as soon as I agreed to go with you, I was set to make my debut in being both a cross-dresser and then a public streaker?'

'That took a lot of imagination. I didn't quite know how I was going to pull it off at first, but the plan turned out to be as cunning as it was brilliant.' Summer gave a little curtsey.

'Well bravo. How'd you know I'd get the tattoo, though?'

'Wounded pride and all that. It was a bit of a risk, I admit, but I had faith in you.'

He looked over his shoulder to see if anyone else was watching from the house, but they'd moved mostly out of view from the kitchen. For some reason, he felt like he was fraternising with the enemy. He looked down at the decked patio and kicked a small stone. 'I mean it about trust, though. You specifically asked me to trust you in London – how do you think I felt when I saw you run off with my clothes? And then turn up later as a DPI employee? How can I really trust you again?'

Summer went up to him and put her thumb and index finger either side of Jon's chin, lifting up his head. 'I asked you to trust me to help get you here, did I not?'

Jon stared into her hazel eyes and for the first time saw no hint of mischief. 'Yeah, I guess.'

'And did I help get you here?'

'Yes, but –'

'So in spite of my methods, in what way did I betray your trust?'

'How about pretending you were going to go on the London Eye with me, stealing all my clothes and faking that tattoo photo?'

'All a means to an end.'

Jon looked towards the sky and shook his head.

'Besides,' Summer went on, 'think of the story you can tell your future kids.'

'There are some things your children are best not knowing.'

'Maybe they'll read your blog one day.'

'I'm definitely not blogging about that.' Jon showed his palm to Summer in a 'stop' gesture.

She looked at it, puzzled. 'What's that mark on your hand? Have they signed you into a cult?'

'What? Something that you don't know about? This sambuca souvenir from the night out won't be in the blog, either.'

'Oh c'mon – that's perfect for the blog.'

'No way. When I get back I have to get another job, thanks to this little competition. I don't want people thinking I'm a party animal or a stupid, clumsy, gullible fool.'

Summer took his hand and began to trace the circle with her finger. 'You are a party animal. You are stupid, clumsy and gullible. But –'

'If this is a pep talk, I've heard better.'

'Let me finish. But I'm sure you are only those things *sometimes*, just like the rest of us. So open up, share your fun experiences. Let everyone see who you really are.'

'Which is...?' Jon felt her finger go round and round the scar on his hand, giving him a pleasant tickling feeling he felt he could have enjoyed for hours.

Summer stared into Jon's eyes, theatrically trying to physically peer inside his mind. 'I'm not sure. I guess I barely know you.'

She kissed his palm and walked back into the house, failing to see a frowning Nicki peering out the far window in the kitchen.

Chapter 18

'THE thrill of the race. Don't you just love it?' Jackson said as he sprinted on the spot. 'Anyone nervous?'

Four weeks into his training, Jon hadn't been worried at the thought of his first race until he'd seen the hundreds of other runners lining up in the warm-up area in Central Park. Nearly every one of them looked a seasoned pro, chatting idly amongst themselves while they casually went through their stretches. On some of the men he'd seen smaller calf muscles on a horse. Even the elderly runners looked in shape and up for it. If it hadn't been for a small man in his fifties stuffing himself with his third bagel within minutes, Jon seriously thought he may come last.

'No-one a bit nervy? Well sorry guys, but I just don't believe ya. But the good news is that it's okay to be nervous, especially as it's your first race. In fact, let your nerves feed your energy. If you can control it, it's like a natural performance-enhancing drug. Talking of which, I forgot to tell you of the drug testing at the end of the race. It's mandatory, so get ready to pee in a cup soon after finishing.'

'You're gonna drug test us? Why?' Natasha said.

'Been secretly spliffing it up, Tasha?' Danny said.

'It's just part of the rules, people, set by DPI,' Jackson said. 'Mr Peabody doesn't want any cheats getting their hands on his prize.'

'Well if I wasn't nervous before, the thought of drinking all this crazy-coloured sports drink, running five miles and then being forced to piss in a cup has made me a little uneasy,' Natasha said.

Jackson stopped his exercises. 'Relax, you'll get used to it after each race. Besides, today should be a walk in the park. Well, a little jog, anyway. We've all gone much further than these five little miles we're gonna do today. It'll be over before you know it.'

Jon only hoped Jackson's last statement would turn out to be true. Sure, they had indeed gone double the distance the week before, but they'd been allowed a few walking periods and had been told the clock wasn't important, as it was just to get the experience of covering the large distance. Today, although the clock didn't matter too much, the presence of five hundred other runners and the prospect of seeing each and every one of them disappear into the distance certainly did. Even if he was only half as knackered at the end of today as he was last week, he was probably looking at a heart and lung transplant, minimum.

'You don't have to worry about the course as there'll be marshals everywhere and you just follow everyone else anyway. Water stations are regularly spaced, so that will give you practice in running and drinking. If you can get more in your mouth than down your vest you're doing well.'

'Jackson – Natasha wants to know if she should spit or swallow?' Kieran said.

Natasha threw a bottle of blue drink at Kieran who managed to dodge it at the last minute.

'Fluid is important,' Jackson said, ignoring Kieran. 'It may be 8am but you know by now how warm it can quickly get on a New York summer's day, and by the looks of the sky, we're in for another hot one. And remember – there's a lot of runners here but don't get intimidated or rushed at the start. Make sure the electronic timing chip on your shoe is secured, as this will record your official time from the moment you cross the start line to the moment you go over the finish time. You'll hear a beep every time you pass over a special mat that'll pick up your unique signal.'

'What about Nicki's chip on her shoulder?' Ceris whispered to Jon.

'I think that's secured for life,' Jon replied.

Nicki may have been installed as second favourite to win, but in terms of popularity, the word back home was that if the programme had a voting out system, she would have been on the plane home by about the second week. They all read each other's blogs, and it was clear from hers that Nicki was only focussed on the winning. Jon, on the other hand, had gained a bit of a cult following, resulting in the odd bit of fan mail.

'So you decided not to wear the dress that your biggest fan sent to you?' Ceris said.

'You know I would have done, but it wasn't official DPI uniform,' Jon said.

'Shame. I'm sure it would have suited you more than Summer's.'

The word of the competition had obviously got to France, and the French couple who had kindly taken the photo of him in a dress had sold it to the English newspapers, most of whom went with a title along the lines of 'Ooh la la!'

'Yeah, I didn't have the hips for that one.'

Ceris smiled. 'I'm sure your new boyfriend would have loved to have seen you run in it, though. Especially with your new beard.'

'Just because they signed it from "Leslie". I'm sure it was from a girl. At least I hope it was. And what's wrong with the beard?'

'Nothing, you look very…rugged.' Ceris was fumbling with a safety pin as she tried to attach a square piece of paper to the vest that she was wearing. 'Can you give me a hand with my running number?'

Jon took the pin from her and pinched a bit of material from her orange vest. 'Hold still a sec.'

'Make sure you don't stab my boob.'

'Why? Will it go pop?'

Ceris waited for him to finish before mock slapping him. 'No, but if I want a little prick I know where to find one.'

Jon left Ceris and looked around at his fellow competitors. Barry finished a banana and stood opposite Jermaine, balancing a hand on his shoulder as he performed a hamstring stretch, Jermaine mirroring.

'Barry,' Jermaine said, 'I don't think I've ever seen a man consume so much fruit.'

'Blame my parents,' Barry said. 'They've run a fruit and veg stall for years down our local market, kind of rubbed off on me.'

'Bet your mum had a nice pear,' Danny said, laughing

as the other two shook their heads. Natasha gave him a little shove and the two began play fighting.

Barry had a strong following due to both his Pakistani and Scottish roots and Jermaine had been promised many supporters from Leeds. Kieran had been given some coverage in America and no doubt would get the support of all the New Yorkers who considered themselves Irish, despite not a single member of their family having set foot on the Emerald Isle for countless generations. Nicki and Arjun were in the middle of their exercise routines next to each other, Nicki keeping a close watch on her main rival.

'Five minutes,' the PA system announced. The ten DPI runners followed Jackson towards the start line which was now obscured by dozens of eager athletes. The leafy trees provided a nice shade from the low morning sun, and the mundane talk about subway closures and last night's TV filled the air with thick New York accents. As he rubbed a light sweat from his face, he could smell the Vaseline on his fingers, Jackson's mandatory running accompaniment to prevent soreness in sensitive areas. He waited in silence, checking his GPS watch and making sure his shoelaces were done up enough but not too tightly. On both sides of where he stood, bare shoulders almost touched his own. A woman with greying hair in front of him gave a big yawn as she tensed her arms upwards. In front of her was a lad who looked to be in his twenties but was wearing a t-shirt that Jon could see featured over a dozen names of races that he had completed across the city. As Jon shook his legs, he realised his calves felt tight, but he didn't know if that was from stretching or whether it was the damage from the previous weeks. He could see some portable toilets some way to his left. Did he need to go? It was probably too late now, he thought, which turned out to be correct as the hooter sounded to start the race.

'Moon Runners – eyes right and don't forget to wave,' Jackson said as he led the group over the start line, pointing at the camera crew on the sidelines. Dozens of shrill beeps could be heard as the runners' chips activated their registration, starting the individual clocks of each runner. Jon scanned the people surrounding the cameramen but couldn't see Summer anywhere. He hadn't seen her since they had talked at the house, but had not been able to get the conversation out of his mind. Her absence today would at least allow him to concentrate on the race and not worry about looking a complete wreck on the finish line. However, even this quick lapse into thinking about Summer led to him being overtaken by eight other runners in the DPI orange, leaving only Tom behind him.

'Let them go off fast – we'll catch 'em later when they start flagging. Us Hertfordshire boys have the better stamina, eh?' Tom said as he jogged alongside Jon.

'Well we certainly don't have the pace,' Jon said as another bunch of local runners jogged past. Jon looked behind him. He could almost count the runners they were beating. It might be a long race, he realised.

At just over halfway, Jon was feeling much better with himself. After worrying about being too slow over the first mile, he picked up the pace and left Tom behind him yelling a warning about hares and tortoises. He cruised past a surprised Natasha and Barry and had his sight set on Ceris's ponytail about twenty metres ahead. Every time he overtook someone, he felt a small energy boost, and it was as if Central Park was now his home running track. The water station had been spectacularly unsuccessful, however. His attempt at grabbing a cup of cold water and downing it without breaking stride led to a slight panic when he thought he might be the first ever person to drown attempting to run five miles.

'See you at the finish,' Jon said as he ran past Ceris, pumping his arms.

'Go on, beardy,' she replied. 'Show us how it's done!'

Four and a half miles in, just half a mile to go, Jon was in trouble. His legs and lungs had conferred and decided that they'd given enough on this little jaunt, and that they would not be supplying the necessary oxygen and power any more. He'd tried some advice Jackson had given all the runners about using different leg muscle sets as he ran when one set got weak, but as he subtly shifted the weight he realised each one was also in agreement with the strike. He recalled a computer game he used to play as a kid – *Daley Thompson's Decathlon* – and how in the 1500 metres poor Daley was left floundering at the end if you'd been too enthusiastic at the start with the speed boost. Jon's own energy bar was now only a few pixels wide.

Natasha had passed him with a smile, Barry with a sympathetic look and even Ceris gave up trying to give him a boost.

'You know what they say,' Tom said as he began to pass Jon, 'hare today, gone tomorrow.'

Jon's only response was wheezing more heavily and to stare at the ground. He didn't dare look behind him. The only way now was to keep going and hope that at least someone who he was ahead of was also in the process of collapsing or about to meet a nasty accident with a rogue rollerblader. He could see the end in sight now, tantalisingly close, yet far away at the same time. Determined not to stop, he focussed on the finish line and just getting one foot in front of the other, knowing that continuing this simple task would indeed eventually get him there. He was now certain that at least nine of his eleven stone had fallen to his legs and was barely going forward when, with about a third of a mile left, he saw an angel. Up ahead was the one person right now that could possibly give Jon the extra strength he needed. As visions go, an old, overweight man in a tight grey vest was not up there with your Archangel Gabriel, but to Jon, Fat Bagel Man was his saviour, someone to guide him home. Jon had barely lifted his head for the last mile and had missed being overtaken by him, but now Jon just had to beat him to the line. He called for reserves, a second wind, the cavalry – anything to make his legs go faster and catch the sweaty man that he was targeting. Jon the survivor now became Jon the hunter. The balding head got nearer as Jon pushed on. There was no park, no crowd, no finish line, only a white, fat, shiny head coming closer into view. He could see its details now – folds in the skin, a deep scar and a faint hairline. His legs were crying out for mercy but he ignored them. Every step was accompanied by a grimace as Jon came to within touching distance. One last effort was all that was needed to overtake. His focus was only on that big, wide head. He was about to make his move when he heard a shrill beeping noise.

The race was over.

Jon lay on his back on a patch of grass, eyes closed. He had somehow managed to stumble there after having a medal put round his neck and a goody bag thrust in his hand by still-eager volunteers. Now he was contemplating spending the rest of his life in the spot, which probably wasn't going to be for too much longer anyway, he figured. The sun that filtered through his shut lids suddenly dimmed.

'Do you need the kiss of life?'

Jon snapped open his eyes to see a beautiful face above him. 'Summer?'

'Because if you do, I better catch that fat man before he leaves. I think he was a doctor.'

Jon sat up. 'I so nearly had him.'

'Well if it's any consolation, I heard him complain that you'd been given the last banana despite him finishing ahead of you.'

'Did I come last?'

'Not all the results are in yet, but out of 520 official starters, it looks like you were 511th. There's a couple more coming in now, being cheered on by their grandchildren.'

'At least I beat the oldies then.'

'Well, not all of them. I saw the "80 And Still Going Strong" team come in a minute or so ahead of you.'

Jon rested his head in his hands as Summer sat down beside him.

'I went off too quickly after the first mile,' Jon said through his fingers. 'I was doing well.'

'I know – I was following everyone's progress on my phone. We brought out an app to link in with the official timings.' She showed Jon. 'I watched your little orange dot move up the field, and then slowly move back down again.'

'Thought you'd missed the race.'

'I almost did. Flew over late last night. You'd all started by the time I'd arrived and I had to get to the finish to see that the interviews were all being organised. They want to have a few words with all the DPI runners, first and – sorry – last. But I did stall them while you recovered.'

'Thanks. Think Mum might have called the British

Embassy and demanded that a crack SAS team storm the house and rescue me tonight if she'd heard my gasping for breath just at the finish.'

'You did okay. You earned this,' Summer said, taking his medal in her hand.

Jon looked down at it. 'Does it have "Thanks for taking part" engraved on it?'

'You finished the race and that's what counts. You don't get a medal for quitting. Given the state of you, I'm proud you carried on.'

'Thanks.'

'Are you ready to face the cameras?' Summer said.

'I suppose I have to, if it's all been planned. I assume they won't be interested in me for much longer.'

'Why not? You have plenty of fans. You're a pin-up boy in the homes of many women.'

'And men, by the sounds of it.' Summer frowned as Jon continued. 'No, I meant in terms of the race, after this performance.'

'There's still two months to go. You'll get fitter and learn from your mistakes.'

'So will everyone else, though.' He looked over to where Jackson was organising a warm-down session. 'Who won today?'

'Nicki pipped Arjun right at the end, Danny third.'

'See? I'm not gonna beat those three. They're younger, fitter and will just get stronger.'

Summer stood up. 'Tell you what, I'll do you a deal. A carrot and a stick thing, only you get the carrot first.'

Jon frowned. 'What's the carrot?'

'It's my day off on Tuesday. We can go into the city and have a fun day out. I've been thinking about London and what you must have gone through, so I suppose I owe you a day out where you get to keep your clothes on.'

'That would be a first. But you mean a night out, though?'

'No, the whole day.'

'I can't. We've got training every day, remember?'

'I can get you out of it. Only if you want to, that is.'

Jon could see Jackson looking over at them, probably annoyed that someone was absent from his stretching masterclass.

'And I should trust a Summer plan because...?'

'Because I always get what I want.'

'I'm sure you do. So what's the stick?'

'That in the next race, you come in the top five.'

Jon painfully got to his feet and snorted. 'Top five? No way that's gonna happen.'

'Well that's nice.' Summer gave him a stern look that he hadn't seen from her before. 'A gal is willing to give up her free day and offers to get you out of the training you oh so love, in return for a commitment to effort...and you won't even try for me?'

'It's not that, it's just fifth place is a bit too –'

'Too what, Jon? Tell me.'

Jon heard himself ask the same question. A whole day with Summer, and he was turning it down because he was too scared he might not be good enough? What if he did get better? The next race was three weeks away and a

155

different distance. He took a long breath out. 'You're right. It's a lovely offer, thank you. I can't promise I can achieve fifth place but I'll give it a shot. The carrot might be worth it.'

Two days later, Jon was wondering whether any carrot was worth being hauled out of the DPI house upside down and having his leg almost ripped off by an enraged Jackson.

Chapter 19

LEAVING Summer to concoct a plan to ensure Jon skived off his training as cleanly as possible was a little like asking a four-year-old to plan next year's national budget. They'd discussed a few ideas, but soon realised that some were not suitable. The idea of Jon feigning sickness was a non-starter, as his self-confessed acting skills made even a porn star's look good. Going completely AWOL would cause too many questions later, and anything involving a family emergency was too much like tempting fate, according to Jon. Summer had gone off to think about it, and later sent a text saying she'd come up with a simple plan that would be plausible and acceptable to everyone. Unfortunately, she'd decided not to tell him anything about the plan itself, so as to add some realistic shock when it started to take place. If Summer wanted surprises, then being woken by a screaming Jackson towering over him had certainly done the job.

'Jon! You're outta here!'

'Wh–' Jon's breath shot out of him as Jackson grabbed his right leg and hung him upside down like a dead rabbit.

'I haven't done anything!'

'You think taking drugs isn't doing anything? You think cheating is acceptable in my team?' Jackson waved his other pile driver of an arm at Jon.

'Drugs? But I haven't taken any drugs?'

'That's not what the tests say. Evidence of performance-enhancing drugs in the urine of a Mr Jon Dunn – that's what I've been told.'

Jon hoped it had better be Summer's plan, otherwise he'd be seriously questioning the source of the Nurofen he'd taken after the race on Sunday. 'There must be some mistake...'

'Really?' Jackson lifted Jon even higher and screamed down into Jon's face, 'There's no smoke without fire in my book. Let's go.'

Given Jackson's passion for drug cheats exceeded his passion for mouthwash, Jon had no alternative but to be hauled unceremoniously to the front door while being verbally abused by Jackson for his alleged misdemeanours. Ceris, Nicki and Danny had all come out of their rooms to see what was going on, but barely had a chance to see the boxer-shorted Jon get thrown out onto the street. A cool breeze swept past his legs and he folded his arms over his bare chest. A limo was waiting by the curb, and although he couldn't see in through the darkened windows, he guessed Summer would be waiting for him inside. As Jackson led him to the car, the driver got out and gave a short nod. Jon recognised him as the chauffeur from London, who proceeded to address them both.

'Thank you, Mr Jones. Mr Dunn – please get in the car and I will drive you to the DPI testing facilities for your follow-up tests.'

'I'm coming with you to ensure you don't bail out en route,' Jackson said.

'I'm sorry, sir, but that is not possible. I have strict instructions to bring him alone.'

'You think I'm going to let this little weasel out of my sight?'

'Sorry sir, but I have my orders.'

Jackson went up and faced the chauffeur. 'Are you telling me you're not allowing me to get in this limousine and escort this weakling excuse of a Limey athlete to ensure justice is served?'

Despite conceding a good six inches in height and even more so in width, the driver stood rock solid. 'Sir, apologies sir, but I have my orders. Mr Dunn will be imprisoned in the car with full door and window locking facilities, I can assure you.'

The toy soldier versus Captain America stand-off ended with Jackson turning around, giving Jon a look that threatened to create its own bruise, before stepping backwards.

'I assume they don't let wild animals in the limo?' Jon whispered. The driver said nothing and opened the door. Jon leapt in, slid along the seats, looked around expectantly...and realised he was alone.

This wasn't exactly what he had expected. Was he really being taken to a testing facility? Sitting almost naked on the cold leather seats, he felt strangely like a white mouse on the way to its new laboratory home. He heard the car doors shut, and moments later the driver's partition was wound down.

'Hello again, sir. Apologies for keeping you waiting back there. Underneath the seat you will find a rucksack with everything I am told you will need today, including clothes. You are also welcome to freshen up using the on-board facilities.'

Jon groped under the seat and found a small bag. 'Thanks...sorry, I didn't catch your name before.'

'Johnson, sir. Just call me Johnson.'

'Okay, thanks Johnson. I don't always leave my house in just my boxers, you know.'

'I'm sure you don't, sir.'

'So where is it that we're really going?'

'The DPI testing facilities. Or so I'm told. It'll be about fifteen minutes.'

Jon opened the main section of the rucksack and found some long cargo shorts, a designer t-shirt, trainers, socks and a pair of Wallace and Gromit boxers. He put all of these on and then opened another section to find a set of DPI running gear, some sunglasses and a compact camera. The last two items brought a bit of relief to him – an indicator, he figured, that this was part of a plan that didn't involve him peeing in a jar and being deported back to England. He examined the camera closely; it was a high-end model and had the kind of cool features that would normally occupy him for hours. However, he tore himself away from it and had a quick face wash and brushed his teeth in what he now assumed was DPI-standard limo facilities. A few minutes later and he was smelling and looking like a rock star. There was still one slight concern, though. He looked around and eventually found an intercom button. 'Johnson?' A few seconds passed.

'Yes sir?'

'I don't suppose you have a toilet in here, do you?'

'I hope you don't want to be sick again, sir. They're still cleaning the first limo.'

'No, I need to pee. Think it was all that excitement.'

'Sorry, sir – no toilet facilities are on board. I do have a flask though, if you are desperate. I can empty out my coffee first.'

It was an option that he gave considerable thought to. 'No, that's okay. I'll hold it, thanks.'

To take his mind off his bladder, he switched on the camera and eventually came across the play mode. Summer's face appeared with a grin so cheesy you could put it on a cracker and have it for supper. Jon laughed to himself and scrolled to the next one – pouting lips, blowing the camera a kiss. The third one was simply a close up of a carrot, and the final one was her in a mirror holding up something written on a notepad which said – back to front – 'See you soon!'.

The car came to a stop on a corner of some small shops, and as Jon presumed this was just part of the journey, he was surprised to hear Johnson getting out of the car. The limo door opened near Jon, and as after a few seconds no-one got in, he took his rucksack and decided to take a peek outside. 'Am I getting out here?'

'Yes, this is the DPI testing facility,' Johnson said. 'So I'm told.'

Jon got out and looked around. A newsagent and a diner was all he could see that even resembled a non-residential building. 'What, here?'

'The instructions were to bring you to this exact spot. I will go now, but have a good day, sir.'

'Thanks Johnson. Guess I'll go find the testing facility.' Jon said goodbye and watched the limo disappear, before deciding that whatever Summer's plan was, it could wait two minutes. He dashed into the diner, asked a passing waitress directions to the gents and relieved himself. On the way out, he stopped when he heard a voice.

'That's a bit rude.' There, in a small booth to his right was Summer.

'Whoa – er, hi,' Jon said.

'Not only did you completely ignore me on the way in and nearly on the way out, but you used the facilities without even ordering anything.'

Jon let go of the door handle and sat down opposite her. She was wearing a tight, pink t-shirt, a green baseball cap, cut-off denim shorts, and was sporting a pair of designer shades. Jon thought she looked like a cool actress in hiding. 'Sorry, wasn't expecting you there. Was running late for a drugs test.'

'Shocking. Who'd have thought that innocent Jon would be taking performance-enhancing drugs?'

'Jackson for a start. He was ready to chop me up and mail me home.'

'Really? Oh yeah – thinking about it, I suppose given his past it's not surprising.' Summer sipped her coffee as Jon waited for her to elaborate. 'Oh, he used to train someone years ago. Great prospect, but later on was found to be using drugs and tried to blame it all on Jackson. I'd forgotten about that.'

'You couldn't have thought of some better plan? One that was slightly less damaging to my reputation and didn't involve threats of castration?'

'Relax, I have it all in hand. It will be announced later

that it was all a mix-up, you'll be fully exonerated and can go back to the house tonight. By the time the rest of the world find out, it will all be sorted anyway.'

'Still sounds a dodgy plan, there'll be questions from everyone.'

'I'll give you the alibi information later, where you've meant to have been all day. Other than that, just be moody, complain about the tester's incompetence and that you want to put it behind you.'

Jon toyed with a napkin. 'What if they find out the truth? It'll look even worse.'

'They won't. I have it covered, trust me.'

'Well I'm here now. Guess I have no choice.' Jon grabbed a menu and slumped back in the plastic chair. 'Breakfast?'

'Not here – I've got somewhere more interesting lined up. We'll get a train up the road to Penn station and start from there. You'll get plenty of exercise, so in some ways you're not even missing out on the training today.'

'You promised me fun, though.'

'I did, and you shall get it.'

When they came out of Penn and on to the Manhattan streets, the temperature was perfect for a quiet morning stroll. Unfortunately, for most of the surrounding New Yorkers, a stroll was not going to get them to their work place on time. The pavements heaved with men in crisp shirts and bright ties, women in power suits and immaculate hair, most clutching varying sizes of coffee mugs and cups with small paper bags of pastries. Snippets of mobile phone conversations passed by Jon's ears from those who walked and talked their way through the crowds. Plans for lunch, dinner, the weekend, and even a desperate plea from one man for his caller to not tell his wife about something. Jon was prepared to start following him just to find out exactly how juicy that something was, but he'd decided to let Summer be his tour guide for the day.

'Where are we going?' Jon said as he saw Summer dart off to her left.

'A good breakfast hangout that I've been to many times, we can chill there. Follow me and try to keep up.'

Jon kept a couple of paces behind Summer as she weaved her way through the human traffic. The roads were busy too, but she often ignored the red pedestrian signals at the cross roads to jog across when the traffic was clear, much to the disgust of the locals who seemed to be more compliant. To Jon, she looked like a creature in her natural habitat. They soon reached a corner of a small green area.

'Here – Bryant Park. We'll grab breakfast, sit out and people watch,' Summer said. 'Hope you're ready to order food New York style.'

Once they had got their food from a nearby shop, they sat down at one of the green metal tables and started to open their bags.

'Well, that's the second time someone's wanted to kill me today,' Jon said as he took out his bagel.

Summer started on her yoghurt. 'If she *had* murdered you, she probably would have got off with a caution. In this city, spending more than half a second deciding on your order is considered a felony in itself, double-so if there's a big queue behind you.'

'They have too much choice here. And what's wrong

with my pronunciation of "butter"?'

'See, you've had it too easy. All that catering we do for you…you haven't really experienced the wonderful New York food culture yet. But you better shape up for lunch, that's all I can say.'

'You could have at least packed me a stab vest,' Jon said, pretending to check his rucksack.

Summer smiled with a spoon in her mouth. The grass area was well-populated with most of the people in groups of two or three sitting down, busy working their way through breakfast. Workers caught up with the latest gossip before going into the office, and youthful tourists made up most of the rest of the collection. One person was completely alone and was going through a series of slow physical exercises.

'So how did you get here, Jon?' Summer said, scooping up more of her pink yoghurt.

Jon looked at her and considered the strange question. 'Can you be more specific?'

'How did you get to this stage of life and end up just drifting along?'

'Who said I was drifting?'

'I've seen the research they've done on everyone. Are you saying you weren't in a rut at work and that you're happy living alone in a flat with just Tiddles for company?'

'*Conan* and I get by just fine, thank you. And I'm not in a rut at work any more, am I?'

'But you were, that's my point. Didn't you want to progress, push yourself before?'

Jon took a bite from his bagel and chewed for a few seconds. 'Been there, done that. Didn't work out.'

Summer just stared back, Jon taking it as his cue to elaborate.

'Four years ago, I got a small promotion to team leader. Within a month, three quarters of my team either handed in their notice or applied for a transfer.'

'What happened? Your idea for Naked Wednesdays not go down too well?'

Jon made an exaggerated frown. 'No, nothing like that. I just kind of froze. Didn't know how to handle them, couldn't deal with it. Got no support from above, either.'

'From above? Maybe you didn't say your prayers,' Summer said, waiting for the next facial expression. 'Still, at least they didn't *all* leave.'

'Jeremy only stayed 'cause he wanted my job and figured the best way to get it would be to stay and make my life hell.' Jon finished his bagel. 'To sum up, the last time I pushed myself I ended up with two weeks off work for stress. After that, a reshuffle and a carefully-arranged new job title left me with a boring, but safe and easy job. It suited me better.'

'So you let one bad experience put you off? Let me guess – you're gonna say the same thing about girls?'

'No. I have three proposals of marriage a day, actually. On average. Becomes tiring after a while. It's just, you know, so hard to choose between the supermodels and the Nobel Prize winners.'

'I can imagine,' Summer said. 'Especially when you aren't awake at the time.'

Jon swept up the crumbs and put them in the bag. He took a big slurp through the straw into his orange juice and looked at Summer. 'I haven't found the right girl yet, that's all. Someone who's not allergic to cats, puts up with me watching football and of course is fluent in Klingon. Having big boobs would just be a bonus.'

Summer laughed. 'So what about Ceris? She seems very friendly around you, and Welsh isn't a million miles away from Klingon, at least in terms of the amount of phlegm used.'

'Ceris? She's cool, but she's like that around everyone. I've fallen for that one before – read something into it that wasn't there. Ended up very messy.'

'Maybe I could do some investigation, find out for you.'

'Nah, I'm good, thanks.' He looked over at the green. 'But what about you?'

'What about me?'

He turned back and saw Summer regarding him with some anxiety. He realised how his last question might have been misconstrued. 'I meant, quit trying to sort out my love life and tell me about yours.'

'Oh. You're just changing the subject, though.'

'No – same subject, just different *subject*,' he said, pointing at her.

'Okay. I guess I haven't found the right man, either. Or girl.'

Jon froze while his mind went off into fantasy land. 'Or girl?'

Summer quickly licked her spoon clean and put it into the empty yoghurt container. 'That's right – "girl". Pays to keep your options open, don't you think? Maybe you're not the only one who likes big boobs.'

Jon studied her for a few seconds. 'Ha! You're lying. I'm not as gullible as you think.'

Summer sat there stone-faced, motionless. Just when Jon had an awful – and yet still fantastic – thought that maybe he had got it wrong, she burst out laughing. 'I knew it,' he said.

'I'm sorry. I couldn't help myself. I wish I'd taken a photo of your face!'

He noticed how cute it was when the top of her nose wrinkled up when she laughed.

'You must be getting better at reading me,' she said.

'Maybe your own Jedi powers are fading.'

She composed herself but kept up a wonderful smile. 'It appears so.'

'Do I get any further detail?'

'On my love life? Let's just say DPI keeps me busy enough as it is, without having to worry about men.' It was her turn to look at the lawn. 'Although I do like how strong *he* is.' The man who was exercising was currently upside down, holding a perfect handstand.

'He's just doing all that for attention,' Jon said.

'Well, it's working.'

Jon picked up the rubbish, got up and placed it in a nearby bin. 'Don't we have a schedule to stick to? Or did it just involve ogling narcissistic men with nothing better to do at nine thirty in the morning than gymnastics?'

'Such fantastic technique.'

'It's just a handstand. Although I'm sure he does a mean cartwheel, too,' Jon said.

'At least he can do it, unlike certain other male members of the species round here.'

'You think I can't?'

'I'm sure you can't.'

He put a hand on his chest. 'Jon Dunn – voted best handstand in the class, aged fourteen.'

Summer eyed him with suspicion. 'Well I have no idea if that's true, but regardless, I'm sure you won't do it.'

Jon sat down again. 'I'll tell you what – if I try it and pull it off, I get to dare you to do something. Agreed?'

'Hmmm, it depends...'

'Oooh – she doesn't like it when she's not in control of what's going to happen. What's the matter, too risky for you? Perhaps you need to phone DPI headquarters to write a script for you?'

'Did someone put an extra spoonful of cockiness in your orange juice? Okay, smartarse, you're on. You know what I'm capable of so you'd better make it good if you wanna challenge me.'

'Oh I will, don't worry.'

'No nudity, though. Been there, done that,' she said.

'Seen it all before. I'll think of much worse.'

She leaned towards him. 'Bring it.'

He mirrored her. 'I will sooo bring it.'

A moment later they started laughing.

'That was so lame,' Summer said.

'I've been over here too long,' Jon said. 'Only one thing to do now...' He got up, stepped towards the lawn and, without losing momentum, bent over until his hands touched the grass and pushed up his legs. It was only when he was completely vertical that he realised he was considerably heavier now than he was in his school days, and that his legs were swinging their way confidently past ninety degrees and showing no sign of stopping. He took evasive action by walking with his hands in the same direction, first just a couple of steps and then a rapid succession of smaller ones until his shape eventually collapsed, bringing his feet down onto something soft that let out a loud 'uummph!' Jon got up and brushed off some loose grass. Curled up, rolling around holding his groin was the gymnast.

'Sorry mate. Didn't mean to catch you. I thought, I, er...I thought I could do it. Obviously not an expert like yourself.'

The man opened his watery eyes which were fuelled by pain and anger. Jon stepped away. 'Sorry again. Hope they're okay, your...you know...I'll just go.' He walked back to a beaming, clapping Summer.

'Wow. That was almost...something,' she said.

'Yeah, well. Bit out of practice.'

'I guess your approach was, "If you can't beat 'em... put 'em out of action and prevent their chances of ever spawning".'

'I think we better get outta here.'

'If it makes you feel any better,' Summer said as she headed off at pace towards uptown, 'you have a much nicer bottom.'

'Thank you,' Jon replied as he started to follow.

'Especially when it's bare and running along the Thames.'

Jon caught up with her. 'Wait a minute. You can't have seen me running naked – I saw you head off with my clothes, which you took to Zu's before your "tattoo".' Jon said the last word whilst making inverted commas with his fingers.

'Ah, you have to thank Daisy for that. After she phoned you and heard that you were planning to run au naturel, she popped down from the bridge and hid with a camera. I think she's a closet voyeur, if you ask me. Anyway, she captured you in all your glory and happened to share it with me.'

Jon closed his eyes for a second. 'Surprised it's not on YouTube yet.'

'We wouldn't do that.'

'Really?'

'No. It would spoil the 3D version we're working on.'

They carried on in silence as Jon tried to work out whether he had any more dignity left to take. It was a humid September morning and his back felt like it was having a sweat shower. Perhaps he should just strip off now, he thought, and let the few remaining people in the Northern Hemisphere that hadn't seen him naked see what they'd missed out on. With Summer around, it was probably only a matter of time, anyway.

'It still counts, though, surely?' he said.

'The handstand?' Summer considered this for a while. 'Yeah, I guess. You tried it and were upright for a second or two. Wouldn't count as a Guinness World Record, but it'll do for me.'

'Great. Why are we headed uptown? Aren't we going up the Empire State Building?' Jon said.

'Empire, Schmempire,' Summer said, with an attempt at a Jewish New York accent. 'There are two main problems

171

with it. One, in summer it's busier than The Vatican when the Pope is in and giving out signed bibles. Two, you can't see one of the most iconic buildings in the world from the top of it – namely itself. Far better in my opinion is the next destination in Summer and Jon's Fun Day Out...the Rockefeller Centre.'

Having walked a few blocks later, Jon was chuckling to himself.

'What's so funny?' Summer asked.

'I've just worked out what your dare is going to be. I just hope it doesn't cause any suicides.'

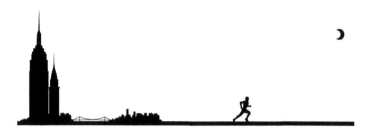

Chapter 20

JON didn't know which part of the view to take a photo of next. From the 'Top of the Rock', as Rockefeller Centre liked to market the rooftop view, the Empire State Building stood magnificently in the foreground, the king piece of the city. Jon was amazed how much it dominated the area. Its queen had to be the Chrysler Building, at this angle peeking out from behind the MetLife building, sunlight dazzling its silver needle against the pure blue sky. In the other direction, Jon had been stunned at the rectangle mass of Central Park. It was as if a designer had used a big sharp knife to cut out a section of the city and had replaced it with an English wood, adding a couple of lakes and a few baseball parks to give it an American flavour. Every hotel and office block around it seemed to lean into it, as if trying to suck the fresh air and peacefulness that was abundant down there. The breeze created a soft backing soundtrack to the voices of the surrounding tourists and the horizon was hazy as it blurred into upstate and beyond.

'Welcome to New York, Jon. Take a good look, as you'll be running through most of it,' Summer said, coming up next to him at the edge.

'It's huge. You can barely see cars down there, let alone people, and yet look at the scale.'

Summer pointed to the bottom left hand corner of the park. 'See there? That's where you'll finish the marathon and that'll be the scene of your greatest victory and your ticket to space.'

Jon tried to imagine himself crossing the line, people cheering from the rooftops that he looked down on now.

'And if I take you here,' Summer continued, taking Jon round to the opposite view, 'you can see the Verrazano-Narrows Bridge, where you'll start in Staten Island.'

Jon peered into the distance at the two towers with an enormous span in between. 'There? That's the bridge? Is that actually in New York still?'

'What did you expect? You must have seen a map of the marathon course. It's not just going round Central Park for 26.2 miles.'

'I know, but seeing a map and seeing it for real are two different things.' Jon felt his calves ache just considering the distance. 'Why did you bring me up here? To inspire me? Did you think up here it would look easier?'

Summer put a hand on his back as he looked out towards the bridge. 'I brought you up here to help prepare you. The whole day is for fun but also for preparation. You need to see what you're facing, to visualise it. You can use these images when you run, tick them off in your mind as you go past.'

'It just seems so...vast. The bridge looks huge in itself.'

'The bridge is awesome – just over one mile of music, views, cool breeze, camaraderie...and all when you're feeling fresh as a daisy. It's a great start, sweeping into Brooklyn, feeling the buzz, knowing you're part of something special.'

Jon jostled for position with a group of Eastern European students and took a photo of the bridge zoomed in and then another at the widest angle. Summer took off her baseball cap which was threatening to make a bid for freedom.

He watched Summer's bronze locks dance around in the light winds as she looked out over Manhattan. 'That sounded like you spoke from experience there.'

She didn't turn round. 'Me? No, I've just been there and watched. Looks amazing, and I've heard lots of accounts from others. Anyway, what about my dare?'

Jon had nearly forgotten about that. From up here, it seemed the whole marathon was just one unachievable dare. 'Will you do whatever I ask?'

'Within reason, yes. We had a deal.'

'Great. There's a risk involved, but fortunately for you, you'll be safe. As I intimated earlier, it might be a problem for others, though.'

'Go on...'

'It's quite simple, really...'

'Cut to the chase.'

'Only take a few minutes...

'Jon...'

'Okay – I dare you to sing *New York, New York* to the whole city from up here. The entire song. Loud.'

Summer pursed her lips. 'I don't do singing.'

'And I don't wear dresses, but hey, roll with the punches.'

'There are dozens of people up here.'

'For the moment, perhaps. The urge to jump may be high by the time you're in full swing.'

'Exactly. I'm sure security would have to stop me, on grounds of safety. I'm sorry Jon, you'll have to think of something else.'

'You're not getting away with it that easy.'

It was about time someone else was on the end of the embarrassment stick, Jon thought. He left Summer by a corner edge and walked off towards a cluster of people. Out of earshot from her, he talked to them, occasionally pointing back to Summer who was satisfyingly looking puzzled by his actions. He got nods from an elderly Japanese couple and three Americans barely out of their teens, two men and one woman. Jon led them all over to Summer who was battling with the wind to make her hair look presentable.

'Everyone, this is Summer,' Jon said. The five strangers said hello in a flurry of waves, slight nods and loud greetings. 'Summer, meet our new friends here. They have all agreed to join you in your sing-song. They know you're nervous but that it's your dream to be up here today and sing it.'

Summer shot Jon a look as if he'd just performed a checkmate, slam-dunk and drop-shot on her. 'Jon, I told you, I don't –'

'I've got the camera ready, so let's do it, baby. *New York, New York!*' Jon pointed the lens at her and switched to video as the others huddled, wrapping their arms round Summer and each other. Jon's smile was as wide as the park. 'Who's gonna start us off?'

One of the American men opened his mouth wide and begun with a much-elongated first word. The camera screen showed Summer looking as comfortable as a vicar in a strip club. Five voices joined in to boom out the second word. Summer just mouthed it while scowling at Jon.

'C'mon honey – I can't hear you!' Jon said, gesticulating at her to get involved.

For the next line, she sang quietly, drowned out by the loud Americans and a high-pitched, wobbly Japanese voice.

'Do the legs,' Jon said, kicking out his left leg to the right and back again, pointing the camera down at their bottom halves. They obliged with vigour, Summer forced to synchronise her slender legs with her new pals.

From the corner of his eye, he could see people starting to gather to see the impromptu show

The next verse had Summer showing a little spark in her eyes, although he still couldn't hear her above the rest.

By the third verse, she'd taken over. Jon could suddenly hear a wonderful voice, powerful and full of control.

She led the six of them – and several other new recruits who didn't want to miss out on the action – sweeping into the slower fourth verse before accelerating into an early finale. Head back, eyes closed, red lips surrounding beautiful top notes, she swung her legs as if she was making her Broadway debut. Her voice was the last to finish the end note, closing with a sharp bow of her head. They hopped around her, cheering and whooping as a round of applause from spectators rang out. Jon kept filming until the crowd broke and Summer looked up, her smile making the rest of the city look in need of a polish. She thanked her choir and then let Jon walk up to her. Her cheeks were crimson, clashing with her pink top.

'You were unbelievable,' Jon said. Summer stared at her feet and grinned. He continued, 'I think one person jumped off in expectation, but he was looking depressed before you started.'

Summer tapped him on the shin with her foot, but didn't reply.

'I thought you said that you didn't do singing?' Jon said.

'I don't. Well, I haven't in a while.'

'You should be on some star search show – "From PR to Popstar".'

Summer's grin faded to a smile. 'I could never be that good. C'mon, we should probably go now, before someone wants an encore.'

Back at street level, they made their way up Fifth Avenue. Summer had been quiet since her performance, but Jon was content at having a silent girl clinging to his arm while walking up the famous street. It reminded him of a room his nan used to have in which everything was always kept absolutely perfect – spotless, with clean lines and the best china on show for all to see. Just like that room, Jon felt he was not meant to be in it, as if someone would come and hustle him down a side street, telling him he should know better. Fashion shops gave him glimpses into the clothing of the rich. Jewellers displayed over-sized pictures of watches only James Bond could possibly wear. Across the street, loud music roared out of a shop with a bare-chested male model at its doors and a huge queue to get inside.

'I think I deserve a present after that performance. Now where can a girl go to get a nice present on Fifth?' Summer said, stopping and looking up.

Jon turned and saw the object of her attentions. Even Jon recognised the cyan of Tiffany's. 'Isn't there an H. Samuel round here instead?'

Summer groaned. 'You can take the guy out of Stevenage...'

Jon allowed Summer a few minutes to window shop before he dragged her away.

'Hey – no fair. A girl can dream, can't she? Maybe one day a handsome prince will buy me a stunning diamond-studded Tiffany's necklace.'

'That's not gonna be today, though. Firstly, I'm no prince, and secondly my credit cards are safely stored at home, due to someone arranging for me to be dragged out in only my underwear this morning.'

'Good point. Still could have offered, though.'

'Well what you gonna do?'

Summer did a little skip. 'How about we fulfil a fantasy of yours?'

'Here? Won't we get arrested?'

'Must you always be so crude? No, I'm talking about something I reckon you must want to do if you're approaching where we're heading.'

Jon looked up the road. He could only see the Apple Store, and didn't recall having any particular fantasy about that or their products.

'I'll give you a big clue.'

Jon waited but Summer said no more. 'Well, give me my clue then,' Jon said.

'I just did. I said I'll give you a "*Big*" clue.'

Jon still had a blank.

'Oh for goodness sake! If we're gonna do this, let's do it properly.' Summer grabbed his hand and led them running towards FAO Schwarz.

The queue for the larger-than-life piano on the upper floor of the toy store could not have been longer if Michael Jackson had phoned ahead to say that he'd really just been in hiding for a while and that his comeback performance would start with a moonwalk on this very keyboard. Jon folded his arms. 'It was a nice idea, but I'm not gonna be able to get on until October at this rate.' He watched as a couple of kids ran back and forth over the large keys on the floor while their parents recorded the action. 'How did you know anyway?'

'That you wanted to go on it? You said in your survey that one of your favourite films was *Big*, so tell me what person watched that film and didn't want to be Tom Hanks and play on this piano?'

'Weren't no queue in the film, though. Stupid kids. They weren't even born when it came out.'

Summer could see that the two young attendants were having difficulty getting the children off once they were on it. 'Why don't we push in?'

'We can't. We're English – we're programmed to obey a queuing system. It's in our genes. You can't fight nature.'

'Dare you.'

'Summer...'

'Bottom line: we haven't got time for this. I've got much more to show you in New York. We either leave now and you miss out on a secret ambition of yours, or you storm the piano in the honour of every kid who never asked to grow up.'

Jon heard the uncoordinated random notes of twins who looked barely over three years old. In terms of situations, being shouted at by a couple of adolescent shop workers and making an unwanted cameo in a family video was, appropriately enough to Jon, child's play. Before he knew it, he was taking off his shoes, handing them, his rucksack and his camera to Summer, and was running towards the exit side of the keyboard. 'Sorry folks, gotta be done!' No-one stopped him as he got past the barrier, skidding a little until he was lined up with the length of the keyboard. The twins and the whole of the queue could only watch in amazement as Jon propelled himself on the keys, plink-plonking to half way before skidding and sliding on his side to the other end, finishing up arms spread out shouting, 'Ta-da!' Amongst shocked faces, Jon caught a glimpse of a camera flash and Summer disappearing as he was hauled to his feet by a security guard.

'Nice stunt, you jerk. I think you'd better leave the store for the real kids.'

Jon had been waiting outside the toy store for about fifteen minutes, which wouldn't have been so bad had he not just been in his socks. Any thought of sneaking back in was stopped by a guard at the front of the store who, although dressed in a toy soldier costume, must have been approaching seven-feet tall even without the large hat. Jon faced outward and scanned the street before he felt a soft tap on his shoulder. Jon spun round to see an enormous teddy bear in front of him.

'Hello,' the bear appeared to say. 'I'm looking for my owner, about your height and no shoes.'

Summer peeked out from behind the bear. 'Sorry it took a while – long queue. Here, take him – he's been dying to meet you.'

Jon's face was engulfed in light brown fur as Summer shoved the bear at him. He grabbed it, only just managing to put both arms around it, and then sat it down on the pavement. 'Did this bear eat Goldilocks or something?'

'You have to carry him around for the rest of the day,' Summer said.

'Why me? You bought him. Thanks for waiting for me, by the way. In case you didn't know, I got thrown out for unwanted behaviour.'

'Oh, I saw them escort someone out when I'd just joined the queue to pay. Figured if it was you, you'd be okay.'

'Oh, cheers.'

'You're welcome. Can't say I blame them, though. You did kind of leg sweep one of the kids with your slide.'

'He'll survive. Might have a fear of playing the piano for the rest of his life, though.'

Summer started walking off. 'C'mon – put your shoes on and pick up your teddy. We've a tram to catch.'

'Tram? I thought we were in New York, not San Francisco.'

'You'll see. It's time to meet your nemesis.'

When they arrived at their next destination, Jon's eyes lit up as he saw their next mode of transport. 'Spider-Man!'

Summer frowned as she peered into the bright red metal aerial tram car as it glided into the station on its eternal loop to and from Roosevelt Island. 'Where?'

'I mean, this is the cable car from the first Spidey film. Cool.'

They got onto the tram, getting a seat right at the front so that he, Summer and Hanks – named by Jon on the way to the tram's entrance on 60th Street – were all getting a great view as they left Manhattan and swooped up towards the small island.

'I'm sorry – was I supposed to have packed your Spider-Man tights?' Summer said.

'Let me guess,' Jon said as he looked out the window. 'More footage from Daisy Films?'

'It was a bit blurry, you running so fast from that copper and all, but it certainly was a look.'

'I'm surprised they let a fugitive like me in the States.'

'I know, Jon Dunn: America's Most Wanted.'

The gentle, peaceful ride continued as the tram hauled itself to its peak over the East River.

'So where's this nemesis of mine? Is he going to attack the tram?' Jon said, pretending to look for villains who might be clinging on to the side of the car in waiting.

'There, to your right – that's your nemesis. The Queensboro Bridge.'

Jon took in the light-brown structure running parallel to the tram's cables, stretching out over and beyond Roosevelt Island and into Queens. Hundreds of girders criss-crossed above several lanes of cars like a cat's cradle canopy made of steel, sections of it arcing upwards towards one tower, before falling down the other side and on to the next. If the bridges of Manhattan were boxers, its bulk would definitely have it slugging it out in the heavyweight division. 'What's so special about this? It's big and ugly but I'm not exactly gonna paint a picture of it.'

'It's evil,' Summer said, deadpan.

'The Verrazano-Narrows looks evil, out there light years away from the finish. This one, we'll come out into

Manhattan after crossing it, won't we? Looks okay to me.'

'That's if you make it across. It's alive. It preys on the weak and saps their strength. No-one makes a sound when they cross it for fear of angering it. You reach it after fifteen long miles and it opens its throat and swallows you.' Summer watched as the tram descended, taking them lower than the bridge. 'Time passes more slowly in there. A second inside there is longer than outside, I swear. You pray for the exit but it is always round the bend beyond.'

Jon studied Summer's face as she stared out. 'Quit the melodrama,' Jon said. 'I get it – I'll take it a bit easy and dig deep with my legs.'

Summer hugged Hanks. 'It's not physical, Jon. You don't beat the marathon here with your legs – you beat it with your mind. I'm showing you this as you need to be ready when you reach it. If you're not prepared mentally for Queensboro Bridge then you will crawl into Manhattan with your mind in pieces.'

They didn't say anything else to each other as they got off the tram and onto the island. Summer took the bear and walked off fast to a path alongside the river, Jon trying to keep up. The sound of a ringing phone made her come to a halt and she took her mobile out of her pocket. It continued to ring as she glanced at the number and moaned. 'My boss, Charles. Give me a couple of minutes, will you?'

Jon put his rucksack down next to the bear as Summer walked off. He gazed across to the skyscrapers they'd left behind, and took a picture of the twin points of the Empire State and Chrysler Buildings that could be seen close together at this angle, like weapons guarding the city from invaders. Five minutes later, she returned. 'Everything good?' Jon said.

'Nothing for you to worry about, just wanted to know how Operation BJ was going.'

Jon let his eyebrows do the asking.

'It's my perv boss's idea of a joke. BJ in this case actually stands for Ben Johnson, as in the sprinter who got banned for taking drugs at the 1988 Olympics. That's the code we have to use. He just wanted to know how I was handling the whole drugs test issue with you.'

'He knows about it?'

'Of course he knows about it. It was kinda his idea.'

'What you mean *his* idea? I thought you planned all this?'

Summer perched herself on the concrete edge of the path. 'I did plan this, to a degree. Look, I wanted to find a way to take you out and have a full day together, but I couldn't come up with anything. Then I thought about the drugs tests you lot do and...well, I also saw an opportunity.'

'For what?'

She sighed. 'I've said to you before that we're under pressure to make this whole thing work, attract interest, raise the profile of DPI through the roof. Everyone loved the start and will be excited for the actual race, but right now it's a little flat. Sponsorship has been down and there's been a bit of force to create a bit more interest. I put the idea into his head and he came up with the plan.'

'So you created a scandal, involving me, just to help push up the share price?'

'A scandal that will be proved to be nothing, a mistake. It'll create a bit of gossip, a touch of excitement and then will all be forgotten. In the meantime, DPI are happy as it gets us in the news and people talking about the marathon again.'

'And the whole world thinks I'm a drug cheat right now? Great.'

'No – we won't release it until tomorrow. By that time, we'll have it sorted here anyway.'

'You better. I have a reputation you know.' Jon looked at Hanks. At least the bear knew he was being bought to be played with.

Summer's phone rang again. She looked at the number and then at Jon. 'Just go with it, please.' She pressed a button and put the phone to her ear, 'Hi Ceris…yeah, Jon's fine. We're pretty sure it's all a mistake…no…he's not the type…yes, he's around here somewhere, hang on a min…' She put her hand over the mouthpiece and thrust the phone at Jon. 'Just be vague, reassure her, tell her you're just waiting.'

Jon kept the conversation with Ceris short, doing as he was told, calming her and trying to make her feel that everything was fine, that it was all a misunderstanding, proved by the simple fact that his last race showed that he was about as much performance-enhanced as a twenty-year-old whippet with three legs and arthritis.

'Do you think she bought it?' Summer said after Jon had handed back the phone.

'I hope so. Don't want the whole house thinking I'm pulling a Lance Armstrong.'

'I'm sure Ceris will champion your innocence to everyone.'

Jon sighed. 'Another nice mess you've gotten me into,' he said before heading off to walk along the river, leaving Summer trailing behind with Hanks. He watched a couple of pleasure boats go past before creeping up on a seagull for a close-up with its city background. Jon nodded respectfully at an elderly Asian man who was performing graceful T'ai Chi moves under a tree.

'It's a bit different over here,' Jon said, gesturing towards the main island as Summer appeared at his shoulder. 'Another world from over there.'

'True, but not a great choice of food here, though. You hungry yet?'

It was just gone one o'clock. 'I could eat soon, yeah. Hanks says he needs to stock up before hibernation, too.' He picked up a paw and the pair carried Hanks between them, swinging him like a fat, hairy child.

'Well I hope you both like burgers, because I've got a great place lined up for lunch.'

'Cool. Where are we going?'

'Over on 56th Street. We'll catch the train back, now that you've scoped out the enemy.'

From down here, Jon thought the bridge looked like a part of an ancient roller coaster. He could scarcely imagine that in just over a month he would be running over it in one of the biggest races in the world.

After struggling with Hanks through the exit turnstiles and appearing back in Manhattan out of the depths of the subway system, they took a walk one block down and stopped part way down the street.

'This is the place. Best burgers in town,' Summer said, facing a set of revolving doors.

'Here? But it looks like a hotel.'

'That's because it *is* a hotel. An extremely nice French one.'

'I'm not exactly dressed for some posh a la carte

restaurant. Shorts, t-shirt and a big mammal under my arm.'

'Hanks has a bowtie on – he'll be fine for the three of us. Trust me.'

'Oh in that case, I'll go find the nearest Mac D's.'

Summer rolled her eyes and grabbed his hand.

'You'll see. I might not look like it, but I love a good burger.'

They went through the doors and walked onto a black and white patterned marble floor. Tall mirrors flanked them as they stepped into an open lobby which seemed more like part of a cathedral than a focal point for a hotel, let alone a fast food joint. The clientele drifted past ignoring them, as a couple checked in at reception with suitcases seemingly more expensive than the sum total of everything Jon owned. Summer headed towards a wall of red curtains hanging from the high ceiling, and they disappeared into a small corridor that ran alongside it. On the wall at the end stood a small, yellow and orange neon sign depicting a steaming burger with an arrow pointing to the right. When they reached it, it wasn't exactly what Jon expected. Just yards away from the grandeur of a reception chiselled in France, was a small slice of American dining done how they do it best – fast and loud. From the back of a long queue towards a small counter, he could see wood-panelled walls covered in posters and graffiti. The dim lights and packed tables contrasted with the brightness and space of the lobby outside. An old blues track rang out and he could hear the names of customers being barked out to collect their orders.

'Let me get this straight – we were in New York, then somehow got transported to France, and now we're back in New York again?' Jon said.

'Yep. It's like a bubble in the space-time continuum. But forget that, because you need to sort out your order. It's pretty simple – up there's your choices.'

Jon asked her what she was having as he studied the hand-written menu pinned up high. 'And where are we going to sit? It's packed.' He couldn't see any room between the tables, on the tables or even under them.

'We'll find somewhere. People have to go sometime,' Summer said.

As they approached the counter together, Summer opened her mouth to give her order but Jon got in first.

'I'll have a cheeseburger, well-done with the works, and my lady friend here will have a cheeseburger, medium-well, lettuce, "tom-may-toe", onion and mustard. We'll have two lots of fries, two beers and the name's Jon.'

Summer smiled at her star pupil.

Jon kept a straight face as he added, 'Do you give discounts to women who can't go anywhere without their bears?'

They ended up squeezing onto a table with four Swedish girls, who giggled at the bear sitting on Jon's shoulders.

'I don't think Hanks is very impressed at not getting his own seat,' Jon said to Summer.

'Ah, you two look very cute together,' she said.

Jon picked up a couple of fries. 'Thanks for lunch,' he said.

'You're welcome. Nice bit of assertive ordering back there. You might just survive here after all.'

'I had a good teacher.'

'Of course it might have helped had you had any money to pay with.'

Jon squeezed tomato sauce in between his burger and bun. 'You love all this.'

'All what?'

'All this control. Having to pay for me everywhere, buying the clothes I'm wearing, leading me to unknown places.'

'Yeah – you ma bitch.'

He took a bite of his burger and gave her his best evil stare. 'Kudos on the food, though.'

Jon noticed that all the girls he'd ever had a meal with seemed to eat daintily, no matter what the food type. Whilst spaghetti would be painted all over Jon's chin and turn his shirt into a Jackson Pollock, the girl would always end up exactly as she'd come in. Summer was no different, making light work of her meal without either the roll disintegrating or sauce going anywhere except its intended destination. Jon, on the other hand, looked like he'd just sat down in a two-year-old's highchair, minus the bib. He ate all the individual pieces of bun and meat left over and attempted to take care of the aftermath with three napkins. An involuntary burp was quickly followed by an apology.

'And you haven't got a girlfriend...why?' she said.

'What you see is what you get, baby. If you don't like it, you know where the door is.' Jon rested his head back on Hanks.

'Maybe I will. Not sure if I can be seen in public with two animals at once.'

'And you're so perfect?'

'Of course. But then I haven't got a beard to collect crumbs in.'

Jon ruffled his chin with his hand, dislodging a few flakes of bread. He grabbed the squeezy tomato sauce bottle. 'You wouldn't look so perfect with the latest craze in makeup.'

'You wouldn't dare.'

He held the bottle out and aimed the nozzle at her. 'Wouldn't I?'

'No.'

He went to fake a squeeze but pushed too hard, shooting out a stream of red sauce right into Summer's face. She just sat there, eyes shut as red streaks made their way down her cheeks, like a bad zombie make-up job. The Swedish girls gasped. Jon put down the bottle, grabbed some tissues and offered them to her. 'I'm sorry, I didn't mean to –' He was interrupted by a blast of mustard to the face. Sliding the yellow gunge off onto a napkin he said, 'Okay, we're even now, I'm sor –' Another attack from Summer, this time from the red bottle and to his t-shirt. Jon took the top of the salt shaker and threw a handful of salt over her t-shirt, but at the same time she made a line of mustard on his arm, turning it into jumbo-sized hotdog. He retaliated by taking off her baseball cap, emptying the remainder of the tomato sauce into it and handing it back to her. Their exchange had now attracted attention from all the surrounding tables, some people laughing, some looking disdainfully at two grown adults acting worse than a couple of monkeys. A nearby customer had taken a bit of damage from a ricochet and was starting to complain.

The cashier looked over. 'Hey! Kate and Wills over there – move your asses and let house-trained people sit down.'

Summer looked guiltily at Jon. 'The natives are getting restless. Time to go, methinks.'

The Swedes were quick to move out of the way of a gooey Jon, who had to resort to lifting Hanks above his head to get out of the tight space. Summer had apologised and was making her way to the exit. When they met again, the sight of Jon appearing to have been shot and dragging along the giant bear by one paw with his hotdog arm in the middle of the posh lobby made Summer bend forwards in laughter.

'Y–you know…what…' Summer was laughing so hard she could barely get any words out. 'You know what you… look like?'

Jon just stood there and waited for the obviously hilarious comment to come.

'You…you look like Christopher Robin…with a bit of *Platoon* and *Castaway* thrown in!' She had to crouch down as big guffaws came thundering out, echoing up and around the large hall. Jon let go of Hanks and walked off nonchalantly to the reception desk. 'Excuse me – could you tell me where the bathroom is? I need to freshen up a little.' The startled receptionist pointed down towards the exit.

'Merci,' Jon said.

They came back five minutes later with clean faces and Jon with the same large red stain on his t-shirt, except it had been completely wet through in the failed attempt at cleaning it. 'You're gonna get me barred from every place in this city,' Jon said to a now composed Summer.

'Me? You started it. Well at least you had the sense to not change into your DPI running top.'

'Suppose I have to stay undercover.'

'Definitely. We'll have to buy you something else, though. You still look a mess.'

'Hanks somehow managed to avoid everything. Could be a lucky bear.'

'With you as his owner? I'm not so sure,' Summer said as they went out of the building.

They chose a tacky souvenir shop to buy a traditional 'I heart NY' white t-shirt for Jon. He asked the old woman behind the register if she minded him putting it on right there, and she agreed, perhaps a bit too vigorously for his liking. He took off his soiled top, put it in a plastic bag and quickly into his rucksack. As he was slipping the t-shirt over his head, he heard the camera shutter go.

'Hey!' he said, now fully clothed. 'So what do you think?'

'Super cool. Take a look in the mirror.'

He walked over to a mirror that had above it a TV which he vaguely noticed was showing a news channel. After studying his reflection and being satisfied with the outcome, he happened to look up. He stood there rigid at the woman who was being interviewed. 'Mum?'

Chapter 21

DOUG slammed his glove hard into the punch bag. 'It's days like this when you wonder if the rest of the planet are complete morons.'

Kyle, his personal trainer, steadied the bag in readiness for another volley, hoping that he was an exception to Doug's statement.

'Here's me, and what do I bring to the world? I'll tell you what – passion.' Doug drew back his arm and struck again. 'Vision.' He continued to punctuate each word with a blow to the long, red bag hanging from the gym's ceiling. 'Ideas...plans.' He jogged on the spot, sweating hard. 'And above all else – the guts to make it happen.' Behind the bag, Kyle was knocked back by a rapid series of thumping blows into its centre. He'd been hoping for an early night catching up with the evening's football until Doug demanded they had a late session at his house. When Kyle arrived, Doug looked like he was ready to go ten rounds with a tiger who hadn't eaten all week.

'I should be revered, hailed as a pioneer, shouldn't I?' Doug shot out a few light jabs. 'And with my money, I should be able to get what I want, don't you think?' The jabs got harder. 'Pads please, Kyle.'

Kyle held up his padded hands for Doug to aim at.

'But no, there are always people who want you to fail. Bored in their own pitiful, tiny existences, their only crumb of comfort is to try to stop others from succeeding.' Uppercuts slammed into the pads, jerking his trainer's hands backwards with each connection as globules of sweat shot out from his brow. He continued with the punches for a further five minutes before removing his gloves and grabbing the skipping rope.

The day had started brightly with a message from Dmitri telling Doug that he would not be suing DPI for breach of an agreement to send him to the Moon, not that he was worried his Russian ex-friend had any case whatsoever. What was much more grating, however, was the news that Dmitri was investing his money in another rival project, one that he was promoting to all and sundry as making Doug's plans look as sophisticated as a *Blue Peter* demonstration. Worse was to follow – Dmitri's connections, which Doug had initially utilised to help the company that was constructing his rocket, were now appearing to be less than cooperative in supplying the Russian spacecraft parts that were to be used. DPI had foregone cutting-edge technology that was still in development, instead using tried-and-trusted equipment to ensure a quick turn-around. The time for new tech would come for sure, and was included in his future plans, but for now the existence of the Moon mission relied on a mishmash of current and old modules to come together. Without these, there was nothing more than a half-baked future museum piece.

Doug took a breather from the skipping. Kyle was preparing the weights which were next in his boss's routine.

'What do you think of the whole competition, the marathon idea?' Doug said.

Kyle adjusted a bench while he thought. 'Think it's a great idea, boss. Can't wait to see who wins.'

'Exactly. Capturing the imagination of the nation. Dmitri's going around saying it's a childish venture dreamt up by me just to spite him. He's even had the audacity to suggest to the papers that I may renege on the deal with the winner and go myself.'

'Sounds like slander to me, boss.'

'Our lawyers are looking into it. Spent all day trying to undo all the damage that damn ruski is doing.'

'So you don't fancy the trip yourself?' Kyle said.

'Don't you start. I'd love to go up there but it's not about me.' He went over and lay on the press bench. 'Besides, at the rate it's going, I'm not sure I'd trust the contraption they're building.'

After several repetitions with the weights, Doug realised just how bad his last statement might have sounded. Kyle had been with him for fifteen years and was paid handsomely, but right now Doug wasn't confident of completely trusting anyone.

'I only joke about the rocket, Kyle. You can't go into space with an oversized washing up bottle and some double-sided sticky tape and hope for the best. We'll get the parts and build a rocket safe enough to fly the Queen round the Moon and back.'

Doug knew that the rocket had to be his priority right now, ensuring that it could still be built and to schedule. He'd have little time for anything else over the coming weeks, so he had to be certain that everything else was running smoothly. To cap a fine day, he'd been caught by journalists halfway round his afternoon jog, demanding to know how the drug cheating scandal would affect the competition going forward. He would have had a perfectly-tailored answer prepared, if only he'd had the slightest idea of what they were referring to. After eventually getting all the details, it left him more than a little uneasy about it all. He was deciding the course of action he was going to take as he stepped on the treadmill.

'These are my plans, Kyle, this is my vision.' He held down a button as the running belt whirred into life. 'Nothing and nobody is going to get in my way.'

Chapter 22

BY the time the woman in the souvenir shop had found the remote control for the TV and had turned it up, Jon's mum had vanished from the screens and baseball was being shown. Jon's pleas for the live feed to be rewound were rejected on the grounds that, in her opinion, it was impossible to rewind TV and that he was stupid to even ask for such witchcraft.

Jon turned to Summer, who had tried to put a comforting hand on his arm. 'Do you have even the slightest idea why my mum – in England – would be appearing on American TV?'

'I can guess, but let me find out for sure first,' Summer said.

She slapped down a ten-dollar bill on the counter for Jon's t-shirt and went outside to make a phone call. Jon was right behind her and watched intently as she waited to be connected. He'd only seen about twenty seconds of silent TV footage of what looked like an interview, but it didn't exactly appear as if she was being enthusiastically positive about her son. Jon suddenly felt naked away from his phone.

'Charles is not answering, which is strange. More than strange, seeing as he is always contactable on at least one of his three numbers.' Summer spun her phone around in her hand a few times. 'I'll try Leona.'

Leona's phone turned out to be repeatedly engaged, so Summer tried another contact in the London office. She got through, and after a few minutes asking short questions and doing a lot of listening, she ended the call and handed the phone to Jon. 'I think you'll need to speak to your parents once I've filled you in.'

'What's happened? Are they okay? What is it?'

'Yes, they're fine. At least I think so. Maybe just a little concerned and upset.'

'I get the feeling it's not about the sauce fight we've just had.'

'No. It's what I feared – they know you failed the drugs test.'

'What? You told me – barely two hours ago – that you wouldn't release it until tomorrow.' He stared at Summer. 'How the heck can anyone know?'

'It got out.'

'No shit. How?'

'The media picked up on something. We should have monitored it and caught it before it got noticed, but it looks like my team were slacking.'

'What was the "something"?'

'A blog entry. Someone from the house blogged about your grand exit this morning. Jackson was controlled and didn't say anything to anyone, but it didn't stop the blogger quoting some of his rage when he was with you. The BBC read it, did some investigation and created a story. Must've been picked up over here, too, due to our links.'

'And part of the investigation was to speak to my mum on what she thought of her youngest son trying to cheat his way round New York?'

'Yeah. I'm sorry, Jon.'

'"Trust me" you said. Once again that's worked out stunningly well for me.'

He'd got used to the fact that he was in the public eye, but it still didn't feel real, so far away from home. Seeing his mum being grilled by a journalist out for blood brought the whole situation right on his doorstep again. 'Why are you sorry? You and your boss have got your little PR stunt, created a little stir and no-one's been hurt except insignificant me and my family. Perfect day for DPI, really.'

'Jon, I never intended –'

'Save it – I'm phoning Mum.' He dropped his rucksack and walked off while dialling his parents' number.

'Mum? It's Jon. I need to explain everything.'

'What's going on there?' his mum said. 'Everyone's accusing you of being a cheat. Tell me that isn't so.'

'It's not, it's all a mistake. I haven't taken anything, I promise, Mum. It was a bad plan that went wrong.'

After telling his mum all about Summer's plan and that he had been a good boy after all, she seemed a lot happier.

'That's what I told them,' his mum said, 'that you didn't need to take performance drugs, that you were perfectly capable of winning on your own.'

'I'm not so sure about that, but thanks for believing in me.'

'This Summer woman…is she the same one who got you into difficulty with the police?'

'That was all sorted out as I said before, but yes, it's the same girl.'

'She sounds like trouble.'

'She is a bit. Means well, though. I guess.'

'Still, she must like you if she went to all this effort just to spend a day out with you.'

He glanced back to see her still waiting half a block away, looking towards Jon. When she realised he was looking her way, she held up Hanks and waved his paw. 'Maybe. I never know with women, though.'

'Is she pretty?'

'Yeah, very.'

'Does she like your beard?'

'Says she does.'

'Well then, you never know. Just be careful, if she's one of those "wild childs".'

'Okay, Mum.'

'And steer clear of that Nicki. She definitely is trouble, judging from what she wrote about you.'

It didn't take a genius to work out who the blogger was, thought Jon. He was sure she took great delight in seeing a competitor potentially being kicked out, even one as unthreatening as Jon. He looked forward to reading her literary delights later. 'I'll keep my distance, don't worry. Anyway, how's Dad? And is Conan still coping without me?'

'Your father is currently out on a run, and Conan is

loving the extra chicken I bring round on Monday mornings after the roast.'

Jon paused to try to process the information. 'Dad's out on a *what?*'

'A run. He's taken up jogging. Nothing too strenuous, not like you, but just a little run along the cycle tracks round here. Said you'd inspired him.'

Jon finished his call and strolled back to Summer. Of all the surprises today, perhaps the thought of his dad frightening little old ladies walking their dogs as he puffed past them in his shorts was probably the biggest one of all. Summer took the phone back and read a text that had come in.

'They're releasing the results to clear your name in a couple of hours,' she said.

'Really? Oh that's so very nice of them.' He picked up his rucksack. 'This was a stupid plan, Summer. I'm sure you loved all the drama and risk of it, but it hasn't exactly worked out well for me, has it? Cheers for using me in your little game.'

For the first time, Summer didn't have a response. He expected a dose of humour or an outburst of how she thought that it was all trivial in the grand scheme of things, but she just looked away silently.

'I guess I'm not always in complete control of matters,' she finally said after a minute of standing around. 'The last thing I ever wanted to do was mess up your life. I just wanted to help you with your running in a way that Jackson or nutrition guides couldn't. We've been throwing together this plan at light speed ever since Peabody had his great idea, and everything had worked out until today.

I just got caught out, swept away in the momentum.' She rubbed his arm. 'I am sorry.'

Jon knew the universal truth that a man could not stay mad with an attractive woman that he hadn't slept with while she was stroking his arm. 'Yeah, well. Let's just go home.'

'It's only the middle of the afternoon. Technically you should still be at the lab for a while yet. If you can put up with me for a bit longer, we could go to Brooklyn and then head off later from there.'

Jon took a deep breath through his nose and exhaled. 'I suppose. One condition, though – no dares, games, tricks or surprises. Just a normal trip, doing normal things.'

'Deal. Just you, me and the bear behaving ourselves.'

They found the subway again and headed off to the Manhattan entrance of the Brooklyn Bridge. They arrived at the start of the footpath across it and Jon started taking photos almost immediately.

'Just like in the movies, eh?' Summer said.

'I didn't realise it was so big, so elegant,' Jon replied. 'Not like that Queensboro bridge. This one has class.'

'Definitely. Shame you don't get to run over it in the marathon, but at least we can walk across it. More good exercise for you.'

Jon admired the symmetry of the steel support cables and the arched supports of New York's finest bridge, stopping every few metres to photograph it from different angles. 'One of us together?' Jon said, leaning into Summer and getting a selfie.

'Save some shots for the other side. Wait till you get a load of the view from over there,' Summer said.

As they followed the bridge's arc over the East River, the southern tip of Manhattan came into full view, ending in a stretch of water that eventually surrounded Liberty Island, where Jon could see the lady herself holding the torch to the heavens. Standing on the old bridge, looking across to the most famous welcome to a port in the world, Jon was reminded of just how much history there was in this place.

'I hear they list your name in *The New York Times* if you finish the marathon,' Jon said.

'Yeah, provided you're not in the last lot of stragglers that they run out of room to print. But you'll get plenty of coverage regardless of position, if I have anything to do with it,' Summer said, standing next to Jon, looking out.

'So, did you make it?'

'Make what?' Summer turned to Jon.

'The paper, when you ran New York. And don't say you haven't, because I can tell.'

The sound of the traffic below filled the silence before Summer spoke. 'Perhaps it's a girl's prerogative to keep that to herself.'

'Sorry, my mistake. You have a file on me that would make MI5 look ignorant but I'm not allowed to pry into the life of a precious DPI employee.'

'It's got nothing to do with DPI.'

'Then tell me, let me in.'

'It's just...bad experiences, that's all.'

The sensible part of Jon was telling him to drop it, but he wasn't listening. 'So you're gonna hide it all from me? I'll just add it to the list of things I haven't a clue about you. Heaven forbid I might actually know the real Summer.'

'Jon, don't push it.'

'Why? We're meant to be friends aren't we? You know what? I don't even know your last name.' Jon let out an exasperated laugh. 'Over a month since I met you and I haven't even been privileged to be told that simple fact. And now you want to hold back telling me about something I might have an interest in – that might actually help me – just because you struggled in one race?'

'It's complicated. I –'

'Complicated?' Jon was too far down the tracks now to pull back. 'Am I too stupid to understand? Or don't you trust me enough?'

'I do but –'

'Or is it another one of those games we said we weren't going to play? Guess the Summer Secret of the New York Marathon.' He made a deep sound of a buzzer with his throat. 'I know – she wasn't as good as she thought she was and trailed in 40,000th.'

'It wasn't just one race, you arsehole!' Summer shoved the bear at Jon and started to walk off before spinning round. 'It was three, okay? Three. Three times I tried to tackle this course and three times I failed. Every bloody time I ended up a mess on the roadside. So yes, Jon, you could say I have run it. Happy now? Glad you are in on my little, so-called secret?'

Jon watched the tears streak down her face and then stood rooted as she marched off.

He kept his distance throughout the rest of the bridge crossing. Summer hadn't looked back once, and yet Jon's eyes never left her lonely figure weaving through slow-moving sightseers and dawdling commuters. As he approached the end of the bridge, he felt like a wad of gum on its boards, grey and trodden on in disgust. She went out of sight after she left the bridge exit, causing Jon a slight panic. He'd assumed that the protocol would be to give her space, let her wait for him and then they would talk. She'd hared off, which now left him wondering whether the rules stated that he should have run up and thrown himself at her feet for forgiveness, preferably acquiring flowers on the way. This last thought led to further alarm in the fact that he was still penniless and didn't quite know how he was meant to go back to Long Beach. He started to break into a light jog until he got to the end of the bridge, where he spotted her again, heading right. Transferring to a fast walk, he caught up with her on Brooklyn Promenade, leaning on the railings staring across towards Manhattan.

'Excuse me,' Jon said, 'have you seen an arsehole round here? Carrying a big bear, looking very sorry for himself. He might have jumped into the Hudson.'

Summer stayed still. 'If the arsehole had jumped off the bridge, it would be into the East River. Unfortunately there haven't been any sightings of alligators there for a while.'

'I guess divers recovering his body would find he entered the water with both feet having been placed firmly in his mouth just moments before.'

She turned to see his pale, worried face. 'I guess he wasn't to know.'

'I'm sorry, Summer.'

'Breeze,' she said.

Jon switched to a confused expression. 'Huh?'

'That's my last name.'

'Breeze? As in...'

'The wind.'

'I see. So you're…'

'Summer Breeze, yep. You have a problem with that?'

Actually no, thought Jon. It was probably the most wonderful name he'd ever heard. 'It suits you.'

'Thanks. I changed it via Deed Poll a while ago. Summer's original, though.'

'Well, Miss Breeze, I'm sorry if I made you feel bad.'

'Who says I'm a Miss?'

Jon stared at her, saying nothing.

'It's okay, I'm joking. I'm not married. Tell you what – if you let me buy you a drink, I'll tell you all about the marathons.'

Jon agreed, relieved to be able to spend more time with her, and after the long walk, time off his feet. They found an outside table in a café on Montague Street, running perpendicular to the promenade. Summer ordered two virgin cocktails and proceeded to tell Jon her marathon stories.

'It isn't pretty,' she started. 'I'd already done a couple of London ones by the time I was twenty-one, my second one finishing in just over four and a quarter hours. I was confident of going quicker, and didn't want a year to try again, so I managed to get a charity place and applied for New York later that same year.'

For this conversation, Jon had decided to give his vocal chords some much-needed timeout.

'I kept pushing myself harder and harder in training without really strengthening my muscles, just running day after day. When I came to New York in November I was convinced I was ready, but my body was knackered and just couldn't take the punishment. My left knee gave out around twenty miles and I limped on until almost fainting with the pain. I struggled on for another mile before getting medical help who advised me to quit. I ignored them, and collapsed fifty metres later.'

This time it was Jon who offered a consoling hand, and was warmly surprised when she gripped it tightly. She continued. 'Next year, I entered again and I was a lot more cautious in the build-up and my training was going to plan. My dad and best friend came over to support me, and everything was set. That was until race day, when I woke up at 3am to hear moaning coming from my dad's hotel room next door. With my best friend's bed also empty next to me, I put two and two together and got four, which given the nature of their six month affair I soon discovered, was entirely correct.'

As the waiter bought the drinks to the table, her last sentence lingered in the air like the smell from a rancid fish. Jon squeezed her hand, hoping that it wasn't going to get worse.

'So you can imagine I was a little upset when I crossed the start line. I absolutely hammered the first half – did a 1:30. And then came Queensboro.' She sipped the yellow drink through her straw as her brown eyes became shiny. 'I'd used up nearly all my energy by the time I got to the bridge and it just killed me. I came out of it to the cheering crowds and all I could think of by then was how I'd been let down by the two fans who were supposed to have come to watch me. At that moment, I felt so utterly alone that I just gave up, my legs buckled and I woke up in hospital.'

'You don't have to go on if you don't want to,' Jon said, taking a big gulp out of his own drink.

'That's okay. The third one happened three years ago. Took me a while to get the courage again but I didn't let it put me off. Came over here alone and was having a brilliant run until Queensboro.'

'The monster got you again?' Jon's heart was quickening at the prospect of another horror story of the bridge he was already dreading going over.

'Kind of. Took on too much fluid in the miles before it, got through it okay but had to pee just afterwards. Was so excited at getting past that damned bridge that upon entering a Portaloo, I tripped over the step of it, smashed my knee up on the ground and ended up head first in the toilet hole.'

Jon let out a burst of laughter, immediately regretted it and was about to apologise profusely when Summer started to laugh hard. The café's outside tables were nearly full, despite the humidity creeping up as the day entered evening. Summer's long laugh attracted attention from a few customers, perhaps eager to be in on the joke.

'It was so pathetic,' she said when she'd calmed down a little. 'I was in so much pain due to my knee that I couldn't lift myself up to get my head out. The screams must have freaked out the people in the adjoining loos.'

Jon grinned. 'That might explain your hair colour. They put a lot of chemicals down those toilets.'

Summer swatted him with the back of her hand. 'It wasn't *that* far down the hole, thank you. They managed to get me out but my knee had swollen up like it was growing its own head, so that was the end of my race.'

'Wow. So do you think you'll ever run it again?' Jon said.

'And tempt fate again? I dunno. There's a part of me that wants to – unfinished business and all that – but my knee's pretty messed up though, hence why I just do yoga these days. But you should never quit just because of a few setbacks. That's what I preach and that's what I do. Well, nowadays anyway.'

Jon looked at her. 'The singing? You were very good back there. Did you quit a singing career?'

'What is this – Confession Time?'

'Am I right, though?'

'Did I give it away?' Summer swung her legs back and forth. 'I always thought I had a good voice but was dissuaded from pursuing it further by a jealous boyfriend. Even after I saw the light and dumped him I never went back to it. Today was my first public appearance since.'

'Not bad for a comeback.'

'Thanks. I had potential. Think that's why I like this assignment, helping people achieve their own potential.'

She finished her drink. 'So, have my sorry tales of marathon woe totally put you off?'

'Well, let me see…I learned not to train too hard, never to underestimate the libido of one's parents and that it's probably safer to hold it in for twenty-six miles than to tackle the deadly Portaloos.'

'Sir, if I may say so, I've taught you well.'

'And I shall conquer New York for you, my lady.'

They ordered more drinks and traded other embarrassing stories while watching the Brooklyn street get busier.

Summer had promised Jon one final treat before they headed back, a cheesy New York must-do while they were here. Jon had correctly guessed that she had meant a walk along the Brooklyn Heights promenade, facing arguably the most famous skyline in the world. They settled the drinks bill and set off, holding hands indirectly via the paws of Hanks slung in between them.

The scene reminded Jon of a play with no actors – the stage was Manhattan with its expensive ensemble of skyscrapers, framed with Brooklyn Bridge to the right and the Statue of Liberty far away to the left. White boats trailed past to create a realistic, alive harbour, and the orange Staten Island Ferry chugged slowly out of shot. The audience sat in two rows of benches along the promenade, the front row offering ring-side seats by the railings, with a second row further back to relax under the shade of the leafy trees. In between, was a wide walkway which people flowed down. Those that were seated talked, ate and stared across, waiting for the show to begin.

'This is my favourite time of day here,' Summer said. 'When the sun goes down it takes all the colour of Manhattan with it, turning the city into a brown, grey blandness. Then the magic starts.'

Jon wished that the magic might extend the day, that perhaps the night would not quite arrive, just hint at it and remain in a blue-black freeze-frame that kept them in this moment. As they walked along, they spotted lovers young and old holding hands, leaning on each other or simply just being comfortable in silence as they watched the sun go down together. He'd put his sunglasses on to protect from the glare of the low sun, but also secretly to admire Summer as they strolled together. There was a serenity about her, Jon noticed, as if happy with this moment, this spot and her place in the world. Despite all the bad times the big city had given her, she hadn't lost her love for it.

'So what do you think of this place?' Summer said, stopping to lean over the railings.

'Fantastic views.' He stopped to take a photo, filling the frame almost entirely with her face.

At first, Jon found himself a little disappointed with her choice of location, hoping for something more secluded to end the day. He'd realised that this was likely to be the best it would get in terms of time he would be able to spend with her alone, so when they got to the water's front and saw the whole city and its dog out to join them, he saw his hopes of privacy dashed. However, Summer had a knack of creating a bubble around them, and before long he became oblivious to the waves of joggers, kids pulling stunts on bikes and love-struck couples surrounding them.

She turned round and spotted an opening in one of the rear benches. She jogged up to claim it, beckoning Jon behind her. They sat next to each other, legs touching, Summer wrapping her arms round the bear on her lap. The warmth of her leg seemed to raise his entire body temperature by a couple of degrees. She smiled but said nothing, watching as the sun gradually sunk, bleeding all the colour from the stage.

Jon always thought life was about these moments, the ones that come along so rarely you daren't blink in case you miss something. He wanted to write down every detail, every feeling, every thought in his head. Here he was, a thousand miles from home with a woman he hardly knew and yet Jon felt as comfortable as he would in his own bed at home. Just as the buildings were seemingly about to be faded out into the background, the first specks of light in the windows started appearing. People had begun pointing at the first signs of night. An artist had arrived and started sketching out the bold lines of the skyline. Summer rested her head on Jon's shoulder.

'Am I okay here?' she said.

Funny, thought Jon. They'd seen each other naked and yet this was by far their most intimate moment. 'You're fine. Hanks might get a bit jealous, though.'

'I'm just tired. It's been a long day,' she said.

'Do we have to go back?'

'Do you really want me to think of another plan to stay out?'

Half of him was willing to swim across to Manhattan if it involved extending their time together. 'No, I know what your plans are like.'

They sat there watching the city gradually come to life again, as if the night shift had turned up and begun turning on the lights one by one. The last of the orange sky was being pushed over the horizon as the march of dark blue continued, contrasting the skyscrapers as they started to light up. Jon heard a muffled ringing from nearby. Summer ignored her mobile when it rang in her purse, but when another call followed almost immediately, it alarmed her enough to see who was ringing. As she picked it up and read the display, the caller hung up.

'Something up?' Jon said, on seeing a frown appear on her normally smooth forehead.

'I'm not sure. I don't usually get a call from the big boss, especially when it's this late in England.' Summer jerked in reflex as the phone rang again in her hands. She took a deep breath and answered. 'Hello, Mr Peabody...'

Summer sat firm on the bench next to Jon throughout the entire one minute conversation, near enough for him to hear the tone of the head of DPI to work out that he wasn't happy. Judging from her failed attempts at interjecting or explaining, it was always destined to be a one-way call. When the shouting stopped, Summer agreed that she understood everything, before the call was abruptly ended. She sat there staring at the phone, hands shaking, before finally saying, 'The bastard!'

'What's Dougie Boy done now?'

'Not him – Charles, my boss. Apparently he didn't mention the drugs test idea with Peabody, which was very convenient because it didn't go down at all well with the big man, especially since the leak. What an utter bastard.'

'I thought any publicity was good publicity?'

'Not when Peabody's unhappy with the idea. Rat-face Charles decided to inform him that he had zero knowledge of it, that it was solely my idea and that I'd carried it out without letting him know.'

'Oh. In that case, I agree. Bastard.'

'How could he? I'm gonna tear a strip off him when I see him, listen to his whiny excuses on how he had to save his arse. I want compensation for being the fall guy in this.'

'Ring him tomorrow and let him have it big style.'

'I can't.' Summer looked him in the eyes and ran a hand down the side of his face, stroking his beard. 'I've been called back. Flight's booked at nine thirty tomorrow morning. I've been pulled off the competition.'

Chapter 23

JON'S nipples were bearing the brunt of the morning rain as it lashed through his vest, causing it to rub against them like a cheese grater. His shoes were two puddles wrapped in canvas, splashing with every step on the asphalt. Up ahead, through a coating of sweat and water, his eyes could see blurry figures gradually getting bigger. Wind slapped against his face and legs, toying with him by pushing him left before receding at the exact moment he fought back to the right, causing him to stumble as if he were drunk. Four miles in with six to go, Jon could not have been more wet if he'd jumped into the Atlantic Ocean. And yet he was loving it.

The race in the Hamptons was their second out of four planned before the marathon, six weeks before the big day. It had promised stunning views over a beautiful course, but right now Jon thought he could have been somewhere in monsoon season. The freakish weather for this time of year at the east end of Long Island had been attributed to the tail of Hurricane Wendy that had ventured near this side of America. Jackson had ordered all coats and covers to be abandoned before they stepped into the start area, saying that this would make excellent preparation in case the heavens opened during the marathon. Jon had been carefully planning for the race, working out the correct pace in order to get his desired time. More importantly, he'd been assessing his competitors, evaluating their training and figuring out how he might beat some of them. He may not have seen Summer for nearly three weeks, but he was determined to fulfil his side of the agreement for their day out and claim a top five finish for her. Perhaps it was having this clear target, or from two weeks of no distractions, or maybe it was just the others not coping as well in the conditions, but Jon was comfortably in sixth place amongst the orange shirts and still had plenty left in him.

The crowds were sparse, which was to be expected given the conditions, and the only non-runners Jon met were those under umbrellas handing out liquid refreshments at the designated refuelling stations. He took a cup of water and got a natural top up as he continued to run with it for a few yards before slamming the contents towards his face without dropping his speed. The five-mile marker came into view, but Jon kept in mind some advice Summer had sent in an email during her absence – don't celebrate halfway, as it just means you've got to do what you've just done all again, except this time with a lot less energy. It had been one of the few emails he'd received from her since she'd been dragged away. The last he heard, she was still toeing the company line and protecting her boss, for whatever reason. Perhaps she was biding her time to gain an advantage, Jon thought. There was no sign she'd be allowed back, so Jon had quashed any thoughts of what might have been and had worked hard on his training. Something must have gone right as he now found himself alongside a familiar but soggy ponytail.

'I'd have thought this would make you feel right at home,' Jon shouted across as he got level.

'Oh hiya. You're doing well,' Ceris said between breaths. 'Struggling a little, me. You go on. Don't overdo it this time, though.'

'I won't. See you at the end. And don't drown out here.'

After his last race, his brother had sent him a fridge magnet with a phrase written on it: 'You learn more from a defeat than a victory', and despite feeling bitter about a gift from a man whose own career had had success stamped all over it, he'd taken the phrase on board. Jon's pace was steady, and he was saving a kick for the final quarter of a mile. The race still contained nearly a thousand other competitors, so there were plenty of other targets to pick off as he progressed up the field. Battling the elements seemed to take his mind off the process of running, and he let his legs fall into an easy rhythm. He was pretty certain Nicki was ahead of him, with the usual suspects of Arjun and Danny no doubt leading the way with her. Kieran had overtaken him at the start but hadn't got too far in front, so Jon guessed it was him in the orange vest he could vaguely see three hundred metres ahead.

The tree-lined paths offered little protection from the rain, not that Jon thought that he could get any wetter; even if it stopped now he would still be soaked by the finish line. He passed a cluster of houses before turning into a small bay in which several boats were being tossed around in the wind, indignant at their treatment in what was barely autumn. The terrain was thankfully mainly flat, and with his constant pace, Jon found himself overtaking at least a dozen people in a five-minute period as the conditions took their toll on others. As he passed a farm to his left and rounded a bend, he was within a short spurt of Kieran. He hadn't seen a mile marker for a while, but assumed he was about three miles from the end. Why stop at fifth place? Jon thought. Kieran had proved to be strong in training so far, so Jon was a little surprised to see him apparently suffering here. A minute later he caught him up.

'You okay?' Jon said.

'Jesus – Jon. Am I doing so bad that even you're over-taking me?'

'I'm just having a good run, that's all.'

'Must be those drugs kicking in, eh?'

'Look, for the umpteenth time, it was a contaminated sample.'

'Yeah, yeah. I'm sure those official results were fake.'

Jon may have been cleared, but the potential for good-humoured jibes based on his story apparently had a half-life that rivalled plutonium.

'It was probably as Natasha said – a DPI publicity stunt.'

'That's your story, anyway.' Kieran winced. 'Trouble with my calf. Can't go much faster than this now.'

'Do you mind if I carry on?' Jon said.

'Do I have a choice? Just make sure you save a towel for me.'

Thinking about Kieran's calf problem made Jon become more aware of his own body, which after an ignorant last few miles was a bit of a shock. His calves also felt tight, like someone was inside pulling on his muscles, and the outside of his upper right leg was stiffening up. Jackson had told them to both listen to and ignore their bodies. Most aches could be ignored, the pain overridden by the brain, but anything serious must be monitored. Trouble was, it all relied on experience to recognise the type of pain that the signals from your body were giving you, something Jon was still learning. When he listened to reports from his feet, he could picture the blisters growing with each step. His lower back was grumbling and his nipples were communicating through bloody stains, clashing with his vest. He was suddenly filled with self-doubt. This last mile had taken ages. What if he got severe cramp, leaving him screaming in agony by the roadside? Perhaps his right leg would stiffen up so much he'd have to get a parrot and an eye-patch to complete the look. He had to focus on something else. Thoughts of his parents offered no great support. He flushed Summer out of his mind as soon as she appeared within it, worried that thoughts of her would send him dreaming until he unwittingly slowed to a casual pace. Then there was Nicki. Always competitive, hungry, determined to win. Why couldn't he compete with her? Despite her icy attitude towards him, although thawing, she had the right attitude for this competition.

'One mile to go!'

Jon stumbled for a few steps in surprise at this shout as a race marshal grinned and clapped as Jon passed. One mile? thought Jon. He must have missed the last two markers, lost in his own thoughts. The rain had eased to a light drizzle, and he took a Gatorade from the next station to fuel him for the last time. He tried to think of Nicki's figure from behind which would be somewhere ahead, imagining catching and overtaking it, seeing her face. Looking down at his pace watch, he realised he was going quicker than his goal pace. He wanted to go for it, to press on hard and see who he could catch. His thoughts turned to the fridge magnet. They'd gone up to thirteen miles in training, and one thing he had learned from that particularly difficult run was that a mile at the end of a long distance is a lot longer than a mile at the start. He had to be disciplined, kick much later, pace it right until the end. Wait another five minutes, then push it to the finish. Whilst he was working all this out, he was oblivious to the fact that just behind him, some runners actually had the audacity to plan on overtaking him, including two in soaked DPI vests.

Jon recognised his surroundings as those that they'd started in, which, given the looped course, meant he was nearing the finish. His legs felt as if they had weights strapped to them, and after nearly an hour and a half of running, his chest was worryingly wheezy, to the point where his mum would have definitely kept him in bed for the week. He should have been happy to cruise at this speed and finish in a good time, but the sight of a labouring Danny ahead was like a hare to a greyhound. As he pressed harder, he reckoned he may still have had enough distance to run Danny down before the end. Third was in his sights.

'Oi! Come back, you,' said a Geordie voice behind him.

Jon whipped his neck around to see Natasha and Kieran in a splashing pursuit. His look of total surprise gave Kieran a big grin.

'Second wind!' Kieran shouted as he got closer. 'Natasha promised a leg massage if I beat you.'

This can't be happening, screamed Jon inside. He was supposed to be challenging for third, not contemplating the prospect of coming sixth. No, sixth just wouldn't cut it, would not be deserving and was not the deal he'd had with Summer, whether she was here or not. As they both came up to his shoulder, Jon kicked for home. He pumped his arms harder and just stared ahead, praying for the finish line to appear and not to be overtaken by anyone he knew. Danny had sped up ahead, enjoying his own fast finish, leaving Jon clinging on to fourth at best. He knew he should look round, but was scared to see. His muscles ached as he passed a couple of men, and could hear the cheers of a small crowd ahead. He dared a look behind and saw Kieran ten metres back, having broken from Natasha. Somehow, Jon found another level of energy from somewhere and burst ahead. When the finish line loomed large in his vision, he glanced back and saw Kieran the same distance back, pain clearly on his face. Jackson stood at the finish, clapping and nodding. As Jon crossed the line, he punched the air as if he'd won.

Holding a bagel ready and squirting Gatorade into his mouth like it was champagne, Jon went up to Arjun who had already stripped off his top and was towelling down.

'Did you beat the Wicked Witch of the East?' Jon said.

'Nicki? Yeah, done her in the last twenty. Don't think she was too happy about it. What happened to you? I thought I was hallucinating, seeing you come in…what, fifth?'

'Fourth. Just call me Rain Man.'

Jackson had gathered everyone's bags together by the side of the car park and Jon was looking forward to a warm, dry top, trousers and in fact anything that didn't make him feel like a walking puddle. He delved into his holdall and laid his 'I heart NY' t-shirt out on top. There had been no medals given out for this race, but the free towel handed out to all finishers was even more welcome round his neck. He removed his vest and rubbed his towel over his back, chest and hair in slow motion as his shoulders complained at the extra work they were forced to do. His chest was bright red and his nipples were standing up, surrounded by congealed blood. Slapping on a couple of plasters and looking forward to a long, hot shower later, he slipped on his t-shirt. It felt like he'd just put on the king's robes. The rain had been reduced to a few spits, but not enough to threaten his newly-acquired dry upper body status. Next for an upgrade were his feet, which he fully expected to see turned into shrivelled up, wrinkly pieces of meat when he took off his shoes and socks. Slapping them down onto firm ground, even if wet, felt like a luxury. He wrapped a towel tightly round his waist and shed the last of his clothes. The DPI shorts would have to be kept, but he was considering throwing away his pants; he couldn't imagine their stench as they lay in a curled, soggy mess by his feet.

'Need someone to hold your towel?' Nicki said as she approached and stood close to him, fully changed into her dry set of clothes, bag over her shoulder.

'Er, no thanks. I think I can manage.' Jon wanted to dry himself thoroughly in all the important places, but the thought of Nicki watching him led him to a slow rub of his legs instead.

'Your fourth place was very impressive,' she said. 'Maybe you've got more stamina than I thought.'

Jon clung tightly to his towel and said, 'Thanks. Guess I was up for it today. Congrats on your second place.'

Nicki stopped smiling. 'Not exactly my best race. Thought I had the lanky git but he had more kick than a vindaloo.'

'Sorry you lost, then,' Jon said, changing tactic.

'I don't see it as losing,' she replied. As quickly as the scowl appeared, it morphed into something approaching enlightenment. 'I see it as not winning...but a chance for revenge next time.'

'Arjun's gonna be tough to beat over twenty-six miles.'

'Nah, reckon I can take him. Might have to be looking over my shoulder at you, though, at this rate.'

'Anyway,' Jon said, trying to look like he needed a little privacy, 'I'm dying to dive into something dry, so will catch you later, I'm sure.'

Nicki glanced to her left and right before stepping closer to Jon. 'We should talk. I know the plan is for everyone to go out later for an afternoon stroll along the beach, but make some excuse and stay behind. I'm sure you can think of something suitable – you're good at that.'

Nicki walked off leaving Jon with another chill down his back.

The euphoria of his high finish had worn off by the time they reached home. They'd stepped off the minibus that had taken them there and disembarked with all the speed and vocal displeasure of an octogenarian tour group. Jon tried to use the two-hour journey back to get some rest, but had drifted in and out of sleep. Each time he'd started to lose consciousness, he was snapped awake by recalling Nicki's strange proposition. It was with some trepidation that when Arjun and Danny started cajoling everyone to go out to stretch their tired muscles with them, Nicki had insisted that she was staying.

'What about the bearded hustler?' Arjun said.

Jon flicked a look to Nicki. Here was a perfect way to get out of a talk with her, but after replaying their conversation in his mind, his gut instinct was that it would happen sometime anyway, and that he might as well get it over with. 'I can't, man. Blisters are absolutely killing me. Maybe later.'

After a quarter of an hour and a couple of last-minute pleas for Jon to join them, the others departed, leaving Jon alone downstairs when Nicki headed up to her room.

He picked up a running magazine and had started to flick through it when he heard Nicki shout from upstairs for him to help her with something. What started out as a slight knot in his stomach grew into a coiled ball of fear by the time he'd reached her bedroom. She was sitting cross-legged on her bed, laptop open and facing her. 'Hi. Sit down.'

Jon perched on the corner of the bed, thankful he was near the door if he needed a quick getaway. 'Okay Nicki, what's up?'

'Where'd you get your t-shirt from?' Nicki said, her face as innocent as a child's.

The question sent a jolt of anxiety through his body. He stood up, pulled the t-shirt down tightly and examined it as if he'd never seen it before. 'This? I thought I'd said? From one of the shops on the main street, can't remember the name. I know it's a bit tacky but –'

'Oh. That's strange.'

C'mon, thought Jon. It was a simple lie. She couldn't possibly know or care otherwise. 'Strange? Why's that?'

'Because here it looks like you bought it in a shop in Manhattan.' She rotated the laptop so that Jon could see it. On the screen was a photo he recognised as Summer's shot of him in the shop with it half over his head, just before he purchased it. He had full-on nausea now.

'I mean, I wasn't sure at first, but if you zoom in on the shop window you can make out the Manhattan address,' Nicki said.

For once, a part of his brain had quickly come up with a plausible excuse, but it had been slapped down by the logical part which pointed out that the much more pressing concern was that Nicki had somehow got her mitts on that picture. 'Where –'

'Did I get this from? From the same place as this...oh, and this...and, yes...this.'

Jon appeared on the *Big* piano, at the top of the Rockefeller and finally on Brooklyn Heights promenade, as a close-up next to Summer. He felt like he was running in mid-air, the cliff edge having crumbled beneath him.

'Seems to me like you and Summer did quite a bit of sightseeing together. Look at the happy couple.' She'd pulled up another arm's length one of them on Brooklyn Bridge, taken just before Summer had stormed off.

'It's not what you think...'

'But what I can't understand is the date...it said these were taken on the day you were in the lab, getting tested again. Surely that can't be right?'

Jon snapped the laptop lid down and got to his feet. 'All right, you got me. We didn't exactly spend the whole day in the lab. We went out into Manhattan and saw a few things. Not exactly a crime, is it?' His heart was beating as fast as it had been at the peak of the race.

'So the second batch of cleared results were faked?'

Was that what this was all about? She still thought he had cheated? 'No, not exactly. There was no second test as it wasn't needed. I was always clean.' He continued to fill her in on the true turn of events.

By the time he finished, she was performing a slow clap. 'Bravo! Great plan, Bonnie and Clyde.'

'Well it would have been a tad easier if a certain someone hadn't decided to blab all over the Internet about it,' Jon said.

'Bet they'd have a field day if they knew the truth. Drugs test a total sham? A competitor and a loyal DPI worker in a shameful love tryst? And who knows what other help she's giving you.'

'It wasn't like that. It was just a day out and nothing even happened. We're just friends, and she's back in England now, off the competition, as you know.'

'I'm not sure what I know, with all these secrets,' Nicki said, lying back on the bed.

'Where'd you get the photos from anyway?'

'The other day I'd left my laptop's charger downstairs and so went into your room to borrow yours. Saw your camera lying on the bed and thought I'd take a peek at what lame photos you'd been taking. Must say I was rather intrigued at what I found.'

Jon looked down at the laptop.

'And if you're thinking of throwing it out the window, don't bother,' she said. 'I've got plenty of backups.'

'So what now?' Jon said. 'What do you want from me?'

Nicki cleared the laptop from the bed and stood in front of Jon. Being almost half a foot taller than her, he looked down into her brown eyes, waiting for the blackmail. When it came, it was not quite what he expected. She grabbed hold of her thin, black sweater and lifted it clean over her head. She stood before him in a lacy black bra, his gaze momentarily slipping towards her cleavage. 'Like I said, I want you to help me with something.' Her tracksuit bottoms were pulled to the floor and she stepped out of them to reveal matching knickers.

Jon took a step back. He wanted to look away, but the shock just left him staring at her petite frame.

'It's been nearly two months away now. A girl has needs.'

She put both hands on Jon's shoulders.

'W–what about your boyfriend?'

'Not here, is he? No visits makes Nicki a frustrated girl. I'm sure you can help me out.' She placed her palm between his legs and began to stroke it up and down.

He fought against several conflicting primal urges. 'Nicki, I can't…it's not –'

She leaned up and caught his ear lobe between her teeth, then relaxed it and said, 'Let's make this simple – all I require from you is to lie down and think of England, I'll do the rest. Alternatively, I have a new blog entry ready to go at a press of a button, pictures and all. So, what do you say, stud?'

Chapter 24

JON realised just how difficult it was to think straight while he was being stroked in the long-neglected parts of his anatomy by a girl in her underwear. His brain was being pumped full of chemicals and the overriding message that was trying to flood his thoughts was that there were, in fact, no other thoughts at all, and there was nothing else in the entire world for Jon to worry about. It was a compelling argument, and the memories of what the result would be if he just let things happen certainly presented to Jon a highly desirable outcome that he would be a fool not to take. He had been looking away, but now he looked down into her brown eyes and saw under the thin layer of lust a burning desire for power, the anticipation of having total control.

'I can't do this,' Jon said, pushing her away so that they were now two steps apart.

'Really? Certainly didn't feel like you weren't up for it.'

Jon covered his hands over his bulging tracksuit, silently apologising to it for the false hope. 'Yeah, well... it's been a while for me too. But the point is, it's not right. You're blackmailing me for sex.' The last words hung in the air strangely, as if a phrase from a foreign language Jon had no right to know.

'Call it what you like,' Nicki said, reaching up behind her back, 'but the bottom line is we both get laid and no-one gets hurt.' Her bra fell to the floor, revealing her small, but perfectly rounded breasts. Jon felt the invisible pull of his hands towards them. He shut his eyes, kept them closed and breathed out.

'Nicki, it's wrong. You've treated me like shit from day one. I'm not gonna sleep with you just because you're a bit horny.'

'Aren't you forgetting the photos? I don't think you have a choice, Jonny Boy.'

'You wouldn't –' As he opened his eyes again, his view was now of a fully-naked Nicki, hands on hips, standing up with her legs spread. His groin was screaming at him to lose this argument and repent later.

'Why wouldn't I go public? If I don't get what I want, then at least I can stuff your chances a bit more. Truth is, I wasn't bothered about you before, but now…I don't know, you're surprising me. I want to win this and I'll do what needs to be done.'

'You don't *need* to do this. Summer and I…we were doing nothing wrong. She's a great girl.'

'Nothing wrong? Great girl? Really? Wonder if her husband thinks the same?'

Jon blinked and took half a step backward. 'Husband? She's not married.'

Nicki smiled. 'No? Is that what she told you?'

Jon was motionless, silent. He could hear Summer's words in Brooklyn, her resolute statement of being single.

Nicki walked forward until her breasts were slightly touching Jon's chest. 'Poor Jon – deceived by the beautiful, flame-haired temptress. I checked up on your girlfriend, and found that she is very much married – in fact, only six months ago.'

'I don't believe you,' Jon said as he stepped back once again. 'That's crap. You're just –'

'Google it yourself. Go on – it's all there with just a little bit of digging. She changed her name recently, which made it harder, but it's all there.'

Summer Breeze, thought Jon. Maybe if her husband had an awful-sounding surname, she may have changed hers… 'No, she wouldn't lie…we talked a lot that day, she opened up and –'

'Oh for fuck's sake, you idiot! As they say over here, wake up and smell the *cawfee*. She's DPI, check out the back of your neck – she got you branded, got DPI all over the newspapers thanks to manipulating you, humiliating you, upsetting your parents, and now that her job's done, she's conveniently back safe and sound at home.'

The blood had drained from his groin and made its way up to his neck, making his tattoo throb as if it had been done yesterday. The champions of Summer in his mind were beginning to lose the will for battle.

'Bet she told you she loved that stupid beard? How many lies did she tell you, Jon?' Nicki swept him around and threw him on his back onto the bed. He was still fully clothed, but through his thin tracksuit bottoms he could feel her warmth as she straddled him. His blood rerouted again.

'I may be a bitch at times, but I say it how it is. You know I have a boyfriend, because I haven't hidden it. I don't have to lie to get my way.'

'I'm sure he'd love to hear about how faithful you've been,' Jon said.

'I don't suppose he would, but then I don't really give a toss. I'm sure there'll be plenty of interest in me once I win. I'll have my pick of men I'm sure, but right now the only one that can satisfy me is you, I'm afraid.'

Jon felt her pussy push down and slide over his covered erection. Stifling a moan, he could feel the strength in her thighs gripping his own. Looking up at her athletic body, her pert breasts invitingly within touching distance, his desire and disappointment were sweeping away all his self-control like a flash flood.

'Come on, big boy, we're virtually there already. Let me have my way with you and I'll promise not to break the story of your pathetic little crush on Mrs Breeze.'

'No!' Jon reached up and shoved her aside, rolling off the bed in the other direction. 'I wouldn't trust your word for a second. I gotta find out for myself.' He stormed out of her room as best as he could, given the disabling feature in his pants.

'Whatever, Jon,' she shouted back. 'I'll still be here, naked, waiting for you when you realise the truth.'

He stumbled into his room and grabbed his phone. It would be some kind of mistake, or a trick by Nicki, he was certain. His heartbeat increased as the ringing tone echoed in his ear. After just one ring, she answered.

'Hello, Summer speaking?'

'Hi Summer, it's Jon. I –'

'Fooled you! This is my answerphone. I'm not able to take your call at the moment but if you leave a message after the beep I'll get back to –'

'Shit!' Jon quickly ended the called. He wasn't ready to speak to her, let alone leave a coherent message. His ribcage was still taking a pounding from his heart as he thought about what to do next. He didn't want to trawl the Internet on what might be a waste of time, especially when he could just get confirmation from the source. Bringing up her contact details, he saw a second number – her desk phone. She'd told Jon it was rare she'd actually be at her desk, but as the alternative right now was an agonising wait over email, he tried it. After about half a dozen rings, it was picked up.

'Hello?' Unless Summer had acquired a deep male voice in his absence, Jon guessed it wasn't her on the other end.

'Hi…er, it's…er…I was looking for Summer?'

'Summer? Nah, not here.'

'Oh. Do you know where she might be?'

'Not a clue. But then that's women for you, always going off without telling you where they're going, or how much of your money they're spending.'

'Yeah.' Jon let out a fake laugh, followed by a long period of silence as he struggled to think of what he could possibly get out of this conversation.

'Sorry, who's this?' the deep voice said.

'Mr…Hanks.' Jon winced at his lack of creativity.

'I'm assuming that you're not *Tom* Hanks?'

'No, no. Just a friend of Summer's. So do you work with her?'

'You could say that – I'm her boss, Charles.'

Jon almost dropped the phone at hearing his name. He

didn't know whether her desk phone would have caller ID, or whether it would matter, but he couldn't pass up the opportunity. 'I see. Shame about her having to come off the Moon Runners project, wasn't it?'

'Suppose so. Not my decision, though. Look, she's not here and I'm a busy man so –'

'Funny thing, she claimed the drugs test thing was your idea.'

Jon heard Charles breathe closer to the phone. 'Mr Hanks, I don't know who you are, but that's company business.'

'Only, from my viewpoint it looks like you screwed her over.'

'Yeah? Well you're entitled to your opinion, but my advice to you is to take what Summer says with a pinch of salt. I only wish that someone had said that to me before I married her.'

Jon didn't hear Charles say goodbye or put down the phone, he just stood there holding the mobile, posing like a waxwork museum piece. A whole minute later, he dropped the phone onto the bed. He caught sight of himself in the mirror. Nicki was right – he did look ridiculous with a beard. He left his room and marched towards the bathroom. Jon heard the satisfying buzz of the electric shaver as it removed each patch of hair. Summer had probably only been humouring him when she'd said that she liked it. Or maybe it was a blatant lie, just like all the others. What else had she lied about? The beard was half gone now, and Jon turned his face from side to side to see a before-and-after effect. Perhaps all her marathon stories were there just to make him feel better, he thought. But why did it bother him so much? It wasn't as if anything had really happened, that they were ever together. He didn't owe her anything. Besides, she was gone now. A vision of Nicki waiting for him on her bed appeared in his head. He'd laid low these last few weeks and had progressed extremely well, free from the distractions and media interest. If Nicki released those pictures and a story, he knew it would only stir things up and put him in a bad light again. With his face now smooth, he stared into the mirror. There was only one thing for it, he decided. Grabbing a running top, he sprinted downstairs, away from Nicki's room, into the living room, donned his trainers and headed out.

Despite his morning exertions, Jon's legs ran up the ramp to the promenade at a pace normally suited to one of Jackson's sprint sections. He had no idea of what distance he wanted to cover, it just felt good to be another step away from the house. Dark clouds hung low over the sea, but there was just enough of a break in them to illuminate the wooden walkway and adjacent sand in afternoon sun. The wind slapped into his face, stinging the newly-uncovered skin, whipping the beads of sweat trickling down from his brow and spreading salt into his pores. This was real, he thought. Nothing fake here, no lies – just him running through the elements. This is how life should be, he thought – uncomplicated. He gazed across at a couple walking along the sea edge holding hands and wondered how many secrets they were keeping from each other. Or they could be miles away from their partners, having an illicit affair, unbeknown to everyone else watching. Maybe you could never really know someone, never truly trust what they say, only choose to believe and hope you're right. He turned his attention forward again and saw a woman in pink shorts and a matching vest coming straight towards him, headphones dangling from her ears. They were on the same running line, but Jon thought that for once the girl could dance to his tune and make way for him. With twenty metres between them, he was unsure if she'd seen him through her sunglasses, but he remained on his course. Jon thought that she might be in her early forties, trying to look younger. As the distance halved, she didn't look like moving, although Jon was sure she must have seen him by now. She wasn't going to move – why would she? He was only Jon after all, he thought. He breathed out hard and swung sharply to his right...just as she nipped out to her left. In the ultimate nightmare scenario in a game of chicken, they collided while trying to make way for the other one, obeying Newton's third law in a satisfying crash of heads and arms, followed by a simultaneous fall onto the boardwalk.

'What the hell were you playing at?' the woman said, rubbing her head before picking up and inspecting her headphones.

'Sorry,' Jon said. 'I was trying to avoid you.'

'You were? Perhaps try a little earlier next time, hey, honey?'

'Why should I have moved earlier? You could have moved as well.'

She swiped at her Barbie-pink clothes, brushing off dirt, and got to her feet. 'If you hadn't noticed, mister, I'm a lady. It would have been nice if the gentleman – and I say that loosely – had made way for her.'

Jon was about to reply when she stuck up a hand, palm out vertically, fiddled with a gadget on her sleeve and went off, leaving him lying there watching her bouncy bottom disappearing in the direction he'd just come.

'Just perfect,' Jon said aloud to no-one. He went to get up, but a shooting pain in his right knee stopped him, causing him to roll back to a sitting position. A quick prodding examination seemed to indicate no serious injury, but the side of his knee was tender as a result of the collision. Jon rubbed at it, trying to ease the pain. He gingerly got up, avoiding putting any weight on it and tried to walk one step. It didn't feel too bad, so he took a few more steps. A slight pain, perhaps something he could run off, he reckoned. He began to slowly jog again, but the pain was more acute than a normal ache and wasn't going away. He was now stuck between a house he didn't want to return to, and the open path he could no longer run down. Remembering Jackson's advice, and knowing this was an unplanned run after a long distance a few hours before, he reluctantly chose to head back to the house.

The ice pack was cold and uncomfortable against his knee, but at least it was numbing the pain. He'd taken shortcuts back to the house, but it had still taken him twenty minutes to return. A cab would have been better, but he'd rushed out with no money and had visions of being held captive in the taxi for ransom until the driver got his five dollars. The house was still empty, presumably bar a frustrated and naked Nicki, somewhere silently plotting how to ensnare her next prey. Honest and up-front Nicki, never one to hide her fangs. Still, he thought, on the bright side, he had upped his naked woman count by one today. He picked up his phone and saw a text that had come in from Kieran a few minutes ago, inviting them down to the diner if they wanted, no doubt led there by the Irishman's insatiable appetite for pancakes. It was too far to hobble, so Jon decided to make his way up to his room instead and crash for a few hours to allow the pain to subside. Just as he'd reached the first floor, he was pounced upon.

'Come to your senses yet?' Nicki stood in the doorframe

of her room with a nightdress that didn't quite meet in the middle.

Jon stared at her. 'Congratulations – it seems you were right.'

'See? So I was telling the truth and your precious Summer was lying. Who's the bitch now?'

'Yeah well, Jon meets woman, woman hurts Jon. Mentally or physically, it doesn't matter.' Jon waggled his leg to show his ice pack. 'Same old.'

Nicki walked up to him. 'A woman bashed up your knee? What did you do to her – steal her Ladyshave?'

'We collided. It's just bruised, I think.'

'It makes you look younger, you know.'

'An ice pack?'

'No, stupid – *sans* beard.' She reached up and stroked his cheek. 'Poor little gullible Jon. I'm so sorry about Summer.'

'But not sorry enough to not publish your carefully crafted story about us.'

Nicki looked down at the stair carpet. 'What can I say? I'm a bad girl. I like to get what I want. But perhaps I can hold off being bad for you. Don't want to give you a bruised ego to go with that knee.'

'So should I be thanking you for offering not to black-mail me yet?'

'Probably not. But you know, there's no-one around and the offer's still open.' She leaned in and gave him a kiss on his cheek, before walking back to her room. As she got to the door, she let her nightdress fall down her back, and as she walked into the room she called back, 'I can always start and you join me later.'

Jon stood there, both cheeks still feeling the sensation of her touch. He looked at the steep stairs to his floor and flexed his knee, frowning in pain. He'd got hurt, disappointed and bruised today. Maybe it wasn't such a bad idea to put himself first for once and have a little pleasure.

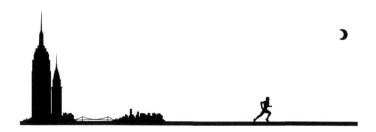

Chapter 25

'NOW that was a splendid meal,' Doug said to himself, leaning back in his chair. He wanted to thank the chef on his excellent culinary skills, but as the pilot had just indicated that they were likely to hit a spot of turbulence soon, he decided against summoning him to his seat. The meal was by far the easiest, least stressful interaction that he had experienced in the last forty-eight hours. He still didn't know whether his trip to China had been a success or a disaster.

His wife often called him stubborn, a trait that he always reminded her was one of the main reasons he had got to where he was now. He was rarely wrong, and had been fortunate enough to make his mistakes when he was younger – when the stakes were lower – and learn from them. Whenever his instincts told him he was right, he would carry on in the face of mounting pressure and doubt from others. Nothing of significant size had had to be aborted or radically changed as a result of him being wrong. So as he sat watching the sun gradually winning its battle with his plane in the quest for the horizon, it was a unique feeling of defeat that was threatening to plague every cell in his body. China had promised to be his saviour, hanging a rope in the dark of the pit whose edge he was clinging on, pushed there by his previously good friend Dmitri. Thanks to the Russian's disruption, the original plan for the rocket's construction was as likely to happen as an Elvis comeback on *The X Factor*. True to his threats, companies had been 'persuaded' by Dmitri not to cooperate with Doug, thus making the required parts impossible to source. With the Americans brushing him off and the Europeans too quarrelsome to work with, the grandiose Moon trip which Doug had promoted to everyone had been left in tatters, until a Chinese company had stepped in with surprising news.

It shouldn't have been surprising really, thought Doug, as he took another gin and tonic from the stewardess. China had put someone in space in 2003, had previously announced ambitious plans for a space station and then Moon and even Mars landings. They wanted to prove to the world what they could do, to show that they really were living up to their potential, that China was the future. With a population of over a billion people, they certainly had the resources, and had shown vision and determination to achieve much in recent decades. Despite a greater transparency, China was still subject to secrecy, hiding some of its capabilities from the world. America hadn't trusted China with its money for technology in case the subsequent advances found their way into military use. The Chinese government had ploughed on regardless, but eventually looked to private companies to lead the way. When one such company contacted Doug after getting wind of his problems, he was staggered at how far advanced they were. He got out his tablet computer and brought up the video of the rocket they had built, the very one he had seen yesterday. As he spun the 3D image with a hand gesture, he imagined it taking off, DPI logos adorning the sides being picked up by the world's cameras, with a last-minute shot of the crew before they blasted off into history. Doug had been honoured to learn how inspired they had been after his world announcement, so inspired that they wanted to alter their less-ambitious space plans for the rocket and – quite literally – shoot for the Moon. However, what they needed to make it a reality was more money, something Doug happily had in abundance right now. But even the vast amounts he was considering to pump into the project may still have meant compromising on his and others' dreams.

He had been delighted with the way the marathon preparations had been going. The drugs test scandal had been dealt with and the media had been focused on the race itself. Doug had been following the training reports submitted by Jackson every week, read all the race results and even watched some of the TV episodes of life in the New York house, as he was doing now. Although always contactable by mobile wherever he was, even in the air, he liked to switch off his phone when flying and get away from the core business for a while. He watched intently as his runners sat around and chatted about the last race. He wondered whether he would prefer to swap places with them, with their simple lives and so few decisions to make. The enthusiasm and seriousness of the runners pleased Doug; he could see that they weren't in it for a fun run, and that they all wanted to compete. There were some natural runners, too, judging from the training. Jackson had been a star in more ways than one, and was coming good in his promise to make it a real competition. One lad, Jon Dunn, Doug had expected to go home after the initial feedback from Jackson, and yet he seemed to be flourishing right now. Even the drug test business hadn't stopped his progress. That's exactly the spirit Doug wanted to see the competition evoke, to raise people's games beyond their visions of their own limitations. Maybe just winning the race would be enough for them, Doug thought.

As the plane made its gentle descent towards the green fields of south-east England, Doug thought what it might be like to come back to Earth. He imagined plummeting through the atmosphere, the colours, the vibrations, the sheer lunacy of crashing through from the edge of space at speeds almost incomprehensible, all the while praying that the capsule holding you stayed intact so that you would get to tell the most wonderful story of your life. The plan for Doug, however, was to be in mission control, holding his breath for that short, agonising moment in time where radio contact is impossible and the fate of the crew is unknown. The first glimpse of them coming out of the return module, the first handshake and congratulatory hug. But as he watched the clouds rush by the window, he couldn't help transition back to his childhood dreams.

The Chinese had loved the idea of a space tourist going to the Moon. Except...they wanted their tourist – a Chinese man or woman – to be on board. *You give us the money, we'll sort out the passengers*. Doug could keep the marathon idea – it was of no interest to them. He had tried to negotiate, but the price they were asking for complete DPI control was way too much. As it was, Doug knew that it would be extremely tough convincing the shareholders to buy into this new venture anyway, and was going to have to be very creative just to be able to justify the rocket on its own. Doug didn't hold all the cards, and although he was their preferred benefactor, they would happily look at others. So he had a rocket – at a price – but no seat for a Moon Runner, in comparison to his current, cheaper option that had threadbare plans but gave him full control. On one hand, DPI could go into space, be part of sending someone to the Moon and become China's favourite cousin. Or they could wait, keep with the original plans and pray for a miracle. Either way, Doug realised, the Great Space Race was coming to an end.

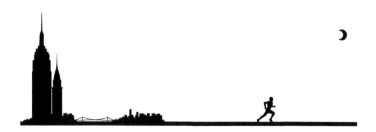

Chapter 26

'**J**ON – why the hell were you hassling my boss? And don't say it wasn't you, *Mr Hanks*.'

After several rings, he had reluctantly decided to answer Summer's call. Cradling the phone between his shoulder and ear, he pulled on his jeans and made his way to his room.

'Boss? Don't you mean your husband?' He could almost hear the calculation of a story in the ensuing silence.

'Did Charles tell you that?'

'Yes. Came as a bit of a surprise, you see. Given the fact that you were categorically single, and all.'

'Jon...it's –'

'Complicated? Ha! Here comes another Summer confession.'

'It's...embarrassing. It wasn't something I wanted to talk about.'

'Don't tell me – you fell in love and later realised you were brother and sister.'

'Ugh, no.'

Jon quickly put on his t-shirt. 'Then maybe you had a glorious wedding but have a rare form of amnesia whereby you erase an entire relationship from your mind and yet keep everything else?'

'Jon, stop it.'

'Well in the absence of the truth – which I'm finding quite hard to come by with you – then I have no choice but to be a little creative.'

'Why are you so bothered with this? You haven't seen me in over two weeks, I thought you'd be getting on fine without me around.'

'Because I cared about you, Summer.' Jon surprised himself with his instant response, then quickly continued, 'Much to my regret, I'm evidently a sucker for a pretty face and a few laughs. I thought after the London debacle that I'd seen the real you in Manhattan, and that despite you having to return, maybe after the marathon we could...I dunno. Obviously I was just a bit of fun, a nice distraction from your hubby for a day.'

'He's not...well, I don't think of him as my husband.'

Jon heard the downstairs door open and the others return from the diner. He was glad that they hadn't come back sooner.

'Right. And so you're not tucked up in bed with him every night? Teddy bear sitting on the side reminding you of the day with nice-but-gullible Jon over here?'

'The truth is, I've only ever tucked up with him for one night. Seemed like a good idea at the time, as did the preceding day's nuptials in Vegas. Unfortunately it turned out to be the most stupid, idiotic, irresponsible thing I've ever, ever done.'

Jon took a while to process this new information. 'So

you married your boss, in Las Vegas on a whim?'

'Yeah. We'd been working for months over there and had just nailed a great campaign. DPI loved us, he'd given me a big raise, the champagne flowed and it seemed the world was ours. He asked me if I was up for some adventure, and I said I was up for anything. When he proposed, I thought it was the coolest thing in the world to do.'

'Until you woke up the next morning?'

'No, the next morning was fine. We strolled around Caesar's Palace like we were the emperor and Cleopatra themselves. What made things a little less than fine was when he pissed off all night and came back to our room at 6am, high on coke, with two strippers.'

'Sounds more like an EastEnders script to me.'

'It's not a joke, it's the truth.'

'But you're still married?'

'Technically, yes. The process of annulment is almost complete, though.'

'And yet you continue to work for him?'

Summer sighed. 'I had disappointed him. He wanted the whole Vegas experience and to come back with a trophy wife he could impress the whole company with. My disgust and refusal to come near him after that night led him to make threats on wrecking my entire career. He still needed me professionally, so we came to an agreement.'

'Sounds a good story.'

'It's not a story. I'm sorry I said that I wasn't married. In my mind, I'm not. I know technically it was a lie, but I didn't want to have to explain all this to you. It wasn't exactly my finest hour.'

He could hear voices pass outside his closed door, so he lowered his voice. 'Maybe what you say is all true but –'

'It is, I swear.'

'– but you're right, it doesn't matter now, does it? You're over there and I'm here, preparing for this marathon and for once in my life really giving something my best shot. I don't need the hassle, don't want to be trying to suss you out all the time, guessing what is and isn't the truth.'

'I'm not like that.'

'I guess I'll never know.' Jon listened to the faint buzz on the line.

'I could come over again,' Summer finally said. 'There's another project in Washington in a week, so I could try and get a plane to JFK and say hi.'

'Don't bother. Jackson's building us up to our peak runs, so gonna be busy.'

'I see.' Jon could hear her softly breathing before she added, 'Hanks is missing you.'

'He's a good bear,' Jon said. 'I'm sure you'll take care of him. Give him a big hug from me.'

'Will do. Get one of the girls to give you a hug. Maybe not Nicki, though. She'd probably want to squeeze you to death.'

Jon thought of what he'd been doing before her call. He guessed it maybe wasn't so clever to be judgemental on a spontaneous decision one might later regret. 'Well, she could be worse.'

'And maybe Cruella de Vil donated to the RSPCA. Make sure you beat her, though.'

'I'll try. I got fourth today, you know.'

'You did? Well done! Even better than fifth. Knew you'd keep your promise. See? I wouldn't ever deserve you.'

Jon smiled. 'Who does, eh?'

They finished up, said their goodbyes and left Jon lying on his bed, staring at the ceiling. He checked his knee and found that it was less painful, although this was largely due to it now being cold and numb. Fancying a bit of male company for a change, he got up and hobbled downstairs.

'What happened to you?' Arjun was lying on a sofa with mug of tea watching American football with Danny.

'My knee? Recovery run, interrupted after ten minutes by Barbie in a mid-life crisis.' Jon was about to explain further when Nicki came down the stairs.

'Are you sure it wasn't Nicki being a bit rough with you?' Danny said, cocking his head towards her as she sat down. Jon and Nicki shot each other a look.

'Yeah, Jonny Boy,' Arjun said, 'while the cats are away...'

'You rumbled us,' Nicki said, putting her hands up. 'Shagged like rabbits until just before you came back.'

Jon stared at her.

'Wow Jon – fourth place and now humping all afternoon. What's your stamina secret?' Danny said.

'The first one was pure hard work. The second one, pure fantasy.'

Had Summer's call come in a minute later however, then he might not have answered it, would have removed his last piece of clothing in Nicki's bed and given her what she wanted.

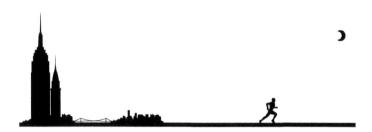

Chapter 27

'YOU'RE such a loser!'

Jon had left it almost two weeks before telling Stu about his nearly moment with Nicki.

'Total, total loser,' Stu continued.

'It was for the best, anyway,' Jon said as he walked on the beach.

'Mate, when you're seconds from getting your end away, you never – and I mean *never* – answer the phone. Whatever it is can wait the one minute – or in my case, a good hour – it takes to perform the necessary.'

'Summer explained a few things to me.'

'You had a heart-to-heart with a girl who's not so much as even kissed you, is thousands of miles away and not likely to see you again, while a girl who, according to you, is absolutely gagging for it, lies naked in her bed, wet, ready and waiting. Hello? McFly?'

'Well I would have taken the opportunity had the call not come in. Don't I get credit for that?'

'That makes it worse! That's like being clear through on goal and then running off to chat to the ball boy.'

Jon kicked at a pebble and saw it skip over the smooth sand and into the water. 'Anyway, she has kissed me – at the London Eye.'

'Yeah, as she stripped you naked and took all your clothes. Mate, you're such a loser.'

Stu had a point, of course. The Summer thing had gone dead, and whether her whole marriage revelation was really the truth wasn't of much consequence now. It had been a bit awkward around Nicki since the near miss, although she had gone out of her way to whisper in his ear a couple of times in passing what he had missed out on, and how much she was enjoying 'special' phone calls with her boyfriend at nights. The real thing was still on offer whenever he manned up, apparently.

'I don't know if I could go that long without a shag. How the heck can you run all those miles when your balls are weighed down that much?' Stu said.

Jon took the opportunity to change the focus from Stu's sex obsession to the half marathon the next day. 'I reckon I might have a chance of third spot tomorrow.'

'I don't know mate, Danny says in his blog he's running well, and Arjun and that teaser Nicki seem to be uncatchable.'

'I have to believe. Plus I have a secret weapon.'

'Go-faster stripes?'

'No – you.'

Passing the two-mile marker in a half marathon wasn't normally a cause of elation for any of the runners, but for the DPI ten taking part in the Long Island Half Marathon, it was certainly special. The mood in the camp in the week had gone from apprehension of the thirteen-mile challenge ahead, to wildly ecstatic at the news that as an unexpected treat, their loved ones were being specially shipped over for the race. Despite all the phone and video calls, recorded messages and even satellite TV links, everyone had buzzed at the thought of seeing some family and friends again.

'Ceris! Oh my god! Oh my god!' A Welsh dragon became a blur as it flew on a flag held by Ceris's sister.

'Gwynny!' Ceris's scream could have carried back to her homeland as she sprinted up to her sister and mum and launched into a three way hug.

There were hugs, tears, high-fives and jumps of delight for all of the runners as they briefly stopped to greet those who they'd been away from for so long. Even Jon was surprised at how long he'd been hugging Stu.

'That's enough, Jon Boy. Don't want everyone to think I'm your gay lover,' Stu said, trying to force himself apart from Jon.

'Sorry mate. Good to see you, that's all.'

'Maybe you can introduce me to that Ceris – she looks excitable.'

'No time for introductions right now. Gotta run – see you in a few miles.' Jon started to run off before shouting back, 'And no funny business with my mum!'

Jon was beaming broadly in the morning sun. All of the DPI runners had quickened their pace since their rendezvous and, despite stopping after different lengths of time, they all seemed to have caught up with each other before the mile was out.

'I'm sure my dad wasn't that bald when I last saw him,' Tom said to Jon as they ran alongside each other.

'You'd better watch out – you're going that way,' Jon replied.

'What happened to your dad? How come your brother made it?'

'That was my mate, Stu. Came over in place of Dad, who wasn't well.'

Jon's mum had told him how eager his dad had been to come over, but had caught a nasty chest cold only a couple of days previously and had decided he could not travel. DPI had organised their own company jets to transfer the friends and relatives across, but could only cater for two per runner. Jon's siblings, it seemed, had far too many commitments at home to accompany his mum for the journey, so he'd been forced to recruit Stu as a last-minute replacement who'd almost jumped down the phone when told of a free trip to the Big Apple.

'How's your mum? Settled down now after the scandal?' Tom said.

'Yeah, always believed I was innocent.'

'What mum doesn't think the sun shines out of her little boy's arse?'

'True. Behind her smiles at seeing me she looked very tired, though.'

'Probably jetlag. Not fair they're only here two nights.'

'Better than nothing. We'll be seeing them again soon, too.'

The route was taking them round a huge park, and DPI had even laid on buggies for the supporters to quickly get from one side to the other to catch the runners at various points. They'd not been allowed to see them before the race, as per strict DPI instructions. The official line was that this was to keep the runners focussed on the preparation, but Jon had agreed with Natasha's cynical comments that it would just make for increased drama in the race. When they saw them again just after the four-mile marker, Jon had run up to give his mum a kiss and he'd also got away with a clean slap to the side of Stu's head. It had made the whole event feel like a fun run, with no-one making an effort to give themselves a good lead. At seven miles, less than two hundred metres separated the last DPI runner from the leader.

'See you at eleven miles!' Stu shouted as Jon ran past waving. 'Give it some Stevenage spirit!'

Jon lengthened his stride and turned on a bit of speed to impress his friend, and was surprised to find himself level with Nicki and Arjun at the front. Instead of keeping level, he continued a few metres ahead and threw up his arms. 'Look at me – I'm winning!'

'Still six to go, hot-shot,' Arjun said, catching him up. 'Feeling good?'

'Indeed, my friend. You?'

'Bit emotional, to be honest. Long time since I saw my wife.'

Jon studied him as he ran next to him. 'Didn't know you were married?'

'Yeah, four years next month.'

'Wow. Closest I've got is a cat. Been together eight years.'

Nicki barged in between them. 'Didn't have you down as a pussy man, Jon.'

Jon continued to look ahead and sped up. 'Anyway, not wasting energy speaking. Gonna run on my own for a bit.'

By mile twelve, Jon had the sudden realisation that he was capable of being the first Moon Runner across the line. The thought of seeing his mum and Stu a mile ago had kept him above his target pace and his mind away from the fatigue in his muscles that had been setting in for some time. With just over one mile left, he had maintained a slight lead over Arjun and Nicki, who seemed to be magnetically connected together. What a time to pull out his first win, he reckoned, in front of his biggest fans and no doubt an interested media. The rise and rise of Jon. The dark horse. One to watch for the marathon. Astronaut-in-waiting. Jon was so busy inventing his own headlines that he almost didn't see Arjun cruise past him. Nicki slid next to Jon.

'You not following?' Jon said.

'Nope. He's kicked too soon.'

'You think?'

'Just a feeling. Reckon I've got this one sewn up.'

Nicki started to get a bit faster, but Jon matched her pace as Arjun continued to get further away. Jackson had told them that they always had more left in them than they thought. If Nicki went, he decided, so would he.

With a quarter of a mile to go in a long, wooded stretch, Nicki and Jon caught Arjun. The cause of his slow-down was evident in his eyes and to everyone's ears. 'Arjun! Arjun! Arjun!' His name beat out relentlessly from his wife and sister ahead at the finish line, both cheering him on and making him a running wreck.

'I'm gone,' he said, looking away with tears streaming down. 'Just go.'

Jon and Nicki exchanged glances and overtook.

'Only one thing better than sex,' Nicki said in between breaths, 'and that's winning.' She was about to shoot away from Jon, but he had pre-empted her strike and kicked for home.

'Go on Jon Boy – do her!' Stu yelled as they passed just ten metres from the line. He could hear his mum clapping and cheering and channelled it into his legs. Nicki was coming back, hands fisted, arms swinging back and forth but Jon was not slowing. The orange tape of the special DPI finish was now held tight across the line, begging for it to be broken by Jon's chest. The win was seconds away, the crowd gone from his ears, Nicki now brushing his elbow. And then the ribbon was broken – Jon's chest snatching the ends away from the smiling female marshals holding them. They stumbled into the finish area, both sucking in air, bending down holding their knees. For Jon, the air had never tasted sweeter.

'Your father will be so proud.' Jon's mum started taking photos of him holding his medal, and every other action he was performing. Apparently, even his post-race stretches were good for the family album.

'Mum, you'll use up all the space on that thing.'

'Nonsense. It's a sixty-four gig card and I can always upload them to the Cloud if I need to make room.'

Jon looked at her suspiciously. 'Okay, who are you and where is my mum?'

'What? You don't think I know anything about cameras?'

Stu cut in. 'I helped her buy a new camera at Heathrow for the visit, and we had a lot of time on the plane for a tutorial. Plus, it took her mind off things.'

'Oh,' Jon said, before adding, 'What things?'

'Er, well, you know,' Stu rubbed his neck. 'The flight? We had a bit of turbulence. Had more ups and downs than my pants.'

'Stuart!' Jon's mum said.

'Sorry Mrs D. I mean, it was a bit rough in places. Had to concentrate on something else. Anyway, I think you are about to experience death by evil stare.' Stu indicated towards Nicki who was lacing up her trainers and looking towards them. Jon went across to her.

'Strange feeling, coming first,' Jon said.

Nicki carried on with her laces.

He tried again, 'I may have won, but it was close. Nothing in it, really.'

'I can't believe I lost to you,' she said standing up. 'Of all the guys – you.'

'I just had a good run, that's all.'

'I meant losing to someone who barely registers as his gender.' Nicki stuffed some clothes into a bag until it was nearly bursting. 'But if I was you,' she continued, 'I'd enjoy the victory now. Might be the last thing you get to celebrate.'

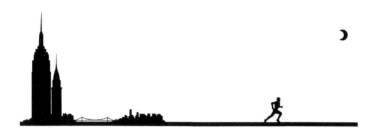

Chapter 28

JON Dunn was the name everyone was talking about. That is, if you believed the hype that was coming out the DPI public relations department and being communicated back to the house. With three and a half weeks to go before the marathon, publicity was going into overdrive, and after Jon's victory the previous Sunday, they'd decided to push him into the limelight. Previously, a lot had been made of Arjun and Nicki's rivalry in races and they had been the favourites for the last two months, but now the man from Hertfordshire was being touted as the dark horse of the DPI runners.

'I think Jon's peaked too soon,' Danny said from the sofa, as he read the latest articles on his tablet.

'Definitely. A true athlete knows how to perform in training to deliver the optimum performance when it actually counts,' Kieran said.

'You two have been reading too many running magazines,' Jon replied.

'Must've been the performance boost from getting rid of the beard. Reduced wind resistance. Bet it *shaves* minutes off over thirteen miles,' Danny said, celebrating his pun.

'Oh the Scouse humour,' Kieran said, shaking his head. 'Tell me again, Jon, why you lost the beard?'

'Felt like a change, that's all,' Jon said.

'I reckon it was because he didn't want to look like his cat,' Danny said, pointing to a photo of Conan.

Jon might have been enjoying an increased profile that week, but for the previous few weeks he had been eclipsed by his cat, who had become a minor Internet celebrity. It had started when Jon had posted on his blog about Conan, after DPI had encouraged them to write about themselves and their home lives one week, as opposed to endless details of their training. Whether it was due to his unusual film star name or his photo, but when a fan – with obviously way too much free time – had set up a website dedicated to the imagined adventures of Conan, he had rapidly achieved a cult following. You could buy Conan mugs, t-shirts and running vests. One person had even sent Jon a knitted Conan scarf, and he'd found one site where there was talk of a design starting for cartoon Conan knickers.

One person had not joined the Conan fan club, though: the owner of a house that was down the road from Jon had recognised Conan and had set up a webcam in his own garden to catch the cat using his garden as a toilet. Obviously Conan had a thing for prized azaleas, as despite a lot of attempts at protecting them, the owner had daily videos of Conan happily squatting away while he was at work. Jon had repeatedly left messages to apologise, but said that there was little he could do as cats were prone to do their own thing where they wanted. However, as embarrassing as it was, at least Jon was able to log on and see that Conan was all right. That was until now.

'Leave Conan out of it. I'm a bit worried about him, actually,' Jon said.

'How come?' Danny said. 'Worried he might have more fans than you?'

'No, he's gone missing. No-one's seem him in three days, and it's unlike him to just disappear.'

'Have you tried his agent?'

'Funny. I suppose he's just gone off for a few days. He's done that once or twice before, but not for years.'

Ceris and Barry came in from the kitchen and sat down, each with a bowl of fruit salad.

'Could be poison,' Kieran said. 'You hear tales of sick bastards who poison cats.'

'Kieran!' shouted Ceris. 'Conan still missing? Don't listen to him. I'm sure he'll turn up as cats do, wondering what all the fuss is about.'

'Or trapped,' Kieran continued. 'Someone's garage, van, shed...'

'Kieran!' Ceris prodded her fork into his leg.

'Ow! Just saying, that's all.'

'Well I hope he does turn up soon. Can't be easy for you being so far away from him, especially living in this house with *some* people.' Ceris narrowed her eyes at Kieran who returned an innocent shrug.

'It's okay,' Jon said. 'If he's hungry, he'll turn up. I'll give Mum a call and get an update.' Jon went upstairs and dialled home.

'So you haven't seen him at all?' Jon said.

'No dear, sorry. He'll be all right, though.'

'Well, you don't know that. He could be stuck some-where.'

'Don't be silly. He's not a kitten any more.'

'But still…could you check with a few neighbours for me? See if they've seen or heard him?'

'Jon, I haven't got time to run a full search and rescue. He's a cat, they wander off once in a while. He'll be back.'

'I'm not asking you to roam the streets for hours, Mum, just knock on a few doors.'

'I'm not bothering your neighbours. Besides, I don't know who lives there. Might be all sorts.'

'Well ask Dad to do it then.'

'Dad's…still recovering. From his cold.'

Jon paused to think when he'd last spoken to his dad. It must have been over a week now. 'Can I speak to him?'

'No, no you can't. He's…asleep.'

'But it's what, eight o'clock there? He's never in bed that early.'

'He's recovering, you know what colds are like to us oldies.'

'You're not that old. Thought Dad was fit as a fiddle now, with all the running he was doing.'

'Yes, well he won't be doing any of that again.'

Jon remembered her trying to ban his dad from ever fishing again, after returning drenched and shivering after one trip. 'Sounded like he was getting into it, so I'm sure he'll be back on the pavements soon.'

'Look love, I'd better go. I've got a mountain of ironing to do. Still catching up from New York.'

'So what do you think I should do about Conan?' Jon said, trying to get something constructive out of the call.

'Oh I don't know...why don't you try phoning the police? I've got to go, see you soon. You take good care of yourself. Bye.'

Returning downstairs, Jon slumped in a chair in the corner of the room and closed his eyes. Jermaine, Barry, Ceris and Nicki were all watching some trashy American afternoon soap in the opposite corner. It was only after a while that he found himself holding a photo he'd picked up in his room. Ceris came over and sat in front of him, cross-legged. 'Did you talk to your mum?'

'Yeah. No sign of Conan and she doesn't exactly seem willing to get CSI on the case. Probably had to go off and polish one of my brother's trophies.'

'Is that your family?' she asked.

Jon sat up a little and handed her the photo. 'Yeah. Just trying to remember what Dad looks like, been so long.'

'Is this the famous Conan?' Ceris pointed to the cat at the front of the photo and Jon handed it to her.

'The one and only. We had to bribe him with cat nibbles to make him stay for the shot.' Jon leaned forward. 'Ceris, what if my neighbour's done something, you know the one whose garden Conan's always messing in?'

'Do you think he would?'

'I don't know. He's crazy enough to set up a webcam and broadcast it to the world. He's got a motive.'

'Maybe DPI can help?'

'Right, old Dougie will get a satellite launched for me so we can track him.'

'It was just an idea.' Ceris picked at the carpet.

'I know, I'm sorry. I suppose I could tell them and ask their advice. Police might be better. Could be some CCTV footage – a camera got put up in the area last month according to Stu. DPI might even be able to use this for some more publicity.'

Ceris handed back the photo to Jon who stared at it. 'Feel pretty helpless?' she said.

Jon got up. 'I've got to do something. I know it's silly, but it's on my mind and I just have this feeling. I'll go and make some calls.'

As he went to go upstairs again, Jon hadn't noticed that someone else had already sneaked out of the living room and was making her own important phone call in a bedroom.

'Duncan, if you loved me you'd do this for me. We've got him worried, but it could get messy for us.'

Nicki got out a nail file and started on her left hand as she balanced her phone between her neck and shoulder. 'I don't care if you *think* no-one saw you. Knowing your incompetence you probably smiled at the CCTV cameras without realising after you bundled it into the car. The damn thing's too much of liability. Get rid of the kitty.' The nail on her little finger was splitting. 'I need to win this, and I don't want it coming back to me. You know what you gotta do.'

Still frowning at her imperfect nail, she interrupted her boyfriend's pleas. 'Duncan! Someone else will find it and identify it. Don't let me down – just kill the sodding cat.'

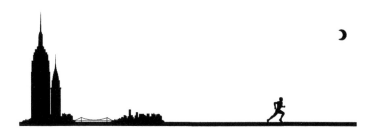

Chapter 29

'**P**USSIES.'

Jackson was addressing the ten runners as they sat huddled around their trainer in Central Park. It was going to be a warm day and the park would no doubt attract a large amount of visitors as people made the most of the weeks before winter came and engulfed New York. However, at 6am the dew sparkled on the grass in the early light and a cool breeze tried its best to jump down the necks of the runners' DPI fleeces.

'Yes...pussies. That's what I thought when I first laid eyes on you lot. But that was two and a half months ago. You've all come a long way since then. Now I regard you as...' he stroked his chin, as if thinking for an inspirational adjective, 'pussies...who can run a bit.'

Jon wondered for the first time whether he might miss Jackson after the marathon. As much as the big lump of meat had indirectly inflicted more pain on Jon's body than he'd ever experienced and had the social skills of a buffalo with a bad cold, he had pushed Jon to achieve far more than he thought he ever could. In three weeks, it would all come to a peak and straight after they would all go their separate ways.

'I hope you're all ready this morning, as today will be the toughest day of your training. This will be your biggest run. Forget the half marathons, even the fifteen miler you've done. We're into serious, leg-killing, energy-sapping, mind-warping distance running. I want you to do twenty miles. If you can't make that – if you're on your knees begging for mercy – then I want eighteen. Because if you can't do this now, then you may as well take your pussy arse home and let the real runners fight over the prize.'

Just the thought of twenty miles made Jon feel queasy. Twenty miles was the sort of distance you would see on a road sign and think is still a fair way to go travelling in a car. Worse was the length of time he'd be on his feet – over three hours, according to the pace Jackson was recommending.

'This is as bad as it will get. It's not a race, so there are no other runners to tag along with. No crowd will be cheering you on. No family, medal or even goodie bag will await you at the finish. Hour after hour you will be putting one foot in front of the other for no other reason than you have to do it.'

As Jackson let his words sink in, Arjun broke the silence. 'Thanks for the motivational speech, boss.'

'You want motivation? How about we try out the staggered starts today?'

'The *what* starts?' Danny said as everyone exchanged puzzled glances.

'Staggered, as in one person sets off one minute ahead of the next. No-one's told you yet about Mr Peabody's idea?' Jackson watched ten heads shake sideways. 'To make it interesting, and to raise more money, the first person to start the marathon will be the one who's raised the most amount of money for their charity. A minute later, the one with the next highest amount raised will start, and so on.'

'That's not fair,' Nicki said.

'Why not?' Ceris said.

'What's raising money for charity got to do with racing?' Nicki replied.

'Could be worse, Nicki,' Danny said. 'Could be based on popularity, then you'd be right stuffed.'

'All right, enough about that. You know the deal, but you won't know your positions until race day. Is that clear? Any questions?'

Jon hugged himself for extra warmth and was silent with everyone else.

'Good,' Jackson said. 'Right, I'm off to the diner but will see you guys again at eight for warm-ups for a nine o'clock start.' He turned and started to head off out of the park.

'What about us?' Arjun said. 'What are we supposed to do for two hours?'

'Whatever you want,' Jackson said without looking back. 'It's preparation for the marathon – lots of sitting and waiting in the cold. Enjoy.'

'I can't believe DPI will treat us like all the other runners,' Natasha said to the group. 'I expected to be tucked up in bed, fast asleep in a plush hotel at 6am and helicoptered in to the start line just before the off.'

'They want us to…' Tom fought to remember the exact words in the email about the events on the day, 'appreciate the whole marathon experience, the same as every one of the fifty thousand athletes taking part.'

'Yeah right, I bet the real celebrities get star treatment. No queuing up for a squirt in a manky Portaloo without any toilet paper for their VIP arses.'

They each had a drawstring bag of clothes and items they would survive on for the day. Jermaine had brought along a few newspapers which he was now sharing with the rest of the group, utilising them as makeshift picnic blankets to sit on to provide some protection from the damp ground. A small table housed a large supply of bagels and hot water for tea and coffee, as well as water and energy drinks. A single, dark-blue portable toilet had been placed twenty metres away from the circle of ten, looking like Doctor Who had come to visit the planet of orange-clad aliens.

'You must be the man to beat, eh, Jon?' Arjun said.

'Nah. Don't fancy it today. Be glad just to make it back alive,' Jon replied.

'Aw, come on Jon. I'm sure Nicki's desperate to get one over you again after last time. Not the same if you're not competing.'

'If his head's not in it, then he's got no chance anyway,' Nicki said.

'It's not a race, though, is it?' Ceris said. 'It's just about getting the miles on the clock.'

'Exactly,' Jon said. He got up and grabbed a bagel from the table, knocking several more onto the floor before apologising.

'Still searching for pussy, Jon?' Kieran said.

'If you mean my cat, yeah. Not been sighted at all.'

'What did the police say?' Ceris said.

'Not much. Apparently they were satisfied that my

neighbour wasn't involved in Conan's disappearance and that he was in fact "perversely missing pitting his wits against the critter".' He decided not to add the recent news that someone had handed in his collar and name tag, found about a mile away from his house. He knew it didn't necessarily mean the cat had come to any harm, but it wasn't an encouraging sign, either.

'He'll turn up, don't worry,' Ceris said. 'Probably sitting on the doorstep, looking as if he'd been away on holiday and wondering what all the fuss was about.'

After finishing a bagel, Jon lay down on the newspapers and tried to pass away the time by thinking of all the possible locations where Conan might be. Over two hours later, Jon was no less comforted.

'Any slower and I'm gonna have to give you a torch for the finish,' Jackson said to Jon who had dropped off considerably from the other nine runners, despite starting fifth in the staggered start. It had only been two miles and the trainer had jogged on the spot for a while until Jon had caught up. 'Problem?'

'No. Pacing it slow. Long run,' Jon said.

'You'll get nowhere at this pace. You're better than this, Jon. Pick it up gradually, half a minute quicker next two miles.'

It didn't feel right, concerning himself about pace in a training run when he had other worries. He'd thought about asking to go home, just for two or three days. He could comb the streets for Conan, call out his name, knock on doors, and search all the likely places a cat could get lost in around where the collar was found. Jon allowed his concern to fuel his legs, and upped his pace so that after eight miles he was comfortably in the middle of the line of runners.

Grabbing a cup of water just after Jackson had indicated the halfway stage, Jon thought about it again. Conan was just a cat, an animal, capable of fending for himself, maybe even finding a new home. Jon let out a little laugh at the thought of Conan nonchalantly chucking off his collar and leaping into the house of a rich widower, into a life of smoked salmon, cushions and a cosy fire. His dad had always told him never to worry about anything out of his control, and this would be a prime candidate for another classic Dad lecture. Not that he'd spoken to him much recently. How long would it be now? Two weeks? Mum always seemed to answer the phone and it seemed she had been fussing round Dad relentlessly after his cold. All the thought of family meant the fifteen-mile mark came up unexpectedly. Suddenly Jon was in unchartered territory.

'Under five to go,' Ceris said to Jon. Arjun, Nicki, Kieran and Danny were ahead of them and Ceris seemed content to run at her own pace and finish in whatever position she ended up with as a result. This suited Jon, so he decided to tag along for as long as his legs could take it. They jogged on in silence, mostly as they knew they needed to reserve all forms of energy, and even one word was a luxury they couldn't afford. But it was more than that – an unspoken connection between two runners that simply said, 'I'll go on if you go on.' By sixteen miles, Jon's autopilot was only interrupted by the sight of the rear of Nicki rapidly coming towards him. She had stopped and was frantically rubbing her left calf. The pair slowed, and as they caught Nicki, Ceris forced out a 'What's up?'

'Nothing,' Nicki said, pushing her hand down harder

over the muscle. 'Just leave me alone, I'll overtake you later.'

Ceris and Jon looked at each other and jogged off.

Somewhere between seventeen and eighteen miles, Ceris looked over her shoulder at Jon. 'You okay?'

One by one, Jon's leg muscles were shutting down. 'Not good. Go on without me.' He shifted his weight and tried to utilise other, slightly fresher muscles, leading to an ungainly gait and a slower pace.

'Sorry,' Ceris said as the gap between them increased. 'Need to keep rhythm. Good luck.' Jon stumbled as his right foot failed to properly clear the ground on its way forward. He looked round to see Nicki still some way behind, probably throwing virtual daggers in his direction.

By eighteen miles, Jon was barely matching walking pace. In an effort to prevent himself grinding completely to a halt, he began to push his now-awkward running style into something resembling a jog.

Half a mile later by a large curb, Jon was screaming in pain, clutching a rapidly-swelling ankle and fearing that his marathon adventure was well and truly over.

Chapter 30

THEY all looked like idiots and they knew it. They'd got used to wearing the orange of DPI over the last few months, mainly due to the well-designed running gear that had been provided. For the six-mile race in Manhattan however – their final race before the marathon two weeks later – the company had decided to do something different.

'Check out Barbarella over there!' Kieran nodded towards Ceris.

'Wow – she's got more curves than a classic Ferrari,' Arjun said.

Ceris strode over to the boys in her tight-fitting outfit. It was a one-piece, padded ensemble, designed to look like a futuristic space jumpsuit, but made from materials that allowed its wearer to comfortably run in it without soaking themselves in sweat. She examined the white fabric, criss-crossed with small orange lightning bolts.

'These costumes were obviously designed by a man. Nothing's been left to the imagination,' Ceris said.

'Oh I dunno,' Kieran said. 'You look like one yummy

Christmas present – one that you know exactly what it is from the wrapping, but you can't open it yet.'

Ceris stuck out her tongue at him and folded her arms. 'I can't believe I have to run in this.'

'Well I think you look stunning, Ceris,' Jermaine said. 'Sporty but glamorous at the same time.'

'Thank you, Jermaine. I'll see how glamorous I look at the end, though.'

'At least you don't look like a space pilot from some tacky futuristic film,' Kieran said.

Everyone's outfits had been tailor-made for each runner, but it was clear that the men's were a lot less prone to revealing the extent of nature's gifts to its owners. They were also the inverse in colour to the women's, with a bright orange suit, white flashes and a white running number across the chest.

'I think the look they're going for is astronauts,' Tom said, sheepishly appearing to join them in his full race outfit, with Nicki alongside him.

'Or stars from a sci-fi porn movie,' Arjun said.

'No pockets, though,' Barry said. 'Where am I supposed to store my banana?'

'Do you really want a response to that?' Danny said.

'Leave it,' Barry replied. 'But at least we're not the only ones here in fancy dress.'

DPI had pulled out all the stops to ensure that a special race had been slotted in before the marathon, one designed to maximise publicity and increase the build-up for the big one a fortnight later. It was an all fancy dress event, organised and paid for entirely by DPI, who had even managed to have some roads temporarily blocked off for the five hundred runners, of which the ten Moon Runners were unashamedly meant to be the main attraction.

'At least you're running.' Jon came over and leaned an elbow on Ceris's shoulder. 'I still have to wear this outfit even with my crutches.'

'Shouldn't you be at home resting your ankle?' Nicki said. 'Don't know why you're still over here anyway, it's obvious you're properly crocked.'

Ceris put an arm round Jon's waist. 'Didn't think he'd get any sympathy from the woman who saw him trip and then just ran past him.'

'It's a competition, Ceris. If, like in a parallel universe or something, you two are battling it out for first place, do you think he will stop and help you out if you fall?' Nicki said.

'I'm just surprised you didn't kick him as you went past.'

Nicki smoothed down her suit. Her body in it was as sharp as her tongue. 'Well sorry if I'm not the little Samaritan that you obviously must be, but you lot are deluded if you think we're all life-long friends in this little adventure. You don't achieve success by being nice. I'm sure Doug Peabody didn't make DPI into what it is by helping his poor competitors along the way.'

'He'll be here later. Maybe you can ask him how many heads he crushed along the way and compare figures.'

Nicki cocked her head and sneered, walking off towards a water stand.

'Dammit,' Arjun said. 'Was hoping for a full-on cat fight there. Jonny Boy – you're not finished yet, are you?'

Jon was about to answer when he caught sight of Leona, microphone in hand, beckoning him to join her.

'Hi Jon, how's the ankle?' Leona pointed the microphone at Jon as the DPI camera switched to him.

'Not so good, unfortunately.'

'We heard it was quite a fall.'

'Well, I was going along, about eighteen miles in, and I just trod on the curb awkwardly, twisted my ankle and landed heavily on it.'

'No plans to sue the state of New York then?'

'Er, no. Just clumsy, I guess.'

'What your fans want to know, though, is...will you be fit enough to enter the marathon in just two weeks' time?'

Jon didn't immediately reply. It was, of course, the only question really worth asking at this stage, and the one he'd been asking himself ever since last Sunday. 'I dunno. It's not looking good.'

'I'm sure DPI has the best medical team looking after you and will get you on that starting line, Jon.' Leona gave a big smile. 'So, what do you think of Arjun? He's most people's tip for the prize. Or how about Nicki?'

'Arjun's a great runner, very strong. I'm not sure about Nicki. She's very determined, but may have weak calves.' He congratulated himself for getting in a cheap dig when she wasn't around to hear.

'Now, any news on Conan? You have got thousands of fans worried about the little tyke's whereabouts.'

'Nothing, I'm afraid.' He turned to the camera. 'If there's anyone out there with any knowledge, any clues, possible sightings, please, please come forward. He means a lot to me, and I just want to know he's safe.'

'Yes,' Leona said, grabbing the camera back, 'and don't forget DPI's one thousand pound reward for information leading to his safe return. Plus, you will get an all-expenses paid trip to New York for the marathon.'

Jon briefly wondered if DPI specialised in headline-grabbing cat-nappings.

'So thanks Jon, and all the best for a speedy recovery. Now let's find Ceris and get her opinion on those amazing outfits.'

Jon hobbled nearby to where the nine other DPI runners were warming up, Jackson once again taking them through their paces. The trainer, he noticed, wasn't kitted out in fancy dress, perhaps due to there not being a big enough design for him, or maybe because there was no-one who valued their life so little as to approach him with the proposal that he wear it. Jon heard a whooshing sound up high and searched the clouds. He could make out an orange helicopter approaching them, slowing as if inspecting the scene below. The PA system announced that this was the arrival of Doug Peabody, who was about to land at the nearby downtown helipad. Jon hadn't seen him since the press conference, with all those revelations about the Moon trip. Most of the concentration had been on the marathon, with little information on the trip itself. He'd spent many hours in his room researching previous Moon trips, dreaming of what it would be like. As he watched the others finish their routines, he could see just how ready they were, prepared for the race and to grab the prize. Energy, suppleness, enthusiasm were in abundance – everything Jon felt he was losing by the minute.

Nicki went to walk past him.

'Watch those dodgy calves,' Jon said.

She stopped. 'It was just a bit of cramp. Unlike some, I still finished the race.'

'It was a training run, and at least I'd done eighteen. Perhaps this rest might do me good.'

'Dream on, loser. Anyway, haven't you got to go home and mourn for your cat?'

'He's not dead. They'll find him.'

Nicki just blinked and resumed her journey to the start. She knew she had a text message confirming otherwise.

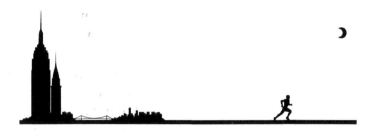

Chapter 31

DOUG had been looking forward to the race all week. He knew he didn't have the time for such a trip, but then he also knew that even if he never slept and installed a commode as his office chair, he would still not be able to complete all the tasks on his list. Today was a brief respite from the chaos of running his company, and a chance to meet the heroes who were living his dream.

'Looks like you've been doing a tremendous job with these ladies and gentlemen.' Doug shook Jackson's hand and slapped him sideways on the shoulder. 'Are they ready for inspection?'

'Primed and ready to go, sir,' Jackson replied, and then took him to the DPI runners.

'First of all,' Doug said, addressing everyone together, 'may I say how wonderful you all look.' There were a few snorts of laughter as they self-consciously looked at themselves in their costumes. 'I can see by your faces that this isn't everyone's idea of Sunday morning pleasure, and I must admit I hadn't realised the women's outfits would be so…exact fitting, but just remember it's all about keeping you and DPI in the news, getting the sponsorship money rolling in and above all – having fun.'

'It could be worse,' Arjun said, 'you could have made us dress up like that.' He pointed towards a runner in a large rhino costume.

'We tried, but unfortunately they didn't have them in orange.' Doug made a few of them smile and went up to each of them for a few words. Jon had stepped back from the others who were due to run, but Doug made an effort to go and see him.

'Ah, Jon. Nice to see you again,' Doug said, greeting Jon with a firm handshake. 'How's the old ankle?'

'Hi, Mr Peabody. Could be better, thanks.' Jon looked down at his heavily-padded foot.

'I'm sure our medical team will sort it out for you and get you back on the run.'

'Maybe. We'll see.'

'No maybe about it. You didn't come all this way to fall at the last hurdle.' He turned round to face them all again. 'Right, better go – I have a race to start. Best of luck, everyone.'

Doug strode his way through jesters with jangly hats, male fairies in pink skirts, Catwoman, Wonder Woman, a walking Chrysler Building and what was probably The Three Stooges tied together at their feet, until he reached a man standing by a stepped platform. They checked their watches, exchanged a few words and, after a minute or so, the man climbed up the steps and introduced Doug. He hoped this was being beamed to China.

'Ladies, gentlemen and other assorted creatures, mythical beasts and inanimate objects.' He waited for the expected laughs. 'May I welcome you all to the first DPI Manhattan 10K.' A round of applause followed. It was a glorious, if surreal, sight of clashing colours, frills, hats and props, and yet underneath were hundreds of runners limbering up, smiling in the autumnal sun. 'Two weeks from now, New York will hold one of the biggest single sporting events in terms of participation – the New York City Marathon. As you should know, we have the Moon Runners here in their final phase of training for that race. Where are you guys?' The nine runners waved, jumped and whooped.

'As you can see – I hope – they're dressed as astronauts. For one of them, they will get to wear the real thing, and the opportunity to go down in history. I am proud to be able to offer it to them, and am honoured and delighted at the commitment they have shown in getting here.' A ripple of applause.

'But today is not just about them. I wanted to provide a race where everyone could join in and have fun. So it is with great pleasure that I give you all 5...4...3...2...1' Doug pressed a hooter in the air and the first line of people dressed in less-restrictive outfits surged forward through an arch of orange balloons. He watched everyone pass underneath him, waving to and even saluting his runners as they jogged past, thirty seconds after the initial group. After the last runner went by dressed as Mr. Stay Puft, Doug stepped down and met Jackson.

'We have a buggy waiting for you, sir,' Jackson said. 'We can take you to the halfway stage to see the runners there.'

Doug smiled and nodded, following Jackson a short way to where a driver was waiting in a white cart that looked like it had been stolen from an airport. Doug got in and waited for Jackson to join him. When the trainer closed the door without getting in, Jackson answered Doug's quizzical expression.

'I prefer to run. I'll catch the space cadets at two miles, meet you over at three.'

With that, he ran off via a short-cut, leaving Doug alone in the back, facing behind as the cart started off. As they pulled away, Doug saw an isolated, orange figure on crutches. 'Driver – could you please swing it around? I want to pick up someone.'

'I guess I did feel a bit useless, standing there with nothing to do,' Jon said, having gratefully accepted the offer of a lift. The two men sat opposite each other as the cart gradually made its way round a grassy area.

'I fully appreciate that it's not fun, being out injured. Occasionally, it happened to me of course,' Doug said.

'How did you handle it?'

'Listened to what the doctor told me.' Doug saw Jon nodding. 'Then, on the whole, ignored it.'

Jon laughed. 'They've said I might be able to run on it in two weeks, but no-one thinks it'll last the marathon.'

'Who cares what they think – do *you* think it can last the marathon?' He studied Jon's face as he thought about the question.

'Honestly? No, I don't.'

'Well then, that's easy to fix. You see no-one can really know for sure – it's your body, your marathon. Just start believing. If you don't believe, then it's not going to happen. But this isn't Father Christmas we're talking about – the opposite can be true. If you believe, then it very much *can* happen.'

'I might risk damaging it further, though. So they said to me. Is it really worth the pain?'

'Tell me Jon – do you really want to go to the Moon? How much do you want it?'

Jon fiddled with the zip on his costume. 'My parents gave me a certificate on my tenth birthday, saying I now owned an acre of the Moon. Dad pointed out to me the spot where it was that night under a blue-black sky. Every time the Moon phase uncovered my little plot, I would lean out the window and imagine standing on it, looking back at Earth. I'd love the chance to see it, Mr Peabody.'

Doug breathed in deeply and leaned forward, lowering his voice so only Jon would hear. 'Can I tell you something?'

'Sure,' Jon said, looking a little worried.

'I have a problem. A huge problem. Bigger than a blister, a sore calf or a dodgy ankle. My reputation is on the line. Vast amounts of money are involved. Dmitri – my competitor – might not be too far behind me, and right now I don't exactly know how to solve my problem. So I'm taking a risk, a gamble, a real do-or-die move. And do you know why?'

Jon shook his head.

'Because the risk is so very much worth the reward. Because I believe it's the right thing to do. Because I'll regret it forever if I just take the easy way out.'

Jon looked into Doug's eyes and then out onto the park.

Doug leaned back. 'Do you ever play poker, Jon?'

'A bit. Texas Hold'em with my mates occasionally.'

'You and me – we're both pot-committed right now. We've put so much into the bet that it would be unwise to walk away. We know we've got good hands but suddenly we're not sure we can win. Maybe if we stay in we'll lose. But one thing is sure: if we fold, lose we most definitely will.'

Jon smiled.

'Is that funny?' asked Doug.

'No, it's just…you sounded like Yoda there.'

Doug laughed and slapped his thighs with both hands. 'I've been called a lot of things in my time…'

'I'm sorry, I didn't mean any offence, I –'

'It's okay, none taken.' Doug composed himself. 'Just think about it, that's all. Oh, and another thing – seeing as I'm meant to be a wise old man giving advice to a young *Padawan* – use a mantra.'

'A what?'

'A mantra, a chant, a phrase – something that'll keep you running when times are really tough. Say it over and over and the magic will work. You may be racing nine others, but the real battle is against your own mind. Win that, and you stand a chance. Look into it and get yourself one.'

Jon nodded. They carried on in silence for a minute. Up ahead, Jon could see that they were catching the runners. 'So why aren't you racing today?'

Doug opened his mouth to give his answer but stopped, before saying, 'You know what? I don't know.' His legs suddenly felt uncomfortable. 'I guess I didn't think about it, didn't bring any running gear.'

'So you're saying the great Doug Peabody forgot his kit? That even he couldn't borrow something and teach us all a thing or two?'

Doug stared at Jon. He couldn't remember the last time he'd been spoken to like this by someone who wasn't his peer. 'You're right. My God, you're right. We're runners. I'm a runner and I've organised a race that I'm not even in.' He turned round. 'Driver – change of plan. Take us back to the start line please as fast as you can. I've got some catching up to do!'

If there ever was a race to run in your business clothes, then a fancy dress one would be a good candidate, Doug thought as he crossed the start. Shirt sleeves rolled up, suit jacket tied to his neck like a cape, the only new kit he was wearing was a pair of running shoes which he obtained from a donor who was more than pleased to accept a pair of five-hundred-pound Italian shoes in return. He felt just as ridiculous as the half-chicken, half-Staten Island ferry man he had recently overtaken. The TV cameras hadn't caught wind of his antics yet and most of the crowd in the first two miles had moved on, but this was all good to Doug – the race was all about everyone else, after all. For once, he was content just to be a sideshow. He was going far too fast to maintain his usual 10K pace, especially with only the merest of stretches before he'd run off, but what a thrill! From being transported from place to place, guided, led, ushered, told where he had to be, shoved in cars, helicopters, buggies…to being free to run with the breeze through his hair, sweat making a mockery of his tailored shirt and as care-free as a child. 'Isn't this fantastic?' he shouted to a surprised marshal as he ran past. He glided past an egg, Superman with cramp and both Batman and Robin, encouraging them all as he overtook. At halfway, he saw Jon, who he had asked to be ferried around in the buggy.

'Go on Dougie! I mean – Mr Peabody!' Jon shouted.

Doug waved and laughed to himself. Perfect, he thought. At this moment he was 'Dougie', just wrapped in a Mr Peabody outfit.

At four miles, the media had realised what was going on and had sent cameramen racing back down the course to see the one-man circus for themselves. Doug suspected that his PR team were having a meltdown right now, cursing their leader for not letting them in on the non-existent plan. They should know to expect the unexpected from him by now, he reckoned. He had slowed down to a more casual pace after his fast start, regretting he'd not made time recently for training runs.

'Don't worry about me,' Doug said to the cameras as he removed his suit jacket and tie and untucked his shirt. 'Catch me at the end – the Moon Runners and everyone else are the stars. Go on – go!'

Regardless of his instructions, he was a big enough story to be tracked throughout. Jogging the last half mile to great applause, he looked like a schoolboy running home for tea. He had stopped several times to help struggling runners, and even joined in as a fourth Stooge along the way. When he crossed the finish line a good twenty minutes after his DPI runners, he bent over and grasped his knees. Before he knew it, a medal hung round his neck. Leona came rushing over, 'Mr Peabody – congratulations! However, I didn't see an email about your intentions to run.'

'That's probably because,' Doug said, trying to get his breath back, 'I hadn't intended to run. Someone gave me a wake-up call.'

'Oh, I see. Well…we still managed to get you in action for most of it.'

'Enough about me – how are my runners?'

'I think the boys struggled with the suits a little more than the girls. Nicki won by some distance, although I'm not sure if the others were really trying to win.'

'Good, good. As long as they all enjoyed themselves.'

'I'm sure they did, sir. They're waiting to see you at the changing area.'

'Great. I'll go over soon. Hang on – Jon! Jon!' Doug had spotted Jon making his way to the other runners and jogged up to him.

'Mr Peabody,' Jon said as Doug caught him. 'You might start a new trend in office sportswear.'

'You think? I'll get my guys to speak to Nike in the morning.' Doug shook Jon's hand. 'I just wanted to thank you for rominding mo why I am doing all this.'

'Some would say you did it for publicity, to promote DPI.'

'Indeed. But what do you think, Jon?'

'That it's true.'

Doug waited for what he hoped would be an addendum.

'But,' Jon continued, 'I can see you have a real passion, too. You can't fake that.'

Doug nodded. 'I'm going to do my damned best to solve my big problem. Are you back in the game?'

Jon looked down at his ankle and then back at a beaming, re-energised Doug. 'Well how else am I gonna get to the Moon?'

Chapter 32

'**Y**OU guys had better practise seeing this sight.' Nicki held up an article in the New York Times with a small picture of her crossing the line celebrating. 'Because you're gonna be seeing it again in less than two weeks.'

It was the Tuesday after the race and they'd all been given a rest day at the house.

'I don't think so, Nicola. I wasn't even trying on Sunday,' Arjun said as he tried to find out if there was English football on any channel.

'Only my mum calls me Nicola, and then only when I've done something bad.'

'Which must be quite frequent, I bet,' Ceris said, raising her eyebrows.

'Anyway, even if you did try, Arjun, I doubt you'd have caught me. Don't reckon you've got it mentally.'

'You certainly win in the mental stakes, Nic-o-la,' Arjun said.

'It's *Nicki*. You're just jealous. Reckon I'll look good in a space suit.'

Jon couldn't help joining in. 'You wouldn't survive the

journey. They'll shove you in an escape pod before you get out of the Earth's atmosphere.'

Arjun and Ceris both laughed.

'At least I have a chance,' Nicki said to Jon. 'You might have just crawled over the line by the time we're all flying back.' She got up, grabbed Ceris's toy dragon and threw it towards Jon. 'Here, take Dewi. Looks like you'll need a new pet.' She ignored the glares as she went into the kitchen.

'Here we go – Birmingham versus Villa. Just in time,' Arjun said, as the kick-off appeared on the big screen.

Jon tossed Dewi up a few times and caught him. 'I'm going up to my room to do some exercises, hopefully strengthen the ankle.'

'Don't let the sour bitch get you down. Conan will be okay, and your ankle will heal in time,' Ceris said.

'Don't worry, I'm staying positive. Just don't think I can stand the excitement of a Midlands derby in the cup. It's got nil-nil and penalties written all over it.'

'No way, man. Three-nil Birmingham all day,' Arjun said.

Jon went upstairs and was halfway through his exercise plan when his mobile rang. It was an English number he didn't recognise. 'Hello?'

'Hey stranger.'

'Summer?'

'The one and only. How's things? Is that ankle any better?'

'Wow, yeah, I mean...the swelling's gone down but I haven't put much weight on it yet.' He tried to recall their last conversation. 'How was Washington?'

'It went well, thanks. See? That's what I like about you

Jon – you remember things like that. However, I didn't phone up to chat about work – I've got some important news.'

'You're having your boss's baby?'

Summer sighed. 'And then there's the unsubtle side of you that I'm not so keen on.'

'Sorry, just kinda came out.'

'Actually, the annulment has finally been sorted.'

A part of Jon that he thought he'd lost high-fived itself. 'Cool, I'm happy for you, I guess.'

'But that's not the news I need to tell you about. Something much better. Are you alone?'

Jon checked his bedroom door was shut. 'Yeah, go ahead.'

'I've found Conan.'

Jon's heart quickened. 'Really?'

'Yep. Safe and well.'

'Are you sure? Where? How? It's definitely Conan?'

'I can email you a photo if you want, but comparing him to all the photos you released it's definitely a match. Plus I met his cat-napper.'

'What? He was taken? Who by? Is he all right?'

'Relax – as I said, he's fine. Glad to be home, by the looks of it. It's a bit of a story, so sit tight.'

Jon thought for a second. 'When you say home, do you mean my flat?'

'Yes, I'm here in your flat with Conan, who's on his second helping of cat nibbles.'

He suddenly had an overwhelming urge to pack up and catch the next flight home. 'How'd you get in?'

'Your mother gave me the key.'

'Oh. But...don't take this the wrong way, but why would my mother just give you my key?'

'As I said, a bit of a story...'

As Summer went on, Jon was amazed to hear that she had been taking an active interest in Conan's disappearance. She had put up posters around the town, knocked on doors, even given his neighbour with the garden webcam a grilling. After getting nowhere, she decided to think a little differently, which led her to Nicki.

'What's she got to do with it?' asked Jon.

'It was a wild guess. The disappearance happened so soon after you beat her, and even without speaking to you I knew she wouldn't be happy with that. You were suddenly a challenger, Jon. I did a little digging and found she had a boyfriend. I figured a girl as nice as Nicki might not have too many friends, so perhaps her boyfriend would be an ideal accomplice.'

'You saying Nicki got her boyfriend to take Conan? I thought she lived in Nottingham?'

'She does, and so does he. Conan went on a long trip.'

'So you just went up there on a hunch that he might be there?' Jon asked.

'Not quite. I made a contact via the website who helped me acquire the details of his address, and also some credit card transactions he'd made.'

'Jesus. I won't ask exactly how they did that. Hang on – what website?'

'Conan's.' Summer made a little cough. 'Okay, look – Conan's website? The one with the imagined adventures? That's me.'

'Seriously? You did that?'

'Yep. I saw your blog on him and got drawn into it. A few people had done tributes to him and one night I just got imagining and it turned into the website.'

'Wow.'

'Anyway, I had problems with the site and one of the forum users helped, and it turned out he knew a lot about other things, too.'

'You said about credit card transactions?'

'I thought it was strange that someone in Nottingham just happened to fill up petrol over a hundred miles away in Stevenage twice, once near the disappearance and another on the day his collar was found.'

'Son of a bitch! Make that – boyfriend of a bitch. Why would she do that? Actually, don't answer that.' Beating her in a race and denying her sex were two reasons, he thought. Being pure evil was a certain third.

'So I went up there, used my charm to schmooze my way into the house and, lo and behold, I found Conan.'

'That's brilliant, Summer. So I guess the police are dealing with it now?'

'Um, not exactly.'

'What do you mean? Surely he'd get charged, implicate Nicki and we'll stuff both of them.'

'None of that is guaranteed. He cracked when I pushed him about Conan, admitting that he'd taken him. But he said he'd deny that Nicki told him to do it.'

'But why? I'd dump the blame on her before they even started reading me my rights.'

'Because he's scared of her. He's so wrapped around her little finger he's taken root in it. And even if he did somehow dob her in, she'd probably deny it, say it was all his fault. He made a point to say there was no evidence of her involvement.'

Jon got off the bed and looked out towards a grey sky. 'So now what?'

'We need to get proof that she was involved, let her implicate herself. Duncan – her boyfriend – said he would keep up the pretence to Nicki that Conan was dead for the moment so –'

'Whoa, wait a minute – dead? Why would Nicki think he was dead?'

'Ah, yes, the icing on the cake. Nicki ordered Duncan to get rid of the cat to avoid anyone finding the evidence and possibly tracing it back to her.'

Jon was momentarily speechless. He wanted to go downstairs and strangle her until she was blue, and then carry on some more. 'I can't fucking believe this. She'd have killed Conan?'

'Putting my Wicked Witch of Nottingham hat on, I guess she had a point – the very fact Conan was still alive and in her boyfriend's house confirmed the whole story. Heartless, but not stupid. Fortunately for you and Conan, Duncan's a wimp who couldn't go through with it. Not that he could tell Nicki that.'

'I'll just confront her, have it out. Blast her with the facts.' Jon walked around his bed and back again. 'She'll crack, or...I'll tell Doug and get her thrown out the competition.'

'No, Jon. You need to calm down. That could all backfire and achieve nothing.'

Jon thumped a wall. 'But I have to –'

'I have a plan.'

'Unless it involves getting her thrown in jail or subjecting her to unprecedented pain, then I'm not interested.'

'If you can stay calm, live with this knowledge for a while, we can get her…really get her.'

'No, we need to act now. She ain't getting away with this, Summer. I won't let her.'

'She won't get away with it. I know I've said this before, but you're gonna have to trust –'

'The only thing I trust right now is my instinct to go kill her.'

'Jon, I want to nail her almost as much as you do.'

'So when exactly do you suggest?'

'Race day. She wants to win so badly, we'll hit her where and when it really hurts.'

Jon thought about it. 'So I have to keep this in for a week and a half?'

'Afraid so. Still, you know what they say…' Summer cleared her throat nosily.

'No, what's that?'

'BortaS bIr jablu'DI' reH QaQqu' nay.'

Jon momentarily thought she'd lost it, before suddenly recognising the phrase and wondering if he'd crossed into a parallel dimension. 'Was that…Klingon?'

'Was that right? Please say that was right as I've been practising for an hour and think that I just killed my throat. I was hoping you'd like it.'

Jon wasn't sad enough to know the entire Klingon

language, but a few choice phrases had been committed to memory from his *Star Trek*-obsessed teenage years. 'It's not the literal translation, but was that, "Revenge is a dish best served cold"?'

'Hey – I did it!'

Jon heard her clapping herself down the phone. 'Wow,' Jon said. 'So is this a new course you're taking or are you a Trekkie?'

'That was especially for you. Anyway, focus. We'll keep the secret for the moment, keep Conan inside so he's not spotted and then go ahead with the plan, which I'll tell you about later. Got lots to sort out, so speak to you soon.'

With that, she went, leaving Jon to lie down on his bed and try to absorb everything that had hit him during the conversation while also trying not to worry about how a plan devised by a Klingon-speaking Summer might end up.

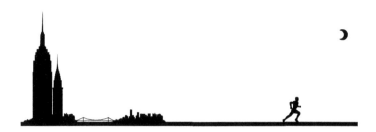

Chapter 33

WITH three days to go, Jon was looking forward to the big race day for the first time in ages. He'd done everything he had been told to protect and nurse his ankle back to fitness, and had every therapy DPI could arrange. The rest had done his leg muscles good, too. Visits to the swimming pool and using various cross-trainers had maintained his overall fitness to the extent where he felt fresh and prepared. All he needed was a couple of light runs to test the ankle and he'd be ready, although quite what ready was when the task was to run twenty-six miles for the first time, Jon didn't know.

With Conan out of harm's way, his mind was much clearer, although he tried as much as possible to avoid being in the same room as Nicki for fear of launching into a tirade of abuse. When they did have to share the same space, he kept well clear of sharp objects. The mood all round had shifted to one of anticipation; with the miles done and stored in their legs, the runners sat around like students waiting for exam day. Jackson had spoken to them about how to prepare physically and mentally on the day, and Leona had briefed them on the processes, the media responsibilities they had and what would happen if they won. This had later led to serious discussions between the ten about the Moon trip, now that the prize was in touching distance. Everyone was cool, excited, nervous and ready for the challenge, winding down the few days before Sunday.

On Thursday, that all changed when Arjun was sent flying over the bonnet of a Ford Fusion.

'You should see my x-ray – it's wicked!' Arjun said as everyone crowded round his hospital bed that afternoon.

'Jackson says he can still get you round the course with some high-intensity training and a few painkillers they use for elephants,' Danny said.

Arjun patted his leg cast. 'Us Brummies are tough, but not that tough. Looks like you've all got a chance now.' There was some shifting of feet. They could try to deny it, but everyone knew that a part of them was secretly relieved that the favourite was now out of the picture.

'What happened, exactly?' asked Natasha.

'It was stupid, really. I just went for a slow jog to loosen up the muscles, went to cross the road and looked in the wrong direction. Next thing I know I'm flying over the bonnet, into the air, thinking, "I'm in a little trouble here..."' Arjun shook his head. 'Crossed that road a dozen times, just made one mistake.'

'Don't you feel cheated?' Jermaine said. 'Like life's dealt you the worst card at the worst moment possible?'

'Nah. Don't get me wrong, I'm gutted at not being able to run, but it just wasn't meant to be, was it? Besides, could've been worse – could have been injured after twenty-five miles.'

'I'm so sorry, Arjun,' Ceris said. 'It won't be the same out there, just the nine of us.'

'What she means is that she'll miss looking at your arse,' Kieran said.

'Oh well, if I want another arse to stare at, I've always got your face,' Ceris replied, looking at Kieran.

'I had a video call from Peabody, said he was gutted for me but that I would be his guest of honour for the day.'

'He's actually quite decent, you know. Underneath the mad ideas,' Jon said.

'Yeah I noticed you two were rather pally at the end of the last race,' Nicki said.

'Ah, is the new favourite jealous?' Jon said.

'Not at all. Unless he was arranging to give you a bionic foot there's not much he can do to help you.'

'Jon's got nothing to lose,' Tom said. 'Nor have I – no-one expects either of us to win now so the pressure's off. Might just count for us.' He winked towards Jon.

'Well I'm hoping it'll be cold on the day. No-one copes better in the cold than us Geordies,' Natasha said.

The banter continued, until everyone had not only staked their case but had also played down their chances. The only thing they could all agree on was how unlucky Arjun had been.

After the hospital visit, Jon had decided to call his parents to update them on the latest events.

'Dad? Well, this is a first. Since when did Mum allow you to pick up?'

'Hi Jon. I managed to persuade her to get out of the house with your aunt for an hour. They've gone white-water rafting. Or maybe to the cinema. So, how's the leg?

Are you phoning to say you're giving up?'

'No, of course not. It's nowhere near one hundred percent, but I'm going to give it my best shot.'

'Winning's out of the question, though, I assume. Never mind.'

Jon shook his head. 'You never know, Arjun's just been injured and he's out of the race.'

'Oh. That's a shame. He had potential.'

And me? thought Jon. 'Well, there's only eight to beat now, and I'm hoping to nobble Nicki after what she's done.'

'Yes, she's a bad one, all right. Sounds like she'll beat you if you don't do something.'

'There's a plan, apparently.'

'Good, you need one. Of course, I'm sure everyone else will be stronger than you, you know, after your injury.'

Jon made a mental note to not make his dad his personal coach after getting home. 'Maybe I'll surprise you.'

'Maybe. So what's this plan?'

'I don't know yet. Summer's sorting it out, which is a little scary but –'

'Summer's a good girl. I like her.'

Jon frowned. He'd assumed his mum would have dealt with her over Conan. 'Oh, you met her?'

'Of course. She's been fantastic, helping with everything after my heart attack.'

Jon heard the blood rush in his ears for what seemed like minutes. 'Your what?'

'Oh, Jon, I–I'm sorry. I forgot. I–I–'

302

'You've had a heart attack?'

The pause was filled with weighty anticipation. 'We didn't want to worry you. It was weeks ago, but now –'

'Weeks ago?' Jon rose to his feet. 'You had a heart attack weeks ago and you didn't think I'd want to know?'

'I'm fine now, it was nothing. I didn't die, did I? I'm still here.'

'Dad – I should have been there!' Jon's vision started to get blurry.

'Your mum and I didn't want to upset you, affect your training. You had some crucial runs coming up, and then the whole Conan thing –'

'Sod the competition! As for Conan, I can't believe I thought Mum was not bothering enough with him – she must have been worried sick with you.' Another thought entered his head, and his face went white. He had to know. 'Dad, did you...have the attack when you were running?'

With every millisecond that passed without a reply, tears slid down Jon's face. He knew it. His influence, his own running, the race, and reports of how fit he was getting had all inspired his father who had lived quite happily for over sixty years on the couch to get up and emulate his son to the point he had nearly run himself into his grave.

'It was all my own doing,' his dad said. 'Bit silly at my age to start, in hindsight. Got me out of the house from under Mum's feet, though.'

'B–but if it wasn't for me, you'd never –'

'It's not your fault, could never be your fault.'

'No, I–I entered this, and I...I put you at risk, and Conan and –'

'Oh for crying out loud, Jon. Don't you see? Don't you get it? I was proud of you. I know a father should always be proud of his son but up to now you've always hidden, been frightened to take a step into the unknown. And yet this race, this competition…it's…it's made you come alive, made you push yourself.'

Jon wiped at his cheeks as his dad continued, 'I realised after all my own preaching I was just wasting away myself. Too cosy in retirement. I took up running after hearing about your efforts and you know what? It felt amazing. I felt young again, ready to conquer the world.'

'R–really?'

'Well, I did until I collapsed running past the football ground just before the Saturday kick-off. Gave the travelling Millwall fans something to laugh at for a minute, though.'

Jon blubbed a half-laugh. 'I don't…I don't know what to say.'

'Neither did they, once they saw it was serious. I'm sure I got a round of applause as I went into the ambulance.'

'Dad…'

'Look, I guess I've played down this marathon thing to you. At first, I didn't think you'd stick it out, but then I heard how well you were doing. With the injury, I didn't want you to get your hopes up, but what do I know?'

Jon composed himself enough to listen to his Dad's accounts of what happened at the hospital, how he was treating it as just a warning and how Jon's mum had wanted to wrap him in cotton wool and keep him inside, as well as protecting Jon from it all. It was only after this that he remembered the comments about Summer.

'Ah, Summer Breeze,' Jon's dad said. 'Is there a better

name for someone to meet after you've had a heart attack?'

'But how did she come into it?'

'Let me see…did you know about my heart attack?'

'No, until now, obviously.'

'Exactly.'

Jon searched for a clue to no avail.

'She helped keep it a secret, stopped it from getting out and inevitably back to you,' he said.

'But…how? She wasn't on the project any more. Peabody removed her from it weeks before.'

'Bit of luck. Local press sniffed around for a story, recognised my surname and phoned up their DPI PR contact for further details without knowing Summer had moved on. She then took over and ensured a media blackout, at our request.'

'Wow. She did all that for us?'

'Yep. Said she thought she owed us one, what with the drugs test thing.'

'I guess.'

'One more thing…'

'Dad…' Jon wasn't sure if he could handle any more revelations.

'You have to pretend to Mum that you don't know about all this.'

'C'mon Dad, no more secrets now. It just gets all messy.'

'Just promise.'

'Why?'

'Why do you think? If she knew I'd told you I'd nearly died she'll bloody well kill me.'

There was no way Jon could stay in the house after he had finished talking to his dad, so despite the weather, he went out on his own for a slow jog. Thick grey clouds swept over him as he ran along the promenade, sending down a drizzle that was trying its best to get through his beanie hat. A black waterproof running jacket and blue scarf kept out the worst of it, the latter wrapped round his face so that only a narrow band of flesh around his eyes was exposed. The wind came off the sea, pushing him sideways, sometimes gently as if guiding, other times causing him to veer wildly to his right.

'Keep going, you can do it, you have the strength, you have the strength,' Jon said out loud through his scarf as he slowly plodded on.

'First sign of madness, you know,' Ceris said as she pulled up alongside him.

'Oh, hi. Where did you come from?'

'Thought you might like some company. And to look after you in case that ankle goes again. But it seems I might have to watch your mental state.'

'Oh, you mean my mantra? That's my magic spell to repeat in the marathon.'

Ceris nodded under a yellow bobble hat and let Jon continue.

'Wanted something simple and easy to repeat in a rhythm. My ankle's gonna complain at some point, so I need to override the pain. You know, despite the crowds, the other runners and beautiful scenery, there will be points when we'll only exist in our minds, the only sounds we'll hear will be the constant screams of pain, doubts, orders to cease and rest. Nowhere to run inside our minds – we have to fight, Ceris.'

'Wow. What have you been reading?' she said, watching white puffs of air escape from Jon's mouth as he stared forward, slightly speeding up.

'Sorry, I'm in one of those moods. Just heard my dad's had a heart attack.'

'Oh my God, Jon.' Ceris reached out and out a hand on his shoulder. 'Is he...?'

'No, no, he's fine now, don't worry.' Jon turned and smiled. 'It's just...I feel different somehow. I've always had this image of him in a steel cage, impervious to harm, forovor there.'

'But he pulled through. You Dunn men are obviously made of strong stuff.'

'Maybe.'

'Will he be able to come over for the race?'

Jon laughed. 'His exact words were, "Son, I'll be there – even if I have to pack my own defibrillator."'

The two of them continued with just the sound of their trainers constantly hitting the boardwalk planks filling the air. Jon now pictured his dad's face as one of hope, instead of the disappointment that had always chiselled his features in Jon's mind. It was unfamiliar to him, and it would take some time to work it out.

The wind whipped the rain into their eyes, making the sea a blur against the darkening sky.

'You had enough?' Ceris said. 'Any darker and they'll send out a search party for us.'

Jon agreed and they turned for home.

'So do you think about winning?' Ceris said a short while later.

'Me? I'll give it a shot. If the ankle holds up.'

'If you're in it, you can win it. That's my new motto.'

'You been getting lessons from Peabody?'

Ceris frowned at Jon. 'Nope. But I've always been scared to push myself, so this time I'm going for it. Ceris the Astronaut. How cool would that be?'

Jon thought of the prize again. At times during training, it felt irrelevant in comparison to the race. 'Very cool. That's if Peabody can make it happen.'

'You sound like Natasha,' Ceris said as they surprised a couple of seagulls who took to the air. 'Well I'm putting my faith in him to deliver. How hard can it be?'

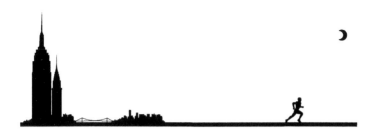

Chapter 34

A lot of people within DPI considered Doug to be inspirational, a pioneer, even a maverick. Some people thought he was crazy, careless and a liability to the company. Doug was having one of those days where the people of the latter persuasion would be running around saying, 'I told you so' and working out how to get the loopy CEO out of the company before he brought it all down. It was just as well that those people were not here to see what game he was playing. And that game was chess.

As ideas go, he thought it was ingenious. Doug had worked hard with the Chinese company to negotiate the deal for DPI to use their rocket, to have their logo painted on the side, to be huge sponsors of mankind's first trip back to the Moon. The trouble was, they had still insisted on a Chinese national going along instead of one of the Moon Runners, which they had only half-promised could go in a later launch. Despite all the angles Doug gave them – including an outlandish bluffed promise to get them the football World Cup in twelve years' time – they hadn't budged an inch. That was until he attacked his counterpart's true competitive nature and challenged him to a game of chess. If Doug won, he proposed, he would get to choose who goes on the flight. If he lost, not only would the Chinese get to choose, but Doug would also be forced to double his investment. 'Think how much more you could prove to the world – how great your company, your nation, is with that extra money,' he had said. A bit of boasting of Doug's own chess skills followed and, much to his amazement, they had agreed and shaken on it. Of course, Doug knew it was a huge risk, but with the recent news that Dmitri's own space plans were now subject to delays, he realised it was time to go in for the kill. The Russian's tenacity and resourcefulness had made him a good ally over the years, but Doug had also seen his dark, underhand side when things didn't go his way. Doug wanted to strike now to leave Dmitri no choice but to see him triumph against all the obstacles put in front of him. His lawyer drew up the agreement in secret, although not until he had handed in his resignation twice and threatened to get Doug committed to a psychiatric ward.

'Your daughter has excellent taste,' Mr Hu said, gesturing towards the chess set that Doug had provided. Doug had conceded home advantage but was allowed to bring the set of his choice, so he had chosen Amber's board and pieces – wooden and classically simple. He decided not to let on how close she'd been to beating him on this very set only last month. The board was placed on a small chrome table in a room that had been emptied except for the board and the two chairs sitting opposite each other. The substantial stake had warranted the minimum of distractions. Mr Hu held out his palms, one holding a white pawn, the other a black. 'May I take it you trust me to do the honours?'

Doug nodded, and his opponent put his hands behind

his back, kept them for a few seconds and then presented them back to Doug, arms extended out in front of him, his fists closed. Doug looked at each fist. It would be only a slender advantage to choose the white pawn and to make the first move in the game, but he wanted all the help he could get. When he accepted that he did not have the gift of x-ray vision, he pointed to Mr Hu's left hand, which he opened.

'Black. You shall go second,' Mr Hu said, replacing the pawns on the board and rotating it so that the white pieces were on his side. 'Good luck, Mr Peabody.' After a moment's thought, he pushed his king's pawn two spaces forward.

'I believe you make your own luck, Mr Hu,' replied Doug, and mirrored his opponent's move.

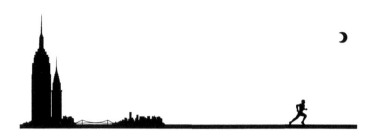

Chapter 35

'**R**ISE and shine people – today's the day you get to haul your arses round this great city for twenty-six and a bit miles.'

As alarms clocks go, Jackson was up there with the loudest. Just in case no-one had heard his subtle wake-up call and felt the ground shake as he stomped around the house, he banged a big fist repeatedly on everyone's door until they answered.

'Okay, okay, I'm awake,' Jon shouted. He turned over in bed and stared at the clock until the figures eventually came into focus – 4:00.

'Breakfast will be in twenty minutes,' Jackson yelled to everyone. 'It is not optional, and anyone not downstairs by then will be dragged down by me no matter what.'

Jon regarded any rise out of bed at a time that started with a number less than six as only suitable if a nice long holiday awaited him soon after. As he lay in bed, snug under a winter duvet, the possibility of him lining up on the start line of a marathon in just four and a half hours in flimsy running gear seemed as likely a prospect as turning over and seeing Scarlett Johansson had slipped in next to him while he was asleep. Not that he didn't know what he had to do – everything had been written down in checklist form, all clothes and items had been laid out ready for him so he could just go through the motions without even thinking. Still, it all depended on the very first thing on the list which was to get up, and despite several brain signals urging his body on, he just lay there. He wasn't tired, quite the contrary – he was now wide awake – it was just that he wasn't quite ready to face what would certainly be the most painful day of his entire life.

'Aw, you spoilt my fun,' Jackson said as Jon came downstairs into the kitchen. The clocked showed 4:19. Everyone else had assembled and was in various states of preparing and eating their breakfasts. 'Remember – nothing new. Just stick to whatever you've eaten for breakfast in your training. Today is not – I repeat not – the day to try anything new. No new food, drink, clothes, deodorant – hell, even nail polish.'

'That scuppers your makeover, Danny,' Kieran said. A Shredded Wheat came flying over.

'Eat well, hydrate well. Sports drinks all round, noting carefully which type to have and when. What you do now will affect you when you run, so don't ruin your chances by sneaking in a beer,' Jackson said.

'Who has beer for breakfast? Even I couldn't face that,' Kieran said.

'I know what you Brits are like. Probably put it on your cereal back home.'

'I could have a beer,' Arjun said. 'Or even the champagne that I saw found its way in last night.'

'Can't touch that, I've got to spray it all over everyone,

314

you know, on my victory celebrations,' Ceris said.

'Nice of you to get up early and join us, mate,' Tom said to Arjun.

'Well, wasn't sure if Mr Motivator here included me in his threats, so thought I'd better join in. Plus, I get to see you all off before the limo collects me later.'

'Think of us when you're quaffing champers as we slog around the five boroughs,' Tom said.

Jon looked down into his bowl of cereal. They had rehearsed this day, getting up this early, but he had been hungry then. The carb-loading from the previous days made him feel full already, and the contents of his bowl looked way too much to fit in, especially when his stomach wasn't usually open for another couple of hours at the earliest. He dunked his spoon in it and pushed the food around. Looking up, he saw everyone tucking in, forcing it down, doing what they knew they had to do.

Jackson spotted Jon's lack of eating. 'Jon – it's been a few years since I played planes and trains with my kids' food, but if that's what I have to do to get you fuelled for the race...'

'Maybe he has a few butterflies in his little tummy, bless his poor soul,' Nicki said, shovelling in another mouthful of grey porridge.

Jon started to eat. Whatever happens in the race, he thought, he certainly wasn't going to let her win at the breakfast table.

The coach journey from Long Island was a long and silent one. The start of the marathon was at Fort Wadsworth on Staten Island to their west, whose main entrance by road was the Verrazano-Narrows Bridge, the very bridge that they would run their first mile over and which would be closed shortly before the race to traffic. DPI organisers had wanted to avoid this bottleneck and also provide the runners with a true New York marathon experience with the main alternative – arriving on the island on the famous Staten Island ferry that leaves lower Manhattan. There had initially been more moans from the group about how a helicopter would have been so much more appropriate for the esteemed DPI runners, but once inside the spacious, comfy coach, they had all separated and found their own window seat. Danny, Kieran, Natasha and Barry all put on headphones and zoned out to their music, Barry with a small bag of red grapes. Ceris and Tom curled up on their seats and tried to get in a bit of extra sleep. Jermaine started reading *The Great Gatsby*, while both Nicki and Jon stared out at the waking of the city that supposedly never sleeps. There was a part of Jon that wanted the journey to go on forever, or at least go round the whole city, the whole state if need be, and return to the house promising that they'd do the marathon thing another day. He was safe here, nothing to do, no effort required, no pain to endure. Watching locals stroll along the paths, walking their dogs and going about their mundane morning business made Jon wish he was like them, free to start a day which didn't guarantee unimaginable effort on his behalf.

'Okay children, we're almost here,' Jackson said as they approached the ferry terminal. 'Make sure you've got all your belongings because you won't be seeing this warm, cosy coach again.'

When they stopped, Jon grabbed his standard-issue marathon clear plastic bag and followed everyone else out of the coach. He put on his hat and zipped up his jacket, jiggling his legs in the cool air. The sun had started its ascent behind a covering of grey which was threatening to agree to the forecasters' grim prediction of rain. Jackson led the group to the entrance of the terminal, unmistakable in the huge letters spelling out its name, balanced in a curve on the edge of the awning. Jon looked behind and around him. All he could see was thin people in tracksuit bottoms and tights, smart athletic tops in every colour imaginable and running trainers on every foot. It was as if the port were a magnet for runners, drawing them in from the land, bleeding the city of its fittest. Inside, the waiting room was a bowl of white noise as people chatted while they stood and sat, waiting for the next ferry to arrive. When Jon tried to tune in to the conversations, he was surprised to hear so many foreign accents. It was clear from the body language, however, that nearly everyone was talking about running. Some stood and casually stretched, others tucked in to bagels and even coffee. Everyone looked like they were professionals, as if it were just another race day on the calendar, a mere twenty-six miles ahead of them that would be entered into their running logs and put down as a fun day. The exception to the rule was a man who stood barely five-feet tall and almost as wide, dressed in a black duffel coat and woollen hat, holding on to a coffee for warmth, with all the looks of a local going to work who was in the middle of watching his town get invaded. As the Moon Runners gathered together dressed in their orange gear from neck to ankle, Jon felt like an intruder himself.

'Do you realise what you've let yourself in for?' an elderly lady asked Jon as he stood at the back of the ferry looking out at Manhattan as it gradually grew smaller.

'A marathon?' Jon replied. Despite having a body that looked like it might be whipped off the boat by the wind any second, her clothing suggested she was somehow also a runner, and one who Jon expected was about to offload a lifetime's worth of experience.

'Pain, that's what.'

Jon waited for more, but she just patted him on the shoulder, nodded and stared into the distance. 'Um, okay…thanks for the insight.'

Ceris came bounding up. 'Hiya. What you up to?' she said.

'Bonding with the professionals, getting valuable tips. You?'

'Just taking it all in, you know. Oh, you've got to see this – look over there!'

Ceris pointed towards the ferry that was about to pass them in the opposite direction. 'Have you seen the side of it?'

Jon looked at the lumbering orange ferry. It had a huge DPI logo on it.

'They don't miss a trick, do they?' Ceris said.

'It's like they own the colour orange. Their marketing team's a bunch of kids, just stamping anything that moves with their colour,' Jon said.

'Apparently our ferry also says, "Proud to be ferrying the Moon Runners for the Great Space Race".'

For the first time in a while, Jon recalled his tattoo and wondered how he would feel with it after all this was done.

'You got a camera?' Ceris asked. 'We have to have a photo of us with the Statue of Liberty.'

'Do we have to? I may just go back inside.'

'Come on, you gotta have one for the New York scrapbook.'

Jon took his camera from his bag and they went to the side of the boat as New York's most famous attraction got nearer.

'She's not very big,' Jon said.

'I think of her as the skyscrapers' little sister.'

'I bet she's seen a few people go past in her time.'

'None like us, though,' Ceris replied, before asking a fellow runner to help with the photo. He examined the camera and took several minutes to compose the shot and work out what to press. When he had taken the shot of them both and handed the camera back, Jon looked at the result on its screen.

'I'm sorry mate,' Jon said to the guy who'd taken the shot, 'but have you never taken a photo before? Look at this – you can't even see the statue behind us. Where's your brain?'

'I – I'm sorry,' the guy replied.

'It's bloody useless! You're supposed to capture the famous landmark in the background. Even a child would know that.'

Ceris glared at Jon and took him further up along the side of the ferry away from the other runner. 'What the hell was that about?'

Jon looked down and played with his camera. 'Nothing. I just wanted a good shot, that's all.'

'Nothing? And I'm about to jump over and swim the rest of the way,' Ceris said. 'Jon, I'm not stupid. You need to relax.'

'I'm sorry. I thought I was okay. Didn't mean to snap. Guess I still have a lot on my mind.'

Ceris rubbed his arm, tilting her head in sympathy. 'I understand. But first, go back over there and apologise. You never know what karma may do, otherwise you'll probably trip over a plastic cup he throws down after twenty miles. Second, blot out all thoughts other than the race. Banish the negative. It can all wait until afterwards.'

'Yeah, I suppose you're right. I'll apologise.' Jon looked back towards him. 'Might still give him some advice on composition, though.'

Once they'd arrived at Fort Wadsworth, it wasn't difficult to spot the DPI tent in the start area – it was, of course, the obligatory orange colour and had DPI logos on it, but it was also blaring out a compilation of songs that had the word 'moon' in them. Add to that the almost life-size photos of each runner on both sides of the canvas, and Jackson had no problem leading them straight to it. They had all been surprised just how vast the start area was. After walking to the security turnstiles, they had been led to a huge complex spread over a grassed park area, split into different zones, each with a colour as its name and its own unique starting point to allow the separation of over fifty thousand people. This year had been specially arranged via DPI so that a small zone – unsurprisingly named the Orange Zone – had been allocated purely for DPI runners, with everyone else split into four others.

One of the most visually impressive aspects of the area was the amount of portable toilets that were available. An entire row lined one hedge, viewed at one angle seemingly stretching out towards infinity. With still two hours to go before the first wave of runners started, it was still nowhere near full. Jon tried to imagine the fields being populated by fifty thousand people. Most people, it seemed, didn't have the luxury of a tent, so they huddled on the grass, wrapped up and shivering like the annual general meeting of the homeless. Jon expected the DPI tent to be heated, contain some nice padded chairs and perhaps even a TV or two, so he was a bit surprised when they arrived.

'Is this it?' Danny said.

'Just a groundsheet? And the rest is coming when?' Natasha asked.

'If you were expecting a film-star trailer then I'm sorry,' Jackson said. 'Mr Peabody's orders: make sure the runners experience the marathon like everyone else, just as I prepared you for in the park.'

'That was weeks ago, it's flipping freezing now,' Natasha said, to general nodding around her.

'I guessed you lot were still pussies.' Jackson smiled. 'Sit down, take a snack and I'll be back.'

Jon grabbed a bagel and a glass of Gatorade and sat down on the floor. It was dry, but still cold. They had a while before they had to change into the clothes they would start with, the rest of their stuff was to be put in their bags which would be sent to the finish to wait for them. A few minutes later, Jackson re-appeared with two large cardboard boxes and dumped them on the floor. 'Here – seeing as it's our last day together, I've got you a present. Just keep it on the down-low with Mr Peabody.'

Natasha opened a box and pulled out something blue and padded.

'Sleeping bags!' Everyone gathered round to take one, Natasha the first to dive in hers. 'Ah, so warm.'

'One last thing – I know you may have seen the many Portaloos around here, but believe me – there ain't nowhere near fifty thousand of them, and when this place fills up, demand is high. I know you Brits like to queue, but there's a limit.' He pointed behind the tent. 'That's why your second and last luxury today is that row of nine there, one dedicated to each of you.' Gasps of glee met his ears, particularly from the girls. 'Enjoy your personal thrones, I'll be back later for your final warm-ups. Watch out for Leona who'll bring the media round later.'

They all gave their thanks to their trainer.

'Oh, and if anyone asks, you didn't get them from me, okay?' Jackson said, walking away.

'Where would we be without Sergeant Major Jackson, eh?' Danny said to the group.

'Cold, unfit and fighting each other for the loo,' Ceris said as she got in her sleeping bag and pulled the drawstring tight so it wrapped around her.

'I don't know about you lot, but I'm gonna have a dump and then settle down for a little shut-eye,' Kieran said, walking off to the toilets.

'Charming. Do tell us all about it when you get back,' Ceris said.

Jon laid out his sleeping bag and was about to climb into it when his phone vibrated against his leg. By the time he had retrieved it from his pocket, it had stopped, the screen showing an American mobile number he didn't recognise. Just as he was trying to guess who might be trying to wish him good luck, he received a text. It was Summer, wanting to discuss the plan to deal with Nicki. Jon felt a twinge in his bowels. With the prospect of running over twenty-six miles ahead of him, dealing with another obstacle wasn't what he needed right now. He glanced over to see Nicki who was also staring at her mobile, seemingly very happy at its contents. Marathon or no marathon, he knew he had to nail her. Jon wanted to ensure he was fully focused and prepared for whatever plan Summer had concocted, so he decided to first sample the delights of the portable toilets, sending a text to her saying he'd call in fifteen minutes. He waited until Kieran returned – just in case his own toilet was inconveniently placed next door – and then headed off. The toilet was hardly the most luxurious facility he'd ever been in, but it was clean, had a seat, toilet paper and even a means to access water, fulfilling all his basic needs. While he sat and waited for nature to take its course, he started to visualise the start line, the first bridge and all the miles that lay after it. None of these thoughts were conducive to the completion of his current task however, or indeed even the start of it. When his phone started to ring again, he instinctively reached for it and answered. 'Hello?'

'Jon? It's Summer. It's been over fifteen minutes so I decided to call.'

'Oh, right. Sorry. I've...er...been delayed.'

'Why do you sound like you're in a cupboard?'

'Must be a dodgy line. Transatlantic calls and all that.' Jon thought about opening the door a little.

'No, can't be that. Anyway, we need to discuss the plan. We need to do it soon.'

'How soon?'

'Five minutes.'

'Ah. Right.'

'Is there a problem? Don't tell me you're busy? I thought you'd just be tucked up in your sleeping bag by now.'

'No, no problem. Of course I'll be ready.' Jon told his body to reschedule its movements until a little later. 'How do you know we've got sleeping bags?'

'Because I've just seen Jackson. He told me.'

'Ah, I see.' Jon stood and was about to get dressed again before the situation suddenly became clear to him. 'You've just seen him? Here? That's means...'

'I hope your legs are quicker than your brain. Yes, silly, I'm at Fort Wadsworth and on my way to see you.'

Jon reached down to grab the waist of his tracksuit bottoms in one hand while holding the phone in the other. 'Here? So you're coming to our tent? Now?'

'No, I've got a temporary one set up nearby. I'll send Leona to get you and Nicki.'

'What's the plan then?' Jon slipped as he pulled up his trousers, pushing a hand out in front of him to steady himself, which only resulted in the cubicle lurching dangerously forward. He leaned back and it settled back into position as he let out a sigh of relief.

'Are you sure you're ready?' Summer said.

'One hundred percent. Just tell me the plan.'

'We're going to confront her. I spoke to her wimpy boyfriend, Duncan, last night and he's on our side. We'll force her to quit or we'll reveal all.'

'And you think that will work? I know what she's like.'

'Of course it will. She'll hate it, but she'll have nowhere to run, literally.'

Jon had made himself presentable again and slowly stepped out of the cubicle. As he began to walk back to the group, he could see Leona approaching from the other side. 'Okay, let's do this.'

He hung up and returned to find everyone in their sleeping bags in various states of relaxation.

'Jonny Boy – you forgot to do up your flies,' Danny said, pointing to Jon's crotch. Jon instantly went red as he looked down and turned away to adjust them, followed by another wave of blood to his face as he realised he was wearing a tracksuit. He returned to face Danny. 'Highly original.'

Leona had reached them. 'Old ones are the best, eh, Danny? Anyway, who's up for some interviews?' She continued to explain that she would take them in twos for some press interviews in a nearby tent, starting with Jormaine and Barry. Nicki and Jon were to follow, something which made Nicki smile so wickedly at Jon, he felt Halloween had come a week late.

When Leona came back and beckoned them to follow her, the pair walked in silence for the two minutes it took to reach a small white tent. In it was a single table, one empty chair on one side and two chairs on the other, one of which was occupied by Summer.

'Hi Jon, Nicki. Sit down, please,' Summer said. Jon sat next to Summer, leaving Nicki to sit opposite them as Leona left them alone.

'Summer Breeze,' Nicki said. 'I thought you'd been banned from our competition for your incompetence over Jon's drug fiasco.'

Summer folded her arms. 'Nicki, I'm not going to drag this out as there's a marathon to be run. All I have to say is that we know about the cat.'

Nicki leaned back in her chair. 'Cat? You mean Jon's little Conan? Please tell me they've found him?'

'As a matter of fact, they have. Alive.'

'Well thank God for that. You must have been worried sick, poor little thing, missing for weeks.'

'Cut the crap. We know you took him.'

'Me?' Nicki put one hand on her chest. 'How on earth could I possibly do that? I've been here in New York, remember?'

'We both know you got your boyfriend to do it. Duncan. Nice chap, if a little dim, going out with a bitch like you.'

Jon was balancing his feelings of anger over Nicki's denials and his arousal by Summer's attack. He tried to keep focussed.

'Nice story, Breezy girl, but I think you'll find I had nothing to do with it.'

'Duncan says otherwise. Sold you out. Is willing to tell the police everything.'

Nicki adjusted herself in her seat and folded her arms. 'Really? You see that's real strange.' She paused for a few seconds. 'When did you speak to him?'

'Late last night. I reckon he was looking forward to stitching you up. He can finish with you and then move on to someone better, more...human.'

'Ah, Summer. If only you knew him as well as I do. You see, he phoned me only half an hour ago and told me all about your little scheme. Seems he had a change of heart, a realisation of where his loyalties really lie.'

'You're bluffing.'

'You wish. You want to go to Peabody and get me thrown out of the race, don't you? I bet you even think that with me out, your precious Jon can win. Ha!' Nicki snorted a laugh. 'You guys crack me up.'

Summer looked at Jon. If this was where he was meant to come in and trump Nicki with a mystery card, she was about to be disappointed. 'Why'd you do it, Nicki? Was I really a threat? You even told Duncan to kill Conan, you twisted bitch! How could you do that? How could you even consider that? He's my cat, for fuck's sake.'

'What can I say? You tell me he's safe and sound now, so I guess there's no real harm done. I'm sure Duncan will testify how Summer tried to set me up to help her boyfriend...perhaps even imply that you staged the whole thing yourself.'

'Do you really want to win this race so badly that you'll lie, cheat and potentially murder innocent animals for it?' Jon said, his face now red with anger.

'You never know,' Nicki said as she got up, 'perhaps the zero gravity will make Nicki a good girl. Now, where's the TV crew? I can't wait to tell them how confident I am.'

After she left, Summer rubbed her hands down her face. 'I can't believe that spineless, piece of –'

'He must be as deranged as her,' Jon said.

'He promised!' The table shook from the impact of her fist. 'I had her stuffed. I had it all worked out, everyone against her, she would've had no choice but to quit.'

'Well it didn't work, did it? She's gonna get away with it.'

'I thought I had her. I set up a monitor on her emails, but it all boiled down to him giving evidence, which he assured me he would.'

'Unfortunately, she has this effect on men. Like poison.'

'I'm sorry, Jon. I've let you down again.' She reached out to touch his hand, true regret in her eyes.

'Don't ever say that! That's enough, Summer. You have done so much to help me. You found Conan and were wonderful to my family with Dad's heart attack. I can't ever thank you enough for all that.'

Summer blinked a few times. 'You know about that?'

'Yes. I found out two days ago. Dad slipped up.'

She cupped both hands round his. 'Are you okay with it? He's fine, you know.'

Jon nodded. 'I know. He said he was coming today, although wasn't going to rush around the whole of the city to see me, so will be with Mum at Central Park.'

'He's a great bloke. Like father, like son.'

'He's a big fan of you, too.' She smiled as he added, 'Like father, like son.'

Leona made a discreet cough at the side of the tent. 'Summer? Sorry, the BBC want to speak to Jon.'

Summer looked down at the table and smoothly withdrew her hands from Jon.

'Right. Looks like I'm up,' Jon said, standing up.

'I'd better go, too. I'll try to get in near the start and wave you off. And I'm sorry about Nicki.'

'You tried. Should've known...your plans have the success rate of a British ski-jumper.'

Summer stuck out her tongue. 'Only one thing left now, I'm afraid.'

'And that is?'

'Run the race of your life and beat the bitch.'

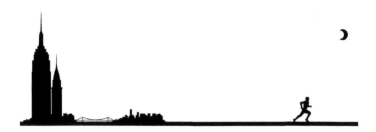

Chapter 36

'WELCOME, ladies and gentlemen, to a most unique event – a separate competition within the world's greatest race. Arguably, there has been no bigger prize in the field of sport.'

Standing within sight of the start line, surrounded by press and a large crowd wrapped in scarves and thick coats, Jon listened to the announcer's words and felt as if he had climbed into a TV screen. He was standing there in a pair of shorts so light they didn't feel like they were being worn, trainers with more technology than his car, and a sweat-wicking, chafe-resistant, ultra-performance, micro-fibre runner's vest with 'DPI 6 – JON' printed across it. He had swapped software testing with marathon running; the roundabouts of Stevenage with the skyscrapers of New York; hiding from a promotion to chasing a prize that was – literally – out of this world. And he wanted to pee again.

The waiting time in the tent had flown by. Nicki had been unbearable after he had returned, saying how wonderful and strong she felt, ready to conquer the city. She had even started singing along to *Bad Moon Rising* when it came on. Jackson had them all stretched and had gone through last minute reminders on the race. Jon had taken on liquids as advised, but either it was nerves or the fact that he was bitterly cold having just taken off his sweater under DPI orders, that his bladder was begging him for one last stop before they set off. He hoped it was just his mind playing tricks and that as soon as he got going he'd be fine. He reckoned that they'd run over the Verranzo-Narrows bridge and eventually be caught by the professional men and the first wave of normal runners who would be released soon after. With all that excitement, he was sure it would take his mind off of it. For now, he tried to ignore his bladder and continue to listen to the announcer above him on a large platform.

'Below me are the nine contenders for the prize. To my side, is the tenth – Arjun – who as you should know, unfortunately fractured his leg on Thursday.' There were some sympathetic noises before a small out-break of clapping. 'I'll allow him to say a few words of encouragement to the team.'

Arjun took the microphone. 'Hey guys!' He waved to the DPI runners who were doing their best to limber up and keep warm but still acknowledged him. 'You all know I was gonna win it, so if you fancy giving the prize to me anyway, I'll be at the finish.' A light wave of groans followed before he continued, 'Anyways, I wish you all the best of luck. Run hard, run fast and may the best Moon Runner win!' Everyone clapped as he handed the stage back to the announcer.

'I also have here Mr Doug Peabody, Chief Executive Officer of Douglas Peabody International, the reason why we have this competition and this wonderful prize.'

Doug stepped forward and took the microphone. 'This race is neither DPI's nor mine – it's yours, so I shall keep this short.' Jon clapped the loudest. 'You are ready. You are strong. You can achieve it. Expect pain. Expect support. Expect a journey like no other. Have fun, my Moon Runners...and good luck!'

Doug handed back to the announcer as the applause died down. 'Thank you Mr Peabody. And now information on the staggered starts. As you should know, the runner who has attracted the highest figure for their charity via the DPI website will start first. A minute later, the one with the second-most raised will start, with the runner who has raised the least, starting eight minutes behind the first runner.'

The runners stopped stretching and looked at each other. 'So who's going to be playing catch-up?' Danny said.

'But to keep you in suspense a little while longer, I will only announce and start one person at a time. So listen up after you start – if you can – to find out who's going to be chasing you down.'

'Eight minutes is a lot to make up,' Ceris said. 'I got just about everyone in Wales to sponsor me, so I hope that will do it.'

The announcer continued. 'All this means that our very first runner who raised the most for his charity, Dreams Come True, is ...Jon Dunn.'

Jon froze. Was that right? Top fundraiser?

'Go Jon!' Kieran said. 'Maybe all that Conan publicity helped.'

'Jon? Would you make your way to the start line now and be the first official DPI runner to take on the New York City Marathon!'

Jon realised he had no choice. What he wanted to say was, 'Thanks, but I'll just pop to the loo first. Swap me with Kieran or someone,' but he assumed that after all this organisation that wouldn't be a goer. A big digital clock hung above the start line that would count down to the time the next runner would set off. As he started walking, it went from 0:00:30 to 0:00:29.

'May the best man or woman win!' Jermaine said.

'Go on Jon!' Ceris shouted.

'Just keep looking over your shoulder,' Nicki said.

Jon couldn't hear any other shouts above the cheer that had gone up as he made it to the line. He looked up and saw the bridge stretch out before him like a driveway to a giant's castle. The incline of the span hid the real length and covered up the city in front of it. As a chilly wind flew into his shorts and snapped at his arms, Jon suddenly felt very alone.

'3...'

This was it, thought Jon.

'2...'

What he had trained for.

'1...'

Hours of hard work and pain coming up.

A loud hooter sounded and jolted Jon into action. He started his stopwatch and began to run alone, *Johnny B. Goode* appropriately blasting out of two huge speakers. Cameramen jogged alongside and a motorcycle went out in front with a camera facing backwards towards him. His legs felt like the wheels on a toy car that had been dragged backwards, coiled springs now let loose. All the warnings of going off too fast with everyone else were redundant, but he knew he still had to contend with the sheer, almost overpowering, excitement of actually starting the race. He checked his watched for pace and adjusted his stride according to his target rate. 26.2 miles stretched out in front of him. Perhaps four hours on his feet. He was finally in the last leg of the competition.

Well, thought Jon. At least he was in the lead.

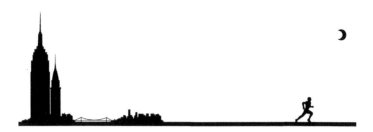

Chapter 37

THE sound of the second hooter caused Jon to stumble and almost lose his footing. He'd barely drawn breath, let alone got round the sweeping curve to his left that was the start of the bridge and yet already there was someone chasing him down. He glanced backwards and saw the blonde head of Ceris. At least it wasn't Nicki, although she would no doubt want to hunt him down like a lion would an antelope, so Jon figured he would not be alone for too many miles. Another hooter soon sounded. Jon thought he may have heard Tom's name. It was hard to predict what pace the others would go at – although they had all started off fairly evenly in terms of fitness and had had the same training, everyone had kept their target finish time a secret from each other. Jon was aiming at completing in just under four hours, so had a nine-minute mile strategy. No more, no less – just keep a steady nine-minute pace from the first to the last mile. He didn't know if that would be enough, but given his fragile state, that was all he could hope for. He consulted his watch as another blast came to announce the next DPI starter. Jackson had worked with them individually to see that their goals were realistic. Everyone knew that the marathon distance would be a leveller no matter what they'd picked – anything after eighteen miles would probably all come down to who would have enough mental strength to go on and win. However, for the next few miles the difference in paces and staggered start would make things exciting – and DPI would not have it any other way.

The view from the Verrazano-Narrows bridge made up for any effort required on the incline to its peak. The south end of Manhattan revealed itself to Jon like a woman undressing – the top appeared first and the rest was gradually exposed as he went higher until he could see her in her full glory. She beckoned him to join her, but he knew that he would have to traverse through two more boroughs before they would meet again. Just give me a few hours and I'll be there, he thought. The Hudson was below him, reflecting the clear skies above. He could see a tug boat proudly shooting jets of water from its bows in recognition of the marathon. If he'd had his camera, he would have no doubt stopped to take some photos. In fact, he thought, this is such a momentous day that he should be photo-logging his entire journey, with a bit of video thrown in. A helicopter buzzed overhead to remind him that he wasn't exactly running it untracked.

The one-mile marker came up so quickly that he had to check that he hadn't exceeded his self-imposed speed limit. He was still on target. One down, twenty-five and a bit to go. The music behind him was fading and he realised that the other eight runners had probably started. Becoming aware of his own feet slapping against the concrete, he dared not look behind at the trail of orange that was out to get him. As he carried on the bridge via its welcome descent into the awaiting Brooklyn, he performed a few mental checks on himself. Firstly, the ankle was holding up without any complaint. While this pleased Jon, he was not going to get carried away – he was guessing the time would eventually come when it would take centre stage in his body's grand production of pain. His legs were a little heavy, but getting used to the running after a quiet week of exercise. He was in great shape and would have been extremely happy as he cruised into Brooklyn if he hadn't been reminded by his very last check that he still very much needed to go to the toilet.

'Go on Jon!' a voice from the crowd shouted.

'Jonny Boy – you can do it!'

'This race is yours, Jon!'

Whether it was the wait to finally see another runner after the professional women had run past – having started ten minutes earlier and been twice as quick – or whether DPI PR had done its job superbly, the Brooklyn crowd were wild at the sight of Jon. He had barely entered the crowded area before he was being beckoned to high-five both kids and adults alike who were sticking out their hands as if the president were coming to town. Young women with prams waved and cheered, middle-aged men clapped with true admiration in their eyes, men whooped as if Jon were a rap star come to sing at their local. Kids screamed to near ear-piercing pitches. Jon had never heard his name being repeated so much in such a short space of time. There were even banners, some just celebrating the Great Space Race, but the odd one was runner-specific. Jon smiled and blew a kiss at two young women who shared a banner which simply had the three huge letters of 'J O N', jumping up and down at his response. New York was crazy. Everyone was insane. It was as if it was his personal victory parade or a lap of honour, albeit one almighty lap. Up ahead, he could see a water station, where a line of helpers looked down the course, dozens of green cups on the table readily prepared.

Which person would he grace with his order? From a few metres back, he picked out a pretty blonde woman who was beaming towards him. Concentrating purely on her outstretched arm, he ran past the rejects to the chosen one, grabbed the cup, thanked her and carried on in one swift motion. He was coming up to two miles and still in the lead, running fluidly, deftly holding a cup of water with the crowd's rapturous encouragement in his ears. He carefully took some well-practised sips and threw the cup on the floor to the side. The marathon was his – his to enjoy, his to celebrate with the crowd and his to lose. And if he hadn't looked back that very minute, he might have enjoyed it for even longer.

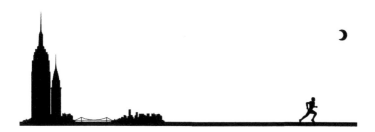

Chapter 38

THE sight of Tom's figure striding in his direction in the middle of the road behind him wasn't entirely surprising or alarming to Jon. It was difficult to estimate the time difference from his perspective viewpoint, but he realised that Tom had probably had Jon in his sights for some time after his two minutes delayed start and was pushing it gradually. The real problem was that just over Tom's shoulder was Nicki. Although he didn't know exactly when she would have started, Jon had spent some time in the second mile calculating that even at a slightly quicker pace, with a few minutes to make up she might catch him after around six miles. However, at the rate she was going now she was likely to overtake at three. Just three miles in and already the one person who he didn't want ahead of him was about to jog past, no doubt with an expression that would gain her the Smuggest Athlete of the Year award. Jon considered his options. Could she keep up that pace? Should he be matching it? What was the point in running a perfect nine-minute mile race when by the time he'd finished she had got the medal, t-shirt, banana and ticket to space? Perhaps he could go faster, before she arrived. That would frustrate her, maybe use up more of her energy. It would also use up more of his, and tear up his game plan, the only game plan he had for a distance he'd never tackled before. He glanced behind again. Tom had vanished – hidden by the now-larger figure of Nicki in front of him.

'Go Nicki!'

'You can catch him, girl!'

Jon had heard that there could be a million people out on the streets across the course. Resenting every single one of them who might cheer on Nicki would be a waste of effort, but it was something Jon had started. She didn't deserve any support, the would-be cat killer. If only they knew. Already he felt he had sped up a little, his engine revving as if wanting to drive on and leave Nicki with a face-full of his dust. Should he let her go? She may have come unhinged, seen the dot of Jon ahead of her and homed in on him, recklessly disregarding her tactics, driven to crack his confidence. Or perhaps she was following her tactics precisely. Jon had seen a marathon where the leader had streaked out so far in advance she'd looked impossible to catch, only to see her being hauled in within the last mile. The thought of him passing Nicki on the last half mile as she looked on in agony, unable to respond, desperately clawing at him to come back, was one hell of a vision. He looked back again – she was within talking distance, eyes wide with anticipation. Could he take the risk and let her freely overtake? Should he put up a fight? As he looked ahead, there was only one move to make. He darted to his right and straight into a portable toilet.

He knew it was only going to last a minute, but the joy of unloading a full bladder coupled with the satisfaction of not allowing Nicki to enjoy her moment of overtaking, produced a natural high for Jon. For a brief second, he thought about staying in the sanctuary of the toilet, away from the madness and the work ahead, but he knew he was always going back. He slid the door catch, burst out on to the streets once more and launched into a jog again.

'I'm back!' he said to the crowd, waving his arms in the air and then supplying some more high-fives.

'Hope you washed your hands,' one joker shouted out.

Ahead, he could see Tom, and just beyond him, Nicki. Looking behind, he could see Ceris wave at him from about a hundred metres back. This was good, he thought. He could keep Tom in his sights, continue at his target pace and let Nicki go off and do her suicidal pace until she burned out. All he had to do was keep going.

At five miles, Jon realised he wasn't an athlete. He shouldn't have even considered himself as a runner. At best, he was a jogger, plodding along in a fun run that just happened to have an edge to nine of its competitors. The real runners were the professionals, who had started to pass Jon as if he were a lamp post. Jackson had woven sprint sessions into their training – high intensity, fast sprints for thirty seconds building up to three minutes as they grew stronger. Jon remembered giving it all he had, relatively fresh after just a few miles of jogging, and continuing until he was out of breath. His mile pace for that period of time had been six minutes – lightning quick in Jon's book. And yet, if he had tried that pace now, gave it his maximum, burning all his energy in one glorious burst of speed, he would still have got nowhere near the pace of the pro men. They were just phenomenal – half-men, half-gazelles. They glided past silently, like a car going downhill whose handbrake had failed. A group of five had come by first, bunched together so closely it was as if they were best friends going out on a Sunday morning run together. Although the DPI runners were all dressed identically within each sex, these elite runners differed in their attire, showing that there was no standard, optimum marathon wear. Two donned stripy hats, one had long, white compression socks and several wore sponsored arm warmers. Trainers were bright red, green, yellow, all probably to be discarded after this race. Following the lead group were a chasing pack of about ten hopefuls who were in turn leading a string of others. Jon was in awe of their speed and their effortless style as he moved over to let them pass. One had kindly patted Jon on the back as he went past, briefly looking over his shoulder to give a thumbs up. Jon did the same and just about made out a British flag on his back as he started to disappear in the distance. He may not have been racing them, but he was still competing in the same race as Olympians, record holders, national heroes and future stars.

'Caught you!'

'Whoa, hiya,' Jon said, as he was joined by Ceris. 'There goes my head start, I guess.'

'I went off a bit slower, but have just sped up,' Ceris said. 'Saw you ahead and thought it would be nice to run together for a while.'

'Yeah, sure. Anyway, they say if you can't have a conversation while running, you're going too fast.'

'True, just don't expect a long debate.'

Although he knew he was racing against her, at only a fifth of the way into the race, he was more than happy to run with her.

'So Tom and Nicki went after you?' Jon asked.

'Yep. Barry reckoned he'll be last. Not sure where the others will be, but at least we're ahead of Kieran and Danny for the moment.'

'Let's hope their pace isn't too much faster. I'm happy at nine-minute miles.'

'Shouldn't you be planning on getting ahead? Catching Miss Bitchy and Tom-Nice-But-Boring?'

Jon had noticed Tom was still going strong. 'It's early days. Biding my time. Had my loo break and not had to up my pace to catch anyone, unlike everyone else.'

'So you gonna rocl them in later, eh?'

'Something like that. Pray for Danny and Kieran to wear themselves out battling each other, leaving us to fight it to the finish.'

'I'd love that. Don't think it'll work out like that, though.'

'Why not?'

'You didn't see Nicki by the start line, she was possessed. I can't even see her now, she's so far in front.'

Jon strained to see ahead of him but couldn't see any glint of orange past Tom, despite the long road and a slight downhill. He didn't need to look at his watch to feel he was still running his target pace, such was the rhythm he'd got into. 'I got to play it my way,' Jon said. 'No point in following and burning out with her.'

Ceris didn't reply and they carried on in silence.

Brooklyn was rocking to the many bands that were entertaining both spectators and runners. He heard the *Rocky* theme tune for the third time that day, but still it never ceased to cause a ripple of excitement down Jon's spine. If there had been some steps to run up, he would have happily scaled them and jumped off. He remembered Doug's announcement in the boardroom in what seemed like another lifetime. The elite athletes had passed, but there was still a steady stream of sub-elite and simply damn fast runners that were overtaking, and the course was now filling up a little, adding to the atmosphere. The crowd competed with the bands with an accompaniment of their own, using cowbells, vuvuzelas, wooden clappers and above all, their voices. Not everything was inspirational, however.

'Run!'

'Go on, you orange freaks!'

'Nicki's sooo got you beat, guys!'

'Do you think she paid him to say that?' Jon said, thumbing towards the guy who leaned forward for that last comment.

'Probably,' Ceris replied. 'Hey – you know what I've just realised? We might not overtake anyone else from now on.'

Jon thought about it. It was perfectly logical, just unexpected to Jon. He'd been at the front of everyone, aside from the professional women, the wheelchair and the handcycle racers. Everyone who had overtaken Jon would have been scheduled to run much faster, so it was likely that unless anyone else broke down, they would forever be getting further and further down the field.

'Well, that's a depressing thought,' Jon said. He checked the mileage. 'Well, we're a quarter of the way through.'

'Or to put it another way,' Ceris said, 'there's still three quarters of the marathon left.'

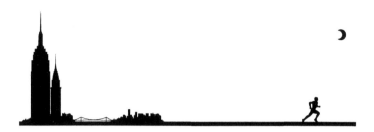

Chapter 39

'**A**RE you sure we haven't taken a wrong turn?' Jon said.

It was fair to say that the marathon in that particular part of Brooklyn wasn't high on everyone's list to see. The bands had disappeared and the crowd had thinned so much it barely deserved the term. The near-silence seemed unnatural.

'Hasidic Jews. Big community of them here,' Ceris said.

It felt to Jon as if he were trespassing on their turf, taking a shortcut they weren't supposed to take. Not that there was any animosity towards the runners, just a stark contrast to the enthusiasm that seemed to have swept every New Yorker in the previous nine miles. A mutual intrigue existed – men dressed in long, dark overcoats watched as the runners went by, as they in turn stared back. Most just went about their usual Sunday business, dressed immaculately, if rather in monochrome compared to the orange and other garish colours that were coming through.

'Bet you don't see many of them in Wales,' Jon said.

'Funnily enough, I do. Usually hundreds of them come over to Aberystwyth each summer to enjoy our wonderful seaside town.'

'Really? Wow. They've got some great beards going on here,' Jon said.

'I wonder what they think of us?' Ceris said.

'Look at us – it's a Sunday morning in November and we're dressed in vests and shorts, putting ourselves through totally unnecessary pain for hours on end. No wonder they stop and stare.'

On the kerb ahead, two children held out their hands over the road, holding out lollipops. When Jon and Ceris reached them he took one. 'Thanks,' he said. As they carried on, Jon felt more at ease, as if this area were a welcome break from all the noise of the previous miles.

As if to make up for the quietness of Jewish area, the next neighbourhood was going overboard. Fuelled by the sight of a good flow of impressive runners and now the appearance of the DPI runners coming through, the crowds were getting excited.

'Jonny...Jonny...Jonny...' chanted a crowd up ahead.

'Do you hear that?' Ceris asked Jon.

'Is that for me? I can't be the only Jon running New York today.'

As they got nearer, it became pretty evident who the crowd was supporting. A banner about two metres tall was being lofted high in the air.

'Oh my God – is that...is that Conan?' Jon said. The banner was in the shape of a cat, superbly drawn as a caricature of his pet. As they got nearer, the cheering increased from a group of about ten people in their late teens. The banner was being waved crazily in the air by two men dressed in full cat outfits who both waved furry paws at Jon as he ran towards them.

'We love you Jon!'

'Conan rocks! Yeah!'

'We'll find Conan! Don't worry!'

They screamed as Jon put up a hand to acknowledge them.

Ceris nudged Jon in their direction. 'Go over and see your fans.'

Jon ran over and exchanged a few hand slaps and even a passing kiss from one girl. He left them and caught up with Ceris.

'Well aren't you Mr Popular?' Ceris said.

'Well, me and my cat.'

'No-one's found him yet?'

Jon looked at Ceris. 'Yes they have, actually. He's fine.'

'That's great! Why didn't you say anything?'

'It's…complicated. Long story. Involves Nicki, funnily enough. Tell you later.'

'Nicki?' She waited for Jon to elaborate but he kept quiet. 'Perhaps I don't want to know. Glad he's all right, though. I hear he's a global superstar now.'

'Looks like it. Crazy. Maybe I should sell his image rights after this – he could have his own cartoon series.'

'If you win this, who knows what DPI might do to help you promote it.'

'Look – we're in double figures.' Jon pointed to a large round sign that displayed a big '10' on it. Ten miles, sixteen to go. Sixteen sounded a long way to go to Jon. A huge effort would be required just to run sixteen miles, let alone start doing it after having run ten.

'How are you feeling?' Ceris asked.

'Ankle's a little sore, calves a bit tight but generally not bad, considering. You?'

'Okay, not great. Not sure I can handle this pace, though. Wanted to hold a bit back for second half.'

'Want me to slow down a little for a while?'

'Nah. If you're feeling good then you should go on. You need to catch The Girl With No Shame.'

'She's way ahead now.'

'If you don't run off and leave me right this minute, I'll kick your arse right here in front of everyone.' She gave him a playful punch on the arm.

'Okay, as long as you're sure.'

'Yes! Now go!' Jon started to go off. 'Wait –' Ceris reached down into her shorts. 'Here – take him.' She handed Jon a small toy dragon.

Jon took it. 'Dewi?'

'Dewi Junior. Dewi himself was a little too big to carry round in my shorts for twenty-six miles. Set him on to Nicki when you catch her.'

'I will. Thanks, Ceris.' Jon tucked the stuffed toy into one of his pockets. 'You can catch me later.'

'Or maybe not – look!' Ceris pointed to a big fire truck that was parked by the edge of the course, surrounded by over a dozen firemen all in uniform. The sight was too much for Ceris, as she darted left and ran straight towards them. Jon carried on running but watched as the blonde was mobbed by the group of FDNY's finest.

The slight but steady incline from ten miles was not welcomed by Jon. He could feel a blister developing on the little toe of his left foot, both calves were giving out a constant dull pain and his right groin muscle was a little stiff. Worse was that Danny was now alongside him, looking in far better shape. Jon could only hope Danny was good at hiding the pain.

'I feel great!' Danny said. 'First ten's been easy. Lucky you'd got five minutes on me, eh?'

'Long way to go yet, Danny Boy.'

'Yeah maybe, but I'll be third now and storming it. Look, I'm gonna crack on and catch the other two.'

'Anyone else behind?'

'Kieran's not far behind. We just overtook Ceris wearing a fireman's hat, for some reason. Think Tasha's behind her. No sign of Jermaine or Barry. Anyway – hope the ankle's okay. May the *fourth* be with you!'

With little effort, Danny cruised past Jon and into a crowd of faster runners ahead. Jon was back on his own, and now in fourth place. He turned his head and caught a flash of orange somewhere down the hill that could have been Kieran. Maybe his strategy was wrong, he thought. With Arjun out of contention, he had been focussing on Nicki, who was not only apparently racing ahead with a comfortable lead but was also the carrot for everyone else to chase, too. Still plenty of miles left, though. If he pushed it now and tried to keep up with Danny, then he would surely pay for it later. If he had to kick, he could do it nearer the end, burning the energy he was saving now, reeling in the stragglers. That's assuming he hadn't burnt all his energy by then or that his ankle wasn't going to be shot to pieces. The time on his watch showed he'd been on his feet for over an hour and a half. What would nearly four hours of constant pounding on concrete do to it?

The Brooklyn crowds were still thick as he swept past eleven miles. Jon grabbed a sports drink from a large green cup thrust out at him and proceeded to splash most of it down his vest. Usually flat and reliable, the ground around the drinks station became a different surface altogether. The floor was littered with cups and liquid as runners took what refreshment they could and discarded the container almost immediately by dropping it by their side. The slipperiness of the cups and stickiness of the drink led to an erratic terrain, and Jon carefully jogged through until the cups became sporadic and the road dominated once again. He could feel his trainers stick to the ground, giving his muscles that little bit more work to do. Just when he thought he had got past the worst, he got a face full of liquid.

'Sorry buddy.' A thin man with grey, army-cut hair gave Jon an embarrassed look. Jon wiped his eyes and chin.

'Should've looked before I threw. Hey – you're one of those Moon Runners!'

Jon nodded. He had decided to cut down on any chat to conserve energy, and had been quite happily running on his own.

'Hey buddy – if I beat you and you win, do I get to go to the Moon?' The man dug his elbow into Jon's arm.

Jon shook his head.

'Of course, you do know why Peabody's really going back up there, don't you buddy?'

'Er, no?' He had no idea what the man was going to say,

but if he called him 'buddy' one more time there could soon be an unfortunate tangling of feet.

'To rescue the aliens.' He looked wide-eyed at Jon, who begun to inch his way to his left. Fifty thousand people in the race and Jon was sitting on the bus next to the weirdo. 'Think about it,' he continued, tapping his right index finger to his temple. 'Think about the commercial value of a real Moon alien. Peabody will be able to hold the world's governments to ransom.'

'They're only going round it. No landing,' Jon said.

'Who's to say that? You don't know that. Why else would they go? DPI don't do jack for no reason, buddy.'

'I'll let you know what I see if I get to go.'

'Dream on, buddy. They'll brainwash you, or kill you or something. You ain't never gonna be able to tell the truth.'

Jon was about to give the guy an 'accidental' trip when he heard a familiar shout from the crowd.

'Jon you big loser!'

He scanned the crowd to his left and saw Stu. Jon raced across to meet his friend, as he waved goodbye to the loony.

Jon shouted at Stu, 'Hey buddy – I mean – mate.'

'Don't come over and chat to me! Piss off back to the course. Nicki's miles ahead and creaming it.'

'Nice to see you, too.'

They briefly bumped knuckles before Jon ran back into the throng of runners. He could see Moon Alien Guy to his far right, so he accelerated a little way on the left to leave him behind him. It was only a brief sighting, but Jon was still smiling at the thought of seeing Stu. Pretty soon he'd be home and they could have beers in a pub and chat for as long as they wanted. He focussed on the image, him demanding Stu was silent as he carefully retold the story of his marathon over a pint and some peanuts. So busy had he been in imagining this, he failed to notice Kieran had sneaked ahead of him on the other side of the road.

Bon Jovi's *Living on a Prayer* was one of Jon's favourite '80s records, but the sound of a live band's singer screaming to remind them all that they were halfway there and therefore another thirteen miles lay ahead of them, was enough to put him off it for life. Did they just play that song all day there? He feared for the spectators' sanity. He agreed with Summer's opinion of not celebrating the halfway point in a marathon, but did congratulate himself on reaching it in five minutes less than two hours. At this pace, even including a slowdown towards the end, he'd get under four hours. Given the fact that thirteen weeks ago neither he nor any other of the DPI runners had done any long distance running, anyone who would beat Jon's four hours would be welcome to the space trip. Unless that was Nicki, in which case he could only hope for some malfunction that would send her hurtling off into deep space with all the oxygen levels of a sealed coffin.

Before he knew it, he had crossed the red Pulaski Bridge and had entered Queens – at long last reaching his third New York borough. The course had flattened out, giving his muscles a much-needed respite. He could feel a throbbing in both Achilles, soreness around his left knee, an ache in his lower back and a slight chaffing of one nipple, despite the presence – last time he checked – of a plaster. All these were in addition to the constant tightness of his calves and quads, as if tiny engineers were busy squeezing his muscles with vices. The crowd were still amazing. National flags were waved from everywhere – stars and stripes were abundant but he recognised Spanish, Mexican, French, Italian and several African ones in just a small section behind the barriers. Whenever a Union Flag or St. George's Cross appeared, Jon acknowledged it and took the cheers. The weather had warmed but the skies took on a more clouded appearance, blotting out the sun and keeping it off his face and arms.

For the first time in hours, Jon could smell something other than sweat and Gatorade – barbecues had been set out on the side and people were dishing out ribs, sausages and burgers. Breakfast for Jon had occurred sometime in the previous millennium, and he was wondering which limb he might cut off for even a burnt offering right now. Manhattan was close, and to his left he could see the Empire State Building and Chrysler jutting out, beckoning him to their island.

If Jon didn't celebrate thirteen miles, then he certainly wasn't going to celebrate the passing of fourteen, purely down to the fact that it led to the thing that he had been trying not to think about – the Queensboro Bridge. When he was eight, Jon and his older brother had sneakily got hold of and watched Stephen King's *IT*. He had been so scared, it had ingrained itself on his brain until well into his teenage years. Summer's portrayal and stories of her Queensboro experiences had, in relation to what he had to undertake, been similarly embedded into his mind since the day she'd told him. This is where it could all go horribly wrong, he thought. The monster could get him, or he could survive only to be ruined for the subsequent eleven or so miles. Maybe it would drain him so much of all pace he would barely get into Manhattan from the Bronx before news of Nicki's win would reach his ears. He knew he needed to be positive, to attack it without fear, but his brain was being overloaded with negative thoughts due to the various damage reports that were coming in from all parts of his body. He looked behind him, and amongst strong-looking runners there was a man in a pink tutu and an elderly lady gaining on him, but he was relieved to see no sign of Kieran. He could also see back to Manhattan, the next borough that they would land into after the Queensboro Bridge. The familiar needle point of the Chrysler disappeared as he turned his head forward again. Why were they running away from Manhattan? It would just mean an even longer journey to and over the bridge. They seemed to be doing a wide loop before they even got onto the bridge, as if the sheer size of it needed a faster run-up. Jon wiped his brow and dangled his arms, shaking them just to do something different to the constant arm-bent, pump-forward action. The bridge was coming in a matter of minutes. He stretched his neck by touching an ear to his shoulder on each side, flexed his back and lifted his knees higher for a couple of strides, all of which were resented by his body. It must be coming round this corner, thought Jon. He was trying to see how the course was bending when he noticed something black jumping out of the crowd, over the barrier and running towards him. As it got nearer, he could see it was someone in a full Catwoman suit.

'Jon! Jon! You're doing fantastic!' A woman screamed from under the costume in a heavily accented voice, her face almost totally covered by the cat mask, goggles and make-up. She started to run with him, putting her arm round his shoulders and giving a kiss on the cheek, leaving a big red imprint of her lips.

'Er…thanks,' was all he could say at this strange but welcome turn of events. He felt the coldness of the touch of PVC against his skin. She put her lips to his ear and whispered, 'You're gonna nail this bridge, Jon. You will beat it. You will get through it.' She moved her head back and let her arm slide down to give him a slap on his bottom. Still running with him, she flashed a smile that Jon recognised.

'Summer?'

'Surprise!'

He looked up and down at her and laughed. 'Nice costume. What are you doing?'

'Just had to be here for you and give you a boost.'

'You're right. Fit girl in tight PVC costume usually does it for me.'

'I needed a disguise – DPI would probably sack me if they knew.' She blew kisses at a couple of runners who had overtaken them, wolf-whistling as they went past.

'Couldn't you have chosen something less... conspicuous?'

'They were right out of Garfield costumes. Thought this would get your blood pumping.' Summer began to puff a little. 'Anyway, I wanted to tell you that you're fifth at the moment. Tom is slowing down and you'll easily pass him. Danny and Kieran are going well, perhaps too well. You can still catch them if you stay strong.'

'Kieran? Thought he was behind me.' Jon took a glance back. 'And Nicki?'

'The little cow is leading but I think she's gone too fast. I don't think she can maintain it.'

'She's pretty determined.'

'Maybe. Look, better go before I get found out. Good luck, oh – and take this.' She undid one of her many zips on her costume and produced something which she thrust in Jon's hand before running back to the crowd. 'You can do it Jon!' she shouted back in the same accent as before.

He watched her wave before she disappeared behind the crowd.

'If that was your girlfriend,' a man in a blue vest said running next to him, 'you are one lucky son of a bitch.'

Jon looked at what Summer had given him. It was a small photo of her holding Conan.

'No, but she gave me her number.' Jon tucked the photo into the second pocket of his shorts.

His smile was halfway over Roosevelt Island already. With Dewi Junior, Summer and Conan all along for the ride, he was feeling invincible.

Chapter 40

JON entered the main part of the bridge, the sky giving way to a metal roof, boxing him in. The crowds had disappeared, as if warned off by an evil presence, but adrenalin was still flowing through his body from seeing Summer. He looked up. Where was the fifteen-mile marker? His ankle gave a little twinge as he continued uphill. Through a group of runners he could now see the next mile sign, wondering if he had enough distance left in the race to rein in four DPI runners. A walking woman came rapidly into view by the side of the concrete barrier that ran alongside him. Jon overtook her, pleased to go ahead of someone else after so long watching backs go out of site. He saw another person struggling not too far away and decided to reel him in too. Just a little change of pace would do it. Breathing heavier, he pushed on ever so slightly and was just about to pass him when his ankle gave him a pain so sharp he winced and brought his leg up again rapidly. The next step was painful but less so, and subsequent ones were subdued, nothing more than dull aches. Sounds of trainers against tarmac echoed round the tunnel-like bridge. There were dozens of runners around him, all slapping heavily against the road. He noticed the different breathing patterns of everyone, some shallow, others forcing the air out like bellows. One man gave a whistle on each exhale, and another was groaning every few seconds. No-one spoke, no band spurred them on, no crowd existed to inspire them through. They were on their own; man and woman against gravity in a dark steel tunnel, like cattle making their slow way to the slaughterhouse. He passed fifteen miles but still the road carried on its incline. What if his ankle gave up now? He slowed and decided to go back to goal pace, but as he looked at his watch, he realised he'd already decelerated below it. The runner he was going to overtake was still within touching distance but he didn't want to risk it again, so he resolved if this mile was to be a bit slower, then so be it. A few seconds won't hurt, he calculated. Still the apex of the bridge could not quite be seen. Just how long was this bridge? His ankle rumbled again, this time not as seriously. What if Summer's curse had been passed on to Jon? If she wasn't running it then maybe the bridge still had to have a sacrifice. No, that was plain daft. His calves felt tight and his quads started to stiffen. Was that the peak up ahead? He manoeuvred a little to try to see between two runners. Steel strut after steel strut passed by to his left. He looked behind him and saw the long slope that he had climbed. All that metal and concrete seemed to pull at him, dragging him down, every step getting heavier on his back and legs. One word came into his head: *Walk*. He envisioned himself walking, relaxing even, just taking it slowly up the rest of the hill. Walking sounded good, he thought. Less pain, less effort. Still moving forward, just a bit easier. Yes, walking sounded better with every stride. He knew there was a part of him that was ready to handle this eventuality. Where was it hiding? A small voice struck back, telling him to keep going. He leaned forward, tried to dig in. The watch showed an extra digit, sending him into ten-minute mile country. *Keep going, you can do it, you have the strength, you have the strength.*

He repeated his mantra to himself in his mind, making the rhythm of the words match his foot strikes. The road began to flatten. Was he going downhill now? His arms were pulling downwards. A few people passed him and he realised he'd slowed down even further. All his energy had been expended on the incline and there was little left to start going down. Still there was comparative silence. No talk, no banter, just the sound of sole on concrete. Jon wanted to shout, to encourage or just to release something audible into the air to break the monotony. He couldn't. Something was gripping at his throat, threatening his air intake. The monster was trying to choke him. But his legs had been programmed for over fifteen miles to keep going automatically no matter what speed. As he got a bit further, he started to gradually accelerate, knowing that First Avenue and sixteen miles awaited. He could hear the crowds now, couldn't he? Or was that just wishful thinking? He was thirsty for cheers, desperate for the encouragement of the crowds. They would frighten the monster, and Jon would have salvation…if only if he could get there. The slope down was long but didn't feel steep, as if Manhattan were sitting higher than Queens and so short-changed visitors of gravity going this way. He could now hear the crowd cheering the escapees, but they were beyond a bend at the end. *Keep going, you can do it.* Teasers of Manhattan flashed by between the steel supports of the bridge. *You have the strength.* Not far to go until he was out of the monster's belly and to the sanctuary of the crowd, whose roar was getting louder with every step. There was the bend, swinging to the right. As the bridge's roof gave way to sky and he emerged into Manhattan, it felt as if someone had removed a veil from his face and turned up the volume. There was colour – several large trees with yellowy-orange leaves greeted him by the side of the road, towering over animated supporters at least six deep, waving national flags full of green, red, white, yellow and blue. Long, thin, orange inflatable tubes were being bashed together to provide extra noise to accompany the cheers, shouts and screams. Cow bells rang out, and old-fashioned car horns made their comedy noises. Relatives craned their necks to see if their loved ones would be next to appear from the bridge. As the runners turned left, Jon swung out wide to the right to be nearer the crowd and was immediately spotted as a DPI runner, increasing the volume even more. He held out his hand, desperate for some human contact after the trials of the bridge, and was duly rewarded by hand slaps from those behind the metal barriers.

'Welcome to Manhattan, Jon Boy!'

'You got it, Jon!'

'Looking good, baby!'

Perhaps the last comment was a little optimistic, Jon thought, but he didn't care. Grown men were clenching their fists, shouting in his face to keep on going. Kids were bouncing and screeching and nearly everyone was clapping, seemingly never stopping. A little girl in brown pigtails, no more than six years old, waved a small Union Flag and threw it at Jon. He caught it and raised it high in the air, her high-pitched screams almost piercing his eardrum. Not one person he passed failed to call out his name. He felt energised again, and started to run off at pace when he saw two sights that fuelled him even more. Firstly, he could see sixteen miles was coming up, which meant that soon he would be into single figures for the distance that was left. Secondly, he could now see Tom walking, just before the drink station ahead.

'You okay, Tom?' Jon said, slowing down as he passed.

'All right, Jon. I'm knackered. That bridge...' Tom was shaking his head, looking down.

'Keep going, right? You can do it.' Jon reached the drinks station and grabbed a cup of water. Given the fact he had already slowed down and that he realised just how much he really needed a drink, Jon decided to stop and walk for a few seconds to ensure he was able to consume the entire cup, as opposed to the usual small percentage he didn't end up wearing. Letting the liquid slide down his throat felt like a reward for his hard work over the previous two miles, and he chucked the cup well out of harm's way with a degree of satisfaction. As he walked, he considered his fourth position and how far the others were ahead. Was he still in with a chance at the prize, or was he competing against the course now? Regardless, he was to press on. He went to run, but nothing happened. The word was back again: *Walk.* His legs had got a taste of walking, and were liking it. It was not as good as *Rest*, but it was a vast improvement. Jon tried again. The signals to run were being ignored, as if his muscles were petulant toddlers. *Walking good, running bad.* No, not good, thought Jon. His calf muscles now each weighed about twenty stone, reporting back that they were clearly unable to perform a running motion again until sometime next year.

'You ain't gonna walk yourself to the Moon, buddy!' Moon Alien Guy ran past, tapping his head again with his finger.

Some switch was flicked inside Jon and his legs started to propel him faster forward until he was at a proper jog again. He looked at his watch and started to gear up towards target pace, saying to himself, 'Follow that loony.'

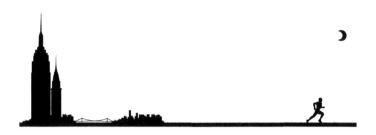

Chapter 41

AFTER his stop and walk, Jon's time for the seventeenth mile had been bad – over a minute and a half over target. Panic hadn't set in, though, and he resisted the urge to try and make it up by running a faster next mile. Within a mile, Jon had caught up with his alien-obsessed friend, overtaking him with a sarcastic, 'Later, buddy,' that he was sure the man hadn't fully appreciated.

Jon remembered from the route map he had been shown that First Avenue stretched all the way up the east side of Manhattan until it met an entrance to the Bronx, where he would meet the twenty-mile mark. It was one long, wide straight that he could see miles into the distance, and he wished he were one of the runners that he could see much further up. Skyscrapers looked on from above on both sides, making him finally feel he was running in proper New York. The crowd was more densely packed on the west side of the road as people came across from the nearby main subway stations. Running in the middle of such a wide road did not give Jon exposure to them, so he gradually angled his way diagonally, dodging runners who were happy to take the shortest route running forward. He noticed that there were little pockets of support for European countries, given away by mass gatherings of flags and colour.

'Go Sweden!' Jon shouted as he ran past a canvas of yellow, all waving flags and shouting back to him. 'Abba rocks!' he added, a little ashamedly. As he continued up the avenue, he slapped hands, took the encouragement and put his hand up to acknowledge the support. It was all free fuel, he thought, giving him a little boost and keeping him going. When he saw a large section of orange, two hundred metres in front of him, he got excited at the thought of a mass rank of DPI supporters, but as he drew closer, he realised that it was an enclave of Dutch fans. Still, Jon thought, orange is orange.

'I love Holland!' Tugging on his orange vest like a footballer celebrating a goal, he whipped up the Dutch crowd into a frenzy. A solitary man stood on the corner of one street, his face painted in a white cross with a red background. Around his neck, hanging down to his knees was the biggest cow bell Jon had ever seen, and was being rung loudly by the man using both hands. Jon could hear more chanting up ahead – what were they saying? As he got nearer he recognised it as a name being said over and over: 'Kieran'. Jon moved slightly to his right to get a view round the runners in front. He could see a figure in orange, horribly slumped forward, still jogging but barely able to do justice to the word.

'Kieran – what's up?' Jon slowed down and patted Kieran's back.

'Went for toilet break, but seized up after. Calves are killing me.'

Jon had to really slow down to avoid going too far ahead. 'C'mon, you've got more left in you.'

'Wish I had. I was all set to kick on and destroy you all, but I just…no, you go on ahead, mate.'

Jon wasn't about to argue; it was a competition after

all. The probability that Nicki would stop to see if another DPI runner was okay was about the same as the Queen throwing the winning touchdown in next year's Super Bowl. Jon was now third, just two people between him and the prize. As he ran on, he shut out the cheers, the clapping and even the other runners for a while to think about the race. He could dream about Nicki grinding to a halt as Summer predicted, but that still left Danny, who was several years younger and looked in great condition when he last saw him. Jon was averaging a nine and a half minute mile now, but with just over eight miles left, he was sure that they both couldn't slow down that much for Jon to catch them at that pace. Trouble was, Jon didn't know how much more he could give. He knew that a spurt now could finish him for the last few miles, perhaps ending up like Tom or Kieran. Learning from previous experience, he also could not count out anyone catching him. Ceris had been cautious and may have paced wisely, as well as being the youngest out of them all. He tried to spot any signs of DPI movement behind him, but with more and more runners catching him up, the course was more crowded and they didn't stand out so much now. Jon decided to wait for a while longer before seeing if he could push on, maybe get into the Bronx, rack up twenty miles and focus on the remaining ten kilometres.

'Energy gels are coming up,' a lady in sunglasses and bright green hair said to Jon as she passed him. She looked tough enough to beat Jon in any track and field event he could name. 'Thanks – I need one,' he replied. Making sure he was in position to take one, he ran past and scooped up a chocolate-flavoured gel and a cup of water. The pouch was about two inches long and felt squishy in his fingers as he grabbed the thin neck and ripped it open. Squeezing from the bottom, he pushed the gel out of the packet and into his mouth, releasing the thick, sticky substance onto his tongue. It tasted like the best chocolate cake he'd ever had, topped with the richest, smoothest chocolate icing that'd had triple the amount of sugar poured into it. As he let it go down his throat, he squeezed more, rolling the packet up as he ran to ensure he didn't waste a single gram. His mouth was clogged with the syrupy paste, and it took several glorious attempts of cleaning with his tongue and gulps of water in order to get it all sent down his throat to be processed. It was like passing through a rainbow in a thunderstorm.

The energy in the gel would take a while to kick in, but the sheer delight of a wonderful taste in his mouth kept Jon going as he headed up First Avenue on Manhattan's Upper East Side towards nineteen miles. His calves were at the stage where he would have normally stopped and called it a day. A good run, great workout but time to go home. His left knee was sore around its cap on every stride and was getting worse. His quads felt as if he had a large child balanced on each thigh, and had started to worry that he might not soon be able to lift his legs to make his foot clear the ground to actually run. The crowds were more sporadic here, away from the main attractions of the island, and the longer he ran, the more isolated he felt as faster runners continued to overtake. His head had dropped, no longer focussing on the distance or the road ahead. His view was of the metre in front of him. A tarmac treadmill passed under his feet, grey, mostly featureless, aside from the occasional white written road sign. From the edges of his vision, he could see orange and white traffic cones – taller, fatter relations of their English equivalents. He glanced up at a road crossing and an illuminated red hand was displayed on a sign high above the road. Don't walk. But walking sounds good, thought Jon. His mind started to work on that idea. Two camps gave battle.

Walking is sensible. You'll feel so much better walking.

No, can't. Keep running. You can do it.

Walking is good.

No, must run.

Walk. Walk. WALK.

No. You have the strength.

Quit, then. Quitting is even better.

No, have to run. You have the...

But quitting solves everything. No more pain.

Run.

It's not like we're going to win. Give it up now.

Have to keep running. You have...

Quit.

No!

Quit. Quit. Quiiiiiit.

'Jon! Jon you flippin' zombie! Jon!' Jon snapped his head up and refocused to see Stu standing at the side waving his arms like he wanted to be rescued. Jon raised a hand.

'Come here...oh sod it,' Stu said as he ducked under a barrier and ran at Jon.

Jon wished he had the energy to vocally transmit the amazing feeling at this stage in seeing a familiar face, but all he could manage in return was 'Hi.' Stu started to run with him.

'Look, I know you're probably knackered and all, but Summer's text me. She's a good sort – kudos for getting in there…if you do, that is. Anyway, it's about Nicki. Summer's just seen her at twenty-one. She's broken down big-time, had to stop and get treatment. I've missed Danny but he must be somewhere in between. Jon – you can do this. For once in your sorry life, go all out to win!'

Chapter 42

UPTOWN Manhattan wasn't normally one of Doug's hangouts, but he had chosen a spot specifically to see his runners come from the Bronx and turn into Fifth Avenue towards Central Park. At just after twenty-one miles, this was the business end of the marathon. Many first-time marathoners would come into this section into unknown territory, their bodies never having run this far. The five miles that were left wouldn't seem a manageable chunk at the end of a race, more like an intercontinental hike with a full backpack. Doug wanted to see how much spirit his Moon Runners had left, how much they wanted the win. Secretly, he didn't want to see them fly by waving, confident and striding on at a steady pace. It wasn't the fact that he had often suffered around this mark, more that he wanted to see the runners really work for it, show that they were adding the effort required to finish the job when all effort looked to have been spent. After all that Doug had been through to get here, it was the least they could do, he thought.

Doug had been kept abreast of the latest positions via his phone app and verbal reports of the DPI team scattered around the course. As promised, Arjun had been chauffeured around the course with Doug at various points, and as soon as the first few DPI runners would come through here, Doug and Arjun would make the dash back to the finish to see the final run-in. Despite being on crutches, Arjun was still managing to get around a bit, and was using his usual charm with a group of female supporters about a hundred metres up from where Doug was standing. It was Arjun who had alerted Doug of Nicki's situation, and so Doug had jogged up to see for himself.

'What happened?' Doug asked Arjun.

'I was watching her coming towards me and she seemed to be labouring. Real slow compared to how she was going before. Then there was this big yelp from her – a sickly, painful cry – and she just clutched at her knee.'

'Where is she?'

Arjun pointed to her, sitting on a chair getting an emergency massage to the side of the course. Doug jogged over to her. He knew she was not one of the most popular candidates, but her lust for competition had always impressed him.

'Nicki – how is it?'

Nicki looked up with a bright red face covered in sweat-soaked strands of hair. 'Mr Peabody. I...I'll be fine. It's just –' she screwed up her face, 'it's just a tight muscle.' A medical volunteer was bending down and rubbing frantically at the muscles around her right knee. 'I'm still winning right? Tell me I'm still winning! No-one's come past, have they?'

'No – you had about five minutes on Danny,' Doug said.

'Shitting hell!' Nicki said loudly.

Doug raised his eyebrows.

'I've really got to get going again.' Nicki went to get up but the helper grabbed her leg.

'Sorry, Nicki, but I really think I need to work on it a little bit longer because –'

'Get off me! Get your hands off me! I'm fine, I'm fine. Got a race to win.' Nicki stood and pushed off with her other leg. When her right leg landed on the next stride she screamed in pain again. The helper grabbed her and pushed her back on the chair again.

'You're obviously not ready, miss,' he said.

Nicki crossed her arms and turned her head away, but not before Doug had seen her watery eyes. She certainly had the spirit, he thought. Arjun joined Doug watching her.

'This is so not fair. I was way ahead. Ow! Do you have to push so hard? It's killing me. Probably making it worse,' Nicki said to her helper.

'I'm sorry, but you have to trust me. I am trained at this.'

'Mr Peabody – why haven't you got your DPI medical staff here to treat me, instead of these volunteers? I'm losing time because they're too incompetent to fix me.'

Arjun butted in. 'Whoa, steady on Nicki. The guy's doing the best he can.'

'That's right,' Doug said. 'We can't have DPI staff at every point of the course. These guys are just as good, if not better. Besides, everyone's going to be slowing down from now on.'

'Well, apart from Jon,' Arjun said. 'I hear he's sped up a little.'

'Jon? So what?' Nicki said. 'That muppet must be miles behind. It's Danny and Kieran I've got to worry about.'

'I'm afraid not – Kieran had problems around eighteen miles. Jon's probably coming up to twenty by now, in third.'

'What?' Nicki's eyes were wider than the mile marker signs. 'You've got to be bloody kidding. Right...' She rose to her feet and put one leg forward, tentatively. Putting weight on that, she then swung the other one forward. A slight drawing together of her facial features indicated the step wasn't entirely pain free, but it was enough to warrant her continuing.

'Take it easy for half a mile,' Doug called out to her as she ran slowly back on to the course.

'Well, this certainly mixes it up a bit,' Arjun said. 'Who's your money on, sir?'

Doug put a hand on Arjun's shoulder. 'Money? I think I've gambled enough for one week.'

They didn't have to wait long for Danny to come past, following a pair of handcyclists who were lapping up the crowd's applause.

'Daniel-san!' Arjun shouted as Danny ran by. 'Looking good, mate. She's only a few minutes ahead and struggling – you can do this, man!'

Although Danny was fighting on, Doug recognised the tiredness of a runner in the latter stages of a marathon. He barely acknowledged his friend or the crowd who were shouting out his name all the way along the street. His technique had gone from efficient to functional, simply to keep going. His pace looked to be consistent but not to the peak times Doug had seen logged earlier. Doug had insisted that Jackson go through the whole course with them all to prepare them for what lay ahead, but the truth was by this point, their brains would have been frazzled and unprepared for the long upward slope running alongside Central Park. Would Danny have the heart to not only tackle the hill but to gain on Nicki? Doug reckoned that Nicki would crawl to the finish line if that's what it took to keep going and win.

Doug stood on a raised, portable platform and scanned the road over the heads of the crowds, waiting for Jon to appear. People dashed this way and that, jostling for position to see their runner come through. A man in a bear costume ran through the crowds, brushing behind Doug and almost knocking him off. Doug regained his balance and searched again for Jon. He had been a serious contender in Doug's eyes, despite his recent ankle injury. The charity money had worked out well for Jon, and Doug had been pleased that he had agreed to the idea of the staggered start based on this. He knew of the misfortunes of Jon's cat, and had not been surprised that it had been the one thing that had pushed Jon more into the spotlight, eliciting both sympathy and cash donations. Jon's parents had been charming when Doug had met them two days ago. It was them who had pulled him aside to praise the efforts of Summer, which had led him to agree for her to come over for the marathon, on a strict proviso that she remained impartial. Quite where she was today and what she was doing he didn't want to know. If she had found a way to encourage Jon, though, it didn't look like it had done much good. Over eight minutes had gone by since Nicki had left and still there was no sign of the third-placed runner. Doug contemplated whether he should have organised more visual incentives along the way, a reminder of what was up for grabs. Maybe that would have encouraged the trailing runners. Of course, given the fact that it had all been in the balance less than twenty-four hours previously, he thought it had probably been wise not to agree in advance to the giant inflatable rockets and spaceman balloons across the course. He still didn't quite know how he'd achieved the checkmate, but at least he was confident now on the prize, if not the winner.

'Any news?' Doug said to Arjun.

'Can't see anything,' he replied, craning his torso over the barrier to see. 'But by the sound of the screams, he may just be approaching.'

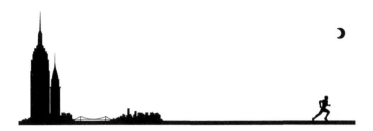

Chapter 43

JON had been cheating. He had also been lying. It was only to himself, but it was still dishonest. His legs had reported unequivocally that they could go no faster than their current pace and, in fact, were likely to get gradually slower. Yep, that was the best Jon was going to get out of them, he was constantly being told. He only discovered this lie after Stu's news about Nicki. Add that to the fact that Stu had mentioned Summer being at mile twenty-one, and lo and behold, the very same legs that were reporting meltdown suddenly had a new lease of life. The renaissance didn't start slowly – it was a whole new gear change. His body had hidden his fifth gear for the past six miles but now had conveniently found it again. Where might he be now if he had got it earlier? Still, the most important thing for Jon was for him to maintain the nine-minute mile speed and not to drop down a gear. The secret, he decided, was rhythm – get the legs going at the required pace and lock on cruise control. They began to act independently while his brain focussed on the challenge ahead. Jon figured that no–one breaks down and just gets up and runs their target pace, at least not without risking another injury. Nicki wouldn't want to stop twice, and so with a good lead was bound to go slower. It would be a big ask with just five and a bit miles left, but with his legs locked at this speed he might just catch her. Danny? Well, he could only hope that he was feeling the strain, too. He took out the photo of Summer and Conan from the pocket of his shorts for inspiration, wishing that he was home with the pair of them.

Turning on to Fifth Avenue brought relief and fear to Jon. He pictured the long straight. Pure maths told him that being on 138th now and going as far south as 59th meant nearly 80 blocks would have to be traversed before he would even get on the back straight in Central Park. But he was finally heading towards the finish, and it was this that he was determined to focus on. He wouldn't count down the number of blocks to go, or the miles left, he would just push along at this speed and keep thinking of the finish.

'It's the Sambuca Kid!' Jon looked to his right and saw Arjun waving a crutch in the air. 'Nine minutes behind Nicki and few less from Danny. But you're looking strong, Jonny Boy!'

He saw Doug next to Arjun, waving and giving a mock salute. Nine minutes. Jon's heart sank a little. That seemed too much to make up this far in. Nearly two minutes a mile. He realised he hadn't seen Summer. He turned his neck and scanned the crowds as he ran, but couldn't see anything. Perhaps she was further up, or disguised again as Wonder Woman or someone, he thought. He wiped his forehead and wondered how he might look. Judging from his matted hair, clothes clinging to him from sweat and a red smudge by his right nipple clashing with the orange vest, he guessed he wouldn't be making too many women swoon. Perhaps he could impress by his running. He started to increase his speed but stopped when his left calf gave out a warning shot. Do not overload. He obeyed, but had now locked in at eight and a half minute mile pace – comparatively sprinting.

Although there were still plenty of runners overtaking him, for the first time in the race he was beginning to go past others regularly. There may have been only two people ahead of him that really mattered, but every struggler that went backwards past his shoulder was a little victory for Jon. But just as you could gain strength from the athletes who are running well, it was easy to get sucked in to the suffering of others. It wasn't so much the walkers that bothered Jon, it was the ones who were going so slowly, their heads down, looking like it would be best to shoot them on the spot and put them out of their misery. One such man with a Union Flag printed on his back and 'Del Boy' written across his shoulders slumped to his haunches just as Jon was approaching.

'C'mon Del Boy! Brits don't quit!' Jon shouted as he ran past, slapping a hand on the stricken man's back and then gesticulating for him to get moving. The crowd had latched on to Jon's attempt to help, and Jon fanned the flames of their support by pushing his palms upwards again and again to get everyone cheering loudly for this guy to get going. Once past, Jon looked back and watched him lunge forward and start running again to a huge cheer. At over six-feet tall, he had a big, lumbering stride and soon caught up again with Jon, before sailing past.

'Well done mate! Keep it going!' Jon shouted. A little disappointingly, there was no acknowledgement from the man, just a cold steel determination in his eyes where he was focussing on getting back in the zone again. Jon was overwhelmed with satisfaction though, like he had achieved a miracle in giving energy to another runner. He may never see him again, never get thanked, perhaps never even be remembered in the haze of suffering, but Jon would know that he had given something back. Jon grinned. He even started to look for others he might be able to help. Why not? He was going well, better than many, and was thrilled by the warmth that had come from his heroics just now. Unfortunately, his body was less than sympathetic to his humanistic cause. It was selfish – it was having a hard enough time keeping itself going as it was, without a load of energy being wasted on someone else. Energy Jon didn't have. The adrenalin that had been used when helping his fellow Brit had run out. His body started to rebel.

Jon stopped breathing.

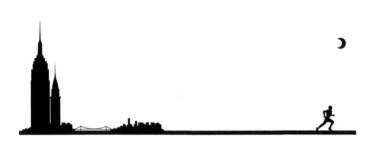

Chapter 44

FOR the first half a second, Jon assumed it was a bit of trapped air in his throat which would instantly clear and allow him to breathe in again. Four seconds later, he realised that it was a little more serious. His windpipe had closed up. Nothing in, nothing out. Still running, Jon demanded more oxygen. It was all around him, everywhere, and all he had to do was open his mouth and suck it in. His head started to feel light. Still no action from his throat. He had no idea what to do. He didn't even know how to jump start his car, so didn't have a clue how to restart what to him had always been an automatic operation. Two more seconds. Or was it a minute? He had to try something. Slowing down, concentrating all his effort on his throat, to his relief he made it open slightly, like a small turn of a stiff screw, and let in a little bit of air to his lungs. But it wasn't enough. Suddenly, there was no race, no people around him, no course, no crowd, just Jon versus his right to take in oxygen and expel carbon dioxide. He was losing the battle. This was it, he thought. Oh shit. Dying in the marathon. One quick faint and then it would be over. Jon Dunn – died chasing his dream.

You have the strength.

His throat opened a bit more. Air flooded in, snatched by his lungs.

Reach your goal.

A breath out, opening it up further. He began to snap back. The sound of the crowd returned to his ears. He was aware he was still running. Gradually, the breathing returned to something close to normal, and Jon cautiously returned to his previous pace. If he died, he thought, perhaps Nicki would scatter his ashes in space. She'd no doubt have great fun pressing the button to send a small capsule of the remains of Jon into the harsh vacuum of space for eternity. He had family, though, friends, a cat. Perhaps it was best to just ensure he survived the marathon.

Stop being such a drama queen, Jon!

A quick jiggle of his head shook out the negative thoughts. He knew that the worst that could happen was that he'd faint, collapse and be instantly rescued by the many staff around. No-one would let him die. Anyway, it was just a one-off, brought on by his well-intentioned but probably ill-advised attempts at heroics. No room for error now, no extra strength for anything else. His legs obeyed and on he went.

Twenty-two miles came and Jon gratefully took another sports drink, letting the cup slip from his hand once he'd consumed enough liquid. Something large by the side of the road about a quarter of mile in front intrigued him. It seemed to be a sign – an orange sign with a DPI logo and words hand-written on it held high in the air. As he got closer, he noticed it disappear, only to reappear with some numbers on it. He made out the words. 'Nicki +7, Danny +4'. Holding the sign was a large tattooed arm of a man standing next to a short, blonde girl who was jumping up and down as if on a trampoline.

'Jon! Jon-Jon-Jon-Jon! Wooo! Jon! You're doing great! Go get 'em!' Daisy yelled as he went past, shoving a large bear wearing a 'I heart NY' t-shirt towards him.

Jon drifted over just in time to wave a thanks to Daisy and give Hanks a high-five. Zu's facial piercings remained undisturbed as he held out a knuckled hand and nodded, which Jon reciprocated, and performed a fist-bump.

'Jon! You can catch them! Summer's at the finish. You can do it – you're my winner, Jon!'

There were four miles left, seven minutes to catch up, but at least he was closing.

The edge of Central Park appeared to Jon's right just before twenty-three miles.

'You know you've got this Jon!'

'Great job!'

'You're crushing it!'

'Do it, man! Do it! Do it! Do it!'

Fifth Avenue was alive with the sound of nutters. Burly men leaned right across the barriers and shouted at Jon with faces so full of passion Jon thought he had just scored the winning home run for their team. People were clapping hard, over and over, relentlessly. They looked him in the eye and showered him with all the hope and best will from their entire beings, projecting power and strength onto him. But it wasn't just for Jon, it was for everyone. Every person who had their name printed on their vest was being encouraged, yelled at, chanted at. Groups of ten, fifteen people jumped up and down cheering at every runner that went by. No-one was left out – even those without the foresight of including their name on their clothing were acknowledged by vest colour, sponsorship names, nationality.

'You're amazing!'

'Come on, hero!'

'You guys are the best!'

Jon thought some of them really ought to have been drug-tested.

'C'mon baldy! There's food at the finish!'

Jon saw a stocky man wave a hand towards the owner of the comment. He looked strangely familiar to Jon from behind, had he seen him before? Then it hit him: Fat Bagel Man. The man who had narrowly beaten Jon in his first race in August was ahead of him. Somehow, this overweight bloke who was at least twenty years his senior had been fast enough to overtake Jon despite a twenty-minute head start. He'd barely lost much weight since, either. He was in some difficulty however, as they started on the long slope that would lead into Central Park, gravity tugging at his ample frame. Jon had his next goal. This time there was more than a few hundred yards for Jon to reel him in, and he once again focused on his bald head glistening with sweat. By twenty-three miles, he was ahead of him. 'Hope you get a banana this time,' Jon said as he passed him, with a bemused look in reply.

Jon had successfully utilised a game plan for hills so far – maintain pace, look down and keep going until it got flatter. Unfortunately for long slopes – like the one he was currently on, between twenty-three and twenty-four – it proved immensely difficult. It was just too damn long.

It barely looked like an incline, but when he looked up it just didn't seem to end. His Achilles and calves were painfully nagging Jon to find a descent, but respite looked far away. Jon wanted to take his last energy gel in the hope that it would carry him through the last few miles, but just the thought of executing the manoeuvre to do it seemed daunting. He would have to reach round to the back of his shorts, find his zip, take out the gel pouch, tear off the top, squeeze the gooey substance into his mouth, swallow it down and then dispose of the wrapper, all while still breathing. Way too complicated and risky, he decided. Breathing and running – that was about his limit right now. Quite frankly, even having his eyes open was an energy-wasting inconvenience, especially with the blinking. Luckily for him, he kept this sense going, as when he next glanced up he could see Danny a hundred metres ahead.

Jon asked his body for more speed, but the request was lost on the way, perhaps filed away in the Humour Department. If there were a Scotty inside him, he had given his captain all the power he could muster. He had no choice but to focus on maintaining this pace and hope it would be enough. He glared at Danny's back, urging him to slow down, pulling himself towards him while dragging him backwards as if using a mental lasso. Sweat was trickling down into his eyebrows, around into his ears, but not even that warranted the effort of a wipe of the face to remove it. A dull ache had spread from the small of his back to his waist. Just for once, he wanted to drop his shoulders and relax. Still Jon kept going, his legs moving as if wound by clockwork, a constant pace up the slope. He was gaining, Danny was appearing larger. He sent telepathic thoughts ahead – *'Don't look round'*. Jon wanted surprise, didn't want Danny to suddenly realise and put a spurt on. He had to catch him soon.

'Danny's toast! Reel him in, Jonny!'

The fans knew the score and they wanted a race. Jon could barely hear himself think above the noise. Faces became blurred, hands held out were left un-slapped as he concentrated on the orange figure in front. Danny was disappearing into Central Park now, leaving Jon an agonising wait until he too would reach that far. It seemed like hours, but when he finally did swing into the park, he could see Danny between him and the twenty-four mile marker. What was a bonus though, was that only a few metres ahead of Danny was Nicki.

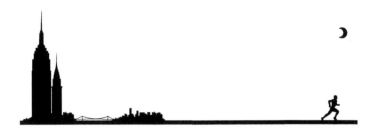

Chapter 45

'**D**O it for Conan!'

'Do it for the Queen!'

'Marry me, Jon!'

The madness seemed to have been cranked up an insanity level or three as Jon ran through Central Park. Even the helpers at the water station cheered and clapped in their blue gloves. It was good to move off the straight of Fifth Avenue into the park and especially onto flat ground, thought Jon. The pavement was still the unrelenting, hard, grey concrete but in his vision there were now patches of green grass under a canopy of yellow trees on the cusp of turning to their stunning late-autumn colours. He had lost sight of Danny and Nicki for a short while, until he got past the twenty-four mile marker and the road turned a bit to the left. When they appeared again, they seemed even closer. To check it wasn't his mind playing games, he watched them go past a Mexican flag and counted the seconds until he reached it. He reckoned about thirty. Half a minute was nothing compared to the gap just a few miles ago. The sound of bongos gave a rhythmic backdrop to the crowd, seemingly in time with Jon's strides. Could he win this? Nicki hadn't looked round yet to see his approach.

He could see he was faster than his two rivals, but knew that he also only had one speed. How much had they got left? Jon imagined racing ahead, only to be left for dead by a final kick he simply couldn't match. Maybe there wasn't any point thinking about it. He would run his race, complete the remaining twenty or so minutes and if they were faster, then so be it. But he was close, so close. He wanted that cigar.

Halfway to mile twenty-five, Jon hit a downhill and decided to make his move on Danny. Nicki had briefly looked round at Danny and responded by moving ahead, leaving him vulnerable to an attack from Jon. Not that Jon did little more than to keep his pace, but an obviously dejected and tired Danny visibly slumped when Jon caught up with him. They exchanged looks, but said nothing. One was on the retreat, the other on the advance, both unknowing what they had left in them. Jon thought about keeping pace with him so they might hunt Nicki as a pair, but Danny's eyes hinted at desperation, as if the road were a treadmill that was on one setting too fast for him. Jon edged past and continued over the undulating and winding route. This time, his head didn't drop – it was focussed solely on Nicki's back. He recalled how cocky she had been when they'd first met on the stairs of the DPI offices. She had worried his mum by revealing the drugs test failure. She had blackmailed him for sex. She had ordered his cat to be killed. It was negative energy, but it had the power to fuel. It worked its way down to his legs and overrode the pain signals. It wasn't much, but it gave him a little boost. They went through twenty-five miles, with Nicki oblivious to his presence. When she grabbed a cup of water, Jon moved out wide. He'd had enough liquid. Taking his chance, he overtook, looking back over his shoulder, giving her the biggest smile of his life.

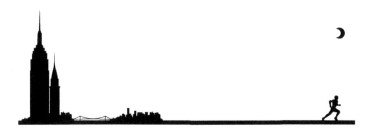

Chapter 46

JON was in the lead. Ahead of him were runners in various states, but none of them wore the DPI orange. The crowd had erupted to his move as if they had put their life savings on a Jon win. Nicki's face as she lowered her cup from her mouth to see Jon ahead of her could have been captured on canvas, framed and displayed in The Met for all time. He could see it now – a whole wall display of ten pictures covering the emotions of that one second. Students would debate each one, examining the subtle differences of the human face, covering shock to anger. But he had to concentrate. He knew right now Nicki would be exploding inside, gathering up all her own energy to come back at Jon. One mile left, nine, maybe ten minutes of running. They had to head out of Central Park, skirt along its south edge before cutting back in to the finish. There was nothing physically in the way of him and the Moon prize now. He wondered what the rocket would look like, how weightlessness might feel. *Concentrate.* He looked behind him and saw Nicki with no less determination than a killer cyborg. If she was in pain, she was hiding it. Jon hadn't forged much of a lead, but kept on with his pace. He wanted to go faster, though. To carve out a demoralising, unassailable gap between them that would coast him to victory. But as he turned right out of the park and onto the road of Central Park South, he found himself running up a hill once more. Within seconds, he was accompanied at his side by Nicki.

Columbus Circle beckoned in the distance, its Trafalgar Square-like column and fountains promising the entrance to the final straight. What was probably half a mile away seemed like a mirage, floating tantalisingly but never getting nearer. Nicki had decided to run next to Jon and not, much to Jon's initial surprise, ahead of him. He didn't look at her, instead staring ahead and working out her motives for such a move. The first explanation was that she'd drawn level and could go no faster. Second, was that she trying to intimidate him by being constantly so close to him. Lastly, he thought, she may have just been toying with him, ready to burst ahead whenever she wanted. People leaned out to encourage both runners, screaming in equal measures of support. Jon may have had the cat voters, but there was enough female support there to cheer on a win for their sex.

The last few handcyclists slowly passed them, every turn of their crank celebrated. He was sure Nicki had more left in her. If it came down to it, he knew she would more than likely be prepared to burst a lung or pull every muscle in her body to cross that line first. But she had a weakness. Jon reckoned that whatever it was that had stopped her four miles ago could easily come back. Perhaps with a bit of pressure, she would snap, quite literally.

'Ladies and gentleman, please make some noise for the leaders of the Great Space Race: Nicki and Jon!' The PA speakers had already been turned up to the maximum to get over the current crowd levels, and its result was like something out of a pop concert. Although there were plenty of runners surrounding them, many breezing past on a late surge to improve their time, most of the crowd on the upper part of the slope were focussing on the DPI leaders. People were chanting their names repeatedly over each other, children rang cowbells with all their might, various inflatable and plastic noise-makers were being deployed within an inch of their manufacturing limits. *Fly Me to the Moon* played over the speakers just in case anyone hadn't quite heard what was going on. The pair had slowed slightly as the hill and nearly twenty-six miles of wear and tear on their bodies took their toll. Jon briefly turned round but could see Danny was some way off. If it had been anyone else beside him, Jon thought he might have agreed a pact to slow down further and save energy for a final sprint, to save the suffering now. His lungs were struggling to get in all the oxygen they needed and he felt a fire in his chest. His calves were as stiff as steel rods, hamstrings wound tight like elastic bands ready to break. Even his buttocks were aching. Just then, Nicki moved forward and sideways to end up directly in front of Jon. His feet were almost touching hers as they struck the pavement each time, but she did not speed up. All he could see was the back of her head as her hair bobbed from side to side from her rhythm. So that was it, he realised – intimidation. She was keeping him behind, daring him to make a move, expend energy or be left blocked and blind. But he wasn't playing her game. He kept behind her, staring at her hair, wanting to reach out and pull it, leaving her sprawling, crying on the floor behind. But he really wanted to win fairly. Let her see the back of his head as he broke the tape at the finish. They reached Columbus Circle, fountains spraying water in the air as they turned sharply right into Central Park.

'You want this, Jon!' shouted a fan as Jon leaned into the corner.

He couldn't think of anything he'd wanted more in his entire life.

Chapter 47

SOMEONE must have measured the distance incorrectly. Surely the finish must be in sight by now? On one hand, coming back into Central Park and having no immediate visibility of the finish was disappointing, but on the other, it still meant Jon had time to catch Nicki. Her little trick at Columbus Circle had given her a five metre lead on him, but she had not increased that since. Here, the crowds were even denser, with people lining up deep into the trees behind orange and blue sponsor hoardings. No-one was silent, few were standing still. The path was spacious, leaving him further from the fans than in the previous stretch outside the park, but he had all the incentive he needed right in front of him. There was only one plan now – wait and kick at the right moment. He didn't want to think about the two major flaws in the plan, though. The fact he didn't know when the right moment would be was dismissed as a minor detail – he would just know. Use the force, perhaps. The other fact was that he didn't know if he had a kick in him. With the last mile marker coming up however, he just had to have one.

It was only the beep of the timing mat that alerted Jon to the fact that he had crossed the twenty-six mile point. Point-two of a mile to go then, thought Jon. Still no finish line in sight, as the course meandered ahead. Nicki was catching up to a slow male handcycle racer who was beginning to struggle on the gentle incline that had unwelcomingly popped up. He was beginning to veer to the right, into the path of Nicki behind him, who was choosing an efficient line for the bends coming up. Head low and facing forward, hands gripping the crank and turning slowly for his final stretch, he was oblivious to the runner behind him. Jon watched the front of the vehicle slide further towards her path, and altered his own route to the left. Nicki kept on going straight.

'Move!' Nicki shouted at the handcyclist. It was enough to get his attention and steer his bike back to the left, but it wasn't enough to get out of her way. Nicki stumbled as the left back wheel came dangerously close to her knee. She reached down, placed a hand on the back of his head and pushed, steering him away from her to the right but sending him towards the barriers. The surrounding crowd gasped as the handcycle wobbled with its rider quickly leaning to the left to leave a wheel almost scraping the sponsor hoardings before coming back on to the course. Nicki had got past unscathed, but her slow-down as a result of the near tangle meant Jon was able to make his move.

This was it, thought Jon. He had sneaked into the lead after what he had just this minute named the Handcycle of Fate which had intervened and given the triple blow to Nicki of distraction, a decrease in speed and a loss in popularity so severe he could even feel hatred being directed towards her. The finish line had to be round the next bend. He looked back and saw her ten metres behind with a huge grimace as she predictably fought back, and could he hear some shouts for Danny further behind? He wanted more – more power, more strength, more speed but had nothing extra to give. He was coming round the bend – surely the last bend now. There was music pumping out, a din of cowbells and claps as the crowd grew. Stands appeared to Jon on both sides, people towering above him, standing and applauding. And then he saw it: the large square arch of the finish, a special one to the right in orange with the DPI logo all along each side, a wide, orange tape strung across the middle all ready to be broken. It was still a hundred metres away but getting larger with every stride. Another glance behind – Nicki was gaining.

You can do it.

He knew his parents would be there somewhere watching. He wanted to win for them, win for his dad, to finally show that he was an achiever.

Fifty metres to go.

You have the strength.

Where's Summer? Could he hear her screaming?

Beat Nicki. Have to beat her. Have to beat her.

But Nicki had come back at Jon and was now level as they both strove for the line. He screamed at his muscles to give him more.   .

Twenty metres.

You can do it!

With every fibre of his being he willed himself to go past Nicki one more time.

Five metres.

Don't let her win. Don't let her win. Do it. You have the...

Jon had the strength.

But so did she.

Edging past with a final desperate dive, Nicki broke the tape.

Jon was left to collapse behind her, over the line and into a heap of despair.

The Great Space Race was finally over.

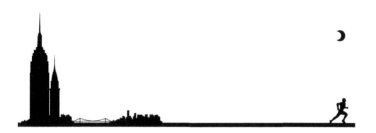

Chapter 48

JON could hear voices. Somewhere in a different world to where he was right now, he was being congratulated, commiserated and told that he really should get on his feet. After he had collapsed over the line, he had ended up on the ground, face down, buried in tarmac. There had been a gentle slap on his shoulder, a ruffle of his hair in an attempt to get him up, but he wasn't moving. He was going to stay there until the continents shifted, he decided. His energy meter was at rock bottom. He had no idea how he was even capable of thinking. Unfortunately, he *was* able to, and all he could think of was that in spite of his absolute best efforts, after the pains, the hope and the immense struggle, he had lost.

Worse, Nicki had won.

He felt himself being lifted up. More voices, this time familiar, male. He felt his arms being stretched out from each side and put over the shoulders of the owners of the two voices. His legs and head dangled like a puppet.

'Jon, you've got to try to walk,' one voice said.

Recognition capabilities returned. Now to try some speech. 'Stu?'

'That's right, mate. Jesus, you're pretty messed up. You did fantastic, though, didn't he, Phil?'

'Amazing. Just under four hours. Dad is so proud of you, Jon.'

His two human crutches, best friend and his brother, took him forward a few steps, his feet dragging along the floor.

'Move those legs, Jon. No wheelchairs for you here,' Stu said, putting one hand under Jon's left knee and pushing his leg forward. He felt his weight go on it. It was like balancing on a tower of jelly.

'That's it, keep going, you'll get some strength back, I promise,' Phil said. 'I'm like this after every triathlon. DPI has its own little area where we'll get you a sports massage. Mum and Dad are there, too. They can't wait to see their hero.'

Heroes don't come second, thought Jon. His head was stooped in the perfect position for a marshal to loop a large medal round his neck. The gold disc swung beneath his chin. Gradually his legs began to form some semblance of useful movement as they moved towards the massage area.

'I think there should be a steward's enquiry.' Jon's dad was standing by a large, beige, leather chair talking to Jon's mum. 'You can't just do that to those wheelchair people. Nicki ought to be ashamed of herself.'

'I think they're called handcycles, love. Anyway, here's the man of the hour!' Jon's mum helped plonk Jon into the chair. It was soft, a little cold but comfortable enough to die in.

'Are you okay, love? I can't believe you did it. I mean – I can, but four hours' running…that's just…incredible,' Jon's mum said, to general nodding around.

Jon's dad crouched down beside the chair. 'That was one hell of a run, son. Whatever they did to fix my heart must've worked, because it survived watching that last sprint.' He put his hand on Jon's arm.

'I'm…I'm sorry I didn't win, Dad.'

There was a sudden outburst of sympathetic noises from everyone. Jon's dad held up a hand to silence them in order to speak again. 'You went for it, that's what counts. I've never been prouder of you.'

Jon thought he might have cried had he had any water left in his body to leak. The sight of a smiling Nicki walking towards them redirected his emotions.

'Sorry to break up this Jerry Springer moment here, but they're dying to hear from the winner – that's me of course – and the runner-up loser in a minute, so best get your massage done quickly.' Nicki disappeared back into a throng of people.

'Phil – you're a lawyer,' Stu said, 'what could you get my sentence down to if I killed her in cold blood here?'

Leona was conducting the live interview, and had been talking to Danny and Kieran who had come in third and fourth respectively while they waited for Jon to become human again. Nicki stood out of shot with a smile that looked like it had been stuck on with superglue. When Jon limped across to Leona and the cameras were fixed on him, Nicki walked up to him, kissed him on the cheek and said loudly, 'Unlucky Jon. It was really close wasn't it? You did so well, pushing me all the way.'

He glanced down at her medal and assessed its throttling capabilities. 'Congratulations,' was all he could return with.

'So Nicki,' Leona said, 'that was one amazing race. Tell me how it feels to know you're going to the Moon.'

'For me, it wasn't about the Moon, it was about winning. I had to focus on the race, give it all I had to beat the others. Plus sponsorship, of course. I'm pleased to have raised so much money for my charity.'

'But you must be delighted to be going into space and becoming the first woman to orbit the Moon!'

'Really? The first? Well, if you put it like that, then yes, I'm delighted.'

'What happened with the handcycle? Looks like you had a spot of bother there,' Leona said.

'Oh my God – that was awful, wasn't it? Is he okay? I've been trying to find him and explain. He just cut in front of me. I was about to fall into him when I tried to steady myself on his shoulders and must've tripped, as the next thing I knew he was careering towards the barrier. They are so, so brave, aren't they? Don't you agree, Jon?' Nicki turned to face him with her angelic façade.

Throwing up on live TV might not be the response DPI would have wanted, Jon reasoned. He decided on a more diplomatic, 'Yeah, very brave.'

Leona kept the microphone with Jon. 'So tell me how you feel coming so close to the prize but in the end losing out by the narrowest of margins.'

'I'm gutted.' He looked down briefly but then faced Leona once more. 'I gave everything. Guess it wasn't enough.'

'So near and yet so far. But well done on second. And our best sponsored runner, too.'

'That's something, I guess.'

'Definitely, Jon. You did them proud. Just think of all the children you've helped. Well, commiserations again, Jon, but a brilliant run.'

Leona wrapped up the interview for the cameras as Nicki was congratulated by various people eager to share the glory or, more likely, to share the publicity. A man in a large bear costume walked up to Nicki and gave her a high-five, put a foil crown on her head and handed her a business card. Jon limped off before he did something he wouldn't regret.

'Care for a drink?'

Jon had been walking back to his family when Summer appeared by his side holding a bottle of red liquid. 'It's got everything a man who's just run over twenty-six miles could need in it.'

'Hey you. Thanks,' he said, accepting it. 'I would have brought something for you, but I'm right out of milk.'

'So you think I pulled off the Catwoman costume?'

'Maybe. You're no Michelle Pfeiffer, though.'

Summer put on her best fake shocked look. 'I would hit you, but you'd probably collapse again. At least you didn't lose your sense of humour out there.'

'Don't suppose you have any cunning plan for Nicki? Any last minute appeal to Doug?'

'I was with him when we saw Nicki do what she did with the handcyclist. As soon as she crossed the line I asked him whether we could disqualify her on account of it.'

'And?'

Summer shook her head. 'He just said after everything he'd been through to ensure DPI had secured the Moon seat, he wasn't going to cause more controversy. Nicki won, so that's who's going. Besides, by the sounds of her interview, she covered her arse quite nicely.'

'You could give her a job in PR.'

'Think she's more cut out to be an estate agent or politician.' Summer smiled. 'Now go enjoy the presentations. I have one last plan to carry out.'

Chapter 49

THE DPI ten stood under a tree while Doug was organising the final preparations for the short ceremony he had promised in recognition of all their achievements. They were all in various conditions of ill health, but for the moment were at least massaged, watered and fed.

'How much do you want for those crutches, Arjun?' Barry said, eating a banana, holding another, with a third poking out of his shorts. He'd limped in last, over forty minutes behind Nicki.

'Going to the highest bidder. Do I hear one hundred pounds?' Arjun said to the group.

'Forget crutches – I could do with a wheelchair,' Tom said.

'You'll soon recover, my friend,' Jermaine said. 'And sorry I overtook you at the end, but my family all had bets on me for a top six finish and I didn't want to disappoint them.'

Ceris was giving Jon a hug. 'Excuse the smell of sweat, but I haven't got my perfume yet,' she said.

'Here – thanks for lending me Dewi Junior,' Jon said

as he removed the small toy dragon from his shorts and handed it to her. 'Didn't do me much good, though.'

'Jon – you were amazing. Second? After all you've been through, that's bloody brilliant.'

'Doesn't feel like brilliant. Well done on your fifth place, though. You must be well chuffed.'

She sniffed her dragon and pulled a face.

'I think he might have to have a bath after all that time down there,' Jon said.

'More like decontamination and a month's quarantine.' She smiled at Jon and placed an arm on his shoulder. 'I'm so sorry you couldn't beat the witch.'

'Yeah, well. Maybe the Moon aliens will capture the rocket and subject her to a lifetime of anal probing.'

Natasha joined them. 'Not sure about probing, but my bum's killing me after all that jigging up and down.'

'Thanks for that information, Tasha. Jon – Moon aliens?'

'A conspiracy theory I learned of today. Best not go there. Let's just say not all runners out there are as sane as us,' Jon replied.

'Don't know if we're any saner. Months of training and hours of hurt for what? Second to last place and a poxy medal,' Natasha said.

'Well I think it was a wonderful experience from start to finish. It's a shame it's all over, really,' Ceris said.

'Hang on – we're being summoned again,' Natasha said, pointing to Leona who was beckoning everyone over towards where Doug was preparing to speak.

'I'm glad it's all over,' Jon said. 'Can't wait to get back to normality.'

A small stage had been erected at the back of the finish area where Doug was standing behind a wooden lectern. The DPI runners had all been seated in line with the stage, five on each side, looking out to an audience of press, family and friends. Dozens of other runners were still finishing the race on the other side of a large mesh fence nearby.

'Ladies and gentleman, as you can see, the marathon in its entirety is far from over. But for these fantastic athletes here, the journey that they unknowingly set out on over three months ago is finally complete. I'll keep this brief,' Doug paused as he turned to look at his runners now all in orange tracksuits, 'because I'm sure they'd all rather be soaking in a bath right now than listening to me. In my eyes, they are all heroes. They came from nowhere, risked their careers, gave up their private lives, left their homes, family and friends thousands of miles away and embarked upon a fitness regime like they had never previously experienced. And all because I had a dream of sending an unknown – a nobody – into space and around the Moon.'

Doug cleared his throat. 'I'm sure you'll agree that they all performed splendidly today in what was an amazing race, better than even I dared to imagine. So before I give out the awards, please show your appreciation of the effort and sheer pleasure they've given us, not only today, but for these last few months – the DPI Ten…the Moon Runners!'

For the first time that day, Jon enjoyed the cheers, shouts and whistles in a rested position. Doug proceeded to present Arjun with a special prize in recognition of his potential shown in training, and his attitude since his accident. Arjun held aloft the gold-plated statue of a man on two crutches and enjoyed his moment like it was the presentation of the World Cup.

'And now we come to the winner. In what was such an

incredible finale, I only wish I had two seats available on the rocket.' He looked down at Jon to his right. 'Jon – you weren't everyone's favourite to win, especially after a late injury, but you showed tremendous heart for the entire race. You should be proud of coming so close to winning that we almost had to resort to a slow-motion replay to decide the winner.'

Jon gave a half smile and took the applause.

Doug turned to Nicki on his left. 'But there can only be one winner. Her sheer tenacity and willingness to win, focus and desire, courage and commitment, led to her just pipping Jon to first place. Therefore, the DPI New York City Marathon Challenge winner and soon-to-be astronaut – Miss Nicki Sizeman.'

Jon did the Oscar nominee failure motions of clapping Nicki as she collected her prize, while simultaneously hoping she would burst into flames. He squeezed his medal tight and summoned his best acting abilities in generating a smile as she accepted the golden, Moon-shaped trophy. He wanted to be far away from here, away from Nicki's gloating face, away from the commiserations and TV cameras. They each had their own hotel room booked in Manhattan and Jon couldn't wait to crash there until sometime next spring.

Leona was saying goodbye to everyone and ensuring everyone had directions and transport to the hotel. Jon was dismayed to hear that they had no other option due to the continuation of the marathon than to take the subway to the hotel, unless they wanted to walk the fifteen blocks. The subway wasn't so much of a problem – more the steps and his complete lack of calf muscles.

Leona came up to Jon. 'You take care of yourself, Jon. You've been a dream to work with.'

'Thanks, Leona.'

'Oh – one more thing. I think they've found a camera of yours. It was left in the changing tent, so you better go get it now. I'll let your parents know you'll be right back.'

'Oh. Can't someone get it for me?'

'Sorry, needs to be verified by you. It's not far.'

'Right now, Leona, everywhere is far.' Jon shuffled off to the large white tent where they'd picked up their bags and had got changed after the race. It had a small flap as an entrance, and when he went inside he was puzzled to see it appeared to be complotoly empty. He was about to curse at having to exercise the muscles he now no longer had in a wasted trip when he heard a voice behind him.

'Welcome to my plan,' Summer said. She proceeded to close the flap, shutting out the mass of people outside.

'Summer – I'm not in the mood for jokes,' Jon said.

'Jokes? Who said this was a joke? Just wanted to get you alone.'

'Look, I just want to go home. Well, hotel home.'

'I know,' Summer said, grabbing his hands. 'You must be absolutely cream-crackered.'

'Did you see her face? Lapping it up.'

'Let the devil have his prize. If she wanted it that much, if she was prepared to do all that she did then –'

'She didn't deserve it! She lied, she cheated, she blackmailed her way to the line. I'm still going to go after her, Summer, for Conan. There must be some emails or phone records or something. She can't get away with it.'

'Jon, I know you're angry, but in the end I guess you could say – as much as I hate to say it – that maybe she was just the best runner.'

'It should have been me.' Jon stared at the floor.

'Let it go, Jon. You can't change what's done.'

'I damn well can't let it go.' Jon shook his hands from hers and looked straight into her eyes. 'All that effort, everything I've done since answering that silly little email in July, all the training, the Conan thing, Dad's heart attack, everything – has all been for nothing. Second place? What the hell's the point of coming second?'

Summer stepped back and slowly breathed out. 'Give me your medal.'

Jon put his hand on it. 'Why?'

'Because I've never got to wear one, remember?'

He took it off and gave it to her.

Summer put it round her neck. 'Thanks. Lighter than I thought.'

Jon watched her examine it closely, running her finger over the embossed design. He suddenly felt naked without it.

'Did you see your time?' she asked.

'No. I vaguely recall someone saying something just after I crossed the line.'

'Three fifty-seven.'

Jon shuffled his feet. 'I guess I did okay. For a beginner marathon runner.'

'Jon – you are so much more than that now.'

Jon gave a little smirk. 'Let me guess – you're about to say that I'm gonna wake up tomorrow and realise just how far I've come, and what a journey it's been. Yeah, yeah.'

'No...I mean now you're a cross-dressing, drug-cheating, z-list celebrity.'

He grabbed at the medal round her neck, brought her face close to his and did what only Marathon Jon could now do.

As their lips parted, Summer stared into his eyes and smiled. 'Wow, looks like a plan of mine actually worked,'

'And I'm still fully clothed.'

'Yeah well...been there, seen that, got the video footage.'

'You might even see it all again one day if you're lucky.'

'Is that so?' Summer stepped back and raised her eyebrows.

'Maybe. That's if I let you apply for the vacant girlfriend position I have available.'

'I'm afraid you'd need a shower before I'd accept,' she said, wrinkling her nose.

'You'd need to promise to behave, though. No deceptions, fake tattoos or marrying your boss again.'

'Oh, I don't know if I can promise all that. That's a risk you'll just have to take.' Summer put the medal back round Jon's neck. 'Think you can handle it?'

'Definitely – I'm a marathon hero now,' he said, looking down at his medal. 'Question is: can you handle me?'

Summer laughed. 'I'll try. Just as long as this isn't an elaborate plan just to get revenge on me for London.'

'Of course not,' Jon said, kissing her once again. 'As someone once said...trust me.'

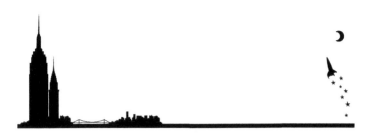

Chapter 50

'10 *SECONDS to launch...'*

Of all the amazing things Doug had done and seen in his life, this very moment had gone straight in at number one. Fridays usually meant tedious board meetings, but today, he was launching a rocket to the Moon. A rocket with huge orange DPI letters running up its side. A rocket containing a very special passenger.

The journey to get to this momentous point had been long and arduous. There had been days when his patience and vision had been tested, but he had never lost belief, never given up, and pushed himself to the edge to achieve his dream. And with Nicki, he got the ultimate reward. To her credit, she had appeared professional from her very first astronaut training day. She had excelled in it, and performed in front of the media as if she were a cross between Amelia Earhart and Princess Diana. But her greatest gift to Doug came from the press conference yesterday.

* * *

'So tell us Nicki – just how excited are you with just twenty-fours to go before launch?'

Nicki leaned into the microphone to reply to the reporter. 'Let's just say I've been looking forward to this moment for a long time.'

'Have you enjoyed the training?'

'Of course. It's been great fun pretending to be an astronaut.'

'So tomorrow are you ready to become the real thing?'

'Well, not exactly.' Nicki paused and took a deep breath, having practised this scene a hundred times in her head.

'Actually – I have a little announcement,' she continued. 'And to help me with this announcement, may I introduce you to…Dmitri Zhirkov.'

* * *

'8…'

The rocket's engines started billowing huge clouds of thick white smoke. Even on the cusp of greatness, Doug was still thinking business. He knew he had fallen foul of a golden business rule: never underestimate your competitor. In Dmitri's attempt to trump the man who scorned and humiliated him, his rival project had seen its scope and expectations grow to such an extent that the Russian was unable to deliver his space programme for another six months. Sabotage had been the only option left.

* * *

Dmitri strode into the studio like a lion about to take over another pride, giving Doug the smuggest of looks. In his hand was a full bottle of whiskey and two tumblers, which he put down in front of Nicki. The press didn't have a clue what was happening, and fired off their cameras in a multitude of directions.

Nicki continued her speech while Dmitri stood beside her, smirking at Doug. 'All I really wanted was to win that marathon, which I did, despite the efforts of the other nine fools. So when Dmitri approached me at the end of the race and offered me an alternative opportunity, I jumped at it. Space? Travel a quarter of a million miles and back in a death trap built by this orange clown?' Nicki pointed towards Doug. 'No thanks. Dmitri gave me a much better offer. I've run...and now I'm taking the money.'

Doug's face was lit up by a barrage of camera flashes.

It was time for Dmitri to take centre stage. 'Douglas, my old friend, my comrade. I commend you on getting this far with your little, imaginative project, I really, really do.' He began to unscrew the top of the whiskey. 'But without your astronaut so close to launch, your plans are somewhat, how you say...buggered?'

* * *

'6...'

The whole Launch Centre shook with the sound of the main engines accelerating towards full thrust. Nicki had given up all this for what? thought Doug. A few million? Dmitri approaching her had been ingenious – how delighted he must have been when he realised that she was just as wicked and corrupt as he was. Evil attracts evil, Doug thought. Of course, Dmitri had just wanted to pull the launch pad from under their rocket, ruining Doug's plans at the last minute with no time to reschedule. Stealing his rival's main selling point was the only way he could buy more time, with a bit of revenge thrown in. Doug's queen had been conquered in what appeared to be a blindsided attack. But Doug had had other valuable pieces on the board that provided him with a strategy to move in for the kill.

* * *

'Dmitri,' he said, clasping his hands together. 'I admire your creativity and sense of drama, I really, really do.'

Doug stood up and walked in front of the table, dragging the focus of the room with every stride. 'And Nicki – well, you certainly had us fooled. All those hours training with us and not a hint of betrayal.' Doug gave three slow claps as Dmitri's bottle hovered over his glass. 'But I'm afraid that this is in fact not a surprise to us at all.'

Dmitri raised an eyebrow as his smile froze. Doug had wanted to appear as if he were bluffing, but he could contain it no longer. 'We've known about your scheme for months. You see Nicki, Jon accepted defeat in the race... but you don't just mess with his cat and get away with it. He wanted to get you, so they did a bit of digging, trying to prove your involvement in little Conan's disappearance. With help from one of my employees, they succeeded in stumbling across an interesting communication between you and Dmitri, two fine specimens of human beings if I may say so. Oh, you remember Summer Breeze, don't you Nicki?' Summer entered the studio from their left with a smile as big as the Milky Way. The result on Nicki's face couldn't have been more intense if Summer had gone up to her and slapped it.

'Well, Mr Peabody,' Summer said as she made her way to Doug's side, 'when you monitor enough emails and scan TV footage, it's amazing what you can find out.'

'Indeed,' Doug added. 'By the way, Dmitri – nice bear costume at the race.'

Dmitri put down the bottle.

'Anyway, I put my own investigation team on it and what do you know? We discovered your diabolical plans. So congratulations on spending what was no doubt a fortune on our phoney astronaut here.'

Nicki shifted uncomfortably in her seat as Dmitri scowled at her and Doug continued. 'Fortunately, we had time to work on a Plan B.' He reached under the table and produced a champagne bottle. 'The launch goes ahead tomorrow as planned.'

* * *

'*4...*'

Doug took a deep breath and thought of the one person without whom he wouldn't be where he was today. The rumours about Jon and Summer and the possible implications of competition impartiality had alarmed Doug, but after Jon had come to him with a very interesting piece of information on the link between Nicki and Dmitri, he hadn't cared one bit about that. Doug took over, had his people action a covert operation to unearth the whole plot and was about to launch a full-scale attack on his nemesis when Summer had suggested something a little more subtle. Nicki's training had continued as if they knew absolutely nothing. The trap had been set, and yesterday it had been sprung.

* * *

The blood had drained so fast from Dmitri's face that Doug thought he was about to see his conquered foe faint. Instead, he slowly got up, took his whiskey bottle, turned around and headed for the door. Seconds later, there was the sound of smashing glass somewhere behind the scenes and a barrage of what Doug recognised as several Russian cusses.

Nicki leapt up from her seat and ran after her benefactor. 'I still get the rest of my money, right?' she screamed down the corridor. 'You still have to pay me! Dmitri?'

Doug waited until there was silence again. 'Well, now that the circus has left town,' he said, addressing the conference once more, 'I can now reveal to you the *real* plans for the launch.' He took the microphone, walked round to the front of the small desk and sat on its edge, facing his eager audience. 'Knowing Nicki was not going to go through with it left us with a small dilemma, namely who was going to replace her as the DPI astronaut. I'd been let down by one of my own Moon Runners. Maybe the whole idea of the race became too important to them. Perhaps this next step was one too far.' Doug let his eyes glance down for a few seconds in silence. 'Did they really want to go? Or should the seat on the rocket – and mankind's first venture in decades towards our only natural satellite – go to someone who really wants it?'

Doug stood up on the desk. 'So what better choice could DPI make than someone who put so much effort into the race, who never gave up and is the real winner of the Great Space Race?' He spread his arms out wide and stared wildly ahead, but saying nothing further as *Space Cowboy* once again provided the back drop.

* * *

'2...'

The Moon Runners watched the rocket in the array of monitors being displayed in the Launch Centre.

'Still reckon they're faking it,' whispered Natasha with half a smile to the others.

* * *

'Mr Peabody?' asked one journalist. 'Are you saying it's you? *You're* going to the Moon?'

Doug gave a huge smile as the photographers lit him up in their most intensive bombardment of flash yet. 'Me? Well, it was my vision, my idea, and all my hard work that got DPI here, wasn't it?' The sound of camera shutters filled the room as Doug led everyone to the precipice of revelation.

'I've wanted to go to the Moon and the stars ever since I first looked up into the night sky. I swore one day I'd make it happen.' Doug put his arms down, paused and turned to look at Summer. 'But this prize deserves someone younger. I'm happy enough to live my dream through another lucky, deserving soul. Summer,' he said, passing the microphone to her, 'would you like to do the honours?'

Summer gripped the microphone. 'Ladies and gentleman, there could really only be one replacement for a task as brave as this one. This man pushed himself far beyond what he thought he was capable of. He survived a family crisis, a dodgy ankle, a cat-napping, excruciating pain and public nakedness.' Summer paused as a murmur swept through the audience. 'So it gives me great pleasure to announce that the person who will become the first DPI astronaut – and all-round nice guy – is none other than our runner-up in the Great Space Race...Mr Jon Dunn!'

As Doug popped the champagne, Jon walked into the studio in full orange astronaut gear, a helmet tucked under his right arm, looking like an extra in *Star Wars* but feeling very much like the hero in his own film.

* * *

'Ignition...'

Jon closed his eyes and prepared for another journey into the unknown.

It was time to make history.

About the Author

Andrew Males lives in Stevenage, south-east England, with his supportive wife, daughter and not-so-supportive cat.

At the age of 15, Andrew wrote down his ambitions in life. Number 6 was: "To be a successful writer of stories." Several years ago he found the list and decided to try to realise that ambition. (Well, it seemed easier than number 3: "To unite the world and make peace.")

26 Miles to the Moon is Andrew's first book. Having slogged through two gruelling New York City Marathons, he decided that it must be far easier and much less painful to write about one instead.

He now knows just how wrong he was.

Follow Andrew on Twitter: @andrewdmales

www.andrewmales.com